THE STANDOFF

DOUBLEDAY

New York
London
Toronto
Sydney
Auckland

THE
STANDOFF

CHUCK HOGAN

PUBLISHED BY DOUBLEDAY
a division of Bantam Doubleday Dell Publishing Group, Inc.
1540 Broadway, New York, New York 10036

DOUBLEDAY and the portrayal of an anchor with a
dolphin are trademarks of Doubleday,
a division of Bantam Doubleday Dell
Publishing Group, Inc.

Book design by Claire Naylon Vaccaro

Library of Congress Cataloging-in-Publication Data
Hogan, Chuck.
The standoff / Chuck Hogan. — 1st ed.
p.   cm.
1. Criminals—Montana—Fiction.   2. Police—Montana—Fiction.
I. Title.
PS3558.O34723S73   1995
813'.54—dc20   94-31987
                                                                    CIP

ISBN 0-385-47716-3
Copyright © 1995 by Chuck Hogan
All Rights Reserved
Printed in the United States of America
April 1995
First Edition
1   3   5   7   9   10   8   6   4   2

FOR
CHARLOTTE BRIGHT

ACKNOWLEDGMENTS

Thanks to Charlotte, my mother and father, Mary, Julie, Charlotte's family, and our entire extended family and friends—no one who has ever tried to write a novel has had better; also, the group at Chef Chow's: Jon Blake, Sara Foster, Monica Gambino, Mary Ellen Schloss, and especially Peter Kneisel; Deborah Futter and David Gernert at Doubleday; Irene Webb in Hollywood; and most especially, Amanda Urban.

THE STANDOFF

PROLOGUE
Thursday, June 13, 1991

The Retreat

It is an open secret among members of the United States intelligence and law enforcement communities that the Federal Bureau of Investigation maintains a private wing in a mental health facility on a sprawling estate in Chapel Hill, North Carolina.

The Retreat, as it is referred to, survives each fiscal year of hard-line budget negotiations due to a provision in the federal employees' general health plan guaranteeing six months' voluntary treatment for alcohol abuse and mental illness. Diagnosed employees are offered three alternatives: resignation, early retirement, or "compassionate leave."

Special Agent John T. Banish had chosen compassionate leave. He was being discharged now, six months to the day after entering the Retreat. He was healthy again; that was what they told him. Alcoholism seemed to him the only disease that could be talked away.

He was seated in a metal folding chair, one of four arranged in a disjointed semicircle facing Dr. Juliet Reed, resident Chief of Psychiatry. The three other patients, all men younger than Banish, wore cotton hospital-issue blues. Banish wore a suit jacket and tie. His suitcase was set on the floor next to his chair. Dr. Reed wore her usual low heels and a long linen skirt. She was a strict professional but with an encouraging smile. Banish liked Dr. Reed. He just never wanted to see her again.

The rec room was otherwise empty at their regular morning session hour, a television flickering behind them through the wire cage covering its screen. The tile floor smelled of overnight antiseptic, and a wasp of some kind, prevalent in those parts, buzzed and tapped at the high, thickly paned windows, trying to get out.

Dr. Reed made a preliminary notation on her pad of paper, then began upbeat. "We all know that this is John's last day with us," she said.

No response from the others. The obvious was not wasted on these shapeless men. Banish could hear Dr. Reed's wristwatch ticking.

"John is returning to the FBI with no interruption of service time, and will be reinstated at his previous pay grade. That should provide some encouragement to the rest of you, as I realize this has been a topic of concern—"

"He's a pariah," Nettles said matter-of-factly. "We all are."

Dr. Reed scribbled another notation.

Nettles had been a forensics specialist in the Behavioral Sciences section. He hunted serial killers for a living. Something had happened to him during a particularly grisly case in Miami, but his senior position allowed him to opt out of the postcase evaluation designed to flag trauma anomalies; two other agents with him who took the routine eval were fine. It had started, as it always did, with drinking. Then dogs in his neighborhood began disappearing under mysterious circumstances. Then a custodian found two mutilated Doberman pinscher carcasses in a Dumpster in the parking garage underneath the J. Edgar Hoover Building. There was even talk of sexual impropriety.

Dr. Reed said, "We have discussed this many times. There is no reason to expect that John or any one of you will not be allowed to reenter active service—"

"He'll be exiled," Rice said.

Dr. Reed stopped. She rested her arms across the notepad in her lap. " 'Exile' is a strong word, Daniel."

Rice uncrossed his arms. "Everybody in the Bureau knows exactly where we are and why we're here. Who would want to place their life in these hands now?" Ashes trickled from the cigarette butt quivering between his fingers. The drugs made him sound exhausted. "Nothing will be said. Reassignment to a Group 4 Field Office, or a Resident Agency out in the Midwest somewhere—North Dakota, or Oregon, the fringe. Somewhere where they won't hear the chains rattling."

Rice had been working a bank robbery in Minneapolis. A young female teller had been implicated in the heist, suspected of providing her ex-con boyfriend with alarm and vault codes. Rice had made two key procedural mistakes. The first was that he fell in love with the teller. The second was that he conspired to shield her from prosecution by attempting to bring the boyfriend in single-handedly. The boyfriend got to the teller first. Her rape-murder broke Rice into jagged pieces.

Dr. Reed said, "We welcome separation. We welcome some relaxation of duty. No one expects John to jump right back into his role as a hostage negotiator."

"Bullshit," Nettles said, turning in his chair. "All bullshit. I participate here until I'm blue in the face. Everybody knows what I saw in that house in Miami—fine. Banish doesn't say shit. We don't know any more about what went on at the World Financial Center than what we read in the papers."

Dr. Reed said, "No one here claims to be cured. No one here claims to be fully recovered. Your health plan allows for six months of in-patient psychiatric rehabilitation, and that is exactly what John has received. He will, however, be continuing with the writing therapy on his own, and AA meetings three times weekly."

The sun was streaming into the room now. The overhead blowers came on and the ceiling rumbled, obliterating the ticking of Dr.

Reed's watch and the sound of the wasp tapping at the window. Banish, who had been sitting patiently like a man waiting for a train, looked up from his suitcase.

"What about my wife and daughter?" he said.

Dr. Reed turned more toward him. She said, "We've spoken at length about your obsession with them, John."

"All my letters were returned," he said. "You told me you would get in touch with them before my release."

Dr. Reed nodded slightly, watching him. It was professional curiosity. "You do realize that the restraining order is still in effect."

"I just want to know where they are," he said. "I want to know that they're all right."

She studied him. Dr. Reed's job was to be empathetic, to understand his experience without actually experiencing it herself. He watched her try. She was perhaps thirty-five years old. He was fifty-two. She was a licensed psychiatrist. He was a twenty-six-year veteran agent of the Federal Bureau of Investigation.

He was relatively certain that she had never had to bargain for another person's life. He was also reasonably confident that she had never been responsible for the safety of upward of one hundred law enforcement personnel placed under her command. But the one thing about which he was absolutely assured: she had not been with him that night at the World Financial Center.

"I'm sorry, John," she told him. "They're gone. They've moved out of New York. I spoke with your mother-in-law this morning. She said that if you try to contact them in any way, they will have you arrested."

Banish stared, unable at first to focus. He wanted to shake his head, then did not bother. After a while his eyes found the glazed-tile floor.

"Then how the hell do I get out of here?" he said.

He felt walls going up. He felt the weight of all his days pushing him down. The wasp buzzed by him. He looked up and watched it fly across the room, and then the door opened and it was free.

The desk nurse walked in. "Excuse me, Dr. Reed," she said. "There's a woman here to see Agent Banish."

Banish looked over at Dr. Reed and got to his feet. Dr. Reed, puzzled, rose more slowly, stooping to leave her notepad on the seat. Banish stood hopeful, not breathing.

The nurse held the door open and a young woman entered. She was small and thin, Caucasian, in her mid-twenties, with brown hair, blue eyes. Her face looked tired, as though she had been driving or thinking for a long time. She was dressed plainly except for a small, expensive brown leather handbag hanging off her shoulder.

Banish's hope fell. She was neither his wife nor his daughter. The woman entered and crossed to him with a tentative, relieved smile on her face, stopping only a few feet away.

"Agent Banish?" she said. "I'm Lucy Ames."

Banish shook his head. He still did not know her.

"From the World Financial Center," she said. "I was a hostage." The woman was reaching into her handbag. "I just wanted to thank you for saving my life."

She pulled out a gun and fired. It flashed and there was a burning deep in Banish's stomach, a bodywide flare of pain. Then he was on the floor.

Confusion, sounds of a commotion, chairs being overturned. Dr. Reed kneeling over him, screaming for the nurse. Blood on her hands.

Banish looked up past her at the corkboard ceiling. His lips were moving. He was trying to speak. He was trying to say something. He could not believe that he was going to die this way.

Monday, August 2, 1993

Huddleston, Montana

It was a small municipal building, flat-roofed, cement-sided, with dry shrubs lining the entranceway and a pool of gravel that was the parking lot out in front. Beyond the foothills bowing in the distance loomed enormous green-blue mountains, thunderous in their silence, mist shrouding and wisping over their snowcapped peaks like shower steam. The sky was vast and cool blue and broken with clouds.

It was Monday morning. The Border County Sheriff's Department's only utility vehicle, a 1991 Ford Bronco, turned off the two-lane interstate and pulled around into the circular parking lot, rocks popping under its nubby tires. Sheriff Leonard M. Blood stepped out. He walked with an easy rancher's gait, snakeskin cowboy boots crunching gravel to the grassy edge of the lot nearest the cement walkway. Two wooden signs were nailed to stakes there. One read CHIEF OF POLICE. The unblemished front bumper of the chief's car rested not six inches away from it. The other sign read COUNTY SHERIFF. A police cruiser was parked there, bumper dented, grill shorn.

Sheriff Blood surveyed the situation. As with everything else, he strived to fit it in a perspective. A police cruiser parked in his space.

A thing that others would see as trivial, he thought. But line up enough of these affronts, and in ascending order, and you began to realize the difference between a push and a shove.

He turned and started along the pavement toward the entrance, his pace loping, the absence of chinging spurs on his boots nearly palpable. He wore a Resistol cowboy hat—crease greased, brim firm —though he supported none of the other stereotypes of a back-country sheriff, such as chewing tobacco or spitting or being grossly overweight. He was trim and strong enough, with broad forty-year-old shoulders down to which thick crow-black hair hung straight and neat.

He was a Blackfoot Indian of the Blood tribe, his last name likely the result of a botched birth certificate some generations past. The Blackfoot Indians had tamed the land now known as Montana and warred with the Shoshoni tribe of neighboring Idaho. They were expert horsemen who prided themselves on their skill in clean-scalping their enemies. Now Leonard Blood wore a United States Sheriff's star and enjoyed jurisdiction over the northwesternmost county in the established state of Montana. The significance of this struck him every once in a while, sometimes in the shower or out mowing the lawn, or while kicking back on the sofa watching "Jeopardy!"

His distinctive gait and the clop-clopping of his boots in the narrow hallway of the building his office shared with the town police department allowed that his secretary, Marylene, would be looking up and smiling at him from behind her desk as he entered. Marylene was older than he was and sported jangly silver loops hanging off her fleshy earlobes, like those of a veteran waitress. She took some pride in mothering him.

"Morning, Marylene," he said.

"Morning, Sheriff. Coffee's on."

His first official act upon his swearing-in as Sheriff of Border County two years before had been to hire Marylene away from the Mug 'n' Dunk down in Huddleston center. This was a bold stroke, coming on the heels of Blood's surprise grass-roots Indian campaign run out of his bait-and-tackle shop, and locals buzzed for days over the new sheriff's demonstrated canniness. Marylene had that elusive sixth sense, the secret of good coffee. In an age of machines and filters and bean grinds, she was an automatic-drip miracle worker. Sheriff Blood opened the door on his inner office and there sat the mug on top of his desk, proudly steaming. He shed his hat and eased back into his wooden chair. The steam swirled in the sunlight, spiraling up in a fine cyclone and disappearing. He took it hot and black. Marylene's brew was such that it came naturally sweet with neither sugar nor cream. He fingered the warm handle of the mug and turned to the clutter atop his desk.

Front and center on his cup-stained blotter was a one-page regional court order. A legal document, large black type across the top reading NOTICE OF EVICTION. Blood's eyes ran down the page to where it had been signed, stamped, and dated by Judge Jonas D. Leary that previous Friday.

Blood withdrew his finger from the mug handle. He stood. He looked around at his desk and the chairs in his office, the notes to himself tacked up on the walls, the cartons set in the corner. Everything seemed to be in its place. He went to his file cabinets and tugged on each locked drawer, checking the almond finish around the locks for scratches. Then he took the notice and his hat. He let the coffee stand.

His boots clopped down the short connecting hallway to the glass doors of the Huddleston Police Station. He went in past the officer at the front desk without a word and headed for the closed wooden door of the chief's office in back.

Chief of Police Gale C. Moody was facing his window, sitting back in his wide, padded chair and looking out at the mountains and the sun coming up over them, and drinking his own cup of coffee. He swung around slowly, looking at Blood with a tipped head. Only annoyance clouded his disinterest. Moody did subscribe to most of the stereotypes of his profession. On a greasy napkin on his desk was a honey roll that a bear might have half-eaten. His gun belt, notches stretched to a pattern resembling Morse code, hung next to his hat on a rack by the door.

"Most people knock," he said.

Blood went forward and laid the notice down in front of him. "What was this doing on my desk?"

Moody perused it from where he was, without setting down his mug. "Looks to me like an eviction notice," he said. "As the Sheriff of Border County, one of your duties is to serve—"

"I know what my duties are," said Blood. "I asked you what it was doing on my desk."

Moody judged him, then nodded as though slowly remembering. "That came in late Friday. I had one of the boys here run it on down the hall so it wouldn't get misplaced over the weekend. One of the conveniences of policing the county seat, our shared quarters—"

"I keep that door locked," Blood said.

Moody's soft bottom lip shrugged. "I'm sure you do."

"I keep a key, Marylene keeps a key."

Moody just nodded. "That sounds about right."

"What do you know about that cruiser being in my spot out there?"

Moody looked at him. "What cruiser?"

Blood nodded and stiffened up. "What do you think I have?" he said. "You think I have something? And if I did, you think I'd keep it in my office?"

Moody's eyes sparked a bit. He sat to. "You been sheriff here what now, two years? I'm chief of Huddleston some sixteen. You got anything more for me, you come out with it plain. Or else turn around and leave."

Blood shook his head, setting the issue aside. "I need two men and a cruiser."

Moody frowned and squinted. "The hell for?"

"Because I'm a one-man office. Or didn't you and your Samaritans even read that?" He was pointing to the eviction notice.

Moody frowned again, having to set down his coffee mug now

and pick up the notice, hating to be made to play along. Then he read the name there. Then his closed mouth stretched wide.

"I'll be a son of a bitch," he said.

Blood tried to undercut him. "You haven't notified the Marshals Service, then."

Moody was enjoying a great and generous grin. "Glenn Allen Ables," he said, so pleased he almost swallowed the notice. "Tax evasion."

Blood said, "Don't know what Judge Leary's thinking. Two years since Ables defaulted on his bail, and now all of a sudden they realize he hasn't been paying his taxes."

"Judge Leary's senile," said Moody, returning quickly to distaste. Then he leaned back in his chair, as far back as a man of his size was able. He made a show of lacing his thick hands behind his head, his face burning with glee. "Now how exactly you planning on evicting a federal fugitive?" he said.

Rookie officer Brian Kearney drove. Sergeant Carl Haley sat in back with his arms crossed, hat brim set down over his eyes, chin on chest. Sheriff Blood sat up in front. The cruiser's engine lifted, strong. Trees alongside the interstate ran past his window; the mountains walked.

Rookie Kearney was young and eager. He said, "You see helicopters and planes buzzing the mountain every now and again. Government cars driving through town. Sometimes you pick up stuff on the radio, them talking back and forth."

Blood tapped the folded eviction notice against his leg. There were busted peanut shells on the unworn blue floormat.

Kearney said, "Those federal marshals are big-time. Him hiding out there on them, that's some guts."

Sheriff Blood said, "Two years on top of a mountain."

"They say he slips into town sometimes," Kearney said. "People see him at flea markets and such, but I don't know. He's got loyal neighbors, though. You know they bring him his food and mail?"

They passed a road sign that read HUNTERS CHECK YOUR ELK IN HERE. Another showed border distances in miles and kilometers. Blood saw Paradise Ridge off the road up ahead, short and stout and distinctive due to its blunted top, which was flattened like an anthill.

Rookie Kearney said, "All that surveillance and running around. How could it be that so many federal marshals are afraid of just one man?"

Blood looked out the windshield. "It's his family up there with him. The feds storm in there and something goes wrong, think of what the papers would say the next day. They're all for waiting on him to leave there alone. I don't imagine feds much like little kids."

They went on a little farther, the cruiser swallowing up white road lines. Kearney looked across at him. "What are we doing here, then?" he said.

"How's that?"

"Well, why are we here and the marshals not? What are we supposed to be doing?"

"Delivering an eviction notice. Doesn't matter who screwed up or how this got put on Judge Leary's schedule. I tried calling the Marshals Service in Arlington, Virginia, before we left. A very pleasant woman there put me on hold."

Kearney said, "You think he'll try something?"

Blood shook his head. "We'll knock, they'll pretend nobody's home, and we'll nail the notice to the door. We'll do what we have to do but we won't get caught up provoking him."

"We're bringing him his mail too," Kearney said, disappointment in his voice. Then he brightened. "Wonder if the feds ever tried this. Just knocking on his front door and asking him to come out, please. Couldn't you just see us making this bust? I could use some action. Tickets and paperwork coming out of my ears. Got my typing up to forty-per."

Sheriff Blood looked at him. Kearney was staring beyond the road in front of him, viewing some distant heroic act starring himself. These were the aspirations of young men, world-beaters. "You're greener than moss," Blood told him. "You know that? Near as soft too." Rookie Kearney grinned and nodded, sheepish, unapologetic. Blood kept at him. "How's Leslie?" he said. "How's she coming along?"

Kearney's grin vanished. "Seven months now," he said.

Blood said, "Sounds like a case of nerves."

"More than that. It's a nightmare, this thing. You would think seven months is plenty time to get a handle on it. But it's too much for me entirely. More and more I'm thinking like it's all one big mistake."

Sheriff Blood reserved judgment a moment.

"I'm trying to come up with a green deeper than moss," he said. "You're consistent anyway. Smile at a gun barrel, run from your wife. Rookie through and through."

Kearney nodded again as though he understood. They were turning off the interstate now and onto the tree-lined, one-lane county access road leading to Paradise Ridge, rattling in their seats as the cruiser's suspension rocked.

"Sheriff," Kearney said, curious about something now, and so a bit more respectful. "We're talking, right?" He was even trying to look at Blood, his eyes cheating off the narrow grassy road. "What's going on between you and the chief?"

Blood looked at him. It seemed like a genuine question.

"He hates Indians," Blood said. "It may be as simple as that. Some people we just piss off. In any case, I'm sure your veteran partner in back is taking notes."

There was no challenge from Haley. They turned off the county road past a bullet-pocked DEAD END sign and rolled over a groaning iron bridge painted blood-orange to match its rust. Paradise Creek, such as it was, dribbled between two hard brown clay banks beneath.

Great oaks and pines crowded and darkened the rising, winding road. The creek ran parallel and appeared somehow to grow stronger as they climbed, its clay banks spreading wider and filling in between with wet, smoothed rocks; there must have been a runoff somewhere below. Tire ruts in the road were jaundiced and deep.

The road eventually left the creek and snaked up under bright shafts of angled sun, then up and over a steep rise and suddenly into the bright light of a broad, tree-lined clearing. It was a plateau, situated an even third of the way up the mountain, more than seventy-five yards long and roughly oval in shape. The dirt ground was generally even, blotchy all over with straggles of dead straw weeds.

The cruiser rolled halfway in and stopped. Kearney cut the engine and there was a Big Sky silence, no traffic noises or train whistles, no sound even in the distance, nothing whatsoever.

Haley finally stirred in back. "Where's the road?" he grumbled.

Blood was first out of the cruiser. He stood and spotted the opening in the trees leading to the goat path up the mountainside, but it was well overgrown now and impassable, almost as though by design.

Haley, a bullet-headed sergeant with puffs of gray showing over his chiseled ears, got out and saw it too. "Looks like we walk," he said.

Blood tried to take it all in. He breathed the air and tasted nothing familiar. "Used to hunt all over this mountain," he said. "Squirrel, buck, coon. Soft land," he remembered, toeing the cracked earth. "No more."

Haley unlocked the trunk and unlatched and removed the shotgun that was kept there.

"Now hold on," said Blood.

Haley went ahead and pumped the Remington, checking it. "He's barricaded himself up there," he said.

Blood said, "All the more reason to go in cautionary."

Haley looked at him. "I suppose, then," he said, "you got a plan."

A mild challenge from Haley, but Blood had no stomach for it. Haley was a fifty-year-old police sergeant who had pretended to be asleep in the backseat of a car in order to encourage a private conversation. He was a patsy for the chief. Blood thought things over, watching Kearney size up the rest of the mountain—a good mile's hike up a steep grade through high trees.

Blood said, "Maybe something will come to me on the way up."

Haley nodded and shut the trunk and took the 12-gauge with him, and they started around the car toward the edge of the woods until a voice said, "Hold it."

At first Blood wasn't even sure what he had heard. The voice seemed to come from the trees at the foot of the mountain off to their left. It stopped them all, the surprise of it. The tone wasn't particularly commanding, but it was strange. Only darkness beyond the light shafts of the first few rows of oak, like a throat beyond long brown teeth.

"Ables?" Blood said loudly.

A short pause, then the voice again. Forceful, not low. "Hold it right there."

Blood said, "Who is that? Identify yourself."

A second voice then, from their right. "Turn around, get back in your car, and drive on."

Two voices. Blood saw no one. He half-turned and checked behind him. Haley was holding the shotgun out in front, not aimed, about chest-high. Kearney was glancing right to left, his hand lightly on the butt of his still-holstered gun. There was no cover at all in the clearing except for the cruiser.

Blood turned back. He said to the trees, "Now hold on in there. This is Sheriff Leonard M. Blood. I am here on official county business, but it's nothing that can't be talked over civilly. Who is that in there? Am I speaking to Glenn Ables?"

The first voice said, "Get back in your car and drive on."

Blood took a short step forward, not being brave or foolish, but annoyed now, not used to being ordered. He unfolded the legal notice and held it up so as to be seen. "Just hold on in there now," he said. "This here is the sheriff and I've got two police officers with me. Now there's two ways of doing this. There's the hard way, and then there's—"

The first shot cracked out of nowhere and nearly tore the notice from his hands. The second shot slit the air behind him, and Haley yelped and collapsed.

Blood turned fast. Haley's left knee was shattered. He was crumpled onto the ground and bleeding. The third shot struck Kearney's hip radio, propelling the rookie backward and down.

Blood scrambled sliding over the cruiser hood, falling to the hard ground behind. He reached around the front bumper for Kearney, who didn't know he wasn't wounded yet, grabbing the fabric over the rookie's shoulder and dragging him back. Kearney was patting himself frantically all over. Then he saw his gun belt and the cracked-open radio and said, "Holy shit!"

Haley was pulling himself around the rear end of the car by his elbows, on his back. His face was wide with desperation, chin shiny and wet with spit. "Fucking Jesus Christ! Fucking—" He stopped behind the tire and clutched at his knee without actually touching it, blood spilling full out and onto the dry earth like water from a dropped canteen. Haley did not have the shotgun. He was writhing too much for Blood to get at his belt radio.

The woods were silent now except for Haley's keening. Blood had flashes of being surrounded and taking a shot in the back as he reached up and grabbed at the passenger door latch. He got it open between him and Kearney and went in as low as he could against the blue vinyl passenger seat and reached up for the radio handset and pulled it down, sliding back out.

He was yelling into the radio when the windshield exploded, tires blowing out, light caddy shattering into raining fragments, the hood screaming ricochets. Blood got as low to the ground as he could, pulling Kearney down with him, eyes shut, head covered. Reports ripping like sparks in his ears. The cruiser pitched against them, rocking and staggering like some wounded beast. Kicked-up dust lifted and blew overhead as smoke. Then all at once the firing stopped. Haley ceased cursing and the gunshot echoes rippled all along the ridge, fading away. Then everything was quiet again.

Clearing

Blood drove the Bronco up over the rise in the mountain road and into the wide-open clearing. The sun was duller now, and falling. Tree shadows were starting their crawl.

The entire Huddleston Police motor pool was pulled up in there, blue lights turning, all parked askew. There was backup from neighboring towns as well, bringing the total police presence on the mountain to about thirty. Blood saw the car trunks open and uniformed men walking around with shotguns on their hips. In the middle of it all, the shot-to-hell cruiser was only then being hauled up onto a wrecker.

Chief Moody stood apart from the scattered fleet of cruisers, halfway between it and two parked Ford sedans with blue government license plates. The sandy-haired man he was facing wore a brown suit jacket and tie, street shoes, and was backed up by three similarly dressed men. It looked something like a baseball coach beefing with the head umpire.

Blood parked the Bronco and he and Kearney got out and came around in front. "Uh-oh," Kearney said, snapping off his orange hospital bracelet. "Chief's pissed." He viewed the suited strangers with interest. "Who's that?"

Blood said measuredly, "Who do you think?"

Kearney smiled broadly and eagerly. He hurried across the clearing to rejoin the ranks.

Blood remained aloof as always, ambling over toward the fracas, back on an even keel now after time out to collect himself at the hospital. He and Kearney had been forced to go in for observation, then stayed long enough for Kearney to donate blood for Haley, who was in the operating room but otherwise OK.

Blood watched things unfold. Chief Moody had his thumbs wedged in the front of his gun belt when he wasn't pointing and gesturing. It was a jurisdictional dispute. "Maybe you and your boys pulled up on the wrong mountain," he was saying. "This here's a local matter."

The head FBI man with the sandy hair appeared professionally unconcerned. "I carry a UFAP warrant from the U.S. Attorney's Office in Butte," he said. "That's unlawful flight to avoid prosecution."

Moody nodded and said, "Oh, I see. One of your escapees hauls off and pops two of my men, but now you're set to take over."

"He's not ours," the FBI man said. "The United States Marshals Service is charged with apprehending federal fugitives. We're just here to hold the scene for them."

"Well." Moody straightened some then. "In these parts," he said, "in this town, we take care of our own."

The FBI man nodded. "That's why we're here." He eyed the various officers looking on in anticipation. "Instruct your men to stand down."

Some shotgun barrels lowered behind Moody, and most of the visiting police holstered their sidearms. But none of the Huddleston force did. They stiffened up behind their chief, a loyalty of posture that made Moody's barrel chest swell out even more.

"See," said Moody, sporting a smile that was quaint, "there's only four of you."

The FBI man's half grin passed for wild emotion as he shook his head slowly, looking down. One of the agents behind him said aloud, "Small town, small dicks," but the lead agent held up his hand, showing displeasure at the name-calling, though not necessarily disagreement.

Moody burned. "The hell you come up here for anyway?" he said. "He ain't your boy, he ain't mine."

The FBI man said, "We got a call."

Moody looked at him. "A call?"

"A party requesting our presence. They said they were local law."

Moody cocked his head in suspicion, thumbs returning to his belt. "Nobody here called you," he said, looking around. "Who the hell would've called you?"

He was surveying his men for reassurance when his eyes settled finally on Blood. Blood stepped forward. "I called you," he said.

The FBI man turned to him, eyeing the uniform. "Sheriff?"

"Leonard M. Blood."

The agent nodded. "Reginald Perkins, FBI. Special Agent in Charge, Butte, Montana. Local field office for this region."

Moody interrupted loudly. "What the hell is this?"

He was looking at Blood. His eyes were big and wet with anger. Blood turned to him. "There's children up there, Moody. And other families. Look at your men here. Walking around with their safeties off, all anxious. This needs discipline."

Moody came closer and said lowly, "You Indian son of a bitch. First you kneecap one of my men, now you kneecap me."

Blood merely nodded at that. He returned to Perkins. "I called you men from the hospital. He's got loyal neighbors up there."

Perkins nodded. "Fine," he said. "We'll get your statement later."

Blood had been dismissed so fast he didn't even know it. It was remarkable, the ease. He was still looking at Perkins, realizing this, but Perkins's attention was given over now to a gathering rumble coming up the mountain road behind. Blood turned.

The signboard above the broad windshield read CHARTERED in yellow block lettering. The bus, silver and green, airport-style, labored over the rise and halfway into the center of the clearing and stopped there with a gusty sigh. It was full of uniformed men.

The door folded back and open and a black man stepped out. He wore a blue jumpsuit with a black flak vest over it, black boots, a black ballcap with a yellow star insignia, and a holstered sidearm.

He stood for a moment, looking around at the trees and the distant green mountains. The man wore an expression of impatient disbelief. Then he started toward the gathering, keenly aware of his audience, walking slowly, boot-proud, over the dry, weedy dirt. Closer, his skin was richly black, his nose large, lips curled into a no-nonsense grimace. The lettering around the gold star on his ballcap and underneath the badge pinned to his chest read UNITED STATES MARSHAL.

He eyed all, then zeroed in on Perkins and spoke roughly. "FBI?" he said.

Perkins went forward. "Perkins, SAC, Butte."

"Fagin, Deputy Marshal, L.A."

They nodded at each other cursorily, then Fagin stepped off and scanned the clearing again, as though looking for a good place to spit. "Where the fuck am I?" he said.

Perkins said, "You're in Montana. The northwestern corner, a gunshot away from the Canadian border. This is Paradise Ridge."

Fagin squinted up at the small mountain. "Son of a bitch finally forced our hand."

Moody came forward. "This area is secured."

Fagin regarded him and his uniform, then saw Blood.

"Chief of Police," Fagin said. "And a real, live sheriff. Well, how-dee." He sized up all the blue uniforms behind, and the white men wearing them, looking from face to face, his rough voice rising. "Maybe one of you men here can point out to me the Einstein who got it in his fucking head to go knocking on this federal fugitive's fucking front door."

Blood swallowed. He licked his lips and acknowledged a burning on the back of his neck. "That would be me," he said.

Fagin turned back to him, staring, near enough that Blood could smell the tobacco of his last cigar. "Do you know where I spent the last two weeks?" he said, taking another step closer. "I spent the last fourteen fucking days up in the White Mountains of New Hampshire with my Special Ops Group, spending taxpayers' money and freezing my fucking ass preparing for a tactical apprehension operation up here in the Montana hills—a full-blown fucking TAO. We were going to take this motherfucker down."

Blood held his own. "I had a notice to evict," he told him. "That's all I knew."

Fagin nodded, mouth curled, voice low and patronizing. "Well, Kemo Sabe," he said, "I guess the element of surprise is pretty well gone now."

Perkins stepped in then, like a referee. "What's this guy Ables's file?" he said. "We heard weapons."

Fagin broke off slowly from Blood, backing away. "Illegal firearms trafficking, bench warrant default. Dabbles in explosives. Also, civil rights violations. No formal charges, but it's part of his file. Hillbilly Aryan. A known white supremacist."

His words were greeted with neither shock nor surprise from the policemen. Fagin surveyed the assembled uniforms with a sneer that could otherwise have been considered a grin. "And no one says a fucking word," he said.

Fagin looked back at the bus and made a circular motion in the air with his forefinger. Marshals saddled with rifles and gear began climbing out. Fagin said, "All right. We'll bivouac a fire base right here, tents and trailers for an overnight. Clear out this area and start e-vacking the locals." He looked across at Perkins. "This fucker's got his whole family up there," he said. "You're the local negotiator?"

Perkins looked warily around the clearing. "Maybe I'll check with the Bureau on this one," he said.

Wednesday, August 4

Paradise Point

Dawn. Morning comes fast to the top of a mountain, like some-one polishing the great black night sky, revealing it to be blue. Dep-uty Marshal Bascombe's breath swirled in the growing light around him. His thermal underwear was a half size too small and pulled at him in all the wrong places, and his stomach was grumbling again.

He was in the fifth hour of his third surveillance watch. They had come up the mountainside in two-by-two cover formation to a gully thirty-five yards below the cabin. Or was it a ravine? The sides were smooth. Like a trench at this point, cutting horizontally across the mountain, then falling off through the trees and trailing away. Whatever it was, it was not man-made.

He was kneeling down, well hidden, with a good view of the cabin through the trees. He ran his thumb and forefinger along his upper lip, smoothing out his mustache. The boredom of a surveil-lance run. Bascombe looked around for birds. Because there was a deadness in these woods, a stillness, more like December than Au-gust, and there should have been birds. In the hometown of his youth, in rural Maryland, he had walked through the woods to school each day, browner woods than these, and there were hum-mingbirds that darted through the air, careening around tree trunks like bullets with wings. And if he stood still long enough in those woods, a stray hummingbird might careen around him too, mistaking him for a tree and rocketing toward him, jumping from breeze to breeze, and he would shut his eyes and feel it splitting the air around him and hear its small wings, fast like an insect's, fanning a hairpin turn. Then he would open his eyes and watch it darting around tree trunks and away.

So there should have been birds here, and animals, something rustling in the underbrush other than deputy marshals. Squirrels in the trees, brown toads hopping, even coyotes. But—birds. If only to eat up some of the damn bugs.

It was the beginning of the marshals' second full day on the mountain. They slept in cots on pancake mattresses and ate Red Cross "food." They showered eight at a time, one minute lukewarm and two minutes cold. You could go a full wrist rotation between FM radio stations, from French blah-BLAH-blah to Bible readings and doomsday predictions. Hell is a place with no takeout and no classic rock. It's a place full of bugs and no birds. Where the wilderness is silent except for your stomach rumbling and the odd crackle of static through the radio wire in your ear.

He wasn't supposed to wonder what they were doing here. They were watching a cabin. They were watching a cabin in the woods on top of a mountain. There was a man inside the cabin who was a wanted fugitive. They were waiting for him to come out. The woods were filled with armed marshals hiding out behind trees. The marshals were dirty and tired and hungry. When not on watch, they worked down below to make the base area livable, erecting tents, building picnic tables, digging toilet trenches. They had run two weeks of TAO prep drills for this in northern New Hampshire because of the similar terrain. And then there was everything they had gone through just to get into the Special Operations Group itself, the elite tactical unit of the U.S. Marshals Service. The training, the written exams, the psychological evaluations, the endless procedural drills. They were skilled in crowd and riot control, semiautomatic weapons handling, rappelling, land navigation, felony car ap-proach. They were experts in the apprehension of dangerous fugitives, including U.S. fugitives abroad. Like going after Noriega in Panama. That was war—gunfire in the distance, rockets shooting overhead, flares lighting up the night sky. This was a man in a cabin in the woods.

The going-through-the-motions surveillance runs brought back basic training at Camp Beauregard in the bayous of Pineville, and the insects there. The marshlands alive day and night with animal chatter and bird cries. The sweat he swept off his forehead with a full hand, having to billow his T-shirt for ventilation during the drills. The tickle of swamp leaves against his face, and faint, steamy Louisiana music through the trees.

All of which brought him back to the grilled Cajun swordfish at Samo's. His stomach again. He had eaten at Samo's only twice in his lifetime, but some places stay with you. The fat maître d'. The nauti-cal decor, the dark tables with red bulb lighting. The swordfish there —steak of the sea, the waiter called it. Christ, it was delicious. The inside of Bascombe's mouth started to flow, more like sweat than pure saliva. For the first time that shift, he even started to feel a little warm.

He was moving. Lobach flanked his right, crouched near dead tree roots spilling in tangles out of the hard dirt wall. Bascombe shuffled over, bent low, drawing up beside him. He saw himself there in Lobach, a cold man hunched down in a camouflage jump-suit, bulky black Kevlar vest strapped over his shoulders and around his sides, black helmet on his head, a gun belt with a thigh-strapped holster, knee and elbow pads and black gloves, and the white radio wire running from his shoulder up into his ear.

There were few mirrors down at camp, so before each watch the men would pair off and grease-paint each other's faces in camouflag-ing swirls of olive, vine-green, and brown. Bascombe had painted the word *pussy* onto Lobach's forehead without his knowing it. This was their sport. God only knew what he looked like himself.

Bascombe said, "I can get closer."

Lobach was a Texan with close-set eyes. Other than that and the two inches he had on Bascombe, they could have been brothers. In full tactical gear, every marshal looked alike.

"What's to see?" Lobach said with something less than a drawl. "S'all boarded up."

"There's a nice fat tree up there, some fifteen yards."

Lobach was settled back against the sloping dirt. "We have orders," he said.

"I know that. I'm going nutso, though, I gotta do something."

Lobach swatted at the air. "Ain't nothing to see."

"Screw it, then. So maybe I'll ring his doorbell and run."

Lobach's eyes brightened. "You do and you can have my Red Cross rations tonight."

Bascombe was being taunted. "Fuck you," he said.

"What, you want a back rub instead?"

"Fuck you. Texas shithead."

"Baltimore pussy."

"I wouldn't say that."

Bascombe had to look away or else he'd laugh. He looked up at the high branches and the brightening blue sky above. He loved being a U.S. Marshal. He loved the two-hundred-year heritage of the service and the images it brought to people's minds—Gary Cooper, the Wild West—and he loved the respect his gold star garnered. But something else told him he was different from all the others. It was what had driven him to volunteer for the Special Ops team against the wishes of his wife, Laura. This sense of wanting to belong. He was more thoughtful, perhaps, but basically irregular, not of the same fit as the others. He envied their easy camaraderie.

"Hey," he said, turning back. "Remember Samo's?"

Lobach squinted at him in confusion.

Bascombe said, "The blackened swordfish. The dinner special, six ninety-five?"

Lobach just looked at him funny. Bascombe pointed. "That tree right there," he said. "Where the rise starts to level off. Maybe I can get more of the layout."

Lobach swatted again. "Goddamned bugs."

Bascombe got up on his haunches. "I'm going."

He rose, stooping, patted his 9mm, looked over the top of the dirt embankment to make certain the coast was clear, then swung one leg up and over.

He came back down again just as quickly, landing on both feet. "Hey," he said. "Is this a gully or a ravine?"

"Gully," said Lobach. "You can float a boat in a ravine."

Bascombe nodded, satisfied. He pulled tighter on the heel of each of his gloves, then went back over the top.

He straightened up at the first tree, stilling a disturbed branch, and drew his weapon, muzzle down, his gloved index finger extended along the barrel. Lobach showed him nothing, so Bascombe spun off and cross-stepped to the second tree, then diagonally again up the dirt rise to his intended post.

Nothing from Lobach. Bascombe was clear. He took a deep breath, warmed from all the motion, and suddenly smelled pine. Bark bristled against the back of his shoulders.

Arms straight, gun pointed away, he twisted and peered out from behind the fat trunk. He was closer to the cabin than he had thought. It was about twenty-by-twenty feet, a patchwork mishmash of wood grades, mostly plywood. The roof was obtuse and unshingled, windows boarded fast, and a lopsided porch on three uneven steps ran the length of the front. The land fell off beyond, the middle and rear of the cabin standing on graded lengths of wood posts to stay level. Treetops showed behind the roof; there was known to be an outhouse and some small wooden shacks among them. Then rocky cliffs beyond. The only sign of life was a lazy thread of smoke rising out of the stone chimney.

Bascombe stood back against the tree. He relaxed his arms a little and looked around, stamping his feet. He realized then that he could get just as stiff and cold and hungry and bored standing out here. He watched a dead leaf drift to the ground, then looked down the length of the mountain to where the thickening tree trunks ran together into a black wall that eventually blocked his view.

A noise behind him. Something like a thick snap or a click, and he pictured a bird or a squirrel settling on a weak branch. He turned and leaned out again to look.

The front door of the cabin was open. Two men were exiting with automatic weapons, one of them a definite match for Ables's mug shot. Then, behind them, a young girl who looked to be about twelve or thirteen, one of Ables's daughters. The girl had a top-handled rifle slung over her shoulder that was too heavy for her, maybe an AR-15, and was holding on to rope leashes tied to three thin gray dogs.

Bascombe stood back quickly, arms stiff. The blood pulsing now in his temples messed with his hearing, but there was nothing on the marshals' radio net. He looked downland toward the gully, saw no one.

He ducked and leaned out the other way. Through the trees he saw a lone man approaching the cabin. Older, like a neighbor, except that all the mountain residents had long since been evacuated.

Ables, his daughter, and the third armed man—tall, burly, bearded—greeted the older unknown with their guns hanging loose, meeting him near the front right corner of the cabin. They were chewing the fat. Bascombe was too far off to hear anything. The dogs rooted around them, sniffing the dirt hungrily, happy just to be outside.

Bascombe straightened again and squared off to the south. Whatever the hell was going on, he was stuck there, but well out of sight. He was OK. He nodded his head and tried to stay loose, watching the gully for directions.

There was Lobach moving laterally to his right, establishing position. That reassured him. He nodded to himself again.

A single dog barked first, almost playfully. Then all three at once, snarling and gargling and gobbling up air. Like beasts laughing and cursing at the same time, cries choked by collared throats. Then movement, hesitant boot-steps and paws tearing up dirt and brush. Then voices calling out.

Bascombe stiffened. He slipped his finger in over the trigger.

Barking distorted by galloping now, the dogs turned loose. Things happening fast. One dog closer than the others. Furious snarling, paws beating the hard ground like hooves, now nearly upon him. Bascombe stood tight against the tree. He was shaking in anticipation, gun ready.

The lead dog shot past him. Legs blurred, head dipping and rising. Ignored, Bascombe watched it go. Then he realized it was charging the gully and Lobach.

Bascombe's mind went into overdrive. He quickly patted his chest. High-powered rounds wouldn't stop for the vest, he knew. He found his marshal's ID and brought it out fast. Head throbbing, he spun out suddenly into the clear, gun out flat, ID up, exactly as he was trained to do.

"Bascombe, U.S. Marshals! Stop where you are!"

He realized as he did this that no one was able to hear him over the dogs. His ears pounded with such force, he wondered if he was even speaking at all. Still nothing on the radio net. Ables had stopped twenty yards uphill.

"Federal marshals!" he yelled. "Freeze!"

The second dog was upon him. Bascombe sighted and squeezed and kicked off a single round, and the dog yelped and collapsed onto its chest, somersaulting forward and dead.

Bascombe looked back up and reaimed. His ears were ringing and roaring now. The individuals had dropped into defensive positions but the third dog was bearing down on him—jagged teeth, body hurtling forward. Then Bascombe was aware of slots opening in the walls of the cabin beyond, and various-sized gun barrels emerging from them. He wondered briefly what Lobach was doing behind him. But he didn't see the girl until it was too late.

Behind a dead stump, the barrel of the AR-15 resting on top.

Young forehead wrinkled in anger and aim. A few quick bursts. Something hit Bascombe hard in the throat and he pitched back and fell.

He slid back a few feet headfirst, then lay still. He clutched at the dirt and dead leaves under his now-empty hands. He turned his head this way and that way but could not get up. No one was near him and he was dizzy. He needed help. Voices talking in his ear now. There was the *brrpt* of far-off gunfire. A sweet taste in his mouth. The morning sky above. And a bird, a crow, lifting off from the high black branches, frightened by all the noise.

Skull Valley, Montana

Memorandum, SA Coyle to [title and name deleted]: PARASIEGE

Sir:

In reference to your request of 22 October 1993, this confidential report has been compiled from personal recollections and is presented in light of the circumstances and questions surrounding the outcome of operation PARASIEGE and the current ongoing investigation. It is intended neither as a recommendation nor as a conclusion of this agent or of the FBI. Verbal exchanges have been reconstructed and should not be considered verbatim.

On 4 August 1993 at approximately 14:00 hrs. (Mountain Time), Special Agent MARY GRACE COYLE and Special Agent DOUGLAS TAYLOR of the Butte Field Office arrived at the FBI Resident Agency in Skull Valley, Montana. The Skull Valley RA is a solitary one-story, Bureau-provided residence on the outskirts of the town, supported by a single resident agent and identifiable as FBI property only by a mailbox shingle on which is depicted the official FBI emblem.

The Skull Valley RA was originally established in 1971 to monitor and investigate acts of conspiracy and gross theft of government property regarding illegal logging operations in the nearby Fort Belknap Indian Reservation and the Charles M. Russell National Wildlife Refuge. Severe timberland depletion, however, as evidenced by acres of razed hills, had long since driven even legitimate loggers from the region. The current operative function of this RA, therefore, was not immediately apparent.

The Butte Field Office had been out of contact with the Skull Valley RA for at least twenty-four hours (last logged interoffice communication: 23 March). On emergency assignment, SA Coyle and SA Taylor touched down via helicopter and proceeded across the street to the front door of the residence. The telephone wires from the sidewalk poles appeared to be intact and the structure appeared secure.

SA Taylor pressed the doorbell twice without answer. SA Coyle then left the front stoop to investigate further, whereupon she gained visual access into the residence through a front window. Nothing inside appeared to be upset or disturbed. SA Taylor then tried the doorknob and found it to be unlocked. SA Coyle rejoined him on the landing and both agents drew their service weapons and entered the premises.

The front room was neatly if sparely arranged and evidenced no signs of struggle. There were several indications, such as a quality of air consistent with proper ventilation, that the RA had recently been occupied. SA Coyle determined upon cursory examination that the telephone and teletype unit wires had been disconnected from their respective wall sockets. The agents then proceeded further with their investigation.

Of the two inner doorways, one to their immediate right was open. The agents approached with caution and entered a small kitchen, which was found to be unoccupied and undisturbed. As the agents were inspecting detailed meal, work, and sleep charts posted on the kitchen cabinets, dated as recently as the day before, a voice from the main room behind them ordered that they disarm immediately. They were instructed to place their hands behind their heads and to turn around. SA Coyle and SA Taylor had no alternative but to comply.

The individual was armed with a large-caliber handgun. He was a white male, early fifties, six-two, medium build, gray hair, blue eyes, wearing khaki pants and a light plaid shirt, white socks without shoes, wire-rimmed half-glasses, short gray beard. He had entered from the door across the front room behind them. He appeared to be agitated and disoriented, and potentially dangerous.

The individual relieved both agents of their FBI identification, which he read and flipped back against the agents' chests to fall to the floor. He demanded to know their reason for being there. SA Coyle advised the individual that they were federal agents and that the individual was trespassing on federal property. The individual then inquired further, to which SA Coyle responded that she and SA Taylor were investigating the apparent disablement of the RA and the possible disappearance of its resident agent, SA John Banish. SA Coyle then advised the individual to set down his weapon and comply peacefully.

The individual instead proceeded to criticize both agents in a disparaging manner. Specifically, he addressed FBI rules of SOP regarding hostile entry: that all doorways be checked and secured before attempting further examination of the premises; that all agents identify themselves immediately upon entry in a loud and clear manner.

SA Taylor then inquired as to whether the individual himself was Special Agent Banish, to which the individual

replied: "We're all special. The Bureau does not discrimi-
nate." Special Agent JOHN BANISH then lowered his
weapon and returned to the front room. SA Coyle and SA
Taylor followed.

SA Banish positioned himself near the open front door
of the premises. He appeared anxious and uncomfortable.
He advised the agents that the Butte office's cause for alarm
was unfounded, and then invited both to leave. At no time
did he offer any explanation for the disconnected telephone
and teletype units, nor why he apparently had not heard the
helicopter approach, nor why he had not originally answered
the doorbell.

When informed that SA Coyle and SA Taylor carried
orders to transport him for reassignment, SA Banish became
agitated and noticeably confused. He immediately questioned the validity of the orders and disallowed their accu-
racy:

SA COYLE: Are you aware of the Paradise Ridge situa-
tion, sir?
SA BANISH: North of here. Local police shot at.
SA COYLE: A U.S. Marshal was murdered there in a
gunfight this morning. Another marshal is still pinned down
at this hour. Marshals Service Special Operations Group is
attempting a rescue.
SA BANISH: How old was he?
SA COYLE: Sir?
SA BANISH: The dead marshal. How old was he?
SA COYLE: We don't know that, sir.

• After some moments of silence following this irregular
preliminary questioning, SA Banish went on to inquire as to
the relevance of the incident pertaining to himself:

SA COYLE: The suspect in question is a federal fugitive. Further complicating matters are the other individuals barricaded in the cabin with him, sir. Five of them are juveniles, the suspect's own children. The situation is being approached as a hostage-taking.

SA BANISH: This is some kind of mistake.

SA COYLE: No, sir. I have the reassignment orders right here. Skills bank matched you to the subject: age, geographical location, distinguished military service.

SA BANISH: It is a mistake.

SA COYLE: I do not believe so, sir. But mistake or not, the orders have been cut. The case has been upgraded to Special and you have been assigned. You are now the case agent.

SA TAYLOR: Sir, we can help you pack while you shave.

SA BANISH: You don't understand. My work is here.

SA COYLE: Sir. You are a federal hostage negotiator with Special Operations and Research. Your work is in Montana now.

SA BANISH: Who is the current Section Chief?

SA COYLE: Which section, sir?

SA BANISH: Seven. Kidnapping.

SA COYLE: I do not know. But this is being handled by SOARs.

SA BANISH: Who is the current SOARs chief?

SA COYLE: Carlson, sir.

SA BANISH: Division head, then. GID. Is Richardsen still Assistant Director?

SA COYLE: I believe so, sir.

SA BANISH: I will call him.

SA COYLE: You can call from the helicopter, sir.

SA BANISH: You don't understand. I am not boarding that helicopter.

SA Banish was becoming increasingly agitated in both tone and manner. SA Coyle's determination at this point was that SA Banish had become irrational. He was contradicting and refusing reassignment and carrying on in an emotional state. He had since retreated near the unopened door behind him, and by his defensive posture appeared to be attempting to deflect attention and/or access to said room.

SA Coyle once again advised SA Banish that he could contact AD Richardsen in transit. When SA Banish refused, SA Coyle then insisted on packing for him and proceeded through the door in question.

In sharp contrast to the front room, SA Banish's sleeping quarters were in absolute disarray. His bedsheets were tossed, wrinkled articles of clothing hung out of half-open dresser drawers, and an odor of heated staleness was pervasive.

A secretary desk sat under sagging bookshelves in one corner of the room, littered with torn-out sheets of writing paper crossed out and rewritten many times over. On the desk was an oversized dictionary of German-to-English translation and a faded wire-bound notebook filled with foreign verse. The purpose served by these articles remains unknown to this agent.

SA Banish quickly followed SA Coyle inside. He appeared furious and inappropriately secretive, but at once surrendered his opposition and agreed to begin packing, contingent solely upon his being allowed to do so in private.

SA Coyle agreed and withdrew. She and SA Taylor retrieved their service weapons and identification from the kitchen area, again observing the peculiar, detailed lists of food intake, exact length of sleep time, etc. They then returned to the front room to wait for SA Banish to emerge.

Washington, D.C.

Salvatore Richardsen, Assistant Director of the General Investi-
gative Division of the FBI, exited the elevator and was halfway to his
car beneath the J. Edgar Hoover Building when a woman's voice
from an overhead speaker summoned him back to his office for an
urgent call.

Upstairs, Richardsen set his briefcase down on the slate-colored
carpet and stood in his unbuttoned London Fog and punched the
flashing button on his speakerphone.

"Jack," he said, fiddling with the secretary's message note left on
his desk. Very sexy handwriting. Wishful thinking at this point, but
he was definitely interested. He admired her script, trying to imagine
her upright loops and fine trailing swirls curled around the word
cock. "Long time, Jack. Too long. Sounds like you're airborne."

Banish's voice was low and remote over the squawk box. "Sal,"
he said. "What are you doing to me here?"

"It's bad business, Jack. We'll need someone of your caliber out
there."

"Sal, I'm in a helicopter, I can't talk. Listen. I don't think I'm up
to it."

Richardsen licked his warm lips. He frowned. It was impossible
to get an accurate emotional read over the connection, from a helicopter headset to a speakerphone all the way across the country.
Like talking to someone on a car phone in the final lap of the Indy
500.

"Jack," he said, "you have to be up to it. A quagmire up there,
very important to this office, as well as SOARs. You know the
bastard's drawn federal blood."

A pause. The whup-whup of rotor blades and the underlying
whine.

"What about Raleigh?" he heard Banish say.

Richardsen shook his head mildly. In his distraction, he held the pink message slip up to the bright ceiling lights. "He's tied up with that Port Authority thing in Los Angeles," he said.

The way she made a capital *B*. Bold, broad, sweeping strokes. Tough, confident. Take-charge. On top of things, experienced—but with a delicate flow of expression. The same way she moved when she walked down the hall ahead of him. That royal-blue sheath dress she had worn today. He had a brainstorm suddenly. Get something of hers down to Handwriting for a full analysis. To get the inside track on her personality. Something off the top of her desk, maybe.

Richardsen set the message note back down and paced a bit. "Look, Jack," he said. "Everything you need. You call back with the specs. Hostage Rescue is yours if you want it. QB this thing, you know the drills. He's on top of a frigging mountain, so you take your time, run your plays."

"Sal, it's been more than two years."

"Everyone knows that, Jack. I don't mean everyone. But you're out there on the fringe, counting your fingers. Look, Jack. A man of your talents. I have absolute confidence in you here, absolutely. You are the best, I mean that. Now, there's the kids involved, I don't know if you know. That's the other thing. They're armed, all right? His kids carry, that's the report we're getting. He trained them— which is what I mean by a quagmire here. You see how it is? With the hostage scenario, SOARs takes full control. We can't afford to ride along with the Marshals on this one, too much at stake. External Affairs knows it's a nightmare going in. That's the main thing. If there's any shooting to be done, make sure it's the Marshals doing it. We don't want to get drawn into a gun battle with little kids. So— they're hostages. All right? That's priority one."

"Sal," Banish said, "you offer me whatever I need, then you handcuff me to a chair. I have to go into this with a clear head."

Richardsen grabbed his football off the shelf. "You make like

I'm throwing you to the lions here, Jack. This is your job, this is what you did so damn well in New York for eleven years. So you're coming back off injured reserve. OK, great—big comeback here."

"Sal. Jesus."

"Just talk him down, Jack. Get him off that fucking mountain, effect the arrest. Bring the bastard to the bar of justice. I mean it, free rein. I don't care how you run things. And look—if the hijacking thing resolves itself soon, maybe we can release Raleigh. Hell—you trained him, right? Jack, I gotta go."

"Sal, listen. Just tell me. Is this a push? Do they want me to resign?"

Richardsen stopped where he was. Even with all the interference, he heard it that time, the desperation in Banish's voice. Richardsen frowned harshly.

"Jack," he said, "we want your expertise here. We want that bag of tricks you've got in your head. Christ, Jack—a man's dead and there are kids in mortal danger up there. All right? Jack—all right?"

Whup-whup.

"You are the best, Jack, the best there is. Just forget New York. Put it all behind you. Starting fresh here. My number two will be in later, so you call him with your laundry list. The SAC out there is Perkins, Butte. All right? All right. Keep in touch, Jack."

Richardsen punched the button and the red light went off. He remained staring at the box a moment, then moved away. He turned his old college football over in his hands. The leather was cracking, its bladder gone soft. He recalled hours spent sitting at the foot of the metal frame bed in his little room at Fordham, thinking about the next game, and the hands that used to hold that ball—tight-skinned, trim-knuckled, ringless fingers—gripping it, turning it, tossing it up and down. It was the last time he could remember his priorities ever matching his responsibilities.

For anyone else, protesting or refusing an assignment would be cause for immediate termination. But the word had come down on his old friend Jack Banish and all the head cases ripe for wrongful termination lawsuits. Sal Richardsen cupped the football in his right hand. He set his feet and momentarily drew his arm back for a dramatic, game-winning Hail Mary. Then he went across the room and returned the football to its wooden stand on the shelf. He threw away the message note and picked up his briefcase and headed for the door. They had needed a negotiator on the scene ASAP. Whoever had screwed up, it was the kind of mistake that could cost a man his career. Banish was mistakenly listed on the active roster and SOARs had geographically matched him to the crisis perpetrator, and Carlson at Quantico hadn't gone through Richardsen himself or known enough to override. So the order had been cut and the great machine set into motion. Stopping Banish now would have thrown the entire operation to a grinding halt, and there was simply no time for that. The crisis was current and ongoing. Richardsen realized that he would have to keep close tabs on this one, very close tabs. He would give it some thought on the long ride out to Rockville.

Clearing

The helicopter touched down cleanly but its roaring engine did not stop. Banish stepped out into the clearing behind Coyle and Taylor, ducking to avoid the beating rotor blades. Two U.S. Marshals in camouflage and greasepaint passed him. He turned and watched as they loaded aboard a leaden, sheet-covered stretcher. Then the whupping roar lifted again and the helicopter spun lazily overhead, tucking its nose and beating away.

Banish straightened and watched it go. His ears rang hollow from the sudden absence of noise, as though hearing an unfelt wind. His newly shaved cheeks stung in the cool air. There was a light drizzle, fog hanging in the trees. A tan jacket hung hanger-stiff under his FBI slicker, holster straps tight around his shoulders and under his arms. Three men coming toward him. Agents. Banish hoped he had his game face on.

The lead one swept back his sandy hair and introduced himself as Perkins. His relief at Banish's arrival was evident in his manner. "We've had some death here," he said.

Banish bristled. The dead man leaving the mountain was immediately his responsibility. He had become the case agent as soon as his feet touched ground.

"The other marshal?" he said.

"Coming down now. He's OK. Was pinned down by gunfire from inside the cabin. Special Ops Group leader is debriefing his men AWS."

As we speak, recalled Banish. The wonky acronyms, the lingo. He looked around as they crossed the dampened clearing. The sky was clouding over and the mountaintop was obscured by fog. He counted three large canvas tents and ten recreational trailers. There were temporary latrine sheds and a row of support vehicles, including a fire engine and a Red Cross food truck. Men in riot gear, suits, police uniforms, military camouflage, and civilian clothes wandered about, some carrying cups of coffee, others guns. Despite the neat arrangement of the parked vehicles and the general complacency of the men, there was no real order here as far as Banish could see.

He tried to organize his thoughts. The remoteness of the plateau clearing offered certain tactical advantages, among them the ability to maintain a large operation without significant disruption of civilian life, a secure and centralized location, and the benefit of removing a potentially hazardous situation from the public eye. Disadvantages would include exposure to the elements, lack of expedient access to the actual crisis scene, and the danger of removing a potentially hazardous situation from the public eye.

He turned his focus to Perkins. The man from Butte was practiced and smooth. A Mormon, likely, the tight-mouthed, tiepin brand of federal agent. As opposed to the Eastern type, ruddy, gray-haired backslappers who still attended their college homecoming each year—the Young Kennedys, they used to be called, the Catholic-school brand of agent, as Banish had once been. Perkins's subordinates wore long-sleeved jerseys under camouflage issue and work boots and FBI shields on ballcaps. Perkins remained in a suit jacket and wore rubbers over shoes. He showed no indication that he had recognized Banish's name, which was mere politeness. It put Banish on guard.

Banish said, "I don't see any telephone lines."

Perkins said, "No electricity either. How much do you know?"

"Nothing. I need to know it all."

Perkins nodded. "You need the file. I can give you a little now. Suspect name is Glenn Allen Ables. Undercover Alcohol, Tobacco, and Firearms agents stung him more than two years ago for trafficking illegal firearms. He put his cabin up for bail and defaulted, and has been holed up here since. A local sheriff trying to serve him with an eviction notice triggered all this. Nine other residents on the mountain, all evacuated two days ago."

"Access?"

"By foot. The path up is impassable."

"How old was the dead marshal?"

Perkins turned to look at him. "I don't know," he said, confused. "Younger."

"Married?"

Perkins, still looking at him, shook his head blankly. "I really wouldn't know."

They were coming up on the canvas tent closest to the foot of the mountain. A group of narrow-eyed marshal sharpshooters, members of the self-named Beloved Order of Long-Rifle Men and Observers, stood outside in the rain with sniper rifles by their sides, waiting.

Raised voices and thick cursing from inside the tent. A table overturned. Then a marshal was backed out forcibly through the tent folds, stumbling to the ground, propelled by a furious older black marshal. The BOLOs moved in quickly to separate the two, restraining the black marshal. The younger marshal slowly got to his feet in the fresh mud, looking stunned. His face and close-set eyes were locked. Banish noticed the word *pussy* dripping off his painted forehead.

The black marshal was yelling through teeth clenched on a lit cheroot. "Fucking bug spray," he said. "On a covert surveillance op, fucking bug spray—" He strained against the arms of the four marshals holding him back. "The fuck were you thinking? This a fucking picnic here?"

"No, sir," croaked the painted marshal.

A flaring shower of tobacco ash as the black marshal got an arm free and whipped his cheroot off the painted marshal's vest. "Fuck me, no sir, you piece of shit. You fucking pussy. You bug-free fucking girl. They scented you. The dogs fucking scented you, you fucking perfume-wearing motherfucker. Bascombe's fucking stung to death and you're goddamn fucking bite-free. I will fucking kill you. Get the fuck out of my sight, I will fucking shoot you myself."

The painted marshal was not breathing now. His mouth was twisted open and he was looking around dog-faced, as though for his dead partner. Then he turned and walked off.

The men released the black marshal but he fought them off anyway. He stalked around and saw a transport Jeep parked nearby and walked up to it and punched the center of the windshield with his gloved fist. It cracked in a fine web burst but did not shatter. Then his big arms dropped at his sides. "Fucking corpse," he muttered.

He turned and saw Banish there with Perkins. The black marshal's eyes were sharp over his frowning mouth, his hair cropped tight under a black ballcap. "What?" he said.

Perkins introduced, too mildly: "Deputy Fagin, head of Marshals Special Ops Group; SA John Banish. Banish is the case agent on this one."

Fagin stopped. "What fucking case agent?"

Perkins stiffened, stumbling over some of the words. "SA Banish is a hostage negotiator with Special Operations and Research—"

"Hostages?" Fagin came forward fast, looking at both of them. "There are no hostages on this mountain. What the fuck is this?"

Banish said, "Tell me what happened up there."

Fagin turned. "Fuck you."

Perkins said, "Now wait a minute—"

Fagin turned to him. "You fucking wait. I don't mind a field division rep up here and I don't mind Bureau deep-pocket help. But this is a U.S. Marshals Service operation."

Perkins shook his head with an expression of tight-faced regret. "Not anymore."

Fagin said, "Bullshit. Ables is a federal fugitive. Recapturing him is Marshal responsibility."

Perkins listed the charges. "Kidnapping, assault on a police officer, assault on a federal agent, murder of a federal agent, conspiracy, conspiracy to commit murder—"

"Bullshit." Fagin stalked away five broad steps, then came right back. Body language punctuated his vehemence. "Bullshit. That's my man flying home under a sheet."

Behind him, the BOLOs stirred with interest and narrow-eyed defiance. Grim, mustached men. But Banish watched everyone with the narrowest eyes of all.

"Was he married?" Banish said.

Fagin looked at Banish. His face seemed ready to explode. "This is your specialist?" he said to Perkins. "What the fuck kind of question is that?"

"Did he have any children?" Banish said.

Fagin looked at him as though he were crazy. His expression as he shook his head was one of broad, taunting confusion.

One of the BOLOs spoke up behind. "He was married," the marshal said. "No kids."

Banish nodded. "Late twenties?"

The BOLO nodded yes.

Banish closed his eyes. He rubbed his forehead, then his temples, then just his eyes with the thumb and finger of his left hand. There was no headache, just a swirl of complications and old, distorted voices. In the darkness he could have been anywhere.

He opened his eyes and was back where he was, the others all staring at him, waiting or annoyed or wondering what the hell. Banish was accustomed to the staring.

He looked at Fagin. "Call your Director," he said. "Get me assigned off this mountain."

Fagin showed him a face. "Fuck you," he said.

Banish shook his head earnestly. "It's all yours. I didn't ask for it and I don't want it. Call him up and get me out of here today."

"Fuck you. You know that's not how it's done."

Banish did know. If it were that easy, he would already have placed the call himself. "Then tell me what happened up there," he said.

Fagin glared. He looked over at Perkins, who showed him nothing. Then he crossed his big arms.

"Routine surveillance-containment, two-by-two cover formation. Two teams flanked laterally in a gully thirty-five yards below the target. Oh-seven-hundred hours, a neighbor approaches the property. Red Cross had been escorting residents up to their homes to feed animals or pick up medicine; this individual somehow slipped away. The suspect, Ables, his brother-in-law Mellis, and one of Ables's daughters all exit with dogs and guns to greet the visitor. The dogs pick up Lobach's scent and charge the gully. Bascombe is positioned behind a tree twenty yards down. The lead dog passes him, going for Lobach. Bascombe jumps out, ID's himself and taps a dog, then takes three quick, two in the chest, one in the throat."

Banish tensed a little, recalling the sensation of lead tearing through skin and muscle. "Armor?" he said.

"Thin ballistic standard. Fucking tin. They're using AR-15s."

"Trigger?"

"Unknown. All three were firing, including the fucking girl. Ten more minutes of swapping shots, then a hose-down from the cabin and all three individuals retreated. The dogs are dead. We can't get to two of them. Cabin fire pinned us down and the fog and terrain eighty-sixed air support. Rescue teams had to hike up. Took three passes to get the body out." Fagin glanced aside again, shaking his head. "Fucking bug spray."

"Your men didn't hit anyone?"

Fagin said, "Unknown at this time."

"The girl," Banish said, pressing him.

Fagin said, "Unknown."

"How old is she?"

Fagin looked incredulous again. "How old? The fuck does it matter, how old?"

"It matters. What are the children's ages?"

"Read the file," Fagin said. "Then you can send them all birthday cards. Meanwhile, we got a fucking situation here."

Banish nodded, but to himself. Too much to handle all at once. He felt suddenly transparent standing there, as though everyone could see right through him. Confidence was crucial to success. Especially the image of confidence. He needed something here. He turned quickly to Perkins. "We'll have a full staging area set up in this clearing—supply trucks, U-Hauls, bulldozers, more trailers, Humvees—everything fully operational by tomorrow A.M."

Then to Fagin, "No more Red Cross walk-ups. Tighten the cabin perimeter and close it to forty yards, no one in or out. Then requisition some legitimate body armor ASAP. When things quiet down, have your men start up a collection for the deceased's wife."

The BOLO said, "Bascombe, sir."

Banish nodded. He was in charge now, he should know the mark's name. "Bascombe," he said.

The BOLOs behind Fagin nodded. Each was a family man, or planned to be, and the scent of death scared them. Nobody wanted to die alone.

Banish felt himself faltering. He had to get away and regroup. He turned and found Agent Coyle and relieved her of his suitcase. "Which trailer is mine?" he said.

Perkins said, "We're tripled up. You can have—"

"I'll have my own. Vacate it and send someone over with the complete file. Where does this road go?"

He was looking back across the clearing to where a Jeep was entering. The Jeep swam a bit in his vision.

Perkins said, "Down to the bridge, where we set up a roadblock. But we only have so many trailers—"

Banish was walking away. He was vaguely aware of Fagin's saying something behind him, swearing. Then, farther away, Banish heard sobbing. He stopped and looked between two trucks and saw Lobach sitting on the wet ground with his head in his hands. Banish looked away fast and kept walking. If there was anything to say, he might have said it. But there was nothing he could say and nothing he could do. Marshal Lobach had made a mistake and another man was dead, and it was something he would taste for the rest of his life. Banish made a mental note to have him dismissed off the mountain.

Marshals Tent

[PARASIEGE, p. 11]

SAC Perkins and Deputy Marshal Fagin remained there watching him walk away. Deputy Marshal Fagin said in a loud manner: "What the fuck was that? The fuck is wrong with this guy?"

Following which, after some consideration, SA Coyle came forward with her observations. She addressed SAC Perkins and detailed the peculiar circumstances regarding SA Banish's transfer. Specifically: that SA Banish drew his service weapon on SAs Coyle and Taylor, that SA Banish showed extraordinary reluctance in accepting reassignment, and that SA Banish had been in contact with AD Richardsen while in transit to request that the transfer order be rescinded.

It was admittedly uncustomary and perhaps of questionable judgment to air such behavioral transgressions in an open forum, but the pertinence of these inappropriate reactions seemed to outweigh discretion.

SAC Perkins then asked for and received this agent's name:

SAC PERKINS: You remember the World Financial Center situation about three years ago?

SA COYLE: I was still in training at Quantico, sir. A guest lecturer from the Bureau came and addressed the pitfalls of that specific situation. As I recall, all hostage negotiation operations and procedures were subsequently reviewed as a result.

DEPUTY MARSHAL FAGIN: That was this guy?

SAC PERKINS: One of the hostages he saved tracked him down one year later and tried to kill him.

DEPUTY MARSHAL FAGIN: Is this some fucking joke? What the fuck are you handing me here? I've got forty fucking men on this mountain.

SAC PERKINS: I informed the SOARs chief that this situation warranted a strategic planning and crisis management specialist. I suppose skills bank matched cop to killer on tangibles alone.

SAC Perkins's slight enthusiasm for a fellow agent was initially confusing. Of the three (unofficial) ways an agent is understood to earn the respect of his colleagues—by shooting a suspect in the line of duty, by being wounded in the line, or by shunning administrative advancement to remain in the field—it appeared that SA Banish had, over the course of his career, fulfilled all three.

Trailer

Banish set his suitcase down on the bed. Four new walls. The trailer looked like half a cheap motel room, the half without the television set. He turned and saw himself reflected in a wall mirror and went and took the mirror down.

The words had come too easily at the marshals tent. Salesman's patter. He feared lapsing back into the old playbook routine. He feared the old confidence.

This was no hostage situation. It wasn't even a barricade case. It was a standoff, the worst parts of both.

He shouldn't think too much. He should act, be moving forward. He took a deep breath and reviewed the old maxims: Discipline is paramount to success; Anticipation is ninety percent of command.

He zipped open his suitcase and turned it over, dumping clothes and toiletries out onto the thickly patterned blanket draped over the low bed.

A knock rattled the aluminum door. It was Coyle, handing him a heavy white legal-sized carton, Ables's file. Banish set it on the floor and returned to the mess on his bed, then realized that Coyle was lingering in the doorway behind. "The situation is stabilized—" she began to say as Banish swung the door shut with his foot. He sifted through his clothes on the bed and found nothing appropriate. As with everything else, he would have to start from scratch.

Staging Area

In a supply truck outside, Banish found a discarded John Deere ballcap and traded his FBI slicker for a camouflage hunting jacket. He slipped his ID inside his breast pocket and stepped out and shut the truck door. Droplets tapped on his shoulders and cap brim, the drizzle becoming full rain.

Men with jobs to do crossed the clearing briskly, ignoring Banish. Among those standing idly, Banish located the local Chief of Police by uniform. He was loose-faced and fat under an open blue slicker. His thumbs hung in his gun belt. Banish approached and got his attention.

"Evening," Banish said.

"Evening," said the chief.

Banish went into his breast pocket. He pulled out his ID.

The chief looked it over, rain popping off the plastic shield. "More FBI?" he said, frowning.

"New case agent," said Banish. "Just wanted to introduce myself to the ranking police official."

He puffed up then. "Moody," he said. "Chief of Police."

Banish took his ID back and dropped his hands into his pockets. "I'll need to address your men. Have them assembled outside the command tent at nineteen hundred hours."

The chief nodded. He was being included now. "We'll be there," he said, his soft chin rising.

Banish walked away.

Mountain Road

The dirt road was winding and stubborn and refused to muddy. A creek ran down along the right, pitted by rain, and the wet mountain air smelled like trees chopped open. Banish thought of ravaged Skull Valley.

He stepped aside to make way for a cruiser transporting three local policemen up to the clearing. They gave a noncommittal salute, the way cops wave to each other. Banish nodded, then stopped and turned and watched them go.

Around a steep bend at the bottom of the road lay a small bridge fashioned of iron beams and sided with pilfered highway railings. Beyond it, a grassy one-lane road ran perpendicular. Four armed marshals stood paired off on the bridge under green ponchos. They were chatting. Yellow police ribbon was woven three times across the bridge front like a lazy spider's web.

More than a dozen protesters stood milling about peacefully on the other side. A passing car slowed to watch and honked its horn in support. Banish took it all in.

A white male in his forties with an overgrown mustache and grass-kneed jeans, holding a simple posterboard sign: GO HOME.

A white female in her thirties holding her young daughter by the hand, standing with a neatly lettered wooden sign propped up against her legs: THIS IS FREEDOM? LEAVE GLENN ABLES ALONE!

A white male in his fifties wearing fatigues, a wool cap, and a lumberjack beard, holding a cardboard sign at his waist and intoning its message: "Rebellion Against Tyranny. Obedience to Yahweh."

Others held candles that flickered in the rain. One man read aloud from a Bible while holding erect a six-foot wooden cross. Banish took note of four individuals huddled off to one side.

He surveyed the shallow creek bed and the cars driving unchecked past the scene, then again the thin tape barrier stretched across the front of the bridge.

No one stopped him on the way back up the road either. Halfway to the clearing, a teenaged male with a shaved white head emerged from the high trees on the right. The youth glanced casually both ways up and down the road, then began toward Banish. He was coatless, wearing a short-sleeved black shirt and black boots and fatigue pants. Hard black tattoos were etched on the white skin of his trim arms, most prominently an ornate swastika and a laughing skull.

"Hey," he said, nodding, neither smiling nor frowning.

"Hey," said Banish.

The youth passed him a folded handbill. Banish noted his sharp-edged rings and scarred knuckles.

"Meeting tonight behind the barricade," the young man said. "Bring a friend."

He turned and walked back into the trees. Banish looked after him, then down at the crude handbill, entitled AMERICA'S PROMISE. He recognized its general slant without having to bring out his glasses, and stuffed it deep into his coat pocket.

Staging Area

Sheriff Blood found himself shaking his head. He was watching uniformed men walking past in groups of four and five like soldiers, and feeling the mountain rumble again as another helicopter landed on the weed field behind him, and choking on Jeep exhaust. He was standing in the rain in the middle of the mountain clearing and actually shaking his head back and forth, slowly, so that the runoff from the brim of his plastic-wrapped cowboy hat ran down his already soaked black hair and trickled into his coat collar—and he was marveling. These were professional movers and the world was full of furniture. He would have to take special care not to be brushed aside.

A man approached him wearing a trucker's cap and an army-style coat. His shoes were muddy, maybe even ruined, and he was soaked through with rain, though it didn't seem to bother him. He was older, fifty, with sharp eyes and a wary face that put Blood immediately on his guard.

Blood turned fully toward him as he came. The stranger nodded in greeting. Blood nodded back.

"Evening," the stranger said. He wore no identification. His hands were open and empty.

"Evening," Blood said.

The stranger made a move for his breast pocket. Blood stiff-armed him, kind of casually, grabbing the man's wrist and sweeping open his own sheriff's coat and baring his .38.

"Easy now," said Blood.

The stranger completed his action, slowly withdrawing a thin billfold and showing Blood his identification card with photo and badge. "FBI," the man said, just as it read on the card in blue block letters.

Blood released the man's wrist and returned his own hands to his coat pockets, but did not take his eyes off the agent, whose name he did not catch.

The agent put away his ID. "Chief of Police didn't even flinch," he said in a rich voice cutting sharply through the spilling rain.

"If it's reaction you wanted," Blood said, "you should have tried reaching for his wallet, not yours."

The agent's eyes went a little narrower, as though reappraising Blood. Seeing them move in his face and betray some of the thinking going on behind them was like watching a rock forget it was a rock and try to speak.

The agent said, "How many skinheads do you have around here, Sheriff?"

Blood figured his face did a little betraying of its own then. "A few," he said. "Our share."

"How many unattended deaths?"

Blood didn't like that question either. The agent had used the local terminology for "unexplained deaths," but it seemed to Blood that he was being talked down to.

"Eight total," Blood said, making as though he had to think about it.

The agent nodded. "How many of those were Indians, like you?"

Small, unshaved hairs stood up on the back of Blood's neck. He made his displeasure evident this time. "Six," he said, further studying the agent's face.

"High percentage," the agent said. "I see this man Ables has quite a following around here."

"He has his supporters."

"Your constituents."

Only then did it dawn on Blood. The two of them had all along been matching wits. This stranger had been running circles around him while Blood was busy playing catch-up Q and A. Now that he knew what the game was, Blood relaxed a little, as was his way, slacking off like a fisherman sitting back in a trawler chair and playing out line.

"You're asking whose side I'm on," he said.

"Just getting the lay of the land," said the agent. "I'm trying to decide whether or not you belong on this mountain."

Blood nodded. Rain pattered the ground and rapped loudly atop his hat. "You like to play games," he said. "You must be in charge now." He pulled the eviction notice out of his pocket and unfolded it slowly in the rain, revealing the bullet hole. "This is my ticket to the big show," he said.

"We'll see about that. Deputies?"

"Nope."

"Up here alone?"

"Yep, but I'm already spoken for."

The agent nodded without remark. "Command tent, seven o'clock," he said, then walked away.

Blood watched him go. He rubbed the back of his neck under his long hair, smoothing over his rancor. The rain came down in strings around him. Unattended deaths. He wanted to know just how this agent had gotten under his skin so quick. Blood promised himself that the next time they locked horns, he would be better prepared.

Command Tent

It was seven o'clock on the dot and Perkins was seated and ready in a folding chair in front. The chicken fricassee which had been perpetrated that evening by the American Red Cross was still very much in his mouth. He took a drink of hot black coffee and swished it around with his tongue, hoping to wash out the filmy taste. Then he looked at the cup. He felt the stickiness of his hand. It was a cold-drink cup that the Red Cross had given him, and the hot coffee was softening it, sweating the outside and melting the inner coating, so that small slicks of wax now floated on the surface of the liquid. He frowned and stood, holding the cup away from his clothes, trying not to draw any attention to himself. He set the mess in a plastic-lined wastebasket and then sat back down, scraping his pasty tongue with his front teeth.

His Assistant Special Agent in Charge, Hardy, sat behind him flipping pages in a small notebook. Fagin sat to Perkins's far left, still wearing his cap, vest, and all his gear, at least twenty pounds of extra weight hanging on his frame. He was blowing thick white cheroot smoke and his legs were spread broadly off the edge of the folding chair for maximum comfort. It was a good show. Anyone who expended that much energy trying to convince people he was a maverick had to be a real ass, never mind in the wrong profession. The U.S. Marshals were known as team players through and through. The operation was full FBI jurisdiction now, the marshals present only under Banish's command, thereby diminishing Fagin's role and strengthening Perkins's position as the number-two man on the mountain.

The Spokane FBI Field Office was also represented, as were Montana Resident Agencies such as Kalispell, Missoula, and Great Falls. Lower-echelon Bureau and Marshal supervisory officials occupied the rest of the folding chairs.

The tent was drafty, sheets of rain blowing and rippling the tightly stretched roof and side walls. Unshaded bulbs were strung overhead and the work light was spotty, the slightest movement followed by three or four different shadows. Wires from facsimile machines and computers and telephones snaked along the lumpy canvas floor, and a generator rumbled somewhere outside, beyond the rear wall they were facing. The enlarged flyby surveillance photograph hanging on the wall showed in grainy black and white the cabin and its grounds, including the wide, elevated back porch on which Glenn Ables could be seen standing, small but unmistakable, giving the helicopter the finger.

Banish entered at five after seven. He passed around photographs first. Perkins had already reacquainted himself with the family bios and was prepared for any queries. Ables looked like a cocky little so-and-so in his two-year-old front and side mug shots. Blond buzz haircut, squirrel eyes, arrow nose, long ears, and a wide, grinning chin. Challenging the camera, not just standing in front of it. A bantamweight, short and wiry, early forties. The kind of man who gets a few in him and goes around picking fights just to prove how scrappy he is.

The eight-by-ten of Marjorie Ables entering the Montana courthouse on the day of her husband's arraignment showed a heavy woman in her thirties wearing a frock coat, sunglasses, and a dark curly wig. She had lost her hair during chemotherapy treatment following the removal of a throat tumor that had claimed her voice in late 1987. Her hair had never grown back.

Then grade school portraits. The oldest, Rebecca, then ten, now fourteen, wearing small yellow ribbons over elastic bands in her braids, and one large ribbon tied in a loose bow under her blouse collar; and Judith, then eight, now twelve, the one thought to have participated in the shootout, hair mussed and smile awry. Both had been removed from public schooling by their parents the year following these portraits. Another black-and-white flyby photo, only four months old, showed Ruth, nine, and Esther, five, playing around one of the shacks on the grounds behind the family cabin. Ruth could be seen wearing a small-caliber handgun strapped to her hip. The fifth child and only son, Amos, eighteen months, had been born in exile. No photographs were available.

Perkins chewed on his coated tongue, passing the pictures back to ASAC Hardy and turning in his seat to give Banish his full and complete attention. Banish seemed a cranky old soldier—just a few years from mandatory retirement at age fifty-seven—but the suddenness of his reactivation must have meant that he had AD Richardsen's ear. Perkins had heard that Richardsen and Banish had graduated from the academy together, which counted for a lot.

Banish started. "This will be brief," he said. "The Bureau code name for this operation will be PARASIEGE." He spelled it out. Pens scribbled behind. Perkins hoped that his crossed arms indicated his senior position here. "Office of origin will be Butte. Faxes, memoranda, field reports, telexes, 302s—everything crosses my desk, everything sees my initials."

Perkins disliked the case going on his field office's books, but Banish's initials would make it all right. The OO designation meant that all paperwork would be routed through Butte. If things were to go badly, the "special case" status and the case agent's corresponding initials made outright failure ultimately Banish's responsibility; but if things went right, Perkins's office would be indicated on every relevant piece of paper, private and public, issued in relation to operation PARASIEGE.

In the meantime, Banish could expect to be initialing reports twenty-four hours a day. Perkins knew the mass of paperwork an operation like this could generate.

Banish indicated an imaginary line triangulating the rear fifth of the tent. "This area here will be partitioned off to form my private office," he said, then went on to detail the equipment and supplies he required. Perkins recalled the first rule of reassignment: Reorganize your new office. A power trick, a way of asserting your authority— though the way Banish was describing it, he seemed more interested in having a place to hide.

"My operating name will be 'Chief Negotiator SA Bob Watson.' Once communication is established, I will be the only one talking to Ables. I will be the sole negotiator and Ables's only link to the outside. I will not, at any time, come into physical contact with Ables. I will not at any time come into contact with any released hostages either, nor will I participate in or effect any arrests."

Perkins recognized this as Bureau negotiator standard operating procedure, though for Fagin it probably pegged Banish as a coward. Perkins, however, saw right through Banish's fire-and-brimstone bluster to a tremendous, brassy ego.

"All Bureau reports and/or summaries will go out over my operating name, with initials JB attached. Press briefings, as and if deemed necessary by me, will be conducted by SAC Perkins."

Perkins crossed his legs. That was a plum. He had to try hard not to let on that he was buzzed. Washington frowned upon news exposure and press conferences, but they sure as hell watched them.

"I've called FBI Hostage Rescue Team off alert status for now. This is not currently a rescue situation and having them here on twenty-four-hour standby could only escalate things. Marshals Service Special Operations Group under Deputy Supervisor Fagin will arrange perimeter cabin surveillance and containment, as well as staging-area security. If the curtain goes up, your men are in first."

"That's how we like it," Fagin said.

"On my order alone," said Banish.

Perkins anticipated a blowout, but Fagin was remarkably self-contained. "I will do the job I was sent here to do," he said.

Banish continued. "As of twenty-two hundred hours, Bureau and Marshals Service radios will network on a common Justice Department frequency. Beginning at midnight, airspace within a two-mile radius of Paradise Ridge will be closed to all private and commercial aircraft. At first light I want engineers here looking over that bridge. We're bringing in a lot of heavy equipment, so I want reassurances. Tomorrow A.M. we begin rebuilding and widening the path up the mountain to the cabin. Hire a local contractor but keep them on a short leash." He looked up. "Now we update. Ables's food and water supply."

Perkins uncrossed his legs. He sat up straight and spoke first, not quickly but with assurance. "Self-sufficient," he said. "Chickens, some animals, a garden. Water from two fifty-gallon drums."

"Outdoor?"

"Outdoor and aboveground."

Banish considered that. "Five young children in the residence," he said. "We'll hold off on taking out the water as long as we can. Plumbing?"

"Outdoor. Primitive."

"Put a couple of rounds in the door tomorrow to remind them that we are here. We would not want anybody wandering around outside. Nearby structures?"

Perkins said, "Some barns, sheds, chicken coops. As far as we know, all run-down and all abandoned. Other than that, he owns the mountaintop. Nearest residence was seventy-five yards down, and all have been evacuated."

Banish put on his half-glasses and picked a fax up off the table.

"I assume everyone here has seen the preliminary on Marshal Bascombe: .223 caliber, consistent with a Colt AR-15 semi. And based on field reports, and the rounds we pulled out of the trees today: .30-06s, .30-30s, 9 millimeters, grease guns, buckshot, mini M-1s, and automatic weaponry, probably submachine guns like the ones he sold to Alcohol, Tobacco, and Firearms." Banish stopped then and removed his glasses. He scanned the men.

Perkins explained, "ATF was supposed to be here."

Banish frowned. "I want the arresting agents here tomorrow morning. So: confirmed stockpiled weaponry and ammunition inside. That's an arsenal. Everyone should be aware. Now," he said, searching through papers on the table desk, "who else do we have confirmed in there with them?"

Perkins said, "Two pairs of in-laws. The wife's brother and sister-in-law, the Newlands. Which doesn't check, because they feud with Ables. Mormons from Provo and reputedly unsympathetic, so they may simply have picked the wrong week to visit. We're working on photos. Also Ables's sister, Michelle, and her husband, Charles Mellis. The Mellises are known sympathizers and have been sharing the five-room cabin with the family for more than a year now."

Banish found what he was looking for and read it at arm's length. "Charles Maynard Mellis. One prior, assault on a police officer, 1990. Probation." He put it down again, satisfied. "That's a lot of people in a cabin with not much food or water, and no plumbing."

Perkins raised an issue. "National Guard," he said.

"No," said Banish. "No weekend warriors. Amend that—I want two helicopter pilots only, not from this immediate area, and two UH-1s. We'll need light air support."

Perkins had something else for him. "We do have nine evacuated families who feel the Red Cross is doing more for us than for them, and didn't mind saying as much on the local TV news last night."

Banish frowned again. "Set them all up in campers somewhere away from the barricade. Other questions?"

Perkins sat back, satisfied, having distinguished himself here. Banish obviously was not a details man. This was a major operation in which, regardless of the outcome, Perkins's support talents would be recognized in D.C. And appreciated. He would make certain that his name crossed AD Richardsen's lips favorably.

To his left, Fagin sat up in his folding chair. "I have a question," he said, speaking mouthfuls of thick smoke, then finishing off the cheroot and killing it under his boot tread. "Why all the pussy-footing around?"

Banish said, "You know why."

"Because this guy's hiding behind his family?"

"The children's safety is our primary concern." Banish addressed the entire tent. "Be advised, the children are presumed to be armed and are by all accounts unfriendly. Everything we do here is designed to avoid the kill-or-be-killed confrontation. That should be perfectly clear to everyone. This man is hiding behind his family because he knows it will work, and it is working. That is why we cannot go in and get him. That is why we must make him come out to us."

Perkins became distracted by a low, garbled buzzing noise. It was the white wire receiver whispering in Fagin's ear. A few other heads turned as well, while Fagin sat there impassively. Perkins decided that he must have one too.

Banish was summing up. "First step tomorrow morning is to establish communication. Ables does not have a telephone, so arrangements are being made to deliver one to him. No television either, although flyby surveillance did pick up a large antenna"—Banish pointed to the backdrop photo—"and he is believed to have an adequate in-house generator. We are as yet without encryption here, and Ables's military specialty was electronics, so he may be monitoring our broadcasts. Radio use will therefore be kept to a minimum. Be advised, he's a combat veteran, so he's used to being messed with. He may even try messing with us."

Perkins said, "We're still holding that neighbor, Deke Belcher. The one who walked away from the Red Cross group and met Ables before the shootout."

Banish said, "What's his story?"

"He says he didn't do anything. He says it's his land up there and he's walked that mountain every day of his life."

Banish was impatient. "Sweat him overnight," he said. "I'll question tomorrow with local law present. I want town police posted down at the bridge barricade, backed up by marshals. Familiar faces should cool off the locals for a while."

Fagin said, "Just tell them to stay out of my way."

Banish was done and reaching for his raincoat, inviting Fagin to follow him outside. "Tell them yourself."

Staging Area

They were going on a half hour now in the rain and everyone was beefing. The man next to him stamped his feet and said, "This is bullshit," but Brian Kearney was keeping quiet. Just like down at the station, it was easy to jump into these grumblings. Everyone getting united against a common evil like the town council, the lack of air-conditioning in the cruisers, or the rain. One voice started it, backed up by another, and another, like a house of cards built in the breakroom between shifts, and it could even get kind of fun, everybody throwing in his two cents' worth, louder and louder, complaint upon complaint, the argument growing and growing. It was happening in this situation now. About the way things were being handled. About how Ables was just a guy with his back to the wall, and who wouldn't have acted differently? No one liked that Haley got shot in the knee, but they blamed the sheriff for that. And on and on. Not that any of them had actually been there. Not that any of them had gotten shot at. Sometimes this griping seemed like their full-time work.

Brian had always been lucky. Taking a bullet in the hip radio like that. Those types of things always happened to him. Not lottery-lucky, just dumb-lucky. Like being let off the school bus right before that car plowed into it. Like transporting a prisoner to the hospital and Brian's appendix bursting in the admitting room. Like going to the wrong funeral home for a wake and mistakenly offering his condolences to the dead stranger's daughter, and then their getting to talking, and she eventually becoming his wife. And now again, here it was: two months after sending in his application to the FBI, the FBI had come to him.

So Brian was keeping quiet and waiting. It was pitch-black outside the large tent they called the command tent, and the rain was falling straight and loud and never letting up. It ran in a stream off his chin. His uniform and longjohns were soaked through and he was shivering. But the way Brian managed to stick it out quietly was by seeing it all as a test, thinking somewhat biblically now. Funny and strange how the things you pay no attention to in Sunday school stick with you.

Chief Moody was ripped, all the complaints now beginning to fall back on him—as in, Who called this meeting? He was pacing back and forth like a bear in a blue raincoat and swearing to himself, rain smacking off his lips like spit. Nobody liked to look like a fool, the chief even less so. He'd been up and down like a seesaw all day. When Brian first approached him after getting back from the hospital about needing a new radio, the chief shouted him out of his face. Then when Brian tried again before dinner, the chief straightaway handed him his. And that dinner, served off the back of a Red Cross truck—that might have been another test.

So there they were, thirty police officers standing with hands in pockets and shoulders shrugged against the rain, and all of them complaining. Maybe they had forgotten what it was to be a police officer, Brian thought, being so long into it themselves. Or maybe none of them quite saw what it was that was going on. There was no ambition in these men, none whatsoever, except to get out of that rain.

The FBI. The Federal Bureau of Investigation. Major leaguers, come to play in a weed field. Unbelievable that Sheriff Blood had called them in. The chief would surely have him for it. The sheriff was standing off to the side now, kind of as usual. The type to barely even pay attention to a thing, and wind up remembering more about it than you did. He'd glance sidelong at a tree, if at all, and then three hours later give you a leaf count if you asked for it. The only man Brian knew who could seem as though he were reclining while standing up. And even there in that rain—he might as well have been leaning back against a post fence, one foot on the low rail, arms spread wide, switching a strand of straw in his mouth and being warmed by the afternoon sun. All those lazy Indians you hear about, that type of personality, Sheriff Blood played that for his own.

The federal men finally emerged from the tent and fanned out, most walking off, busy men with specific government duties. Three remained. The chief stopped his pacing and went right over to the lead agent. He said to him, "Seven-thirty, for Christ's sake."

The lead agent showed no concern at all. "Have your men line up," he said.

Brian braced himself against the rain and stepped right into what became the front line. Other grumbling officers, including those from nearby Crater and Little Elk and Simston, drifted into some order beside and behind him.

The lead agent was older, with a high, serious forehead under an FBI cap and serious lines in his face. He stood upright and tall and his pullover rain-thing hung straight down to his knees. Behind him and to his side stood the black marshal with the military cadence, the impressive one who had first gotten off that bus. His uniform and big, crossed arms were blurred under a long, transparent plastic poncho. The other FBI agent, the one named Perkins, had a plain face of lightly colored freckles, and a disappearing way about him that made him easily forgotten. They were none of them under the age of forty. They looked like ordinary men, and only the marshal seemed to be carrying a holster bulge. Nothing like you see in the movies.

The lead agent waited without expression even after the local men were all assembled and still, as though collecting his thoughts. "My name is Special Agent John Banish," he said above the dark rain. "Before we begin, I want to make a few things clear. I understand there has been some disagreement as to our methods here. Some mitigating circumstances that some of you think we as outsiders may be overlooking. If anyone has anything to say, an opposing viewpoint or a suggestion you think might help—now is the time."

That was a little surprising—their being so open to suggestions. There were some shifts in posture in the lines. Some turned heads.

Agent Banish said, "Speak up," his voice clear and stern through the rain, yet mildly encouraging.

Sergeant Polchrist somehow was nudged forward without anybody actually touching him. Brian, looking straight ahead, saw the sarge only peripherally. Some untaken vote had nominated him spokesman for the corps.

"I think maybe Ables is getting a bad shake up there," Sergeant Polchrist said. "Sure, he shouldn'ta shot a cop, but who can't say he weren't provoked."

Agent Banish nodded. He was looking off somewhere else and considering this. Something about the whole thing wasn't right, but Brian couldn't tell yet what was happening. Agent Banish said, "Fair enough. Anyone else?" There was clear silent support for Polchrist's statement in the form of more posture changes, but no one else actually took a step forward. Agent Banish said, "How about a show of hands."

Polchrist's went up into the rain—he being the leader now—and then another, then more. Agent Banish was having trouble seeing the whole group. "Hands, move out to the side," he suggested.

One by one, a total of seven of the thirty sergeants and officers stepped out of formation to the right. Agent Banish waited until they were all gathered near the tent. Then he said, "You seven are dismissed."

At first it wasn't clear. Dismissed from the meeting? Then Agent Banish said, "Next. Three men in a cruiser waved to me on the mountain road earlier today." He scanned the group and pointed out the three men. "I was dressed in civilian clothes without any outward identification. Dismissed."

Now it was serious. It was obvious that those three were off the mountain for good. Shit, Brian thought. Shit. Shit. Like the first hour of basic training again—not knowing at all what they wanted from you, and it feeding your general fear. Whatever happened, whatever this Agent Banish was up to, Brian was keeping his head low.

"Now, married men," he was saying, "men with families. Hands."

Brian didn't know. He thought it might be a trick, like some kind of reversal. Like all the married men would stay. But he didn't know what the right answer was. His right hand ground into his thigh.

In the rain around Brian, hands went up slowly, almost timidly. He would kick himself fifty times and probably forever if he was wrong.

Agent Banish waited until everybody had made up his mind. "Negotiations could drag on for days," he said. "No place for a man with a wife and responsibilities. All dismissed."

Brian breathed. The general reaction of the men was stunned silence, their soaked bodies moving through the dwindling ranks and out to the side. He couldn't tell how many of them were left in formation—many less than half—afraid even to turn his head. But it wasn't over yet. Now Agent Banish was walking down the line, eyeing each man one at a time. He was saying, seemingly at random, "Dismissed."

Brian straightened himself up. He tried to look as determined as he could, he tried to look impressive. Agent Banish was coming. Brian was second to last in the front line. He squared his shoulders and tipped up his chin. Then he remembered his wedding band.

This was a man who would notice a thing like that. And there were the two others, Agent Perkins and the black marshal, watching everybody at once.

Brian flicked at the ring with his thumb. It didn't budge. He was trying hard not to be noticed. Agent Banish was coming. Brian became flushed, his mindset suddenly thrown from wanting to be chosen to not wanting to get caught. He never took the ring off. He never had a reason to.

He flicked at it again, and rubbed. The black marshal was staring right at him. Agent Banish was approaching and saying, "Dismissed. Dismissed." Why would this FBI man really care if a cop was married or not? Brian made a fist and dug at his skin.

It budged. The ring turned on the base of his finger. He was prying at it, twisting it over and over. Agent Banish was close. Brian opened his hand and worked the ring loose and up to his middle knuckle, prying it, pulling on the thing. He wrenched it up over the joint and off his finger and slipped it into his raincoat pocket just as Agent Banish dismissed the man before him.

Then he was there. He was right there in front of Brian. The rain was loud on his shoulders and spilling off his cap brim and down into his face. Brian tried not to look at him directly, but failed. Agent Banish stood there before him like a ghost. His face was deep-lined and shadowed, breath steaming out of his nose. His eyes caught what little light there was and drilled it into Brian. These were eyes that had seen a lot. Brian felt as though he were nothing to them. He knew he was breathing too much, too fast. He feared his mouth was hanging wide open. So much steam in front of his face, he thought he might be melting. Agent Banish was looking right at him.

Then Agent Banish passed on to the last man and dismissed him. Brian did not know what to do. It took the greatest effort of his life just to remain standing there and not jump up or fall over. He was suddenly exhilarated. He had merely not been dismissed, and yet it felt as though he had been chosen. He wanted to know why. He wanted to know, who was this man Banish?

His breath created a fog around his head. Agent Banish was in front again, speaking now, and Brian fought to concentrate, his mind whirring on and on. "Like it or not, you are all here as volunteers," Agent Banish was saying. "This is a federal matter now. I am an FBI hostage negotiator, the case agent for this operation."

Chief Moody had been waiting along the sidelines, becoming increasingly pissed off. "Negotiator?" he said now, coming forward through the dark rain, his coat collar up around his ears. His voice was full of exaggerated disbelief. "What's this here? We don't truck with criminals in these parts."

Agent Banish turned and met him with his eyes. "That's why you are wearing a uniform and I am in charge," he said. "You are dismissed."

The chief double-taked him. So did just about everyone else. "The hell I am," said the chief, more surprised than defiant. "That may be all right for the others, but this here's the Chief of Police."

Agent Banish said, "This mountain is off a county road. That's Sheriff Department's jurisdiction. The U.S. Marshals will escort you and your men to the bridge."

The chief looked as though he had been punched in the face. He was off the mountain. Just like that. Brian could sense everyone straightening up then. It had become clear to all that Agent Banish had the power of life or death on the mountain. He didn't have to be pleasant about it, or even fair. The chief had been dismissed. It was unreal.

Agent Banish went on, talking through the rain. "Glenn Allen Ables is a fugitive arms dealer implicated in the murder of a federal official, and it is the determination of the United States Attorney General's Office that he be brought before the bar of justice. I have been assigned to this mountain to effect his extrication and arrest, and this is a duty from which I cannot and will not be dissuaded or distracted. Two things I do not tolerate: dissension and poor job performance. Is that clear?"

He didn't seem to require an answer. No one offered one anyway, as the black marshal, who had been silent and mostly still throughout the whole thing, but watchful, all of a sudden started off at a brisk stride. He was holding a fingertip against the white wire in his ear.

"Something down at the barricade," he said, passing Agent Banish but otherwise ignoring him.

Agent Banish paused a moment, then started off as well, Agent Perkins following behind. Then the sheriff started away too.

Leaving the chief with no one to yell at. Only then did Brian dare to sneak a quick look around. There were maybe five of them left. He shook his blessed head. He had always been lucky. He just hoped none of the others who knew would tell. He felt in his pocket to make sure the ring was still there and slipped it safely back onto his bare finger for now. He looked up into the rain falling out of the black sky. It all seemed pretty crucial to him. Like it could be his big chance right there. Besides, Leslie was only seven months along. And anyway, Brian figured that even if she couldn't ever forgive him, God certainly would.

Bridge

The number of protesters beyond the barricade had grown to forty. It would continue to rise as the standoff progressed; that was expected. This was something different.

They were gathered in a knot in the center of the road beyond the bridge. Their heads were bowed in the rain and they were silent except for the one voice leading them. They were praying. Old women, skinheads, young couples, children. Individuals wearing paramilitary uniforms with red, white, and blue swastika armbands, right fists raised in Nazi-style salute. All standing reverently, lit by car headlights arranged in a broad semicircle behind them.

The four marshals posted on the bridge looked on silently, shoulders rounded under their ponchos, arms crossed.

Fagin, watching from the Jeep parked in front of Banish, said, "This is the fucking Twilight Zone right here."

Perkins was in the driver's seat next to Banish, shaking his head.

Banish kept both hands in his coat pockets. He was shivering a little, due in part to the rain and the cold mountain air. The sheriff's vehicle rolled up alongside them and Banish looked over at the Indian; for some reason, he did not trust him.

"Locals?" Banish said.

The sheriff looked. "A few."

That meant trouble. If it were just a local event, then it could be contained. But people traveling across a distance came in groups and invariably brought their own agenda. The situation was developing much more quickly than Banish would have liked.

Fagin said back over his shoulder, "The Klan?"

Perkins liked the easy ones. "The Klan is doing all their fighting in court these days," he said. "Same barn, different animal. The town of Crater is about an hour's drive south of here. Headquarters of the White Aryan Resistance. Then there's a locally based splinter group, smaller, even more radical, calling themselves The Truth. Their aim is to establish an independent Aryan homeland made up of the five Northwestern states, but we suspect them of pulling a number of recent armored car robberies south of here, and right now can only guess at what the money's for. Both groups are factions of the pseudotheological supremacist Christian Identity Movement."

Fagin turned back toward him. "The fuck are we talking about here?"

"A separatist network, loosely organized, but united in principle against nonwhites and Jews and others. This whole stretch of the Rockies—no minorities, weak law enforcement—a refuge for outlaws, fanatics, white supremacists."

Banish again looked at the loose web of police ribbon woven across the bridge front. He closed his eyes. His brain was heavy and felt swollen with blood that needed to be drained off. He wanted out. He needed eight hours of recuperative sleep, but his mind was running too hot already. He hoped for two hours, maybe three.

He opened his eyes. Everything was the same except that the trees seemed closer on either side.

"I want the water supply hit tonight," he said.

Fagin needed no more than that, jerking his gearshift into first. "I'll put my best man on it."

Paradise Point

Fagin hiked the last few steps up the wooded mountain. The rain was stopping now but he could barely tell that from where the hell he was, the excess still dripping off the branches and down through the leaves. Fucking trees, he thought. Fucking Montana.

Taber saw him coming and snapped to attention at the rope line. Fagin recognized the fear and eager respect he was accustomed to seeing in the faces of his younger marshals. He handed Taber his Remington 700 sniper rifle and began buckling the rope harness over his shoulders, around his waist, between his legs. Tight fucking thing. Like a goddamn baby seat.

"Outhouse clear?" he said.

Taber snapped, "Yessir."

Fagin took the Remington back and slung it over his shoulder. He handed Taber his ballcap. "Gimme your NVD," he said.

Taber unstrapped his helmet and handed it over. Fucking unwieldy thing. But what was another four or five pounds.

Fagin let his weight stretch the rope taut, then he yanked on the give line and *whoosh*. The counterweight dropped and his feet left the ground and he rode the pulley rope thirty yards straight up the side of the debranched oak. The harness hit the sheave at the top and stopped with a jerk, and big drops of rain from the highest wet leaves fell on him like a flock-load of bird shit, pelting his jumpsuit uniform. Fagin swore quietly into the night. He found the wooden-platform sniper's nest beneath him with his right foot and unbuckled himself and stood free.

He was up in the tree line above the mountain. Fucking thin air, Jesus Christ. The platform was not large, but the tree trunk provided a nice brace. There was a light, chill breeze, the high branches swishing all around him, but it would not be a factor. In the jungle twenty years before, he had humped a .50-cal M-2 on a tripod and splashed down VC guerrillas in rice paddies at ranges of greater than 2200 yards. For this right here, he hadn't even wasted his time zeroing the Remington. A 7.26 round traveling some 50 yards at 2800 feet per second just didn't fucking care. He was there to do some damage.

He looked up overhead. Good Jesus fucking Christ. Fucking stars. All over the place, constellations of them, blinking like fireflies in a motherfucking darkroom. Obscene. And no fucking moon. What the fuck kind of place was this? There were stars in L.A. too, all they did was stop traffic. How the fuck did people get any sleep here? Maybe that's what it was—fucking stars kept them up all night, drove them all fucking goofy. Made them dress up in Nazi costumes and stand out in the rain saying prayers for their fugitive neighbors.

He slung the bolt-action Remington down off his shoulder. In the darkness before him, a few silvery branches wagged in the dim starlight. Beyond that, nothing.

He flipped down Taber's NVD. These night-vision devices were not like the older-generation infrared goggles, with the branch-snapping click and the whir when you turned them on, easy-target red eyes coming at you in the dark. "Passive" was the technology now. Some fifty yards beyond the highlighted, glaring green branches, the outline of the cabin compound now simmered before him in contrasting shades of spectral green. The cabin itself glowed clean, floating in his vision like a house underwater.

He checked first for movement. There was none.

The twin drums sat to the right rear of the cabin, two clear targets shaded green and black. Fagin raised the Remington and sighted the first tank. He didn't even bother to aim carefully. Just fucking squeeze.

The shot echoed sharply off the surrounding mountains. Nice goddamn effect. Fagin watched a phosphorescent green lake spread beneath the drum.

He worked the bolt and sighted the second tank and squeezed again. This one ruptured with a distant hiss and squeal and emptied fast.

Fagin stayed with the Remington, running his sight slowly over the property. A similar piece, a .30-06 Model 70 Winchester, had been his main tour guide in Vietnam. But this new bull barrel was thicker, and floated heavier, cutting down on the kick and holding sight after the shot. A nice solid piece of wood. He liked it. He regripped the smooth forearm. Worked the bolt. Settled into the cheekpiece. Banish giving him orders, he thought. He squeezed twice and double-tapped the outhouse door. Two gaping black chunks appeared, reports kicking off and ripping back into the mountains. Banish leaning on small-town police chiefs for intimidation. Cutting down the head man to show how in control he was, the oldest trick in the book. Fucking FBI taking over.

Then he was sighting the cabin itself, the boarded windows and the front door made plain in varying shades of green and black. So fucking easy, he thought. The old mastery coming over him again. In the jungle he had earned the nickname "Spider" because he was the sniper king, ice-cold and patient and superfucking stealthy. His web was whatever range he elected to zero his weapon to, cast out from his camouflaged promontory nest high atop a numbered hill, a rice paddy kill zone of unseen, whispering fucking death. Fifty-six confirmed kills in two tours of duty. A fucking game to him back then, because he was young and had been top-to-bottom reinvented, forever leaving behind the skinny black kid from Arkansas who begged his mother to sign him over to the U.S. Marines on his seventeenth birthday. The dead-on patience and bold stealth of a young black man having to prove himself in a white world burned within him no more. He was fucking proven. People snapped to his attention now.

He squeezed off one more round, ripping a large chuck of stone from the chimney top. He hoped it dropped into their fireplace, freaking out the kids, and Ables heard it rattling down and fucking choked on whatever White Power bullshit he was preaching in there. He hoped it scared them all fucking shitless.

He knew Banish would be counting shots down below. Fagin wanted to be called on the carpet for this. Fucking Banish, he thought, slinging the Remington back over his shoulder and taking up the soaked rope line harness again in the chill mountain night. Fucking Montana.

Thursday, August 5

Paradise Point

Banish squeezed the trigger and blew into the bullhorn, testing it. He was kneeling by a thick, wet-smelling pine. The rain had ended overnight and the predawn fog was just now rising off the mountaintop, the sun coming up and cutting through the haze. More than fifty marshals and agents in camouflage jumpsuits and flak vests stood, crouched, or knelt in the trees around him, all heavily armed, all aiming across the forty-yard no-man's-land of stumps and scattered trees at the dewy mountain cabin.

"Glenn Allen Ables." Banish's trained voice sounded robotic through the bullhorn. *"This is Special Agent Bob Watson of the Federal Bureau of Investigation. Your cabin is completely surrounded. There is no chance for escape. Listen carefully to my instructions and no one will be hurt. Lay down your weapons and come out one at a time through the front door with your hands empty and up."*

He lowered the bullhorn and eased out the trigger, and waited. The BOLO marshal posted behind him aimed noiselessly. The silence on the mountaintop was profound. Banish pictured the family holed up inside, crouched on the floor beneath the windows, backs to the walls, weapons in hands, hanging on his every word.

The opening speech was very much a formality. Familiar words, recalled like a song lyric from his youth. The past favorite of some forgotten sweetheart. The old routine. He glanced to his right. Fagin was ready in the trees, squatting behind a five-man team of marshals dressed in full riot gear. Banish returned to the bullhorn.

"Occupants of the cabin. Agents of the United States Marshals Service are prepared to deliver to you a telephone. This is not, repeat, not an act of aggression. Any movement or activity from your cabin will be regarded and responded to as a hostile gesture."

Another moment of pure silence, then Banish lowered the bullhorn and nodded across to Fagin, who hand-signaled his group to go. The five-man procedure was brief and efficient. A pair of marshals in black fatigues fronted the team with riot shields, concussion grenades held at the ready in their free hands. A second pair crouch-walked directly behind, M-21s braced against their shoulders, sighting the cabin through the plexi face shields hanging off their helmets. The point man himself was obscured in the middle.

The team advanced in fits and starts. The drop target was fifteen yards before the porch steps. Banish saw Fagin moving ahead to the edge of the no-man's-land, his .44 down at his side. His lips were moving, issuing orders through the radio on his shoulder. Even at that distance, Banish could see the thin black ribbon stripe across Fagin's chest badge, the same as on the BOLO sharpshooter positioned above Banish's head. The sharpshooter was stiffening now, and reaiming.

The team had stopped at the target and were beginning their withdrawal. The cabin showed no sign of life as the ten-legged creature backed away through the trees as slowly and as cautiously as it had approached, past the first twisted dog carcass, past the second, finally reentering the thickened wood where Fagin stood covering them from behind. Banish felt the shoulder of the sharpshooter above him drop ever so slightly.

The throw phone, contained in a plain-looking, hard black plastic carrying case, waterproof and temperature-resistant, sat quietly fifteen yards before the porch.

Banish took up the bullhorn again. *"Glenn Allen Ables. The telephone has been delivered to you. Your physical safety and the safety of your wife and family and relatives are our primary concern. You have my word that you will be allowed to retrieve this portable telephone without harm."* He paused a moment, taking a preliminary read of the situation, considering his final words. *"I know we can reach an acceptable and mutually dignified solution."*

He lowered the bullhorn. Again the woods waited for the cabin.

Nothing. The front door remained shut. No movement or reaction or acknowledgment.

It flashed through Banish's head then that they were already dead in there. That Ables had taken a knife or whatever was handiest and had already massacred the entire family. He saw the death masks of the slaughtered children and the slumped arrangement of their bodies and the bloody defensive marks on their hands and the staring eyes and the gore.

It was a while before Banish released his grip on the bullhorn. He stood then and said to the BOLO behind the tree next to him, "Tell your CO to clear everyone back another ten yards. I want to make it easy for the suspect. Let's give him some room."

Staging Area

Sheriff Blood was leaning against his Bronco holding a Styrofoam cup of Red Cross coffee, which was serviceable in a caffeinated way but lacked the sweetness and texture of Marylene's time-honored brew. He had called her on the police radio first thing that morning and invited her to take a few days off, as he did not think he would be coming in at all the rest of the week. This forecast had required no special divining on his part.

A military tank rolled past him across the clearing. A full-blown U.S. Army tank. It had been brought in on a rumbling flatbed trailer, backed down off a ramp, and loosed to the feds. It lumbered past him now, toward the two National Guard helicopters in the rear. The feds pointed these things around the clearing like Tarzan with his elephants.

From where Blood was standing, near the center of the tree-lined oval clearing and facing the upper two thirds of Paradise Ridge, an entire fleet of parked military vehicles stretched out in a line along a brand-new chain-link fence, like a watch hand pointing to three o'clock. The largest equipment was stored farthest away, green-painted canopy trucks and more flatbeds holding bulky machinery under camouflage nets. The rest of the lineup included Jeeps of various sizes, both covered and uncovered, used mainly for shuttling men back and forth to the bridge at the bottom of Paradise, and sedans and four-wheel-drive Explorers with two or three whip antennas each, all sporting blue government license plates and inspection stickers from different states. Local fire trucks and ambulances were set way down alongside the largest equipment at the farthest right edge of the clearing, Huddleston firemen and Border County Hospital EMTs standing around drinking coffee and earning overtime.

Squarely in front of him, heading out toward what would be about noon, sat four good-sized U-Haul trucks boxed in by the tents. There were seven large tents now, anchor ropes overlapping, sharing between them three or four outdoor generators that hummed and rattled on like well-fed mulchers.

At about the ten o'clock position, wide out to the left near the opening of the road down to the bridge, dozens of trailer barracks sat crammed in like winter specials on a dealership lot. This meant close quarters for the feds, as well as the marshals bunking in the larger tents; Blood had spent the night in his Bronco. At seven o'clock, behind him, agents were busy constructing what looked to be two make-do kitchens. Portable toilets had been trucked in alongside the wooden latrine shed, and a Salvation Army truck now sat squat alongside its sister vehicle, the American Red Cross.

Finally, across the clearing before him, just beyond the tip of midnight at the foot of the rest of Paradise, a dirty orange backhoe ripped at the entrance to the narrow mountain path, beeping as it backed up and dropping its load into a dump truck before digging back into the hard ground full steam ahead. The work crew appeared to be widening the goat path with an eye toward building a road up the mountainside, most likely to allow up some of the larger vehicles. That was a little like widening a drink straw to suck up hamburgers.

Blood shook his head again and finished his coffee and looked around for a garbage can. There was Banish now, coming down out of the trees near the demolition derby, distinct from the other men in blue windbreakers because of the bullhorn in his left hand and the tall, striding figure he cut, moving across the land with clear purpose, seemingly unaware of the clamor and activity and general busywork going on around him. He walked straight over to a large, unmarked six-wheel black van that Blood hadn't noticed previously. It was backed in right up to the foot of the rise along which agents were erecting tall wooden poles and setting up lights and stringing black telephone wire. Banish disappeared behind the van and Blood waited, watching for him to reappear on the other side. He did not. Blood crumpled the empty cup in his right hand and started slowly across the rumbling clearing.

Sound Truck

Banish stood before the open side door of the modified black Econoline van, recalling the long days and longer nights he had spent in a larger, more advanced model, drawn up on the tarmac at La Guardia, or parked around the block from a midtown bank, even pulled up on Liberty Island under the shadow of the big statue. The Hive, as it had been called, a dark, bustling, information-processing brain that Banish had sat at the helm of, receiving information by headphone and issuing orders to the agents buzzing around him.

This Butte unit, however, was without digital recording capability and satellite uplink. It offered only reel-to-reel Dolby equipment, and a six-bank of five-inch monitors numbered beneath with Dymo-embossed labels, and accommodated only two fold-out desktop workstations. But it was just as well. He knew he would seek out instead the privacy and the retreat of his command tent office.

"Everything ready?"

The sound man pulled off his headphones and turned in the swivel chair. "If he picks up," he said.

Banish set the bullhorn mouth-down onto the van floor. He watched Perkins move busily past the front of the van, then stop and nod to himself as he saw Banish. Perkins was wearing a suit jacket and tie, and an ear wire now. A thin newspaper was folded in his right hand. He recognized the sound van as he came up. "Clunky," he said. "Why not just toss a clean cell phone onto the porch and call him direct?"

Banish appreciated the immediate query, inane as it was. It saved him the tedious pleasantry of "Good morning." He said, "No negotiations on an unsecure line."

"The time element, though. Even if outside parties could monitor, don't we want a quick resolution?"

Banish shook his head. "Not at the expense of security."

Perkins handed him the newspaper, folded open to a page. "Local county fishwrap," he said. "Reprint of an interview with Ables from about six months ago. May change your mind."

Banish scanned the article. The slant of the piece was the irony and embarrassment of the United States Government's inability to recapture a hometown federal fugitive whose whereabouts were publicly known. The newspaper was painting a local outlaw as a folk hero for circulation purposes. The reporter had interviewed Ables outside the cabin. In one paragraph, underlined in blue pen, Ables stated that he would not be taken alive.

Banish nodded. It fit the man's profile.

Perkins said, "You don't take that seriously?"

"He's been waiting for this," Banish said, "which is precisely why we don't rush."

Banish looked up to see the Indian sheriff sauntering toward them. Banish asked Perkins what his name was.

"Blood," said Perkins. "He's the one who first called us in."

The Indian approached with his cowboy hat brim low on his forehead. His face was loose and the color of soaked cherry wood, his nose not very prominent. Cleaved lines extended from the corners of his dark eyes and his mouth, and his elbows were comfortably bent, hands fit snugly into the pockets of his tan sheriff's jacket. Brown wool lining made the jacket look soft. "You asked to see me?" he said.

He kept his eyes steadily on Banish. Banish said, "What was the winning slogan?"

The sheriff looked at him. "Come again?"

"Your political campaign. What banner did you run under?"

The sheriff pursed his lips as though recalling it. " 'Blood for Border County,' " he said.

Perkins smiled wanly and looked up at the sky. "Super."

There was a period of silence then, Banish standing there looking at the Indian, who didn't seem to mind, and Perkins between them rocking slowly on the balls of his feet.

"We're going to question a local resident," Perkins said, evidently feeling the need to break the silence. "Then he'll be remanded into your custody."

The Indian figured it out immediately. "Deke Belcher," he said. "You know him?"

The Indian nodded. "Local color. But I wouldn't say he did anything I could hold him on."

Perkins said, "When the federal government is through with Mr. Belcher, that will be your determination."

Banish was still watching the Indian sheriff and thinking that he ought to have appeared more uncomfortable.

Two marshals turned the corner escorting Deke Belcher in handcuffs between them. Belcher was small and grizzled, with stiff white hair and rotted teeth; approximately seventy-five years old. He brightened upon approaching them and grinned excitedly at all the activity going on around the staging area.

"Oughta sell tickets!" he said.

"Mr. Belcher." Perkins nodded after introducing himself. "What did you think you were doing up on top of this mountain yesterday?"

Belcher grinned. "Ain't against the law to walk a man's own land, or visit a neighbor." He looked from face to face with aggressively mirthful eyes. "Anyways, not yet."

"You do understand that a United States Marshal was shot and killed there yesterday."

Belcher mumbled acknowledgment. The man's chattering grin did not go away. "I saw a whole lot of trespassers up there," he said.

Perkins nodded. It was an official nod that gave away nothing while imparting a sense of developing rapport. Perkins executed it better than most. "So you're a close friend of Mr. Ables."

Belcher nodded. "Glenn's a good neighbor. Clean liver. Real high morals. Got to admire a man who don't buckle. Been mooning these marshals since ever." He smiled up at the taller men on either side of him.

Banish said, "He's holding his family hostage up there."

Belcher looked at Banish and shook his grinning head as though he were being teased. "You federal boys all crap out your mouths. Don't you think we're ready for you? Don't you think we know what the hell all this here is?"

Banish said, "Who are 'we'?"

Belcher's face was wide with sly, knowing excitement. "This here is the federal government trying to push us into armed confrontation. So they can rampage through here, taking our guns, killing off our families, imposing their New World Order on us. That's known."

Banish said, "Who is 'us'?"

"See, around here people believe in the right to bear arms. The right to raise a family whatever way they see fit. The right to worship Yashua—your Jesus—however pleases you. This here's the Great Northwest, the last stronghold of pure white freedom in this country. Do you see that? There's a principle involved here." His shackles, clattering as he grew more animated, became suddenly quiet. "I'll say this, though. If Glenn ain't come down off Paradise yet, he ain't never coming down at all. Glenn's willing to die for what he believes in. Big morals, a man of great faith."

He was reveling in the attention, looking from face to face not merely for reaction but also for approval. Banish glanced over at the Indian. His eyes seemed a little brighter under his hat brim, but clearly not from anything he hadn't heard before. The two marshals stood rigidly.

Perkins said, "That would be the Christian Identity faith."

Belcher nodded matter-of-factly. "That's so."

Perkins grandstanding again. "A fundamentalist creed holding that Anglo-Saxons are the only true Israelites and that America is their promised land. That nonwhites are subhumans to be banished from the country."

"Got to watch your separation of church and state there," said Belcher, smiling, pointing. "Glenn likes agreeable people. So do I. The great race war is coming here. Glenn knowed it. He said all along, he said: the first shots'd be fired at his cabin. And now just take a look around you." He was getting worked up again, clattering his handcuffs. "You know the United Nations Tower of Babylon in Jew York City is making all our laws. Twenty-five hundred blue-helmeted troops massing on the Canadian border right now. What does that tell you there? It's coming. See, Glenn's for preserving the white race. He's for the Grand Old America."

Belcher was nodding proudly, looking from face to face. Banish looked him back. He was recalling for some reason a patient at the Retreat, a former doctor in fine physical health who went around telling people that his body was riddled with cancer, describing the entire destructive process in florid detail.

Banish watched Perkins and Sheriff Blood watching Belcher. The sheriff was remarkably nonplussed. Perkins appeared proud of his success in drawing Belcher out—a chatty old fool who could have been drawn out in conversation by a mime. This episode was the sort of thing that Perkins might later try to bring up with Banish as a flint for conversation: "So how about that old guy . . ." But Banish had no interest in cultural oddities or the local color of one wrinkled mountain man. He did not care who hated whom, nor certainly why. The only thing he cared about was the nodding certainty in the old man's voice, and the strong antifederal sentiment behind his words. Banish knew that this man did not stand alone.

Banish looked at Perkins and nodded, and Perkins said, "Thank you, Mr. Belcher, that is all." The marshals led him away.

The Indian sheriff said, "Fifty more just like him living within a few miles of here. And none of them ever broke a law in their life."

Banish turned to the van and rapped twice on its side with a single knuckle. The sound man nodded to him from inside the open door and began cueing up a reel of audiotape.

Paradise Point

The throw phone remained untouched on the ground fifteen yards before the front porch. Banish stood at the imagined border of the roughly forty-yard no-man's-land surrounding the cabin. A loudspeaker was mounted on a steel tripod near him, its legs anchored in the ground, metal flaps turned on either side to direct sound at the cabin.

Banish said into his Motorola walkie-talkie, "Go."

The hard bass beat and repetitive treble patter of urban black music boomed out of the speaker. The deepest bass notes shook the ground where he was standing, and then the rap lyrics began—shouted, abrasive.

Banish got behind the speaker and instructed the sound man by radio. "Twenty-minute loop, followed by ten minutes of silence the first play-through, one minute less each half hour. And req some earplugs for these men up here ASAP."

Fagin was standing apart from his cadre, picking at an unlit cheroot in his hands and frowning at the music. He came forward and said above the noise, "You rattling him so fucking early?"

"I want him to get the phone and tell us to turn off the music," Banish said. "I want him to start making demands."

Fagin was shaking his head. "It's too fucking early," he said.

Banish just nodded. He looked back at the no-man's-land and the two dog carcasses rotting there. They lay ten yards apart, backs tossed wildly, each drawing a distinct black cloud of hungry flies now. In another day or two the stench would be overwhelming.

Banish moved past Fagin to start back down the mountain. "Your kind of music?" he said to him.

Fagin scowled. "I'm the only man on this mountain who hates this fucking music more than Ables does."

Staging Area

Brian Kearney had just come up the road from the bridge, where things were really getting going. The number of protesters there had practically doubled again. Parked cars lined both sides of the grass road now and people were hiking along beside them to the bridge, carrying signs, coolers, picnic baskets. There was plenty of speech-making and milling around in general. The work itself, what Brian and the other four cops were doing in support of the marshals, was pretty much like any other detail he was used to except that, unlike phone company workers or road repairmen, the marshals didn't take any time to chew the fat. There was not much else to do on a detail other than drink coffee and stamp your feet, both of which made Brian piss like a fountain angel, which was why he was currently back up at the clearing.

Things were happening there too. He stood back and tried to picture the empty space he once knew. It was continuously rush hour here. And music now too, which was strange, from far off, drifting in and out like someone playing a radio or beating a drum. It seemed to echo off the peaks.

The latrines and the Red Cross truck dispensing coffee and plain donuts were right near each other, to Brian's right as he parked the Jeep at the top of the mountain road, so he didn't have to go far. Men were hammering and constructing two long wooden sheds behind the trucks, and when Brian asked one of them what they were building, the agent looked up and said, "Kitchens." But Brian had to admire their efficiency; ask the Huddleston cops to build their own soup kitchen and forget about it. Obviously the feds were shaping up to be in this for the long haul.

It was two wooden steps up to the latrine, and a thin wooden door that might not stand a storm if they got one. Inside was a narrow row of plastic urinals set one next to the other. It wasn't as private as the Porta-Johns outside, but probably cleaner, Brian figured, and definitely more airy. There were no mirrors, and the one sink basin near the door had an empty mop bucket in it. There was a stained green towel hanging off the sink, and two bulbs in socket cords were strung along the low ceiling where the planks were warped anyway, letting in long streams of slanting daylight. A wave of odor hit Brian that was briny and foul.

There was one person in there already, and as in any public restroom, Brian tried not to look at him first. You don't want to meet a stranger's eye in a public toilet. You want to do what has to be done and then wash up and leave. The guy was maybe four urinals away, right in the middle of the row, so there was plenty of room for Brian to go discreetly two or three away from him on either side. But this person had his back turned to Brian. When he shut the door and the guy didn't even turn around to look, Brian was able to size him up without risk. That was when he realized it was Agent Banish.

His first impulse was to turn right around and leave. As though he might be disturbing the man just by being there. But then Brian stopped himself. It was just the two of them inside there, one on one. Brian figured this was his chance.

He remembered his ring again with a grateful start and slipped it off and dropped it into his pants pocket. He started along the creaking boards, literally swallowing, thinking of what to say. Agent Banish wasn't wearing a ballcap just then, his hair grayed and slightly curling, and he was staring straight ahead at the drab wood wall. He was running his water. Brian made sure to make plenty of noise walking so as not to be thought of as sneaking up on him.

Agent Banish's head didn't turn even as Brian stopped at the urinal next to him. But Brian still couldn't think of anything to say, or how to go about starting, so he just cleared his throat and pulled down his fly and began pretty much as usual. Of course by this point, he didn't have to go anymore. He had forgotten all about that. But it would have looked even stranger if he didn't follow through with procedure, so Brian was standing there with his fly down, facing the wall and smelling the salty odor of the place and waiting for something to happen. He was looking straight ahead just like Agent Banish. He was too intimidated to look any other way. Agent Banish's water splashed in fits and starts and Brian knew then that it was now or never. Brian's father liked to say things, and one of the things he always said was, a man's got to take the initiative in life. Brian knew he wasn't going anywhere, wasn't ever getting out of Huddleston, Montana, if he didn't go to the big table and speak up and ask for his plate of food.

So he finally turned his head. It shocked him how close they were. "Agent Banish," he said, pretending to have just noticed him there. Brian took his right hand and extended it across. "Officer Brian Kearney," he said.

Agent Banish's water stopped. His head turned and his steel-blue eyes drilled Brian, just as they had in the rain the night before. He looked at Brian's open hand and then again at his face, all with an expression of hard-to-believe.

"I just wanted you to know," Brian said, forcing it out bravely, "I'm not like the other cops. I mean, they don't see things the way I do. I mean, I don't see things the way they do. In fact," he managed, "two months ago I filed an FD-646, a Special Agent application. I'm hoping to sign on with the FBI myself."

That was when Agent Banish's eyes darkened. He looked at Brian as though from across some great divide, then his eyes dropped away. He zipped up and walked off without a word, without even washing his hands. The thin door whacked shut behind him.

Sawdust blew through shafts of daylight in his wake. Brian stood there frozen, not sure what to do. Then he zipped up and went right out quick after him.

Agent Banish was striding away fast across the clearing and Brian hurried to catch up, then kept apace at his side. It surprised him that they were about the same height.

"I was one of the officers who got shot at," Brian said quickly, so that Agent Banish would know. "It ricocheted right off my hip radio. Not even a scratch. I guess I've always been lucky—"

Agent Banish stopped then. His face was turned toward the open clearing, eyes reading the activity and the surrounding trees the way people look at words and punctuation and make out a sentence. Brian followed his gaze to where Sheriff Blood was standing across the way.

Agent Banish said, "What's his story?"

He was asking Brian a question. Brian stumbled over the answer, because Agent Banish had asked it, and because Brian was wondering what an FBI hostage negotiator could possibly want with the sheriff.

"Sheriff Blood?" he said. "He doesn't have one."

The answer made little sense even to Brian. Agent Banish was still looking, though. The impression Brian got was of deliberate curiosity, the way big animals sometimes paw at smaller animals before killing them.

Agent Banish said, "What's between him and your Chief of Police?"

Brian kind of squinted then. He was trying to decode Agent Banish's face. "How did you know?" he said.

But it was the wrong thing to do, asking a question of the man, because Agent Banish just turned his head and looked full at Brian, recognizing him then, or maybe just seeing the uniform. "Shouldn't you be down at the barricade?" he said.

"I am. I mean—I was. I came back up on a coffee run for the others, and because I had to take a leak too. You know how it is. Only two things to do on a detail like that, stamp your feet and drink coffee, both of which make—"

Agent Banish was already walking away. Brian stayed put, just watching after him. He didn't know why he was trying to waste Agent Banish's time. These were men of action. They did not stand around talking or stamping their feet or drinking coffee. A man couldn't just go up and ask for their camaraderie. They owned the brand of respect you had to earn.

Brian saw that he had bungled the whole thing pretty well, and actually was starting to feel his water again, but now knew he had to see the sheriff. Sheriff Blood noticed him coming and stopped halfway to his Bronco, and then looked and saw Agent Banish walking off in the other direction. Knowing that the sheriff had seen them standing together put a little more pepper into Brian's stride.

"Brian." The sheriff nodded, in his way, arms crossed and casual. "How're you keeping yourself?"

"Good," Brian said, turning back to look at Agent Banish and prompting the sheriff to do the same. "You know," Brian said, "he was inquiring about you."

Brian stayed looking a while longer, for effect, and then turned back to the sheriff, expecting a few prying questions whereby he might be able to dope out some useful information. Instead, the sheriff was eyeing him with some reproach.

"Ables is the man you ought to be concerned with," he said.

The sheriff seemed almost not to care, but Brian realized he had played it badly, and that if he had turned back and looked at the sheriff right off, he'd probably have seen him surprised or curious or worried or whatever. Brian had to believe that was true. This was the Federal Bureau of Investigation taking a personal interest here.

"So," Sheriff Blood said. "How does it feel being a bachelor again?"

Shit. Brian quickly fished out his ring and pushed it back onto his finger. "You won't say anything to the feds," he half-asked.

The sheriff dropped his hands deep into his coat pockets, a stern look on his face. "How's Leslie getting by?"

Shit again. "To tell the truth," Brian said, knowing how much it sounded like an excuse, "I haven't been able to get away to call."

Now the sheriff was angry. Brian knew that he had lost a wife a few years back, to cancer or something, but it was nothing he had ever spoken of, because they didn't have that kind of relationship. But maybe that was why it always seemed that Brian's marriage and Leslie's pregnant condition were so much on the sheriff's mind. He drew his hand out of his pocket and handed Brian a small ring of keys.

"You go call her from my car," he directed.

Brian nodded and went away and did just that.

Command Tent

[PARASIEGE, p. 23]

SA Banish first entered the command tent that day at approximately 11:00 hrs. SA Coyle, operating in her new capacity as directed by SAC Perkins, caught up with SA Banish halfway to his office. The conversation was brief.

SA COYLE: Two more SAs came in from the Bureau overnight, sir. Behavioral Sciences. They're working up a psychological profile of Ables.

SA BANISH: Fine. Have them chart me his horoscope too.

SA COYLE: And the ATF agents have arrived.

SA Banish became distracted at this point. He was staring at a nearby utility refrigerator stocked with fruit and bottled water for the support personnel. SA Coyle determined that a six-pack of Pabst Blue Ribbon beer set on top of the unit was the focus of SA Banish's interest. SA Coyle advised that item had been delivered by a local physician. She advised that the beverage containers had been tampered with and a narcotic suppressant introduced. She advised that they were being kept on hand in the event that alcoholic beverages were requested by Ables.

SA Banish directed that the item in question be removed immediately from the command tent. He then proceeded without explanation into his office.

Office

Banish sat behind the bound reports and files stacked on his desk and watched the two casually suited agents of the Bureau of Alcohol, Tobacco, and Firearms seated across from him. The FBI and ATF operated under similar charters and therefore often found themselves bumping into each other. The press frequently billed them as rivals, but that was inaccurate: the FBI's annual budget far outreached

ATF's $265 million, thereby eliminating any basis for equitable com-
parison. The real source of interagency contention was procedural.
The ATF thought of themselves as cowboys; the FBI, lawmen.

Jurisdictions overlap and frustrate. The FBI and the U.S. Marshals Service are both divisions of the Justice Department. ATF is
Treasury. It was ATF that, acting on independent information involving weapons and explosives trafficking, carried out the original
sting operation which netted Ables. When Ables defaulted on his
scheduled court appearance, he forfeited his surety, the cabin, and
was declared a federal fugitive. Responsibility for his recapture then
shifted to the Marshals Service. The murder of a federal agent and the
development of a siege situation moved the marker a third and final
time, to the FBI. There was no higher domestic law enforcement
authority.

Both sides were being professionally courteous on this case, and
ATF had so far been forthcoming. Banish did not know if the reason
was internal pressure, media heat, or quiet influence from the long
reach of the U.S. Attorney General's Office, nor did he care. The
Spokane agents seated across his desk, Riga and Crimson, did not
immediately impress him. Riga's broad musculature overcompen-
sated for his short stature. Crimson was quieter, less ethnic, more
helpful.

Riga explained that he had shaved off his mustache and all his
hair at the time of the sting in order to fill the role. "We were White
Aryan Resistance members up from Nevada doing a buy at a road-
house just a few miles from here, a skinhead bar called the Bunker. It
was a prearranged meet set up by our confidential informant inside
the WAR compound. Simple paint-by-numbers. Ables joined us at a
booth, we brokered the deal, paid in cash, then followed him out to
the parking lot and received the merchandise."

Banish said, "He had the guns with him?"

"In his truck. Said he was in a rush. It cost him."

"No explosives?"

"Not this time. You remember Miles City?"

Banish nodded. A few years before, a homemade bomb had exploded overnight in an office building that shared a common wall with the Miles City, Montana, FBI Resident Agency.

Riga said, "They never traced the chemicals, but the detonators were definitely his. He's an electronics freak."

Banish said, "Did he resist?"

"No. Grinning, even. Wouldn't go along with Miranda, though. 'Do you understand these rights as I have read them?' Said he didn't. Wouldn't comply." Riga sat back and crossed his legs. "Just being a Nazi prick."

Banish was jotting this down. "What was the final haul?"

Riga said, "One."

Banish scribbled his notes. "One crate."

"One gun."

Banish stopped writing. He looked at what he had written, looked up at the both of them. "One gun," he said.

Riga smoothed out his thickly halved mustache. "A Beretta Model 12 submachine gun. Forty-round magazine. Fires two 9-millimeter rounds per second. Effective range of more than two hundred yards."

Banish said, "You took him down for one piece."

Crimson leaned forward in his chair. "It's a terrorist weapon, popular in South America and the Middle East. How he got it is another question, but that's no cap toy. We know he's connected. He sold a full gross to The Truth just six months before we nailed him. That's confirmed."

"Then why didn't you get more?"

"It was a virgin meet. He was feeling us out."

"Why didn't you ride him?"

"Our informant advised no. Ables only deals with Aryans. Our cover story was too thin to ride out a long relationship."

Banish just nodded. He was taking a long, burning look around his small office, fighting off some of the same dizziness he had felt when he saw the Pabst. Again he had the sensation, like a farmer stamping out locusts, that things were getting away from him.

So it had been a headline bust. Taking guns away from white hate groups always made the national wires. Must have been nearing budget appropriations time at Treasury. State highway patrolmen refer to it as "getting their period," the rush to meet citation quotas at the end of each month. Every agency was susceptible. Every branch of law enforcement had numbers to crunch.

Banish wanted to invite Riga and Crimson outside. He wanted to show them how their one-gun pinch was working out. But it was all bullshit. Because the past didn't matter. A federal marshal was dead. There were criminals and hostages and lawmen all over the mountain, and the welfare of each and every one of them ultimately fell onto Banish's shoulders. Mitigating circumstances equaled hallway chatter, and Banish put it right out of his mind. He would not allow himself to be dissuaded or distracted from doing his job.

Bronco

Blood didn't like watching Paradise Ridge shrink in his rearview mirror. He was worried that something might happen without him being there. Not that he mattered even a whisker to the overall operation. But he could admit that he was caught up in it. Like a baby-girl-trapped-in-a-well story on TV. You didn't want them to bring that baby up without your being there to see it. Especially if there was a chance that baby might have a gun.

So he was hooked—as were others, by the look of the satellite dishes on the TV trucks they passed out beyond the bridge. That was after driving through the protesters who rushed at the Bronco, hammering on the hood and kicking the car doors as Deke Belcher waved from the passenger seat, their fists pounding on the windows, open-mouthed faces bellowing. The old man smelled of a dull, dirty-sour odor that offended Blood in ever-increasing waves. Out on the interstate Blood rolled down his window. He loosened the plastic wrapper on the pine-scented cardboard tree swinging from his dashboard lighter. Then he pulled the plastic wrapper all the way off.

"You taking me to the pokey?"

That aggressive, mangle-toothed smile. He showed it off to Blood the way children hold up their dirty hands to be washed. Blood had the Bronco up to seventy.

"Can't arrest me," said Deke. "What for?"

"I've got some paperwork to do on you," Blood said, trying to speak without inhaling. "Things that need your signature. Then you're free to go."

Deke nodded and kept smiling and watching out the windshield, content as could be. "How about them federal boys?" he said, shaking his bewildered head as if to say, Hoo-ee. "They don't even know what it is they started. Can't see what it is they're into. You know," he said, turning his head then, "I'll lay a wager it was you that called them in the first place. I'll bet that."

Blood didn't care to bite.

"Because Chief Moody is a man who knows how to handle things around here. You always seem to need help getting things done. Such as, I know you got elected, and you been sheriff here two years—but where's your support now? A sheriff who's Indian? Like putting a rock in charge of a forest, I say. People don't know their place nowadays. But it's happening all over. The country's changed. A cigar-store Injun, a wooden statue, all of a sudden wants to move inside and own the whole damned store. You see there? It's as screwy as that. You might even agree with me. What about them deaths, for example, those Indian boys? Nothing ever came of that, right?"

Blood held his face steady. The back of his neck flared.

"You take an Indian boy who had too much to drink and then goes out walking in the middle of the road. That's hit-and-run, but who could blame a driver for not reporting that? A drunken Indian who walks in front of your car? Who's to blame there? Fact is, your kind favors imbibing, which is a simple thing of nature, and these things just happen."

More bait. The old mountain fool might have been craftier than he seemed. But Blood played his part as Deke rattled on, chewing words.

"You got a pretty good job there anyways. Least you ain't one of them Indians always crying about his homeland. I give you your credit for that. Saying the white man stole it. Hell, we did steal it. We fought you off pretty easy and took your land right out from under you. Because we could, because that's the law of the land. But now here're these Indians trying to change all the laws and take back all the land, and you know who's behind it. The Jew lawyers whispering in their ears, that's who, who could turn a copper penny off near anything. Indians're just too slow to come up with this themselves. You natives should all just be quiet and honor those original treaties. We didn't have to section off those reservations, you know. That was purely generous."

Blood said, "You also capitalized 'Indian.' "

"Do you think, for a second, that if someone couldn't take over this land today, they'd do it? And believe me, they wouldn't go run us off and change the whole country completely around, and then all of a sudden feel sorry for us and change all their new laws and give it back. They'd take it and they'd keep it for their own. And that's what is happening here, right now. That's how we have to stay strong, to preserve ourselves. Sure enough—we could go the way of the red man. Federal government has declared war on the white Christian race. Glenn Ables is just the tip of that iceberg. But don't you think you and your ancestors wouldn't scalp and fight like all hell if you got a second chance? Thing is, there ain't no second chances. That's the way this is. We're preserving our race here and preserving it now. You probably understand that as good as anyone."

Blood wiped a stripe of sweat off his thick upper lip. "I understand you perfectly," he said.

They arrived at the station and Blood turned into the gravel lot. Except for the flag flying high, the place looked closed for the season. It was as though the building had been shut down for high quarantine. As though a fever had broken out across the county.

Deke moved anxiously in his seat. "Just sign some papers?" he said.

"That's right."

"Then I'm free to go."

"That's right."

"Then you'll ride me back on up to Paradise?"

Blood put the Bronco in park and turned off the ignition. He grabbed his hat off the dash and worked the door latch and stepped out quickly, standing on the gravel drive and breathing in the open air. He fixed his hat tightly upon his head and turned around to look back through the open door at Deke.

"Then," Blood told him, "you're on your own."

Paradise Point

Now it was dark. Fucking stars again, and fast-moving black clouds. Night wind fluttering the trees. Fagin looked out and saw his sharpshooters crouched all around him, black forms against the tall black trees and purple night. Other men in the woods too, Bureau agents, in duck boots and down jackets from fucking L.L. Bean. They were working at various stations around the cabin perimeter, making a lot of noise, clanking things, and Fagin was pretty sure he knew what they were up to, and it pissed him off. But fuck it if he'd ask. Banish would keep him in the loop or else.

At least the music was off again. Fagin heard the garbled bullhorn barking and started through the dark trees toward it. On his lunch break he had commandeered an outside line and hit up an FBI contact for info about his new friend, Special Agent John Banish. It seemed that Banish had taken the entire year of 1991 off for compassionate leave—six months more than normally allowed for bereavement—and it was halfway through that when the psycho chick plugged him in the hospital. The circumstances surrounding that incident were vague—purposefully fucking vague—but she put a round so far into his gut that he was nearly fitted for a colostomy bag. He'd been at an inactive one-man Resident Agency somewhere in the middle of Montana since getting out of the hospital, just marking time to retirement. The whole thing stunk. It reeked of meddling and preferential treatment and string-pulling and sticky fingers and all the things about the Bureau that Fagin fucking despised.

A man in an FBI windbreaker was kneeling in the dark at the edge of the kill zone and Fagin thought at first that it was Banish, but upon closer examination saw that it was someone else, an agent in headphones mounting a microphone gun with a parabolic dish. Banish was crouched just beyond him, finishing his bullshit bullhorn spiel. ". . . *lay down your weapons and come out with your hands clasped firmly behind your head.*" He lowered the bullhorn and waited then. "Anything?" he said.

The agent in the headphones was kneeling perfectly still, staring at the ground. "Some scurrying," he said, in inflected Virginian, the accent of preference both for FBI agents and astronauts. "But nothing clear. Those walls may be thicker than we thought."

Fagin squinted into the dark distance. Somewhere among the trees in the starlight before the black cutout of the cabin sat the black plastic phone briefcase, like a big fat fucking piece of cheese.

"So here we are," said Fagin, implying the scope of things. No use fucking around anymore. "You turned a dog-and-pony act into a fucking three-ring circus. Now what?"

Banish stood without turning to look back at Fagin. "Have your men switch off their NVDs."

Fagin scowled. He shook his head in disgust, but it was wasted because all he had was Banish's back. He flicked on his shoulder radio. "This is Fagin," he said. "Everybody click off. Repeat, everybody. We're gonna have a show here."

Banish remained looking straight ahead, waiting another good half a minute, looking for the cabin through the black trees or maybe just watching the night sky. If he wasn't doing it solely to piss Fagin off or to prove how in charge he was, then he was a mope pure and simple. Finally Banish turned his head. He raised his left hand.

Loud metallic clanks sounded all around the mountaintop as switches were thrown and six big stadium lights flashed on, showering the cabin in near daylight. Fagin squinted and raised a gloved hand as his pupils contracted. The lights appeared to be evenly spaced in a wide half-circle, set on raised standards around the convex perimeter of the no-man's-land, and humming. The lit area was washed out and nearly shadowless, the cabin now made plain through the trees.

"That's good," Fagin said. "You're pissing into the fucking wind. And you got me standing right behind you."

Banish's back was in silhouette, the trees and the superbright cabin beyond him, as though he were standing in front of a picture. "Has he broken the phone?" Banish said.

Fagin was still squinting.

"Has he shot at the phone?" Banish said.

Fagin frowned. "Not yet."

Banish nodded. "He'll talk," he said. "They always do."

Then Perkins came up behind Fagin in a hurry. He had run up the mountain and was trying to mask the fact that he was sorely out of breath. "More trouble down at the barricade," he huffed.

Banish stood there, thinking about it some more—fucking mope. He turned finally and looked back at the agent wearing the headphones. "We'll have some more music," he decided. Fagin watched him start back down the mountain with desk agent Perkins. Then the fucking music started up again. Jesus fucking Christ—

Bridge

Used to be, news happened and then it was reported. And that had seemed fair. If a person caught a big fish, there'd be a picture in the newspaper the next day of that person standing on the dock next to his strung-up prize. Before-and-after seemed like the natural progression of a story.

Sheriff Blood looked at the scene being played out beyond the narrow creek bed not twenty yards away. He had always detested the local Montana news programs. Didn't favor the network news much either, but they had less time for shenanigans. He bristled at the idea of creating news, but that's what these people did and that's what they were doing now. They used cameras like sticks, turning them on people and prodding at them. And satellite dishes like sirens. Just after nightfall they had turned their camera lights on the protesters gathered on the far side of the bridge. They wanted a show and they were going to get one. No sense waiting around to see if any fish swam by. They were chumming the waters. They were scooping out blood and guts and dragging a wide net.

There was, of course, another ingredient going here. Whiskey and beer made instant problem-solvers out of the most irascible characters. The Great Clarifier imparted to them the strength and conviction to act decisively upon solutions which just that moment were themselves revealed. That was when your bar fight or homicide or domestic disturbance was most likely to occur.

Some words rose up distinctly above the din. "Get out of our backyards!" they yelled. "Pigs!" And again and again, from one gang of young, angry, swaying men: "The Truth! The Truth!"

"Jesus Christ," said Brian Kearney, watching the crowd all of a sudden surge toward the bridge again. He was gap-mouthed. The marshals who had relieved him of his position on the bridge front were fast-talking into their shoulders, rifles drawn and ready. The convention of protesters had become a legitimate mob.

Lights, people, noise. It was all a great big carnival freakshow. The federal government was the Man with One Hundred Arms, and Glenn Ables was the barker. Kearney could have been holding a pink beehive of cotton candy as he pointed in amazement to a person by the left side of the bridge. "Sheriff," he said. "That guy just chained himself to a tree."

Near the man were a group of people holding up a banner: FEDERAL GOVERNMENT GET OFF OUR LAND!

"Environmentalists," explained Blood.

Kearney was staring at the scene. "Is everybody gone completely off their nut?"

Blood took another sip of coffee and waved away a whirring buffalo fly. A thrown egg landed near them with a dull splash. Blood admired the slanted shape it made, and the manner of its oozing.

"Yep," he said.

Headlights sprayed the crowd then. A Jeep pulled up behind and Kearney turned and so did Blood. It was Banish and Perkins, Perkins driving. Perkins's eyes stayed wide and on the crowd as he stepped out of the Jeep. Banish watched them with more detached concern, sizing up the crowd like a shop owner watching a big sale going on across the street.

Kearney met them first. "There's been some drinking," he explained. He might also have let slip that the earth was round. He handed Banish some of the handbills and newsletters being distributed behind the lines, racist things home-printed under such jagged headings as The Covenant.

Perkins surveyed the swelling mob scene. "Jackals," he said. "Brownshirts."

Banish barely glanced at the handbills Kearney had given him. "What set them off?" he said.

"I'd say it was what just happened with the Mellises," said Kearney. When the agents didn't respond immediately, he added,

"Charles Mellis's parents." But they were just waiting. They weren't looking for a conversation. Banish seemed to be counting heads.

Kearney pushed on. "Mr. Mellis wanted to be let through to talk to you people. I told him that no one gets through, so he went over my head and talked to the marshals, and they said no too. Then a TV crew got Mr. Mellis on camera, standing in front of the bridge, and he told them what had just happened and how he was being treated unfair, and that's when things really started to get ugly. That's when people started to yell."

Perkins pointed and said, "There's Belcher."

Blood looked. Deke was standing near the front of the bridge, grinning wide and adding his hand to the support of a crude cardboard sign that read FEDERAL BUREAU OF INFIDELS.

Blood turned back to find Banish frowning, probably at him. Kearney pushed on, doing his level best, pursuing whatever it was that he was pursuing.

"The thing is, sir, Mr. Mellis knows Glenn Ables. He says that maybe he can get through to him."

Banish dismissed it with a single shake of his head.

"But he says Ables will listen to him. Maybe if they could get to talking, it might ease some things—"

Perkins said, "People always inflate relationships with a hostage-taker during a crisis. Hero mentality."

"But aren't the hostages really only Ables's family?"

Banish shook his head. "No one crosses the police line."

But rookie Kearney wouldn't let go. "I understand that, sir," he said, "but it's the man's son up there. All he wants to do is just talk to someone to find out if his family is all right."

Banish looked hard at Kearney. "No one crosses the police line. Especially family members. Is that clear enough?"

Another egg fell nearby. Banish turned and regarded it with some interest. The yolk spread lazily out of its shell and oozed onto the dirt. He seemed to discover the hate literature in his hand then, and pawned the pamphlets off on Perkins. He looked over at Blood.

"This appears to be a riot," Banish said. "You are the sheriff in this county, aren't you?"

"Thought I was here as an observer," Blood said. "A volunteer, I think was how you put it."

Banish nodded. "I'm wondering why you're here, too," he said. "What's your read on the character of this crowd?"

Blood did not turn back to look. "It's a pretty good cross section, I'd say. We run the gamut up here. These would be resisters, protesters, evaders, constitutionalists, survivalists, separatists. Or do you want me to be more specific?"

Banish didn't say no.

"Home schoolers, tax protesters, old hippies, conspiracy buffs, Vietnam veterans, religious fanatics, radical environmentalists, outlaws, Christian Patriots, assorted mystics and so-called doomsayers, white supremacists, and sure, probably some people from White Aryan Resistance. Some skinhead members of The Truth as well. Did I leave anybody out, Brian?"

Kearney said, "I sure hope not."

Blood said, "A pretty good patchwork of angry special interests. All except for one unifying principle."

Banish said, "Not Glenn Allen Ables."

Blood nodded at that. "Their hatred and distrust of the federal government. Most of them, the locals anyway, that's why they live where they do. Instead of, say, a mining community, this here might be considered a protest community. That's why they're taking this whole thing so personal."

Banish stood there inspecting him, clearly deliberating something. Then he nodded. "All right, Sheriff," he said. "I'm putting you in charge down here, because I don't have another man to spare. I want a local face of authority dealing with these people. I need you to monitor protests and media reports, collect newspapers and all circulated literature, and report twice a day directly to me."

Blood looked at him. "That sounds like quite an honor," he said.

Kearney said, "I'll do it."

Banish said, "It's an important job. If you can't handle it, you will be replaced."

Blood nodded. "I had a paper route once," he said. "I guess I'm qualified."

Kearney said, "What do you need me to do, sir?"

Banish seemed to really notice him only then, and made as though he was giving him some serious thought. He asked him his name and Kearney gave it to him. "I want you to help the sheriff and the marshals here with security," Banish told him. "So that absolutely no one crosses the line. That is of primary importance. I need a liaison to the front here and you two are it."

Kearney said, "Yes, sir," with all the willingness of a good soldier.

Now it was Blood's turn to shake his head. He couldn't help but grin, what with the foolishness going on here amid the chaos all around them.

Banish said, "Something funny, Sheriff?"

"No," Blood said. "I just like watching you boys work." But he couldn't push it too far. Banish was an animal that could turn on him.

Perkins was staring and thinking. "We could try moving back the roadblock," he said.

Banish shook his head. "Too late for that."

Then the crowd was surging again beyond the creek, tangling and pulling like human taffy being made. It swelled dangerously, then crested back, and in the give-and-take an older woman was ungracefully bumped to the ground. She was clearly somebody's grandmother, wearing as she did a blouse and pink polyester slacks and a mop of tightly curled white hair, getting to her hands and knees on the dirt road before the bridge.

She was helped back up by the concerned people on either side of her. Something she had been holding had fallen to the floor of the iron bridge and now she was giving the business to the nearest marshal. He seemed to be offering to retrieve it for her but she was refusing, or insisting—in any case, she was bickering to be let through. Then suddenly the crowd that had knocked her over threw its full support behind her. She brushed off her short coat and motioned over to where Blood and the other three were standing, and the mob rallied loudly behind. This grandmother was a tiger. You had to feel something for the bridge marshal as he turned and looked helplessly back toward them for help.

Blood saw Banish eyeing the scene and frowning bitterly. He clearly wanted to stall things out but the crowd would not quit, their ranting jeers increasing in decibels like a thunderstorm coming over the mountains, until it seemed as though things were just about to break completely out of control. Banish said to Perkins then, under his breath, "Let her through."

Perkins motioned to the marshal. An unforgiving cheer rose from the crowd as the marshal helped her duck under the yellow web of police ribbon and onto the checkpoint bridge. He inspected the package she had dropped, then returned it to her with a polite nod. She thanked him and crossed the iron bridge with an air of pride and determination, like a spy being exchanged between countries, and the crowd behind grew quiet, hanging on the imminent encounter.

She stepped past Blood to get to Perkins, who she assumed was in charge. Banish had moved off to the side. She held in her hands a blue Tupperware bowl covered with tinfoil. The woman peeled back the wrap and revealed a batch of homemade brownies, which she then kindly presented to Perkins.

"I just wanted you to know," she said, "a lot of us Montanans here are behind you boys one hundred percent."

Perkins tried not to look too surprised as he accepted the gift of fresh-baked goods. "Well, that's much appreciated, ma'am," he said.

The grandmother smiled and nodded to the rest of them, then returned to the bridge. The crowd hooted and hollered and a few more eggs were launched. They had been betrayed. In their rush to power they had nominated a representative from the opposing party.

Banish returned. He said to Perkins, "I'll prepare material overnight for a press briefing tomorrow morning to defuse some of this." Then he turned to Blood. "I want an emergency countywide ordinance restricting the sale and consumption of alcohol. Cite threats of violence and public safety. That is within the powers of your office?"

Blood said, "I suppose it is."

Banish nodded. "This ought to send your popularity ratings right through the roof."

Kearney had dipped into the Tupperware container and was now sampling a brownie, and voicing his garbled approval. "Kind old lady," he observed between bites.

Banish had started back to the Jeep. "Probably poisoned," he said over his shoulder.

Kearney stopped chewing.

The Covenant Newsletter

HOLY WAR!
A Call to Arms

The final hour is here. Agents of the Zionist Occupation Government tread upon our soil. They have moved in their tanks and taken up positions all throughout Huddleston. They are massing on Paradise Ridge. Local raids are imminent.

Our nation is in jeopardy. Our people are being taken. The time is NOW for action. Glenn Ables is only the beginning. They want to make an example of Glenn Ables.

The time is NOW to show our strength. They want to ban our guns. Support Compulsory Firearms Ownership!!! It is the ONLY WAY to guarantee your freedom. Your right to own and carry a firearm and defend your family is

GUARANTEED by the Constitution. Stand up for Glenn Ables! If someone trespassed on your private property and shot your dogs dead, you would shoot back too, and it would be within your God-given rights. Keep ammunition well stocked and always keep one gun hidden in the event of an Occupationalist purge. Martial law is imminent. The blue helmets are coming.

This tyranny is not limited to the land of the Great Northwest. The siege on Glenn Ables is just one phase of a series of strategic federal assassinations, beginning with the murder of Order founder Robert Matthews and including the recent massacre at Waco. We must END THIS TYRANNY! If ZOG is allowed to establish a stronghold here at Paradise Ridge, they will rampage throughout Montana and the entire Northwest. THIS IS OUR LAST STAND! We need witnesses on the front lines in the form of freedom-fighting Christian Soldiers. The time is NOW to fortify our charter and establish once and for all time the independent white homeland of Washington, Idaho, Montana, Oregon, and Wyoming, and secure our borders.

They have targeted Glenn Ables because he stands for a way of living that we as members of the White Race believe in and hold to be true. His is a family like anyone else's who moved up here to raise their kids away from the drugs and violence and the crossbreeding of the cities, to try and reclaim a little corner of this great country that was once our own. No decent, moral Christian should have to live next to a bunch of niggers and Jews.

This attack is pure provocation. Hundreds of United Nations agents bankrolled by the money merchants in the East, military helicopters cruising the ridge, armored personnel carriers, hi-tech demolition equipment—all for one man and a simple firearms offense? Pure and murderous provocation. ZOG must be stopped at Paradise Ridge.

We all have guns and are not afraid to use them. We take our orders straight from the Bible, and we know that *Thou shalt not kill* is really *Thou shalt not murder.* Yahweh commanded his people all throughout the Book, *Go out and slay.* In the name of Almighty God, we will do whatever it takes to defend our families and our Christian way of life.

Glenn Ables was not afraid to shout it from the mountaintop. He and his family are a testament to the freedom the federal establishment is here and now trying to take from us by force.

!!!

This is a call to arms. As our forefathers before us threw off the tyranny and oppression of the Kings and Bankers of Europe and established an independent homeland, so must we now rise to the cause. The final hour approaches! A state of war currently exists in America. This is a call to action. Support Glenn Ables. His fight is our fight. Witness him and join him. Get the word out over the wires. Get fax machines if you already don't, get computer modems. Use their technology against them. Send it out over the American Patriotic Fax Network. We must come together now. Let the faithful converge on Paradise Ridge.

KEEP AMERICA PURE!

This is our last stand against the Zionist Government and their New World Order. We will not back down. We must keep our land free. FBI agents are white in color only, and by their fruits ye shall know them. The federal agents here will be held accountable for their crimes. If Glenn Ables is murdered, or if any harm comes to his wife or any one of his five innocent children—then in the name of all that is Christian and Good, the second American Revolution will begin right here. The marauders will be overthrown. That is our covenant.

Friday, August 6

Office

There was nothing from the cabin overnight. Banish could tell that it was morning now by the brighter complexion of the drab canvas walls. In the absence of any real progress, he had devoted himself to paperwork. Photographs of the Newlands, Ables's in-laws on his wife's side, had come in from Provo, along with biographies and neighbor interviews. Craig Newland, Marjorie Ables's brother, had four months earlier put in for a week's vacation from the paper processing plant that employed him. Their Sunoco credit card account showed activity at a station twenty miles outside of Huddleston six days before, a nine-gallon fill-up at 10:37 A.M. on Saturday, July 31. Their 1987 Ford Lynx had been found parked, locked, and empty on one of the access roads adjoining Paradise Ridge, a coffee-stained AAA Triptik highlighting interstates from Utah to Montana discarded on the backseat. By all accounts, the Newlands disliked Glenn Ables but had undertaken the journey north in order to visit Marjorie and the children, whom they had not seen in over four years. They were likely the only true captives in the cabin.

Two Assistant U.S. Attorneys had come in before dawn to brief Banish on the government's formal criminal complaint regarding the shootout. They were going to charge Ables with the murder of Deputy Marshal Bascombe, and Mellis with assault on a federal officer, while reserving future charges against twelve-year-old Judith. The wording of the complaint was important to Banish because filing it with the U.S. District Court in Helena effectively released the FBI version of the initial skirmish into the public domain. The news media could then source the complaint and air previously withheld information. On the other hand, it was a legal document, and any inaccuracies or omissions would hinder the government's case later in court. Banish had spent the better part of two early morning hours going over it with a red pen.

The press situation itself was heating up. The Press Services Office of the External Affairs Division had called overnight from Washington to order a departure from SOP. They had decided that a pool of twenty print reporters and one Associated Press photographer would be allowed access to the staging area that morning. Their concern was that a five-day standoff without any substantive development would move a blacked-out media into broader speculation in the form of opinion pieces concerning transgressions of "the State," or comparisons to similar standoff situations—the MOVE bombing in Philadelphia; Waco—that had ended unfavorably. Traditionally, the longer a siege dragged on, the more law enforcement came to be painted as the instigator. Banish, in order to avoid media disruption of the staging area, had already figured out a way around the command. Perkins was at that hour escorting the press pool up an adjacent mountain, one with a higher ridge and a distant but fair view of Paradise Ridge below.

That had been the only official communication from the Bureau SOG, or seat of government, in Washington, D.C. Nothing from the top brass, and specifically nothing from AD Richardsen. The obvious explanation was that no significant progress had been made. Nothing happens in a hostage negotiation until somebody picks up the phone. Banish had always played the maverick in keeping the Bureau at bay, but for this, his first active assignment in almost three years, he had expected to be kept on a short leash. Not only expected, but anticipated. Even hoped. He wondered then, fleetingly, if there was some other way they were keeping tabs on him.

He stopped what he was doing then and sat back in his chair. As he had done once or twice daily following his release from the hospital, and nearly every other hour since arriving at Paradise Ridge, he took his mental pulse. He was self-evaluating. His reason seemed to him sharp enough. The disruption of his routine at Skull Valley had at first been overwhelming. There, by adhering to strict work, meal, and sleep schedules, removing himself from the constant push-and-pull of everyday life, he had slowly and painstakingly rebuilt his mind. He had lived there inside his head like a man with a white coat and clipboard, tampering with and tempering the dark thoughts and appetites and urges that had nearly consumed him. At Skull Valley he had been his own lab rat. He ran the labyrinths and doled out the cheese. And the Bureau had left him alone there, but perhaps for too long. He saw now that the recovery of his reasoning faculties had left little room for the more gauzy shadings of the mind, such as personality, temperament, character.

Being sprung from that solitude had at first been disorienting, but since arriving on the mountain he felt that he had met each task head-on, managing to adopt a fair shadow of his former working persona. He had picked up all the familiar scents. He was able to function again and recall a detached sort of familiarity, like a dog stumbling upon a forgotten yard, digging for old bones. But he was untested and he knew it. There was, behind every action, the desperate possibility that something crucial or obvious might somehow slip past him. And a certain paranoia he was aware of, a voice muttering in his ear, that was fed by the vacuum of silence from D.C. And above all that, the hope that the call would come relieving him of responsibility, returning him to Skull Valley. But by taking one step back from himself, he was able to keep all this in check.

There was always the concern, however, that the gauge itself might be faulty. That in these steadying self-evaluations, his reason might fail to police itself accurately, and like a man stopping to take his pulse and coming away satisfied, not knowing his second hand was slow, Banish could himself be deceived.

His methods so far seemed to him sound. There was no set playbook for hostage negotiation. There were strategies and there were tactics, but no methodology. Each situation was its own. The negotiator worked to isolate the suspect while at the same time setting himself in a position to wait, psychologically starving out the individual, as here, where Ables had effectively been placed under house arrest. Then the negotiator was left to his own devices. In the days when he was still considered an expert on the subject, in his lectures on tradecraft at the FBI Academy at Quantico, Virginia, Banish had likened the role of Chief Hostage Negotiator to that of a man trying to adjust a roof antenna by himself. You position the antenna, he would tell the trainees, then climb off the roof to check the progress of its reception, then go back up and try something else entirely different again. The analogy made sense in the days when cable television was just a dream and satellite dishes were fifty feet wide. When he was still one of the Young Turks at the Bureau, the best and the brightest who would reestablish the FBI as the world's preeminent law enforcement agency in the post-Vietnam, post-Watergate, antigovernment era. When he was still a family man with a wife and daughter, which had guaranteed that he would never have to adjust a roof antenna alone.

He returned to the work on his desk. The stacks of bound reports and memos and requisition authorizations were like rocks he could hang on to. They were real things he could touch and move with his hands.

These were the idle hours. The stasis when anxiety battled reason and when mistakes were most often made. The downtime that sapped men's spirits. Even unfavorable developments were more welcome. They at least demanded some form of action. Frustration was the hostage negotiator's enemy. Purgatory was hell.

He reinitialed the disclosure sheet he had authored detailing Perkins's guidelines for that morning's press conference, including a formal three-paragraph press release and an annotated cheat sheet of responses to anticipated questions. He was reviewing the marshals' watch summaries for the previous day when he heard laughter coming from outside his office.

Something about it bothered him. When he heard the laughter again, he set down his pen and went out through the canvas flap door into the greater command tent. The agents there were busy at desks littered with soda cans and coffee cups and plastic junk food wrappers from the snacks the supply trucks had brought in. The switchboard desk telephones and the telex and fax machines were up and running. One agent was logging reports into a computer; another, issuing orders over the radio. Only Coyle's chair near the front was empty.

To Banish's right, in the corner near the small utility refrigerator, two Montana state policemen stood engaged in casual conversation, laughing and drinking out of two tall cans of doped Pabst Blue Ribbon.

Banish saw red. He exploded at the stunned men, grabbing their arms and propelling them out of the tent and into the bright light of morning. He emptied the cans there, the smell of the beer salting his nose, then he dressed down the Staties, and then Coyle, who arrived in the middle of it with a cup of coffee in her hand. By the time he was through with her, the Staties had gotten up on their hind legs.

"Look," one said, "we just come off a twelve-hour shift."

Banish said sharply, "No one goes off-duty on this mountain."

The other said, "So you guys in there get cold ones, but not the men out here doing the real work?"

Banish looked down at the dark puddles the beer made in the dirt, the foam along the edges clinging to stray weeds. The beer smell wafting up. His head started to swim. He looked around and noticed a familiar face among the people standing nearby. "Kearney," he barked.

The cop looked startled. "Yessir," he said, coming over.

Banish had to fight to keep himself from yelling. "These two imbeciles are dismissed. I want you personally to see them off the mountain and back to their barracks."

Kearney nodded without question and went off alongside the disgusted troopers.

Banish turned back to Coyle. "Do you have a hearing problem, Agent Coyle?" he said.

Coyle said, "No, sir."

"Do you have a problem following orders?"

"No, sir."

"Well, I don't know who put you in charge of this command tent, but if I have to give one more order twice around here, HEADS WILL ROLL. DO YOU UNDERSTAND ME?"

"Yes, sir."

"WAS THERE ANY PART OF THAT YOU DID NOT UNDERSTAND?"

Coyle swallowed and shook her head. "No, sir," she said.

Banish was nodding. He knew his voice had gotten away from him. He was losing control. He looked to the command tent as a place of refuge. Agents watching from the entrance disappeared back inside. Banish turned and walked off in the opposite direction across the clearing. Men who had stopped there to stare now hustled out of his way.

He was getting away from the smell. The smell of the beer was so thick he could nearly taste it, and if he could taste it, then he could swallow it, so he was getting away from that. He was breathing clean air. It smelled of diesel fuel and exhaust, but it tasted clean, because it did not tempt his immense thirst.

Sound Truck

He came to the sound truck and knocked twice. The agent inside, the sound man, whatever his name was, slid the door open. Rap music beat tinnily from the headphones hanging around his neck. He stepped back to allow Banish inside.

"Anything?" Banish asked.

The sound man shook his head. "Nothing."

Banish did not nod. If there had been any activity whatsoever from the cabin, he would of course have been notified immediately. It was a senseless question. He sat down in the chair nearest the open door. It creaked under him.

The sound man took the other chair. He was quiet, waiting for the senior agent to say something. He tapped two fingers on his fold-down desktop. Finally he came out with what was on his mind. "Why haven't they answered?" he said.

Banish's eyes were closed. His head was bowed. He just shook his head.

After a while the tin music became muffled as the sound man put his headphones back on. Banish opened his eyes and looked up. Surveillance cameras had been installed overnight, the monitor bank on the panel above the sound man's head showing six different scenes in flickering black and white. It took Banish a moment to place each location: the cabin from three strategic angles, one head-on through the trees in front, and two wider pictures more than forty-five degrees each way; a wide view of the bridge and the crowd of protesters at the foot of the mountain; a section of empty road leading up the mountainside; and a high, wide overview of the staging area itself.

Banish thought he could discern the small dark blot the throw phone made on the wavy ground in the trees before the cabin. When the sound man looked up again, Banish caught his eye with a head nod. The sound man pulled off his headphones. "What about the external microphones?" Banish said.

The sound man shook his head. "Nothing between the music. Except once around three in the morning, a marshal taking a piss against a tree."

"My men don't piss on duty," Fagin said.

Banish turned slowly, unimpressed by theatrics. Fagin was standing outside the open van door in full uniform minus his ballcap, a camouflage bandanna wrapped tightly around his hard black head.

"Mighty big squirrels, then," said the sound man in his Virginian accent.

Fagin nodded. "Must fucking be." He stood with his big arms crossed, sizing up both of them. He looked as though he had had a shower. "Beautiful Montana morning," he said, eyes cool and bright. There was something about Fagin that was always coiled.

"Actually," the sound man said, turning more in his chair, "there was one strange thing overnight. A growling sound."

Banish said, "What do you mean?"

"Not from inside the cabin—out there in the no-man's-land. Every once in a while. Guttural noises, deep and fierce."

"Coyotes," Fagin said. "Bloodthirsty sons of bitches. My men see them stalking the perimeter at night through the trees. Yellow fucking eyes, and stealthy. It's the dog meat. Music doesn't scare them anymore."

Fagin's voice trailed off slightly at the end, and then his entire countenance gradually changed, his sharp eyes showing just a touch of vacancy. Then he frowned. He was receiving a transmission in his ear.

He looked up. "Where the fuck's Perkins?"

"With the press," Banish said. "Up there." He motioned toward the adjoining peak.

Fagin said, "Fuck." Then he moved off fast.

Banish turned back around. The sound man was looking at him, but Banish shrugged mildly. Delegation was another part of command. "Put me through," Banish said, lifting the handset off its hook.

The sound man readjusted his headphones, then cut the music with a flip of a switch, cueing Banish to begin.

Banish said flatly, "This is Special Agent Bob Watson." He was watching the cabin on the wavy monitor, the dark blot of the orphan telephone. "Your cabin is completely surrounded. There is no chance for escape . . ."

The Baltimore Sun

HUDDLESTON, Mont., Aug. 7—Federal authorities obtained a murder warrant yesterday against fugitive Glenn Allen Ables in the shooting death of Deputy U.S. Marshal Stanley Bascombe.

FBI agents yesterday continued to surround Ables's remote mountaintop cabin in a tense standoff, wary that a full-scale assault could endanger the lives of the five children living inside.

Ables was indicted two years ago on federal weapons charges. Bascombe was killed during a gun battle touched off when a family dog picked up the scent of four U.S. Marshals conducting what has been described as a routine surveillance in a ravine below Ables's cabin, according to authorities.

Bascombe's body was flown home to Maryland two days ago. He will be eulogized at a service today at St. Paul's Church in Baltimore by E. Walter Leveralt, Director of the U.S. Marshals Service.

Ables, a notorious white supremacist and former Ku Klux Klansman, has been charged with firing the shot that killed Bascombe. Charles Mellis, 29, Ables's brother-in-law and one of four other relatives also hiding out in the cabin, faces a lesser charge of assault on a federal agent.

Authorities reportedly have received no response from the cabin since the initial shooting. They continued yesterday the tense and prolonged process of attempting to lure Ables out of the cabin. "This is not a routine arrest," said Frank Spona, spokesman for the FBI in Washington, D.C. "We will exhaust every possible means we believe will effect a peaceful resolution."

Ables has vowed not to be taken alive.

[The fifth day of the standoff was marked by mounting tension and swirling rumors, according to the Associated Press.

[A bizarre scene unfolded early yesterday as members of the elite U.S. Marshals Special Operations Group arrested five heavily armed men on a mountain road leading to a high ridge overlooking both Ables's secluded cabin and the federal command post. Marshals, who described the young men as members of a neo-Nazi skinhead sect known as The Truth, stopped the Jeep and confiscated at least eight semiautomatic rifles without incident.

[The five men had swastikas painted on their faces, according to eyewitnesses. A banner proclaiming "Great White Revolution" was also recovered.

[Also yesterday, a Helena television station, without identifying its sources, reported that authorities had previously cut the eleven-member family's water supply. Authorities have said that such action would be routine, although they have denied several other media reports, including one broadcast that tear gas canisters had been launched at Ables's cabin.

["We have purposefully and patiently taken no aggressive action," said Reginald Perkins, Special Agent in Charge of the Butte, Montana, FBI Field Office, in the first FBI briefing at Paradise Ridge. "The critical factor in this situation is that there are juveniles in the residence."

[Authorities denied that Ables's continued lawlessness showed ineptitude on their part.

["I see no embarrassment," said Perkins. "This whole prolonged procedure shows only caring on the part of the government. The situation right now is that we care more about the children than Mr. Ables does, and this is a shame."

[Authorities have said they are unsure how many weapons Ables may have stockpiled in the cabin, though it is widely known that his wife and children, ranging in age from 18 months to 14 years, regularly practice target shooting in the area.

["We are prepared to face an arsenal," Perkins said.

[Perkins also said he has no way of knowing how long the standoff will continue. According to the Associated Press, it was not immediately clear whether he was acting as the government's chief negotiator.]

Authorities have established a federal command post on the mountain consisting of at least nine tents, a fleet of military vehicles, several U-Haul trucks, a fire truck, helicopters, and hundreds of police and support personnel. The standoff includes agents of the FBI and the Bureau of Alcohol, Tobacco, and Firearms, U.S. Marshals Service deputies, the Montana State Police, the local Border County Sheriff's Department, and members of the Huddleston town police.

The duration of the siege has done nothing to abate the groundswell of support for Ables in and around this tiny Northwestern hamlet. Local residents, members of various Christian Identity sects, neo-Nazis from neighboring states, and thrill-seekers from all across the country continue to gather daily at the police barricade, heckling vehicles leaving the scene and local police officers posted on the bridge, and occasionally making racist remarks or chanting pro-Aryan slogans.

Ables and his family moved to this remote northern

Montana community from Chicago several years ago. The area is not far from the headquarters of the Church of Christian White Aryan Resistance (WAR), considered to be one of the largest and most active white supremacist organizations in the United States. A delegation of that group late yesterday delivered hate literature to the police barricade at the foot of Paradise Mountain.

Ables has previously denied any association with WAR.

Through it all, Ables, 41, has gone from being a religious and racial extremist to a folk hero among his neighbors. Residents help by delivering mail and groceries up to the fugitive's cabin, which has no electricity or telephone service.

Neighbors described Ables as proud and self-sufficient, someone who before the standoff would take a group of local children fishing.

"Glenn's a man of morals," said Deke Belcher, 77, a neighbor of Ables, who said the FBI and federal marshals should leave the mountain and its residents alone. "He was provoked," said Belcher.

Office

Sheriff Blood entered the command tent and tipped his hat to the agent at the first desk, telling her who he was. She was the no-nonsense type, with a disapproving look and a voice that wore glasses. She seemed more like an agent than a woman, just as the men there seemed more like agents than men. There were two genders on the mountain, agents and everyone else. She inspected the newspapers in his arms, perhaps for a weapon of some kind, aside from the gun he was wearing on his hip, then directed him to the rear of the tent. He tipped his hat to her again and moved on.

The inside of the tent itself was something. A bright, serious place, with agents clicking things into computer keyboards and a general droning noise caused by all the various voices speaking into telephones and radios and to each other all at once. The main attraction stood wide in the center of the tent, a glass or clear plastic half-wall visible from both sides and somehow glowingly lit from within. An agent in black-rimmed glasses was sketching onto it with a kind of crayon pen, adding to the elaborate color-coded diagram overview of the mountaintop and Ables's entire compound, complete with distances and heights and more. It sure did beat drawing maps in the dirt with a stick. Blood felt as though he were in the control room of a submarine heading into war.

There were voices inside the canvas office in back, one of them excited. Blood stopped and debated going in, but there was only the draped flap of canvas and no solid place to knock, so he pushed aside the canvas drape and entered.

The voice that was getting worked up belonged to Perkins, the most animated Blood had yet seen him. He was saying, "I'm up there with twenty newspaper people and no cover and he comes out of nowhere tearing after a Jeep full of neo-Nazis? You know what that was? That was an embarrassment. Fagin is reckless and I don't like it."

Banish was sitting behind a desk inside, Perkins standing with his back mostly toward Blood. Neither acknowledged the intrusion, so Blood stepped fully inside. There was a crooked-arm fluorescent lamp poised like a vulture over the paper stacks on Banish's desk, and a telephone next to a walkie-talkie standing in a battery charger, and electrical wires trailing back under the separating canvas wall. A windbreaker jacket and a pair of boots and a pitcher of water were set on a small wooden stand in the shadowed corner behind.

Banish said, "He did what had to be done."

Perkins was standing between two metal folding chairs set in the cramped area before the desk. "I want to know how they got up there in the first place," he continued. "The press almost got a show up there they never would have forgotten. I'm standing there feeding these scribblers your answers, and all of a sudden there's a stopped

Jeep and marshals everywhere. And an AP photographer clicking away. And me ending up looking like an ass because I don't have a clue as to what the hell is going on. Five kids with swastikas on their faces, semiautomatic rifles, and I'm left holding the ball. That was humiliation." Perkins jabbed at the air before him with his finger.

Banish didn't seem concerned. In fact, he seemed almost bored. "The crazier they appear, the more patient we come off as being," he said. "Anything else?"

Perkins stood there before Banish, clearly fired up now, hands going from fists to open palms and back to fists again at his sides, over and over. It was somehow a personal thing with him. "Do you understand the vantage point they would have had?" he said. "Like fish in a bucket. We're vulnerable up here. Can you see that at all? Do you realize how close we came?"

"Fagin has secured the surrounding mountains," Banish said, still more interested in the work on his desk. "It was an unfortunate incident, but we will benefit from it in the long run, and learn from it."

Perkins nodded, not at all satisfied. "That's it, then," he said. When he received no answer, he went stiffly out past Blood without even a look.

Banish closed his eyes. There were bright pink sores on either side of the bridge of his nose, from a pair of half-glasses overturned on the stacks of reports on the table before him. He appeared to be having a rough time of it. His cheeks, neck, and chin were roughened with a thick peppery stubble, and the harsh light from the lamp looming over his desk washed his skin pale.

He rubbed the sore marks on his nose, then reopened his eyes and put his glasses back on. He picked up a sheaf of papers and continued reading. Blood came ahead to the desk. "Are those my newspapers?" Banish said without looking up.

Blood set them down. "And a fresh batch of these pamphlets."

"Anything else?"

Blood said, "I was out behind enemy lines earlier. I counted cars.

Ninety-eight of them now, from eight different states, and one license plate from Heaven."

Banish nodded dismissively. "We have someone out taking down plate numbers," he said. "Anything else?"

"Well," Blood said, "now that you ask." He pulled a piece of paper from his coat pocket. "Here's a thing that seems to be getting a lot of play down there. Raising a good stink, as far as stinks go." He presented him with a copy of a letter. "I'm sure you can verify the handwriting. It's from Glenn Ables to the pastor over there at the WAR church, dated two years ago this past July. That would place it right before his original arrest. You can read it for yourself. He says an Alcohol, Tobacco, and Firearms agent visited his cabin and tried to strong-arm him into becoming an informer."

Banish barely scanned the revelatory letter and set it aside with the rest, returning to his reading. "Anything else?"

Blood looked at him, looked at the letter. "You don't think that's something," he said.

Banish said, "This is a tactical operation, not an investigation."

Blood's eyes opened a little wider. "Well, even so," he said, "that seems to me like a pretty big fish flopping around right there."

Banish said, "I don't care who did what to whom. I'm here to get a man out of his cabin."

Blood was about to toss off a shrug, then Banish looked up and surprised him with a question. "Is WAR a big concern around here?"

Blood's narrowed a little. "Concern?" he said. "I wouldn't say that exactly."

Banish said, "What would you say to five armed young men with swastikas painted on their faces, not at all intimidated by law enforcement?"

Blood pshawed him. "Jackassery," he said. "Pure childishness. Secret handshakes and such. And carting guns in your truck—around here that's like packing fishing rods. People up here believe generally in four things: family, property, Jesus, and guns. And not necessarily in that order. It doesn't mean you aim to use them on people."

"So it's nothing, then."

Blood improved his posture. "I'm a sworn officer of the law," he said. "I turn a blind eye on nothing worth seeing. But ninety-five percent of it is all jaw. It's talk. Nothing you can arrest anybody for."

"Not unless they violate the letter of the law."

That felt loaded. Blood accepted it gingerly. "That's right," he said. "Like living near a nuclear plant, I suppose. It's right there, so it's always somewhere in your mind, but unless and until it goes off, there isn't anything much you can do."

Banish showed him some distaste then, nodding. "As for that note," he said, "we've seen it before. We also know that Ables disassociated himself from the White Aryan Resistance. He rejected them as too moderate. Anything else?"

Blood stood there. "Guess not," he said.

Banish set aside the sheaf of papers then, and Blood saw photographs underneath, grade school portraits of the Ables children. Banish picked them up and was looking at them intently, which Blood took to mean that it was time for him to leave. He lingered another few moments in case it was another of the agent's games, but Banish was truly absorbed in the photographs and seemingly oblivious to Blood's presence.

On his way back out through the main tent, as he neared the telephone switchboard, Blood saw the agent there acknowledging something through his headset and throwing a series of switches. The woman agent from the entrance noticed this too and discreetly got up from behind her desk and crossed to the switchboard, her badge flap hanging off her skirt belt. "What did he want?" she quietly asked the switchboard agent.

"An outside line. He told me to turn off the recorder."

Whatever was going on, Blood was already at the exit and could stall no longer. He stopped a good distance away outside to think.

There was a wide anthill on the ground by his foot, a herculean effort fashioned of sand of a lighter color than the dirt base it was founded upon. Blood leveled it with a soft swipe of his boot toe. He watched the ants dig out and race around in circles, then he started back down the mountain.

Cincinnati, Ohio

Frank Dewey looked at the telephone on the third ring. The other four lines were already lit up. He had wanted to get away in time for his son's afternoon football practice, but his partner was off on an extended trip to Vegas, mixing business with a little pleasure, and the office was swamped. Dewey had seventeen employees under him, and two part-timers, which was a lot for a Cincinnati professional investigation firm. But business was absolutely booming.

Dewey and Stone Associates specialized in peace-of-mind investigations. In the age of AIDS and personals ads, people were running scared. Courtship was fast becoming a thing of the past. People wanted facts and they wanted them now, and a comprehensive background check in many cases revealed more than years of a relationship ever would. In a matter of days or even hours, Dewey and Stone could distill a person's social, financial, and health status into a concise two-to-three-page report. Five hundred dollars for a simple background check, or seventy-five dollars per hour per operative for a comprehensive investigation, was a small premium to pay for insurance against a relationship ending in disillusionment or even tragedy.

Example. A young woman, the daughter of a friend and business associate, had come into the office two days before requesting a background check on her new boyfriend. There were now two pieces of paper on Dewey's desk. One was a copy of the boyfriend's San Francisco rap sheet, showing two separate arrests for heroin possession in 1989, a year and a half before moving to Cincy. The other was a copy of a recent outpatient receipt from a local clinic that had forwarded blood samples under the boyfriend's Social Security number and a dummy name to a serology clearing house in Philadelphia. The results of the tests were to be mailed back directly to the dummy patient's home address, which was listed as a mail drop two blocks away from the boyfriend's apartment.

The young woman was due in Saturday morning at nine. It satisfied Dewey's personal law of averages: Ninety-five percent of the time, if they're suspicious enough to hire a private investigator, they're probably right.

He checked his watch under his starched blue sleeve cuff, then heard the phone ring again and pressed the button and grabbed up the line. "Dewey and Stone Associates," he said.

"Mr. Dewey."

Dewey recognized the voice immediately. He sat back from his glass-topped desk and folded one leg neatly over the other, adjusting his sleeve cuff back over his gold watchband. This client interested him. Dewey couldn't say why, but he felt a sort of kinship with the guy, one of the few cases he still personally oversaw.

"Mr. Banish," he said. "You're two days late. I thought maybe something happened."

"Something came up."

This guy never missed his twice-monthly call. He never missed a payment. The money was transferred to Dewey and Stone from a local bank account in Cincinnati, but correspondence was mailed out from the firm to a General Delivery address somewhere in the middle of the state of Montana.

"Look, Mr. Banish," said Dewey, sitting forward again, opening a side drawer and fingering through files. "We got to take you off billable hours here. You're a regular client, it's not hard work. I think we could settle on a monthly fee."

"Whatever," Banish said. "Go ahead."

He was impatient and that was unusual. This Banish was a strange guy. Something told Dewey he was ex-cop.

"She's broken it off with her beau," Dewey said, flipping open the file. "We don't know exactly what happened, or why, or how, but they're through. She was back at the piano bar again three nights ago. She requested two songs to be played and stayed about an hour, drank two Manhattans. She left alone."

Banish said, "Good." He said it without much emotion, but it seemed a reasonable enough response regarding one's former wife.

"The downside is, she's smoking again. And not the filters. There may have been more riding on this relationship than we originally thought. Also, she's seriously considering giving up the condo for something smaller."

"Smaller?" said Banish. "What about Nicole?"

Dewey laid it out straight. "Well, that's the thing right there, Mr. Banish," he said. "The big news is that it looks like your daughter is getting married." He opened the file on his desk. "The same guy, the one who works at the radio station. A half-carat." He picked up a copy of the credit card bill. "Just under three grand on his Visa, mail-ordered from Tiffany's in Chicago on the twenty-fifth of July. He signed for delivery on the twenty-eighth."

Dewey sat waiting for a response. Even he couldn't help feeling for the guy. Here was Dewey, a total stranger to these people, and he'd seen the couple together countless times, in fact from their very first date up till now, whereas by all indications Banish hadn't seen his own daughter in more than two years.

So it seemed important to say something here. "He proposed in a restaurant," Dewey said. "One knee, all that. People at the other tables clapped." Nothing came back right away. "Look, Mr. Banish," he said. "I don't ask, because it's not my place, and because my clients are always right. Always. And that hasn't changed. But maybe you could go see them now. Maybe you could at least try giving them a call."

Banish said, "That is not possible."

Again Dewey waited for Banish. And Frank Dewey was not a man normally made uncomfortable. But, whether ex-cop to ex-cop, or father to father, he felt as though he knew this guy. Something here got to him. He thought of his own twelve-year-old son, and football practice, and what Dewey himself stood someday to lose. He sat forward in his chair, checking his watch again. He would get away right after this call.

"You want the usual package?" he said. "Pictures, phone tapes, transcripts?"

After a good long while Banish's voice said, "Just the pictures."

Command Tent

[PARASIEGE, p. 35]
Therefore, it must be assumed that SA Banish willfully and knowingly disobeyed the Press Service Office's command.

Again, SA Banish's judgment and competence were called into question. The near success of a terrorist assault on the federal staging area went all but ignored, while over-worked agents accused of minor logistic transgressions were promptly and publicly disciplined.

Following the extremist incident on the adjoining moun-tain, SA Banish received a local county sheriff in private conference, then placed a long-distance telephone call which, per SA Banish's order, went unmonitored. This accounts for the three-minute tape lapse as reported by investigators. Di-rectly following that conversation, SA Banish departed the command tent without informing SA Coyle of his destina-tion. It is presumed that he withdrew to his private trailer. He did not return to the command tent for a matter of hours.

Staging Area

At dinnertime Sheriff Blood was eating his tin plate serving of meatloaf and rice at a picnic table set apart from the long bench rows of off-duty marshals and agents hungrily chowing down. He was closer to the marshals' row, and the men's displeasure there was apparent. They looked ragged, first of all, as four days of mountain living will do to men accustomed to the city. Even their short-clipped haircuts looked bushy. There are itches you get from mountains that bugs are only a part of, to the point where even Blood himself was feeling a little dusty. He had been living out of the overnight pack he regularly kept with his fishing gear in the back of his Bronco.

So there was that, the griminess settling into pores used to regular and thorough washing, which is why mountain men always rub their arms as though to stay warm. Then there was the aggravation of it all: a prolonged staring match with a man who wouldn't blink, who wouldn't even open his eyes, a criminal who was so close they could just about spit on him without taking a running start. The feeling that they were being shown up, that this man, this criminal, was enjoying some dark chuckling in his cabin at their expense. It was obvious to any eye that these were proud men who did not take affronts kindly. These were men not normally thumbed at. In this you could see the reason that the object of their animosity was starting, like five-day-old cream, to turn.

The top ranks were growing antsy too. Blood was near enough to the black van earlier in the day to hear Banish and Fagin and the sound man entertaining potential strategies. The sound man suggested "insinuating" a listening device into the cabin by way of the chimney, but Banish dismissed it, citing Ables's background in electronics. Then Fagin pushed hard for some sort of gas attack, which Banish rejected as well, saying that the Ables family might have gas masks themselves and, if so, the agents and marshals going in would be facing a slaughter. Banish shot down each proposal similarly, with stubborn reason, and there was nothing Fagin or the sound man could do to change his mind.

Now it was that guard-changing time of day, the period just before dusk when the moon rises high and fat across from the setting sun and things don't seem quite as they should. There was a nip in the air, but it was humid enough still and the bugs came fierce. Brian Kearney appeared with a tin plate and plunked it down across from Blood, his back to the marshals' bench, the rookie unusually quiet and even serious, not saying hello, not given to his normal idle chatter. He ate purposefully and glumly, as though he had deep troubles. He likely was stewing about the way the Mellis family was being treated down below. Blood drew him out only once, about bees, after shooing a yellow jacket off his food.

"I saw a man stung to death once," Kearney said. "In basic training. He was on groundskeeping duty, up on a cherry picker pruning trees, and I guess he must have hit on a hive, because by the time he got down he was completely covered in them. It was a swarm. He was thrashing around and running, I think even trying to scream, and there was that mad droning noise you'd expect. None of us knew what to do. We went and kind of pushed him with poles into a pond right by there, thinking the water would help, but it didn't. I thought a lot about that afterward. What it must have been like to be covered with those bees—they were frenzied—all yellow and black and furry, driving their stingers into him one after the other, and then him going like that into the water. I wonder if he even knew what was happening to him. If he knew why we were all pushing and kicking at him and being so rough."

Blood said, "That's some ugly death."

Kearney was looking down at the table. "Stung more than a thousand times. I never killed a bee since. I know they don't hold grudges, but at the time it seemed like payback, it truly did."

"You mean to say, nature took a hand."

Kearney barely nodded. "And he was a good kid too, he didn't deserve it. A skinny kid. No one deserved that."

Blood was surprised by the hue of Kearney's thoughts. Then they were both distracted by a thick round of laughter from the marshals' bench. A minor uproar, but it was dark laughter, the kind that comes at someone else's expense. The kind that sets you off listening for more. Part of it is the curiosity, the way a barking dog makes you turn on the lights at night. And part of it is the little kid inside that wants to know whether or not they're laughing at you. Blood consciously ignored their comments and monitored them at the same time.

"The man is incompetent," he heard one of them say behind Kearney.

"He's a screwup, I think. He don't know what the hell he's doing."

"He's just stalling for time is all."

"I heard his last negotiation went bad."

Blood watched Kearney stiffen across the table. The rookie's shoulders broadened and thin mists of breath curled out of his mouth. Blood looked him in the eye and there was an acknowledgment without gesture, and then they were both looking at each other and plainly listening.

Another marshal said, "What do you mean?"

"I mean deaths. Hostage deaths. Him blowing the whole thing."

"You gotta be shitting."

Then something Blood couldn't quite hear. Then:

"I hear he drinks."

"Get the fuck out."

"No, wait," said a new voice, indignant. "I seen him taking brew away from some state troopers today."

Kearney's eyes started to glow.

"Probably got into his private cabinet."

"Son of a bitch."

"The selfish bastard."

Kearney put down his fork. He placed his hands flat on the tabletop and made as though he was going to stand. Blood rose just slightly ahead of him, grasping his wrist.

"Let it go," Blood told him. "Not your fight."

It was just a few marshals talking. All were listening, but most of them probably only because they had to, because it was their necks on the line, not because they enjoyed gossip or wanted to hear. There was one talker who seemed to be the ringleader and Blood picked him out from among the others, set back from the bench, holding court. Blood looked around and saw Perkins too, hanging off to one side but well within listening range, not busying himself, not even moving, not doing a damn thing.

Kearney was glowering. To him it was something more than blatant disrespect, beyond outright offense.

"I heard they couldn't can him, so they stuck him out in some dry prairie town where he wouldn't hurt no one. They buried the fucking guy."

"Then what the hell's he doing mixed up in this?"

"Good question. A good fucking question."

Another new voice, doubting. "How do you say you know all this?"

But over him, someone else snapping his fingers in emphasis, rising to the emotion. "This guy could go at any minute—"

"That's not half of it. He did time in a fucking hospital. That's right—but not just any hospital either."

Kearney's eyes were burning right through Blood.

Reactions now. Another voice. "The fuck you talking about?"

"I'm telling you, this guy's three bricks short, he's crazy—"

Kearney shot upright. Before Blood could stop him, he had turned and stepped over the seat bench and was now facing the wide double row of U.S. Marshals. Blood rose behind him.

"Who said that?" Kearney said. His fists were at his sides.

The marshals all stopped and looked over at him. Nobody said anything, but Kearney must have picked out the ringleader right off, probably by the slant of the man's grin.

"Get up," Kearney said.

The marshal just kept grinning at first and looking around at all the others. None of them grinned back. Most were still looking over at Kearney. The marshal sat a bit straighter then, his grin leveling out as he met Kearney's stare, but still he said nothing.

"Get up," Kearney said, voice louder now, nearly menacing.

Blood could tell that Kearney was shaking, but not from fear. He had never seen him like this. This happy-go-lucky kid. Built like a baseball player, and tall, summoning shoulders to fill out his police uniform, and the marshal was seeing this now too.

Blood looked again over at Perkins. He was pretending to be unaware of what was happening. Fagin had entered the bench area from the side, looking on with interest.

The ringleader shrugged up at Kearney. "What's your problem?" he said.

Kearney said, "Get up."

The marshal stood then. He had no other choice. He was grinning at being called out, making as much a joke of it as he could. "What?" he continued, half-mocking. Only the marshals' table now separated them. "What's it to you?"

The men sitting near him pulled gradually away, to get a better view and also to distance themselves. They were going to let this happen. The marshal sensed this and looked around.

"What do you think this here is?" he said to Kearney.

Kearney said, "I'm calling you a liar."

"Brian," Blood said behind him.

"I mean, what the hell do you care," the marshal continued, "what FBI agent drinks and which one don't? What the hell are you? Some hick-town traffic cop."

Kearney's breath was swirling around his head. His voice was somebody else's now. "Take back what you said, or I'll take it back from you."

The marshal tried to rally his mates. "What the hell is this Okie talking about?"

Kearney was remarkably fast crashing over the table to get to the marshal. The others all leapt to their feet but not one interfered. Kearney grabbed the man by the front of his uniform and in one rough move propelled him back against the next parallel table, where the FBI agents quickly cleared out of the way. Blood hurried up and over his own table after them.

Kearney had stopped there, leaning over the marshal bent backward and flat across the tabletop.

"You take it back," he said, breathing hard.

Blood saw the marshal reaching behind him for a glass bottle of ketchup. Blood started toward them fast, but before he could get there Fagin was standing between the two men.

Fagin backed Kearney off with one flat hand and allowed his marshal to get to his feet. The bottle remained on the table. "I like a good fucking brawl as much as the next guy," Fagin announced. "But not here, and not now."

The marshal said, "Sir, you—"

Fagin cut him off. "Dinner's over. Everybody break it up, and I want my overnights up and reporting for duty ASAP."

Kearney started away then, fast. Fagin turned and watched him go. Then he noticed Blood looking across at him. "What the fuck was that all about?" Fagin said. But Blood looked into the man's eyes and saw that he knew.

Command Tent

Brian Kearney walked for a while, and finally when he knew where he was, the high lamps were on and cutting into the twilight falling over the clearing, and he was standing in front of the command tent. He didn't think he'd planned on going there, but now that he was there he realized he probably had. He wanted to warn

Agent Banish somehow. He wanted to warn him that lies were being spread. But as soon as Brian reached the tent, he realized that he had nothing to say. And then he felt even worse. He looked around at the lit clearing and had to ask himself what it was all for. He felt about two inches tall and half as powerful. Right about then, Agent Banish stepped out of the tent in front of him.

Agent Banish was wearing a blue FBI jacket and had a radio in his hand. He looked at Brian strangely, as though he didn't know where he had come from, or maybe Brian had interrupted a train of thought. "What is it?" Agent Banish said.

Brian couldn't even shake his head. He stood there kind of searching Agent Banish's face, studying it for imperfections. It was deep-creased and shadowed, and bruised-looking under the eyes, and his lips were chapped. His shirt collar was sagged and rumpled, and he looked pale, even old. But his chin and cheeks were shaved, and the eyes themselves seemed clear. He was about to say something else, because Brian was paralyzed and simply could not speak, but then like a cat hearing something in the walls, Agent Banish became distracted. He started to glance around the clearing.

Brian looked too. He picked up on the nearby agents touching their ears and moving around, reacting. People starting to scatter throughout the gloomy clearing. Voices being raised.

Agent Banish turned on his radio. "Fagin," he said into it.

After a moment the radio crackled with Marshal Fagin's voice. "We have movement."

Agent Banish's mouth tightened. "The phone?"

"Negative. Southeast side of the compound. Escapees. Three."

Agent Banish said, "Presume complicity. Get up there and bring them in separately and quietly."

He switched off the radio and started away at a brisk pace across the clearing. Brian stood there just long enough to watch him disappear, striding hard into the shadows falling between two high lights, then hurried over to a Jeep to get back down as fast as he could to his assigned post. Things were finally starting to happen, and he knew now that Agent Banish was in full control.

Sound Truck

Perkins was already at the sound truck when Banish arrived. The sound man was seated in front of the monitor bank. Banish climbed inside. His blood was pumping again.

On the monitor showing the artificially bright eastern angle of the mountaintop, a team of marshals was rough-searching three people lying prone on the ground.

Perkins said, "The Newlands and Charles Mellis."

"Escaped or released?"

The sound man said with a shrug, "They just walked out."

Banish watched the monitor a moment longer. "Keep all three separated," he said to Perkins. "Debrief them before you feed them. Read them their rights, then get everything down on tape. Cover it with your 302 and see me after. I want observations and impressions. Then call the U.S. Attorneys. They'll need statements and so on."

Perkins was nodding, taking it all in. "Wait," he said. "We have only two holding tents."

Banish acknowledged this with a frown. "All right," he said. "Clear the personal effects out of my trailer. Put Mellis in there and assign two marshals to guard it full-time." He raised his radio then. "Fagin. Anything?"

Fagin's voice came back from the mountaintop. "Negative."

Banish nodded. He said, "Keep watching."

Sound Truck

Perkins was waiting for Banish outside the sound truck. His ear wire was out and hanging down to his lapel and he was smoking a cigarette. Banish had not smelled tobacco on him before. A roar started up again before they could speak, a UH-1 National Guard helicopter lifting off into the early evening sky and circling away. Dirt swirled up and the clearing shook. Banish would return to his office to find half the papers shaken off his desk again.

Perkins released a sighed stream of smoke out one side of his mouth. "The Newlands check out," he said. "I took them backward and forward through it, the same exact story. Kept in a back room by the rear porch, given bread and fruit and water rations twice daily, but didn't know what was going on inside. Ables purposefully kept them isolated. They said they could hear music playing and the voice on the loudspeaker, but they didn't know what the reaction was. They heard the infant crying every once in a while, but Mrs. Mellis brought them their food and she never said anything."

"So what happened?"

"They said it came out of nowhere. Ables appeared with Charles Mellis and told all three to get their things and go."

"Why not Mellis's wife?"

"Unknown. The Newlands say they don't know much about Mellis, except that he was very tight with Ables. But since the shoot-out, they've been in back of the cabin and everyone else was in the front."

Banish nodded. "What does Mellis say?"

Perkins took another deep drag, blew it out. "He admitted right away to being involved in the shoot-out. I Miranda'd him but he kept right on talking. Said Ables is losing control up there. Said he's not thinking clearly, he's talking to himself, pacing around the cabin, blah, blah, blah. But then a funny thing happened. Mellis figured out that I wasn't Watson and he clammed up. He says he has something important to say, but only to the man in charge."

Banish was shaking his head.

Perkins said, "All he said was that people will get hurt. That's all he would tell me. Ask me, do I believe him? I don't know. My read is that he's serious, at least about refusing to talk to anyone else. He does seem anxious to spill, though."

Banish said, "Out of the question." The negotiator never met with the hostages.

"We need a break here," said Perkins. "The men, everybody, getting very anxious. Maybe you should at least look at the video-tape."

"How does he seem?" Banish said, avoiding.

Perkins twisted apart his shirt collar. "Truthfully, I think Fagin scared him a little up there. But you get past that and he's overly helpful. Like someone with a lot to get off his chest. Like the guy who walks in off the street and says he wants to show you where the bodies are buried."

Banish was frowning and shaking his head again when in the distance they heard the pop-pop of gunfire. Both men looked quickly up toward the mountaintop, which could not be seen from where they were standing. Then more scattered reports.

Perkins flicked away his cigarette and fumbled the wire back into his ear. Banish worked his radio. "Fagin," Banish said.

Fagin's voice came back loud and full of adrenaline. "Shooting out the lights."

Banish heard a burst of reports through the radio and the sound of glass breaking, then Fagin's voice again over it. "Fucking crap-shoot, from holes in the cabin walls."

Banish nodded, pleased. "Good," he told him. "Put that down as their first communication. Hold your fire and get everybody down low."

A pause. "I didn't get that last part."

"You got it all right. Hold your fire and get your men down low. There are still children in there. Pull back when it stops, then get those lights repaired ASAP."

More gunfire and shattering and ricochets through the radio. "*Motherfuckers,*" spat Fagin, muffled.

Banish switched off. Perkins's eyes were attentive and he was standing up straighter in his sagging clothes. "It's working," he said.

Banish showed him no reaction. "Get to the sound truck," he said. "Have him start ringing the telephone again."

Perkins nodded. "You think Ables is losing it?"

Another distant smattering of reports. Banish looked up at the mountain. "No," he said. "I don't think so."

Staging Area

Brian pulled up the Jeep before the tents and hopped out. He could tell just by the look on Mr. and Mrs. Mellis's faces that the sheer magnitude of the staging area—the tents, the vehicles, the equipment—astounded them. It made him see it with fresh eyes again, and he got a bolt of renewed enthusiasm. The FBI in Huddleston. And him involved in the process, dealing with FBI agents, knowing them and being known by name.

He helped Mrs. Mellis out of the Jeep and walked them both toward the far-right tent nearest the chain fence and the long row of service vehicles. They slowed halfway, looking up and squinting as a spotlight swiped the clearing and a huge helicopter roared overhead.

Mr. Mellis was wiping his flat hands on the legs of his trousers. It had been a long wait for them. Brian explained that their son was still under arrest, but that he had asked to see them and the federal authorities had OK'd it. The couple kept nodding their heads, too grateful to quibble. At this point they would take whatever they could get.

Three men emerged from the tent, two tall marshals with Charles Mellis between them. He was a big spud, with a bushy beard and oversized boots, and shackles on his wrists and ankles. Brian had the parents stay where they were, then pulled off to the side himself. The marshals walked their prisoner about halfway, then stopped and undid both sets of cuffs, which Brian thought was a really fine gesture.

Charles Mellis jogged the last few steps into his mother's arms. He towered over her. Her arms went around his hips but her hands didn't touch behind. She was crying and saying his name over and over again, "Charlie, Charlie," and his father, a good-sized guy himself, was smiling and patting his son on the back, and even, it seemed, wiping his eyes.

His mother pulled back to get a better look up at her son, probably to make sure he was all right, and then he was shaking his father's hand and hugging his mother again, holding her head against one of his suspender buckles. Just standing there witnessing it, Brian felt a warm buzz of satisfaction that he had admittedly done nothing to earn.

He was backing away farther, trying to let the family have even more of a private moment, when he saw two men watching from the shadow of a large truck off to the side. Brian instantly recognized the posture of the taller one with his arms crossed as belonging to Agent Banish, and was surprised that he was there watching, even more surprised than he had been when the order came down to the barricade originally to let Mr. and Mrs. Mellis through. Brian moved toward the two men through the shadows under the high lights. He saw that the second expressionless man was Agent Perkins.

Brian was probably too caught up in the moment, but he felt as though he had to thank Agent Banish for doing the right thing. He said to him, "It's a good thing you did here."

Agent Banish showed no reaction. He did not respond or even let on that he had heard. Instead, he said something to Agent Perkins that did not involve Brian. He said, "I'll see him"—almost with an air of regret. Then he turned and walked away.

Trailer

Banish had the two marshals wait outside, then entered his former trailer behind Perkins. Charles Mellis was seated without restraints behind the small wooden table, drumming his thick fingers on its chipped surface. He was big and eager-looking, like some dogs, and the tangled black-red beard hanging from his sideburns and crowding his mouth sprang like a disguise from his pale, freckled baby-face.

His eyes were black and guarded, probably sizing up Banish in comparison to his imagined Watson. He was a big, sloppy kid. He had wrinkled wet lips and knuckles the size of walnuts.

Banish glanced at the bed he had had no luck with. Mellis's feet would hang over the end like tongues.

Banish moved to stand across from him. "Special Agent Bob Watson," he said.

Mellis showed relief. He placed the voice. He was nodding.

Perkins chimed in. "Mr. Mellis, your rights as I explained them to you still stand."

"He's crazy," Mellis blurted. "He's gone off the deep end. And violent."

Banish said, "We know he's violent. Do you mean violent toward his family?"

"Getting there." Mellis nodded. "Sure getting there. And it's a change in him, in who he is, and that's got me worried."

"But everyone else is in good health. The children."

"So far." He nodded.

"Health conditions OK? Enough food, water?"

"Enough for now. Glenn's a survivor. But he's ranting and raving like you wouldn't know."

Mellis was holding Banish's gaze and blinking slowly. He used his arms on the table to help him over the words, occasionally dropping his bearded chin to accentuate what he was saying. He appeared earnest and overly sincere, the way lonely people become when addressed on the witness stand.

Banish said, "I'm going to ask you some direct questions now, Mr. Mellis. Approximately how many guns does Mr. Ables have in the residence?"

Mellis inflated as though he couldn't get the words out, then swept the table with an elaborate arm gesture. "How many do you need?" he said finally, blowing out a breath.

Banish nodded, encouraging him. "Why won't Mr. Ables use the telephone we provided?"

"He don't trust you-all. He says there's a sharpshooter out there waiting to put one in his back. Says if I went out for it, I'd get one in the back. And he says there's poison or gas or something on the mouth part."

"Is he monitoring our transmissions?"

Mellis expelled another breath of relief, as though grateful that the question had been asked. It was easier to betray someone with a nod. "He's got a whole setup in there, he knows all the government frequencies."

Banish's eyes stayed on Mellis's face, trained not to react. "What about your wife, Mr. Mellis?"

"Shelley couldn't leave the kids. Margie's not so good now, her cancer's back, and I knew Shelley wouldn't leave. Margie's stubborn too. Says she's through with hospitals."

"Why are you telling us all this, Mr. Mellis? What do you expect to gain from it?"

Mellis straightened in concern. "Nothing for myself. I didn't shoot nobody up there. Not without being shot at first."

"What happened to make him let you go, then?"

Mellis shook his head. "It finally got so that I just asked him to —can you see what I mean?—and he did. Glenn said he was letting the Newlands go because he couldn't use them for nothing, and I saw that things were getting bad with him, so I asked him if I could just go too. Not that I'm a traitor. I ain't, I am not." He shook his head strenuously back and forth. "And I ain't broke with Glenn either. I ain't stabbing him in the back. But he's got his kids up there under the gun with him now too, and I don't think he's reasoning things so well." He was looking back and forth from Banish to Perkins. "So I thought maybe I could argue his case for him down here. I never told him that, of course. He wouldn't stand for it and he'd probably just as soon shoot me. But when I seen those kids' little faces. They're all my family and I want to do right by them. Because I seen what's coming and it ain't pretty, nor is it safe. Because Glenn don't bend. I see that now, he don't bend for nothing, it's glory or death with him, but still he don't really want to hurt nobody. Truly, he don't. I knowed the man for years. But you're backing him up against a brick wall. You're pushing his fatherhood and his manhood right up in his face and forcing him to do something he don't want to do. Nobody can draw a line in the dirt with Glenn Ables. Not without him stepping over it and going right for your throat. That's why I'm here now and I'm asking you—for them kids up there, and Margie, and my wife, a couple of human lives that maybe don't add up much to you, but to me, they do, a lot. Couldn't you just drop the charges? All he wants is to be left alone up there. All he wants is his land back and his family. If you could just drop the charges before it's too late, and all just go away—"

His eyes were getting damp. He looked as though he wanted to stand, but he didn't, being careful or perhaps just polite. Glistenings of spit speckled the stray whiskers around his mouth.

Banish said, "Is that what you brought me in here to tell me?"

Mellis nodded once. "Yes."

Banish turned to leave. Perkins turned with him and they got as far as the door before Mellis said, "Wait." He said it without rising from his chair, without any urgency. He said it almost sadly. "All right," he said.

They turned. Mellis looked long at Perkins, then looked away. Banish turned to Perkins. He nodded to him. Perkins frowned and stared down at the trailer floor a moment, smiling bitterly, then stepped outside the trailer.

Banish moved closer to Mellis. "That nigger up there on the mountain," Mellis said in confidence, "that big dark one. He got me in the gut with the butt of his rifle when I come out. Had my hands up over my head peaceful and obedient and everything."

Banish said, "So?"

"Just keep him the hell away from me. I mean that."

"You're making threats now, Mr. Mellis?"

"No, sir. I am just telling you straight. I thought maybe you might care. But that ain't what I have to say. You need to understand why I'm saying what I'm saying, though. It's on account of things already going too far and me seeing the toll it's taking on one man." He was looking up at Banish from where he sat. "I'm trying to prevent things here, so that it'll help. But I want you to take that into your decision-making, so that things'll go easier for Glenn when this is all over and done with."

Banish said, "Just tell me what you have to tell me."

"But I'm a man of my word and I want to take you at yours, and have this said in good faith. I don't care for myself. I'm asking you— couldn't you just think of this as coming from Glenn's mouth instead of my own, and take that into your considerations later?"

Banish said patiently, "You'll have to tell me what it is first, Mr. Mellis."

"A claymore mine. A bomb. He's booby-trapped the mountain."

Banish felt the color wash from his face. Training or no training, his head started to buzz.

"Where?" he said as evenly as he could.

"Near the cabin. It's just one."

"Where?"

"Now I'm only saying this in good faith—"

Banish said forcefully, "Where?"

Mellis nodded over his own shoulder. "Up near the cabin. There's no saying exactly, but I could take you up there—"

Banish reached across and grabbed the big kid's flannel collar. "Say exactly," he said.

Mellis looked scared. "It don't have no marker. It's all woods up there. Near a stump and a fallen tree. It's hidden."

"Command-detonated?"

"No—simple trip wire."

"Between the cabin and the lights?"

"Sure." Mellis nodded, blinking.

Banish released him and stood back a few steps. A claymore mine. Banish thought of all the men up there.

Staging Area

Fagin was standing under a high arc light and watching his marshals suiting up Banish in a BDU, a battle dress uniform, black fatigues and a flak jacket and bullet-proof helmet. They were issuing him a 9mm sidearm and having him sign for it.

Fagin said, "This is fucking bullshit."

He looked at the agents and other marshals standing around them, including ever-present Perkins, and then off to the side, being zipped into a similar black BDU suit, Charles fucking Mellis.

Fagin said, "This is fucking goofy, you following him into the woods like this."

"The mountain is secure," Banish said, tugging on his gloves. "He is unarmed. I will be watching him, and your men will be watching us from the trees."

"Fuck it," Fagin said. "I'm going too."

Banish shook his head. "He doesn't like you."

"Doesn't like me? He doesn't *like* me? You think I'm up here to fucking *meet* people?"

"You're staying behind. And I want all your men pulled back another twenty yards."

"Fuck that. Fuck it. I'm in charge of security and I won't allow it."

Banish accepted his weapon and ejected the clip, thumbing out rounds, counting them. "It's real simple," he said. "I am responsible for every man on this mountain. Mellis is the only one who knows where the mine is, and he has agreed to lead me and only me to it. We will climb up the mountain, slip into the no-man's-land, isolate the trip mechanism, and then back off so you and your men can disable it."

Fagin said, "He's bullshitting. He's stalling or something. He's full of shit up to his fucking beard."

Banish said, "If so, then he has nothing to gain except wasting my time. If not, then there's a tree trunk up there with a projectile mine strapped to it. It's on a trip wire a raccoon could trigger and it's facing downhill. That's a widow-maker, Fagin. These woods are full of agents and marshals. Some may be your men, but all of them are mine. The circumstance here is that, for better or for worse, he trusts me. Things might be different if you had thought a moment before suckering him up there."

"Fuck him. Fucking piece of trash."

They handed Banish a flashlight and then the strobe. "What's this?"

"Infrared strobe," Fagin said. "So night-vision can pick you up in the trees if we need to, fast. No fucking lights up there still."

Banish said, "Good. Better cover. And stay off the radio. He's listening in."

"Fuck it," Fagin said, more determined than ever. "I'm going."

Banish didn't answer, reloading the 15-clip and popping it back in and tucking the piece into his holster.

Fagin grabbed him by the shoulder and said, "You listen to me.

I've got a fucking job to do here. The marshals are in charge of security, and I am in charge of the marshals, and that's that. So don't talk to me about widow-makers. I've lost one man already, and I don't care who you are, I'm not losing one more. You are not going up there solo and I'm the best fucking man to go with you."

A voice came up behind Fagin. "I'll go."

Fagin turned to see who it was. He saw the Indian sheriff coming toward them carrying a big Browning 12-gauge.

Banish said immediately, "No way."

Fagin eyed the shotgun and reached for it. The Indian presented it, and Fagin hefted the thing and turned it over in his hands. The semiautomatic Browning shotgun was a sporting piece, but the Indian had stripped down the walnut stock and dulled all the steel parts. He had custom-policed the thing.

"Expensive piece," Fagin said, sighting down the barrel, feeling its weight. "Nice weapon. You come prepared, anyway."

The Indian said, "I know this mountain. I hunted all over it as a boy."

"Negative," Banish said, done suiting up. "This is no photo op. No politicians on the mountain, and no heroes."

The Indian said, "Politicians?"

"That's right. You're not riding to reelection on a short hike up a hill."

This was something here. Fagin rode Banish like a bastard day and night and the mope reacted as though he were asking him for the time. Then the Indian comes up and says word one and Banish runs down his throat.

The Indian was confused. "Two officers in my jurisdiction were shot at—"

"Jurisdiction." Banish was shaking his head. "Now you sound like the police chief. Now all of a sudden you're worried about jurisdiction."

"That's right." The Indian nodded, relaxed but firm. "Because I figure now maybe I can earn my keep up here." He looked around.

"You've all been feeding me these past few days, and it hasn't been particularly good food, but it's kept me from going hungry. And I've been using the facilities here, running up quite a tab. But I am the sheriff of this county and am nobody's lapdog. Now you are climbing up my tree. Now you need me."

Banish said, "Somebody take this man's gun away from him and get him a cold drink."

Fagin had had enough. "Will you two shut up, you fucks. A claymore mine. Eight hundred steel ball bearings blasted into a hundred-fifty-yard kill zone, shredding you to fucking ribbons before you can even think to shit yourself. If one of you bickering girls doesn't know where the fuck he's going, then you're both gonna get there, and awful fucking fast."

Fagin thumbed the marshals over to equip the Indian before Banish could say anything else. Fagin was going to win this one. He was right as rain this time and Banish fucking knew it.

He spoke to one of the other deputy marshals, then issued coded orders over the radio to his men, and by the time he was done the Indian was suited and ready. The three of them walked off toward the trees, all camouflage and dark paint, Banish with the flashlight in his hands and Mellis in between, taller and wider than both. They walked into the dark tree line at the base of the mountain and were gone. It was at least a good fifteen-minute hike up to the zone.

Fagin shook his head. Fucking Banish. Doesn't want to be involved with Tactical, then doesn't want anyone else but himself involved. Crazy fuck.

He saw Perkins drifting over toward him. Perkins was like that, shifty, blowing around and feeling his way into things and then melding with them. A penny boy. A chameleon in a suit and tie, and Fagin could use that. He knew he had a sounding board here.

"Crazy fuck," Fagin said aloud when Perkins was near enough.

Perkins looked at him as though he wasn't sure what Fagin was talking about. "Sorry?"

"Fucking unpredictable," Fagin said. "I don't like that."

Perkins nodded. "Well," he said, a sentence. "Maybe it'll all work out his way in the end."

Fagin looked at him more closely. Perkins was smiling faintly.

"You serve in 'Nam?" Fagin said.

Perkins shook his head.

Fagin nodded back behind them. "When those Hueys take off sometimes, dipping away over the trees, I do get flashes." It was a fertile part of his memory when triggered. "Banish served," he added. "Psyops specialist. Psychological Operations. Propaganda and persuasion."

Perkins nodded slow. "Like Tokyo Rose," he said.

Fucking citizen. "A little more sophisticated than that," Fagin said. "Deception. Head games. The fingernails on the blackboard."

Perkins looked at Fagin. "You have good sources," he said, dropping his hand lightly into his pants pockets and rocking twice on his heels. "From what I understand, Banish was a real asshole before the crack-up too."

Hearing a Mormon trying to swear was like listening to a drunk trying to sing. "At least then," Fagin said, "he was a respected asshole."

They both nearly nodded then, Fagin looking across at the dark trees and Perkins doing the same. Fagin could feel the conversation ending then and them going their separate ways. He was glad.

"You know what?" he said.

Perkins shook his head. "What?"

Fagin spat at a tuft of straw weeds, and missed. "I'm just waiting for him to fuck up."

No-Man's-Land

Banish switched off the flashlight. They were coming up through the trees. Mellis was a few yards ahead of Banish, Blood somewhere behind. The big kid climbed quickly but Banish kept him close and in full view. The wider spacing of the trunks meant that they were near the top. They were into the zone. The spotter marshals sat somewhere high in the trees behind them. Music blared into the no-man's-land from the left.

Mellis covered the uneven, rising ground in broad, lumbering strides, often talking to Banish over his shoulder. "It'll go easier for him now, right? This'll make things easier."

Banish said, "When did you help him set it up?"

"Some months ago. Glenn always knew what was coming. He knew he was being watched. He always said Judgment would come at his front doorstep. The first shots of the final battle would be fired there, he said."

Banish could smell the dogs. "Where did he get the mine?"

"I think he stole it off an army base. Don't know for sure. Looks like a small suitcase without a handle, and curved."

"I know what it looks like," Banish said. "How much farther?"

"I think we're almost there."

The odor of the dogs was pungent and pervasive and Banish directed his breathing through his mouth. "How close are we to the cabin?"

"Maybe fifty yards," said Mellis.

"Twenty-five," said Blood behind them.

Mellis was looking around more now, picking up speed, anxious. Dull moonlight fell more freely through the thinning tree cover. "Almost there," he said. "It'll go better for Glenn, right? Less injuries, less killing?"

"You are doing the right thing," Banish said.

Mellis moving impatiently. "Right around here somewheres."

"Where's the trip?"

"Not sure," Mellis said. "Be careful."

Banish dropped back a bit, allowing Mellis some room as he followed him down and up again over a steep gully. There was a large fallen tree ahead of them and some ragged stumps on the other side. Mellis moved quickly toward it, Banish more cautious behind, glancing around.

Mellis said, "It's right over here."

Mellis reached the fallen tree and climbed over it, disappearing for a moment, then straightened up fast. He turned to face them and there was something black and glimmering in his shaking hands. Banish barely had time to react. Mellis raised the gun and aimed it at Banish's head across the fallen stump. Banish tried to get his hands up. There was a snap and a brilliant flare of white, and the gun muzzle exploded in his face.

Fallen Tree

Banish went down. As though someone had slipped a rope around his neck and yanked it from behind. The shot rang to near deafness in Blood's ears. He was looking down at Banish. Banish was lying in a heap and not moving. Mellis was heaving bursts of mist and giggling nervously at the sight.

Then he looked up at Blood. Blood brought the shotgun level, groping for the trigger. Too late. He took off diving for cover behind a clutch of trees as Mellis fired on him, choking rounds from the handgun and yelling something crazy.

Staging Area

Fagin looked up fast at the racket. His face went taut. "Fucking double-cross!" he said, and started at a run for the Hueys.

Sniper's Nest

Deputy U.S. Marshal Robert Taber scanned the hazy green woods below with his NVD. Radio silence had been broken and there were now twelve different voices yelling at once in his ear. He had heard the gunfire. He was scoping out the woods for individuals. His right hand found his Remington and brought it to his side and felt for the trigger guard. He was breathing short, sharp breaths.

Motion in the trees up ahead. In murky shades of green, two ghostly figures moving along the ground, both racing away about fifteen yards apart, both headed up toward the top of the mountain. Taber saw traded heat bursts corresponding with reports from two different weapons. He sighted one figure, then the other.

He heard his name on the radio and clicked on fast. "I can't tell who's—" he was yelling, then stray rounds sprayed the leafy branches above his head. He ducked and pitched back blindly against the body of the tree.

Paradise Point

Mellis hauling up the mountain, laughing crazily and firing behind him. Blood reloading, weaving tree to tree, shotgun blasting. Mellis was maybe fifteen yards ahead but getting away, galloping hard through the woods while Blood advanced in fits, using the trees for cover and taking fire.

There was a brief respite. Blood, pulse racing, reasoned that Mellis was reloading and so tried to take the advantage, keeping on the pressure with short, sweeping blasts and racing ahead. As the tree spacing grew more generous, affording more and more steely moonlight, Blood could make out the cabin sitting silently in the distance. Then Mellis crossed into view again, firing downhill and chipping away at branches and plugging trees, and Blood spun around fast behind a fat trunk, taking shelter from the hail.

Fallen Tree

He rolled over onto his stomach. He felt his knees and brought them up under him and groped around. There was a buzzing drone in his head so distant that he reasoned it must have been the neighbor's telephone. For some reason it woke him. He reached for the pillow next to his and felt for his wife's shoulder.

Then Banish remembered the woods. He remembered being shot. He flailed around and found the hard, dead bark of the fallen tree next to him.

Banish explored his face with rough, trembling hands. He found no wound there. His heart went cold.

He flapped around. Dark night. Reports cracking under the steady droning. The sickening smell of the dogs. The woods coming alive. He was vulnerable here.

Banish held his hand up in front of his face. Nothing. The woods were pitch-black. He knelt against the felled tree and tried to stand, but could not tell exactly which way was up and then slipped back down again. He landed hard against the dead tree.

Where was Mellis? The son of a bitch. He would get Mellis. He would hunt the bastard down and kill him.

The flashlight. Banish slipped it off his belt and picked at the switch. Nothing. He shook it and felt the batteries click and tried it again. They were dead.

Cabin

They were in a race for the cabin. Blood could hear Mellis's strangled laughter like war whoops behind the stuttered backward cracking of his gun. Blood answered, but as always the woods got in the way and he did more defoliating than anything.

This was his last push. He knew he had but one more chance to cut Mellis down before they reached the cabin. As Blood moved wide to his right, hastily vying for a side shot, he could see the cabin more clearly. He could see now that the near wall was somehow starting to move. Black rectangles appeared in it like slots sliding open. Blood slowed and eventually stopped. He watched gun barrels come poking out. He turned and dove hard behind a deadfall tree.

The firepower was all-out deafening. The mountain filled with noise and rippling echoes and the branches shook, the cabin fire shredding the surrounding trees to mulch and kindling. Hot rounds picked at the dead trunk he was lying behind and pitched splinters into the air, Blood protecting his face with his arms. He stayed down low. He crept longways to a clear spot blocked by standing trees and cautiously put up his head.

He had one hand over his ear and was squinting. It was noise and flame from every side of the cabin, tremendous. The woods were crumbling and staggering around him. Clear enough, then, that the whole thing had been orchestrated. Ables wasn't satisfied with just principles anymore. He wanted lives.

An awful roaring noise, rumbling the very ground, and Blood braced for whatever was coming next. A spotlight pierced the dark scene and then a helicopter rose fast over the trees beyond the cabin, turning and dipping down close for action. It was answering fire, glowing phosphorescent green and ripping the ground and the cabin walls, and Blood stayed where he was just long enough to see Fagin riding shotgun, leaning out of the helicopter door and braced against the skid and howling and tearing away. Then Blood ducked off and started fast down the ravaged slope.

Fallen Tree

Banish had his gun out now. He was listening hard. Nothing through the drone except gun chatter. Sounded like a firefight. Sounded close. Where was Nicole? He couldn't let anything happen to her.

He was stumbling around. He was seeing things in the dark, traces of things, like ghosts drifting down and settling in the blackness in front of him, and he was giving them meaning. He saw Lucy Ames smiling into the sterile rec room of the Retreat. He felt her bullet burrowing deep into him and dropping him to the tile floor. He saw his house on Long Island ripped to pieces inside. He saw the wide, bright trading floor in the World Financial Center, heard the buzzing of hundreds of telephones, saw the blood on the floor. He saw a mother and daughter standing up against a wall, throats cut, necks sliced open. Their mouths were wide. Their tongues were swollen. Their eyes were staring and wet.

"Banish!"

Someone was yelling and near. Banish got a read on the voice and spun and fired. The gun kicked back wildly in his hand. He reaimed as well as he could and then stopped, turning his head, listening for more.

Fallen Tree

Bark chipped off the tree next to Blood and he froze. Banish wasn't dead. He was somehow on his knees on the floor of the woods waving a gun, motioning wildly and mumbling aloud. His flashlight was lying on the ground behind him, illuminating a bright cone of bark trash. He looked this way and that way, but he did not register Blood.

Blood glanced quickly around. The gunfight was going on unseen away from them, occasional stray bullets whistling past, picking off leaves, thumping trunks. Blood bent down carefully. He found a broken piece of squaw wood and tossed it back over Banish's head and Banish turned at the noise and fired twice. By the second shot Blood was upon him, pitching himself sidelong against Banish and knocking him flat against the ground. He kicked the gun free and managed to wrestle one of Banish's arms behind his back. They were rolling around on the ground. Banish was still struggling.

"Banish!" Blood said. "Banish!"

Banish was fighting for Blood's Browning. He had wild strength. Blood managed to force the butt of the shotgun against the back of Banish's neck and then pin his elbows with his knees. Blood kept saying "Banish" over and over again, trying to get through to him, keeping his head pushed into the bark trash on the ground.

That seemed to work. Banish eventually stopped resisting, then relaxed completely. Blood let up on his neck and allowed him to turn over beneath him. There was a glancing dent on the right front of Banish's helmet and a spray pattern of black powder burn over half his face. He had come closer to death than anyone Blood had ever seen. Banish blinked several times, opening and closing his mouth and trying to speak.

"Blood?" he said.

Blood said, "You're all right."

"I can't see."

"You're alive, you're all right."

"I can't see."

"That's just the flash. Come on."

He helped him to his feet and took Banish's arm over his shoulders. Bullets split through the trees. They started to move.

UH-1

Fagin leaned way out of the Huey as it swept wide over the treetops to make another pass. They had the fuckers on the run now. Massive firepower down there, outlying trees being blown back from the cabin as though caught in a storm. It made Fagin howl all the more. He was pumping tracers into the mountaintop, phosphorous-tipped rounds glowing in loud, green streaks, threading their way through the dark night to the target, chewing up cabin wood. Fagin knew what the fuck it was he was feeling, the great spirit having fully arisen within him once again: the glory and majesty of the early days of Vietnam.

Motherfuckers!

His hold line snapped tight around his waist as the bird swooped in low to make another pass. The searchlight came around and found Mellis, unmistakable fucking bearded fucking Mellis, stomping along the side of the cabin and firing blindly over his head. He was galloping for the elevated porch in back. Fagin rolled right and choked the M-60, lighting up the cabin side, tracer fire eating its way into the ground at Mellis's pounding boots, but then the Huey lurched and his kill fire missed its mark, and Mellis reached the rear of the cabin and disappeared under the overhang of the porch. Fagin swore wildly back at the farm-boy pilot. The UH-1 came around again and swung down low and Fagin, screaming now, gave the fucking porch everything he had.

Barn

Blood told him they were taking cover. A structure downland from the cabin, a barn. A few more steps and Banish smelled a musty odor, and then the shooting was not as loud. His head fought the buzzing drone.

He pulled the strobe off his belt and felt it into Blood's hands and told him what to do with it. Blood traded him his flashlight and Banish heard him walk away and outside. There was a low whir as the strobe was switched on.

Banish saw a shadow. He waved the flashlight in front of him and several times, fleetingly in the far corners of his eyes, he saw hints of light. He perceived texture within the blackness. He saw the beam indirectly and, through it, the stripped-back wooden walls of the barn, debris and discard scattered around the dirt floor. His eyesight was beginning to fill back in. He was despondent.

UH-1

Captain Greg Ohmer of the Montana National Guard topped out over the tree cover and throttled hard left to bring the UH-1 back around. There were some zings as the bird took a few sparking hits broadside, and Greg tightened up his grip on the stick, saying "Sweet Jesus Mother of Mary" over and over again in an unnaturally high voice and fighting to hold the shaking helicopter even and low.

Fifty weeks out of the year, Greg Ohmer was the owner and manager of a Burger King franchise in downtown Billings. He had a wife and a nine-year-old daughter and lived in a small house a few miles west of the city. His biggest worry going into this year's two-week tour in the reserves was leaving his restaurant in the hands of his twenty-year-old assistant manager.

Greg Ohmer had not sat in the cockpit of a helicopter for more than three years—and even then only to renew his pilot's license. Patrol missions were one thing, especially during the day, cruising above the mountain ridge and looking out over the blue-green mountains into the snow peaks of British Columbia; Greg had never stopped loving to fly. But these low-maneuver tactical raids under heavy unfriendly fire were something else entirely. He was WAGing it up there, wild-ass-guess flying, piloting via his PAVE nightfall system and recalling his training as he went, watching the altitudinal wind gusts and trying to keep his rotors and his tail fin clear of the treetops, and basically bringing the cranky UH-1 in as tight as possible without choking up the engine or one-eightying out.

He swung around so that Marshal Fagin stayed on the hot side of the bird, then tensed up his shoulders and dipped down into the gauntlet and white-knuckled it on through, muttering to himself as he went. Fagin got off fifty or so unanswered rounds this time, hanging out of the gun door and howling. Greg came out of the pass and realized that the resistance was finally, thank God, falling off. He pulled back on the throttle too sharply and jerked the bird up and clear of the heat. There, from above the dark canopy of tree cover, he noticed a strobe light pulsing faintly downland.

He radioed back to Marshal Fagin. Fagin's reply filled his head and the gray flight helmet he wore. *"Take her the fuck down!"* he bellowed. This Fagin fellow was a psycho son of a bitch. Greg Ohmer eased back on the throttle and the UH-1 swooped wide and out.

Barn

Blood had his Browning up and was standing watch just inside the open doorway. Now that he was able to catch his breath, a clear sense of doom was settling over the barn and himself. It was a debacle. There would be a good load of finger-pointing after a thing like this, and Blood felt that his own performance had been lacking.

He had a shotgun, Mellis had a handgun. He wished sorely that he had done more and wondered if he'd catch any blame. He turned then and looked behind him.

Banish was standing in the center of the barn. His hands were on his hips and his head was low and he was shaking it and blinking, plainly trying to encourage his eyes to see. Now and again he brought up a hand and felt his head. He had unstrapped the helmet and was feeling where Mellis's bullet had glanced him. He was disoriented from the blow, which explained a good deal.

Blood heard the helicopter approaching. He turned and looked up as it slowed to a hover overhead, whipping back the treetops and shaking the ramshackle barn. He saw a man drop out of the open door and watched him rappel down. It was Fagin, a rifle slung over his shoulder. Land marshals emerged from the woods. A spotlight swung over from the helicopter, filling the entrance with blinding white, and Blood backed away inside.

He saw Banish clumsily exploring the barn, his hands helping him to see. It was dusty from disuse and appeared pretty much abandoned, filled with various pieces of refuse like a rusted-out sit-down mower and busted sawhorses, plucked-up tar shingles with nails still stuck in them, stacks of bug-infested wood off to the left, and a discarded plastic gasoline tank cracked up one side. It looked like the community junkhouse. Banish was over by some old rolls of tarpaulin in back, still trying to see.

Fagin entered with the swirling, kicked-up bark trash from the helicopter wind, his rifle at the ready, the harsh spotlight lighting his back and darkening his front. "The fuck happened!" he bellowed. He saw Blood there and came up close enough for Blood to see his shadowed face beyond the light, see it full and big-eyed and hungry. It was the look some animals get after tasting blood. "I want some fucking answers," he said.

Blood said, "It was a trap."

"You're goddamn fucking right it was a trap." Fagin looked up and across at Banish. "The fuck's wrong with him?"

Blood turned to look. Banish was pulling at the tarp now, trying to unroll it.

Fagin said, "Banish. Banish!"

Banish did not answer.

"Fucking mental," said Fagin, stalking around. "Will someone please give me some goddamn fucking answers here?"

Blood remained looking at Banish, realizing then that he was not merely exploring. There was something wrapped up in the tarpaulin and Banish was trying to get at it. Blood started toward him, then Fagin grabbed his arm, stopping him, and Blood made ready to receive the riot act.

Fagin nodded at Blood's leg. "You're hit," he said.

Blood looked down. His black uniform was split across the side of his left thigh and soaked darkly below. He hadn't felt a thing until it was pointed out to him. After that, it began to burn fierce.

Blood pressed his hand above the cut and some dark red washed out. It was not very deep.

He started back toward Banish, favoring the leg. The barn was full of marshals now, and white light from the helicopter, and stirred-up, swirling dust. Fagin came up behind and they both watched Banish pulling at a tight swathe of white sheets rolled within the tarpaulin. His actions grew impatient and finally savage. He wrenched at the bedsheets with his bare hands until they tore apart and came free.

There was an awful puff of smell. Blood didn't need more than a second to recognize the corpse's face. It was a few days gone, lips wrinkled and black, skin sunken, gray. Contact wound through the T-shirt over the heart, eyes filmy and staring up at the rafters.

Fagin backed away covering his nose, saying sharply, "Jesus fucking *Christ*."

Banish just sat back. The Ables girl was lying there dead and stinking and his face got tight, then he made a little fist as though he was going to yell. Instead, he took the fist and pounded it once into the dirt ground.

Saturday, August 7

The tent was in an uproar. Phones buzzing, men yelling. Fagin on his radio, spitting curses, and Perkins shaking his head into a telephone. Facsimile machines tonguing out sheets of paper, and men spreading maps on desks and scribbling onto the elaborate glass-wall diagram. The stale smell of dry sweat and the rumble of helicopters circling overhead. And Blood sitting quietly in the middle of it all, without pants, his wounded leg resting on one of the EMT's chairs, the gash being washed and sewed.

They tied off the black thread and clipped it short. One EMT remained to bandage him while the other two gathered their emergency aid cases and moved through the crowd to the office where Banish was. Blood noticed Fagin coming off his radio across the tent room.

"Fucker got clean away," Fagin said, looking around as though he wanted to hit something.

Perkins turned from the desk he was sitting on and spoke away from his phone. "Where did he get the gun?"

Fagin was pacing between desks, grinding a black-gloved fist into his opened hand. "All a setup," he said. That aspect of it seemed to rile him most.

Perkins said, "But how could they know in the cabin—"

"A setup," Fagin said, pacing faster, "the whole fucking thing. Swift and surgical. He releases Mellis with the in-laws. Shoots out the lights. Then in the downtime confusion before my men can get their NVDs on, he gators out twenty meters and plants the gun. Mellis false-flags Banish with his bullshit mine story—if there was a claymore mine on this mountain, it would be command-detonated and Ables would have lit it off with the rest of his fireworks—then leads him up to the gun site and fucking drops him cold. All fucking planned."

A noisy crash from within Banish's office then, like something being roughly overturned, and a raised, angry voice—Banish, swearing venomously. The two EMTs came hustling out. Only one still had his first-aid kit with him, holding it together awkwardly as though it were a suitcase come unlatched. Behind them, Banish's continuing voice and the fluttering bird-wing sound of papers being hurled. The EMTs met the stunned glances of everyone turning to look their way, then tried to avoid all eyes and moved quietly off to the side.

Then Banish was standing in the canvas office doorway. He appeared strangely calm and stiff, hands open and empty at his sides and his feet spaced evenly apart. His black jumpsuit was off now and his clothes beneath were rumpled, his hair mussed from the removed helmet. The black spray pattern from Mellis's gunfire speckled the right side of his face like soot.

"Perkins," he said, speaking flatly, "have the girl's body airlifted to Helena for autopsy, then begin contacting local hospitals. Have them call in off-duty help and start preparing disaster plans. There's going to be trouble down below. Then call AD Richardsen at home. Give him a full situation report and tell him we need to double our number here ASAP, including Hostage Rescue, and then inform him that it is my recommendation that I be relieved of duty immediately."

He looked over at Fagin. "Nobody fires on that cabin again

without prior authorization from me as long as I am in charge," Banish said. "I don't care what the situation is. There are hostages in there."

Fagin smiled, not happily.

Banish said, "Coyle."

She was standing at the desk by the entrance of the tent. "Yes, sir," she said.

"Get in here," Banish said, and stepped back behind the fold.

Coyle crossed the tent to follow. Perkins looked quickly over at Fagin, who was still looking in the direction of the office and shaking his head. "That fucking kid," Fagin said, drawing his weapon suddenly and inspecting the clip. "They're all gonna go apeshit when this comes out."

Blood lifted his leg off the chair and stood. He pulled his pants up over his bare legs and boxers, taking his time buckling the heavy black leather gun belt, testing his weight. The leg felt good. He fit his cowboy hat back onto his head and walked with a slight limp over to where his Browning was propped up against a desk near Fagin. He took the weapon up by the barrel, knowing he had Fagin's attention now, and therefore that of Perkins, who was still sitting on the desk holding the telephone receiver away from his ear. "Who are the hostages now?" Blood said, and left them to chew on that, heading out of the tent and across the dark clearing to the government Jeep that would take him back down the winding dirt road to the foot of Paradise Ridge.

Office

[PARASIEGE, p. 44]

SA Banish's office was in disarray. The floor space was littered with papers thrown off his desk, and bandages, scissors, and other medical kit supplies lay scattered about the room.

SA Banish himself, however, appeared reasonable and well tempered, even sharp, following his outburst. Except for the gunpowder spray pattern burned into his right cheek and forehead, his appearance and manner actually appeared improved. His queries, as recalled, were succinct and professional.

SA BANISH: We are monitoring the mountaintop for broadcast activity?

SA COYLE: Yes, sir, we are.

SA BANISH: That facet of the operation will be stepped up. I want citizens band radios brought in and monitored on every channel until such time as we can take delivery of scrambling devices. When that happens, I want every channel blocked except emergency channel 9. Reassign personnel as necessary.

SA COYLE: Yes, sir.

SA BANISH: Where precisely was Mellis allowed in the staging area?

SA COYLE: Just one of the holding cells, sir, briefly, before meeting his parents. Aside from your trailer, that is.

SA BANISH: Send down to the bridge barricade for Police Officer Kearney. I want to see him here immediately.

SA COYLE: Yes, sir.

SA Coyle then returned to her desk. SA Banish departed the command tent not more than two minutes later.

Trailer

Banish entered the trailer without a sound. He eased the thin door shut on the overnight activity behind him and stood still, relieved, facing the dead room. The buzzing in his head persisted, fainter now, more remote, but enduring. He indulged himself in it, as well as in the thickened thumping of the pulse in his temples. He fed off the droning rhythm. Its regularity seemed to have the effect of shortening and constricting his physical movements while at the same time freeing his mind for more speculative thoughts. He began prowling methodically about the room.

First to the table, silently, on one knee, examining the unstained underside and each knicked leg. The rust-colored carpeting below was muddied. He could smell Mellis there. He had no anger for him anymore. Mellis was just a pawn and Banish's anger for him had dried up and died. Banish was all determination now. No anger even for himself, or even pity, for being so handily duped. His one crippling flaw had been his overriding concern for his men's safety. He had been much too cautious and too restrained.

He moved to the flat-backed headboard of the bed, carefully probing the unstained side facing the wall, then the paneled wall itself. He slipped a penlight out of his shirt pocket and thumbed the tip, and a narrow, yellow light flared noiselessly. He placed it between his teeth and lay down on his back to explore the dusty underside of the bed.

He ought to have been killed. For being caught flat like that with his pants down around his ankles and his belt buckle clanking behind him, he deserved the ultimate humiliation. Mellis ought not to have missed. But he had—though for this Banish felt neither particularly grateful nor, again, angry. What he felt was engaged. He felt invigorated. As he slid back silently from underneath the bed and continued at the wooden night table, pulling out a small, empty drawer and probing it with the stealth of a cat burglar, he felt a quiet, businesslike ecstasy. Offering his sword to Richardsen had been mere good form, pure bureaucratic chivalry, as he knew that it would take much more than a bungled, nonfatal recon up a mountain to warrant his removal. Banish was well acquainted with the inner workings of the machine. Washington, despite whatever misgivings they may have had about him, would already be moving to shift the blame. Ables was much more dangerous than had originally been anticipated. He was a Vietnam veteran set to kill as many federal agents as possible in order to avenge the death of his daughter. Faulty knowledge from the U.S. Marshals Service had prompted the Bureau to dispatch a negotiator to do what would normally be a strict tactician's job. Now the troops would march in behind him. Now the mountain would be held and bled. Now the hammer would fall.

He also foresaw whispering within the ranks. His men's confidence had certainly suffered and Banish's next order might be questioned. A bold stroke was needed to restore their faith, both in him and in the operation. He was dug in there now, with no reasonable expectation of getting free. Ables had reached out from the cabin and attempted murder. He had taken the battle to Banish, dispatching an assassin to do his bidding. He had failed.

The night table yielded nothing. Banish stood and eased the yellowed shade off the bedside lamp for inspection. The nature of a hostage negotiation dictates that the negotiator begins necessarily two or three steps behind the hostage-taker. Success therefore turns upon the acquisition of knowledge, knowledge of the suspect and complete knowledge of the situation at hand. In every successful negotiation there is a point at which, whether through the astute gathering of information or through timely and significant action, the negotiator overtakes the criminal in terms of control. Because the negotiator is withholding what the suspect ultimately demands—his freedom—this translates into a transfer of dependence wherein the negotiator assumes power. The rest is just patience and allowing the suspect to talk himself out. Banish knew he was not quite there yet. But his renewed stealthiness was showing him the way.

He was as though reborn. He had climbed to the top of the mountain and now saw the situation lying open before him, the stripes of the beast, the task at hand. He was making leaps of pure intellect, as though following a mental map through a minefield. He could anticipate, and counter. He could have the upper hand. He could take significant action.

He left the lamp, turning in the room, and found himself facing himself in the dark trailer, and suddenly the answer was plain. The mirror he had earlier pulled down off the wall. It had been replaced for Mellis's brief occupancy. Banish moved to it, silently, buzzing inside, running his fingers down along the smooth plastic frame, then raising the mirror gently an inch or two off the wall.

The homemade device was no larger than his thumbnail, no thicker than three or four coins. It was black and beetle-shaped and attached to the mirror backing with a small patch of regular adhesive tape, its thin, bare antenna wire rising vertically to the top of the frame.

Banish eased the mirror back against the paneled wall and moved to stand in front of it. The prescience of his actions charged him. Everything was falling together now. Ables's military electronics background. It was the only way the cabin could have known when they were coming.

Banish examined and touched lightly the black powder burn coloring the right side of his face. He ran his fingers through his thick tangle of hair, smoothing it back, then stared deeply into the glass. He recognized that game look, his true command presence. After two long years of slumber. He was his old self once again, full of confidence and cleverness and cold capability; but of self-doubt, and caution, and the cancer of fear—void.

Office

All of a sudden Brian was in the FBI command tent. It was one in the morning but the place was full of activity still, certainly having to do with the shooting that had gone on up at the ridge. The crowd below was worked up, what with the gunshots going off and the helicopters spinning overhead. All Sheriff Blood said when he came down was that Mellis had somehow escaped.

Agent Banish had sent for him specifically. Brian couldn't think of anything he had done wrong and so was going in blind. The command tent inside was exactly the kind of highly charged place he expected it to be. He went in past the agents behind desks, past a glowing wall-sized diagram map that had to be seen to be believed, and past Agent Perkins, sitting on the edge of a desk, staring up at the tent ceiling and speaking into a telephone. Agent Perkins called his wife "honey." He was telling her that he was going to be gone a few more days at least.

Brian reached the dark rear of the tent where there was light coming from under a section of canvas fold. He set himself and straightened up. There was nothing on the canvas door, no name and no bell to push or solid place to knock, so he edged the flap open a bit and stuck his head in.

Agent Banish was sitting back in his chair behind a desk across the small office. He was talking into a speaker telephone, one of those "hands-off" jobs. He saw Brian and nodded and motioned for him to come inside.

It looked as though there had been a fight. Brian moved ahead, nudging aside some important-looking papers with his shoe toe to make a clear space of floor to stand on. The upper right side of Agent Banish's face was singed black, as though he had been burned with something. Still, though, he seemed to be at ease talking to the man on the other end of the telephone.

Agent Banish was saying, "No, Sal. Nothing from the cabin since."

"Damn shame, Jack," said Sal, the volume low, his voice sounding mechanical through the speaker box. "What would you say, then? Would you say we got a Rambo on our hands?"

"I would say we need to be ready for anything here, Sal. Hostage Rescue airborne yet?"

"They'll be there, ready for deploy, by oh-nine-hundred your time. Get them in tight around the cabin and fast. Keep those trigger-happy marshals away. It's big now, Jack—but you know that. Just get him on the phone. Get him talking. We're all rooting for you back here."

Agent Banish nodded and said, "I know you are."

He sat forward and punched a button and hung up. "Kearney," he said, standing and coming around his desk. "Come ahead."

Brian nodded politely but couldn't go any farther without clearing himself a path first. Agent Banish crossed to him instead, stepping boldly over the papers.

"What happened to your face?" said Brian.

Agent Banish waved at his own cheek. "Should work itself out of the skin in a couple of days. How's the situation down at the bridge?"

"Edgy, sir. Tense. They want to know what happened up there."

He nodded. "A mix-up," he said, "but no time to go into it right now." Whatever did happen seemed not very important. Agent Banish got right to the point. "I called you up here because there's something I need you to do."

Brian nodded. "Yes, sir," he said, buoyed.

"Something I need you to do for me."

Brian strengthened his posture. "Whatever you say, sir."

Agent Banish studied his face, then nodded once with a dry kind of satisfied certainty. "Good," he said. He reached into his pants pocket and pulled out a twenty-dollar bill. "A bottle of whiskey. Whatever brand you can find around here. Royal Canadian, I guess."

He pressed the bill into Brian's hand. Brian stood there, looking at the twenty, then looking at Agent Banish again. Brian saw that he was different now somehow. His composure, his expression, the way he was talking. The sharp blue eyes he was holding Brian with.

"It's the middle of the night, sir," Brian said.

Agent Banish nodded coldly. "I figured you would know the area."

This was why he had called Brian in. To run an errand. Brian looked into the agent's eyes, watching him trying to act official and uncaring. Brian realized that those marshals had been right. Agent Banish's face held the pose, but there was clear, devious desperation in his eyes. He was starting to sweat a little.

"Agent Banish, I don't think—"

"Take one of the government cars," he said, talking over Brian. "You'll get through the crowd more easily."

Brian was trapped. He tried to come up with something to say, but Agent Banish sucked the will right out of him.

"When you get back," the agent continued, "we may be needing another man up here in the command tent. Someone who's proven himself to be responsible."

Brian felt a draft run over him. It was like a chill feeling of collapse. Those marshals had been dead-on right and it was killing Brian, standing there in front of Agent Banish. He knew what was being said. Agent Banish was dangling everything he wanted right in front of his face. Either the agent had guessed it somehow, or he was able to open Brian up like a rotten ear of corn and look right into him and see it. Brian couldn't even look Agent Banish in the eye, but the agent didn't seem to care. When Brian swallowed and felt himself wince, he knew that Agent Banish could see whatever sour ambition there was to see in his crushed face. Here was the secret of this agent's strange power. Bargaining and manipulation. His treating Brian like a nothing. It made Brian want to do this thing for him and be recognized. There wasn't anything about it that was fair or right, but it was Brian's big chance and he was signing off on the dotted line by just nodding to the agent there in his office. Agent Banish wanted a bottle of whiskey. Brian saw a long, cold ride ahead of him.

Holding Tent

As directed, Blood entered with Deke, up from the front lines. The leg felt pretty good now and Blood limped only slightly. Banish was already there waiting for them. He was seated at the rectangular table in front, his bent right elbow on the tabletop, cheek and chin resting in his hand. He was in profile, sitting back, looking impassively across the tent at the blank inside of the left canvas wall.

There was a single standing iron-bar cell beyond the table, five or six feet in from each of the three nearest walls of the small tent. It stood about six feet tall and the bars, Blood noticed, were dug or somehow driven into the solid dirt floor. So were the legs of the heavy wooden table Banish was sitting at, and the poles supporting a thin handcuff bar running the length of it behind. Light was provided by two shaded bulbs hanging overhead, and there were two unlit ceiling spotlights turned toward the empty cell.

Deke started off by crowing a little, gesturing toward the mountain. "Some running around there up top," he said to Banish. "Helicopters and such. A good lot of shooting."

Banish turned to look at Deke then, his sooty face revealed. "Nothing for you to be worried about," he said.

Deke whistled and stepped back in surprise and an unchecked bit of pleasure. "Looks like you got the worst of it. Turpentine ought to bring that right off."

Banish said, "I appreciate your concern."

Deke nodded rapidly, slyly. "Glenn got the best of things, didn't he? He's a polecat, I told you. I warned you don't step on his toes. I said he weren't afraid. What happened up top of Paradise? Hellfire, weren't it? Wild stories spreading down below, folks starting to whisper. Near to bursting waiting for some word." He looked at Banish and then at Blood.

"I'll ask the questions," Banish said.

Deke resumed his frisky grin. "You want to know what the talk is down there." He nodded. "Something happened, something you're worried about now, and you want to know what folks are thinking."

Banish shook his head slowly. Blood was noticing now a change in Banish's countenance, a darkening in the man's manner. It included the sullen way in which he regarded old Deke.

"I want to know about Ables's daughter," Banish said. "The oldest one, Rebecca. I want to know if she's developed."

His words put a cold, strange needle into Blood's side, so that Blood couldn't even imagine how the words fell upon Deke's ears, except that, for once, the old fool was at a loss even for chatter.

"Come again?" Deke sputtered.

"Developed," Banish said. "She's fourteen years old. Puberty, breasts. Coming of age. I need to know from you whether or not she is developed."

Blood watched Deke's face redden in disgust. The old man's jaw started to shake before he could get any words out, then the angry quaking spread to his neck and shoulders and chest. "I don't know what the hell you federal boys think—" His rage prevented him from finishing; his face showed him imagining the worst. "That what you spend all your damn time up here thinking about?" he said.

Banish stood up out of his chair. He crossed slowly to Deke and reached out and took the collar of the old man's shirt and twisted it up under the loose flap of his fleshy neck, walking him backward and up against the tight wall of the tent. The old man grabbed at Banish's fist with both hands. He gripped him with his dirty nails, looking up at him widely, but it was all in vain. Banish showed no anger, no haste. Only deliberateness. Deke's eyes gaped as Banish leaned in close.

"You think I'm in this for kicks?" he said. The canvas wall was rippling from Deke's kicking resistance. "One word from me," Banish said, showing him a forefinger up close, "one word, and your little shack up there, everything you own in your rotten little world

—ashes. Rubble. And not a thing you can do about it. Now you answer my goddamn question, and goddamn fast."

Deke was shaking and staring like a small creature about to be consumed. It was Banish's cool restraint that made the encounter so threatening. Blood decided that he had had enough. He stepped back without excusing himself and turned and exited through the tent door.

Two marshals waiting there snapped to attention when Blood emerged, then saw that it was only the sheriff. He acknowledged them with a nodding glance and turned to look off the other way. Blood wasn't so genteel that he couldn't stomach a little law-minded intimidation, but this particular encounter represented a philosophical difference. Blood saw that the way to deal with these people was not to confront them. A direct challenge to them was like questioning a religious man's faith or calling his wife a whore. These were not reasonable people; they were proud people, and their ridiculous pride made them blind. The only way to lose a fistfight with a blind man was to come straight at him.

Banish exited the tent holding Deke ahead of him like a scarecrow. "Take him away," he told the marshals. He turned to Blood then, his face hard-set but otherwise blank.

"It's called COINTELPRO," he said. "Counterintelligence program. Designed to disrupt and discredit the opposition."

Blood looked into his eyes. "What happened to you up on the mountain?"

Banish shook his head, matching Blood's gaze. "You know Mellis was sent down here to kill us."

"He was sent down here to kill you."

"Just follow my lead," Banish said, close enough now that Blood could see the tiny ridges the burnt black powder made in the skin on his face. Banish's expression was clear and commanding and hard as plated steel, as with a few simple words he brought Blood into his great reserve of confidence. "Ables thinks Mellis killed Watson," he said.

Trailer

Banish jiggled the knob of the open door, stepped firmly inside, then pointed at Blood behind him, a prompt.

Blood said, "Do you think he really would have tried to kill us?"

Banish nodded and closed the door behind them with a click, flipping on the light. He held up a hand to hold Blood where he was, then pointed across the trailer to somewhere near the bed.

"I don't see how he could have gotten away with it," Banish said.

Banish nodded deferringly at Blood. Blood looked at him, shrugged lightly, then went with it.

"True enough," he said.

They were moving farther inside. Banish went first, pulling a chair out from under a table, knocking pieces of wood together. He did not sit but instead continued forward, Blood following. Banish turned his head back toward him.

"Well," Banish said, "immunity is a small price to pay to get Ables."

He was walking around the bed, quietly now, circling to the far wall. Blood was behind him.

"True enough," Blood said again, his voice raised a little. "But can you trust him, Agent Watson? What about his wife?"

Banish stopped and indicated with his chin a hanging wall mirror.

Banish said, "I guess Mellis has a thing for the daughter."

They stopped at the mirror. This wasn't exactly what Blood had had in mind. He didn't so much mind a little revenge—Mellis had tried to shoot them both—but Banish's particular brand left a sick feeling in his gut. Still and again, he complied.

"So that's why he wants the others out of the way," Blood said.

He was looking at Banish's reflection. The agent's face showed no change, but the mirror, as with any clear reflective surface, distorted his features ever so slightly, like a wrinkle in an otherwise fine fabric, so that Banish's sooted face took on a kind of hidden snarl. Banish nodded his head in a pleased fashion.

"I guess twelve months together in a cabin will do that," he said.

Outside, Blood stood away from the trailer with his hands deep in his coat pockets while Banish closed and locked the door. There was no sense of victory in Banish's person, no deviousness, no haste. In control and simultaneously out of control. Blood watched him coming toward him through the cold night without a coat on, without even his arms crossed, breath swirling whitely across his face. They were about to go their separate ways.

"What have we done?" Blood asked him quietly.

Banish said, "We just shot their lights out."

Office

He paced. He ran a flat hand across his dry mouth. He had given up trying to work and took instead to walking back and forth and tapping his leg, with frequent side trips to the door flap. He had issued various busying assignments to the remaining overnight personnel to keep them away from the tent, and now that they were all gone, his window of opportunity was wide open and Kearney was nowhere to be found. Banish ran his left hand back through his thick hair and felt the hum rising again in his head. His great and immense thirst.

The old mastery. Things were moving now and he was in complete control. The drink itself meant nothing to him. A small reward. A squirt of grease to lube the few remaining creaks. It would leave him refocused and refreshed for the return to work the next morning. He nodded as he paced, routinely patting his right hand against his leg.

He checked the outer tent again, still empty. Time, time. It had been so long. The cool smoothness of the glass bottle. The snap and paper crinkle of the government seal. The twisting crack of the plastic cap—the genie escaping, the perfume released. The glug of it being poured. He was coming out of the desert. He felt himself finally rising out of the stasis that was Skull Valley. His tongue was a dry bucket in the stone well of his deep and immense thirst.

Footsteps in the outer tent. Quiet footsteps, and Banish started fast toward the door, then retreated instead to stand waiting casually before his desk. The flap was shrugged aside.

Dutiful Kearney. Banish crossed to him, fighting eagerness, fighting joy, but surely smiling and widely, ready to relieve Kearney of the burden of his plain brown package and feel the comforting shift of the liquid inside. Delicious fuel.

But Kearney had a soft look on his face, and when he raised his hands, they were empty. Banish blinked. He looked up at Kearney to see if he had realized his mistake, but Kearney was standing there, that hangdog look on his face, and Banish realized that there had been no mistake.

"I'm sorry, sir," Kearney said, sheepish but resolute. "I couldn't do it. It's not right. Maybe you need help."

Banish went after him. He put him in a choke grip, his forearm pressed against Kearney's neck and pinning him back against a tent pole. It took Kearney by surprise, before he could even save a breath, and his mouth gaped empty.

"Goddamn Boy Scout," Banish said. Kearney put his hands up to Banish's quivering arm but did not fight back, except with his eyes. "I give you a direct order, I don't care, you carry it out to the letter—" Kearney's face turned pink, then red from the strain, lips blue, mouth twisting. Choking, deer-eyed.

"Get off my mountain!" Banish railed, releasing him finally and pulling back. Kearney slumped off to one side, stumbling away from Banish, reeling, his hand at his neck. The young cop stood there sucking air, face pained and twisted and red.

"GET OFF MY MOUNTAIN!"

Kearney pushed aside the canvas flap and stumbled out of the office. Banish turned fast. He went to his desk. He put one hand on the edge and held on, looking about feverishly, his head raging, buzzing.

He cursed Paradise Ridge. He cursed Montana. He flashed on his favorite liquor store in Manhattan, the fifths kept in dark bottles on shelves behind the counter like exotic medicines, neat rows of more than ten deep. He could drive off the mountain right now, he thought, in search of some. But how to explain it. They would be coming back to the command tent any minute.

The command tent. A cold ripple of salvation straightened him up. The beer. The drugged Pabst Blue Ribbon—he didn't care—tall, chilled cans of blue and gold. If Coyle hadn't gotten rid of them yet—

He went out roughly through the canvas fold and into the tent room to the small, humming refrigerator, ripping open the door and rooting through the clinking bottles of clear water and the scattered pieces of fruit. They were gone. The cans of beer were gone. He stood there a moment, frozen, cursing Coyle—then slammed shut the door, rattling the refrigerator, grabbing and shaking the appliance bodily, upsetting its contents, and then, defeated, he slumped over its top, gripping it finally for balance. He swore into his shirt-sleeve. His great goddamn immense thirst. He closed his eyes and felt nothing but emptiness, recalling in the poisoned darkness of his mind the insects that had plagued him throughout his first blurred weeks at the Retreat, the bugs of hysteria—chewing on his skin, racing under the flesh of his arms, feasting on the soft pulp of his brain.

Office

It was a chilly morning after. Perkins crossed the staging area briskly, wearing a navy-blue jacket and a bold necktie for television. Agents had been shipping in hourly from nearby field offices and the busy clearing bore their presence. Rumors abounded as to the previous night's fiasco. While there was great concern over what the reaction to the impending announcement might be, Perkins himself was humming with contentment. He would be the Bureau point man that morning, the vessel through which the FBI's version of the night's events would be presented over the airwaves throughout the country and the world.

He passed the wide mouth of the new mountain road. The contractors had cut deep into the rising timber and torn up and flattened the ground soil in a straight, upward path, and they were now working unseen beyond the crest of Perkins's sight line. He could hear them, though—great noisy machines—and see the dark exhaust smoke puffing. He watched as a treetop high above shook its top branches and then fell. The road was nearly completed. They were closing in on the mountaintop.

Perkins entered the command tent and went straight to the back office and inside, prepared for whichever Banish he would find. The office was cleaned up, papers stacked neatly on the desk, calm order restored. Banish was so intent on his work that he did not notice Perkins's entrance. He looked disheveled, hair tugged-at and roughened, the black powder stain on his face already starting to gray. He was hunched over his work, eyeglasses low on his nose, writing not on white sheets of notepaper, Perkins noticed, but on a separate yellow, leather-bound, legal-sized pad. Perkins advanced and waited for acknowledgment. It was not forthcoming.

"Been here all night?" Perkins said.

Banish looked up fast in surprise and saw him standing there, then returned wordlessly to finish whatever he was working on. When he was done, he set aside the notebook and handed Perkins some typed pages. He coughed into a loose fist, clearing some of the phlegm from his throat and reaching for a glass of water.

"Briefing and Q and A outline," he said, setting the glass back down. "That's as far as we'll go."

Perkins flipped through the pages, nodding. "Right," he said. "Everything else is set for later."

Banish nodded, distracted. "What time is it?"

Perkins checked his watch. "I go on in twenty minutes."

Perkins turned and headed back out of the tent and across the clearing to the waiting Jeeps, covering the pages as he went. It was good work. Perkins couldn't fault the preparation, nor the expertise. It was Banish's sense of procedure that worried him, the way he was handling the cabin, the staging area, and the press, all by remote control—these were dishes he could keep up and spinning only so long. Any spectacular failure following this new escalation—millions of taxpayers' dollars spent, thousands of man-hours committed— would surely touch Perkins as well. He could protect Banish only so far, but if in the end Banish was to topple like one of those unlucky trees, Perkins would make certain he himself was in a good position to yell timber and jump clear.

Sound Truck

Banish entered the sound truck cleaned up and shaved and wearing a fresh white shirt. He was moving slowly, though not because of the buzzing in his head, which remained but no longer compelled him. Morning found him penitent. It was like coming off a powerful drug.

The sound man eyed him as he stepped inside, saying nothing about Banish's burnt face.

"Anything overnight?" Banish said.

The sound man was chewing peppermint-smelling gum, shaking his head. "Not a thing."

"The microphones? Nothing?"

He shook his head. "All quiet on the western front."

Banish took a seat at the other workstation. He stared blankly at the controls. He was thinking about Mellis. "I need my trailer swept for bugs," he said.

The sound man turned and looked at him sideways, chewing. "You mean," he said, "real bugs?"

Banish picked up the handset and flipped the control switches himself, taking in a good, deep breath. "This is Special Agent Bob Watson . . ."

He ran through the speech, changing very little. Best to remain constant, to keep his vocal persona separate from the fury of the previous night's assault. He finished and there was predictably no response. He hung up the handset, noticing a small color monitor playing behind the sound man. It was flashing bits of the press briefing down below: Perkins speaking from behind a podium, various agents flanking the bridge, the angry, stirring crowd.

"I had them bring out a satellite dish from the Seattle office," the sound man said. "CNN was carrying a live feed of the briefing." He glanced at the black-and-white bridge area monitor. "But it looks like he's into the Q and A now."

The monitor shot was too wide. "Can you move that camera?" Banish said.

"Twenty-to-one zoom ratio," the sound man said, turning a dial and tightening the monitor view to frame the bridge and Perkins's back and shoulders at the bottom of the screen and the press corps and the twelve-wheelers and camera towers at the top. Protesters packed the area between. Fists and effigies and signs were raised: FBI BURN IN HELL!   FBI: GUILTY GUILTY GUILTY!   BABY KILLERS.

Suited agents with fingers touching their ear wires filtered conspicuously through the jostling crowd, standing out even on the black-and-white monitor. That was their job this morning, to be a visible presence. Banish said absently, but with a detached certainty as he watched the scene, "There's going to be a disturbance as soon as this ends."

The sound man looked again at the monitor, as though for some explanation, then turned back to the color satellite screen. "They're cutting it down now," he said, nodding, "that's what they're doing. Breaking it down into bites to send out to the affiliates around the country to be folded into feature stories."

He turned up the sound. The screen went dark between broadcast bursts, then a rainbow stripe appeared and a digital counter beeped down from three. There was Perkins behind the Department of Justice/FBI podium, voice weighty, expression grave. "Judith Ables appears to have died of a gunshot wound. It appears she was hit in the initial exchange of gunfire with U.S. Marshals on the fourth of August and died instantly." Then blackness.

"Died instantly," echoed the sound man. Anybody who was ever mistakenly killed by law enforcement had died instantly and painlessly.

Three, two, one: a middle-aged woman with curled brown hair pointing threateningly at the camera. "They killed a twelve-year-old girl over a single gun! We won't stand for it!"

Blackness. Three, two, one: a young close-eyed man in a hunter-green parka shaking an unseen sign. "This right here is the site of the massacre. This is the blood of our children. This is Concord Bridge and they have fired the first shot. What you are seeing right here is the beginning of a great American civil war."

Blackness. Three, two, one: Perkins again. "It must be understood that Glenn Allen Ables and Charles Mellis are charged with serious crimes and pose an immediate threat to the community. Efforts to apprehend them must and will continue." Heard clearly over his voice, from the bulging crowd, defiant cries of "Murderers! Assassins!"

Blackness. Three, two, one: the Mellises, Mrs. Mellis straining to be heard. "We don't know what is happening. The FBI won't tell us.

When we saw Charles, he was fine and just anxious to come on home. I don't know what they're doing to him up there . . ." The picture lingered as Mrs. Mellis wilted and began to cry. Mr. Mellis, in a suit jacket and no tie, tried to comfort her.

Blackness. Three, two, one: Perkins looking stern, elaborating on a question. "We have had reports, unconfirmed at this time, of possible abuse in the household, ongoing over a period of many months."

A reporter yelling, "Sexual abuse?"

Perkins saying, "I can't comment on that at this time," and pointing to another reporter.

Blackness. The sound man said, "Jesus Christ. Is that true?"

Banish's face was hard and tight with disbelief.

Three, two, one: Deke Belcher standing facing the camera, holding a sloppy cardboard sign across his chest: YOUR HOME IS NEXT.

Banish turned away, Perkins's foolish ad-lib ringing in his head. "What the hell is he thinking?" he said.

The sound man said, "That was off-card?"

"Goddammit." Like sand through his fingers. In that one instant it had gone out to television stations in every city in the country, and probably overseas.

The sound man was back watching the black-and-white monitor. Banish saw that Perkins had since stepped down from the podium and agents were now converged on a disturbance near the front of the crowd. Two men were being pulled out and wrestled facedown onto the bridge, and taken into custody.

Banish stood and turned to leave, stepping out of the open van door and hearing the suspension give a bit, creaking. "Hey," said the sound man after him. "What's it like," he said, "being God?"

That stopped Banish, stopped him dead in his tracks ten feet away from the van. He looked up at the new road carved fresh into the mountainside, a helicopter rumbling over the ridge. The clearing overrun with men and machines.

He turned back to the sound man, who was standing in the doorway of the van and smiling offhandedly, merely impressed.

Banish shook his head. "I'm just a federal employee," Banish told him. Then he walked away.

Holding Tent

Banish was outside waiting for Perkins as he walked up. "What the hell was that?" he said.

Perkins's satisfied smile dipped in surprise. "Improvisation," he allowed. "Strategy."

Banish was furious. "If I had wanted that card played, I would have played it myself. You had the goddamn outline right there in front of you."

Perkins raised a flat hand. "You're right in the thick of things now, so you can't see," he said. "But I'm looking at the larger picture." His voice lowered then in confidence and he stepped even closer. "You need an out," he said. "We need an out. The Bureau needs an out if this thing goes wrong. If decisive action has to be taken. This way we're all covered."

Banish nodded. "I see," he said. "You're protecting me now. You've only got my best interests at heart. Otherwise, why would you start making things up off the top of your head like some first-office agent? Why would you raise all our stakes on a wild bluff?" Banish shook his head and pointed. "I don't want to be covered, not by you or anyone else. I don't want any politicians on this mountain. You're losing faith in the operation, Perkins. And you are being insubordinate. If I hear you deviate from that script one more time, I don't care—I'll have Fagin conduct the briefings."

Banish turned and entered the holding tent. Perkins followed soon after but remained out of sight behind. One of the two arrestees from the bridge disturbance sat alone at the heavy table before the empty cell, two agents standing behind him on either side. He was a white male in his mid-to-late thirties, with a shaved head that was strangely pockmarked, probably the result of a childhood disease, hidden sores idly picked off a then-covered scalp. He wore raw black skinhead tattoos on each of his hairless arms, a sleeveless black T-shirt to feature them, blue jeans, black boots. Handcuffs hung empty on the iron bar behind him and he was rubbing his chafed wrists. A thin line of fresh cherry-red blood ran from a half-inch gash over his right temple down to below his bruised right cheek.

Banish brought out his ID. "Banish," he said. "FBI."

The arrestee squirmed, shifting often and shooting side glances up at the agents on either side of him. The bones supporting his face were jagged. A wiry little weasel. "A little rough," he said, dabbing at his face with a tissue, "don't you think?"

Banish said, "You received our message."

"Got myself arrested, didn't I?"

One of the agents beside him said, "He punched a black SA in the mouth, sir."

The arrestee said, "Now listen—I need a plane ticket this time and some seed money. I want outta here for good."

Banish said, "We'll get to that. What are they planning for us?"

The man shifted in his seat, shrugging. "Lots of talk down there. You know—little action. Some kind of presentation, they're calling it."

"Nonviolent?"

"A *pre-sentation,*" the man stressed, then shrugged again. "For now anyway. That's all I know."

"Who?" Banish said. "Locals? WAR? Truth? What?"

"The Aryans," the man said. He was impatient. "Who else, how would I know? They all feed off each other, wackos and patriots alike. Kremmer is supposedly visiting the front tomorrow."

Franklin Kremmer was the sixty-eight-year-old minister of the WAR church. "That's it?" Banish said. "Nothing else being planned?"

"If it is, they don't tell anybody who don't need to know until they need to know. There's no newsletter or nothing. But Kremmer ain't gonna be near no real violence. His shit, it don't stink. Trucks coming in, though, past two days. Ammunition off-loaded."

"Ammunition," Banish said.

"Large caliber, and shells. All legal," the man said. "Just in big amounts, and pricey. Supplies like flashlights, batteries, sleeping bags, first-aid kits."

"What does it mean?"

The man shrugged. "It means they're laying off a lot of money on this shit, how the hell would I know? A lot of Truth boys driving off with it."

"Members of The Truth."

"Hanging around the place the past couple of days. So there. That's something for you, ain't it? That ought to be worth something to you."

Banish held his official gaze. "What about Ables?" he said. "You know him?"

"Seen him around. He's known."

"For selling guns?"

"Yeah, for selling guns. Wants to be an Aryan arms merchant worldwide, that's his kick."

"Everybody has a dream," Banish said. "What did the others think of him?"

"Some laughed. But most were more afraid. Weird fucking guy. If they laughed, it wasn't when he was around."

"What did you think?"

The man scoffed and looked off a moment. "A nut. Like a lot of them, believes in UFOs and shit. Drove a nice truck, though. Until I bought it off him after he got pinched. Said he wouldn't be needing it no more. Now look, man—that's all I know." He sat up straighter, opening his hands on the table as though he were presenting something. "So how about it?"

Banish said, "How about what?"

"A plane ticket, man. Get me the fuck outta here."

"A plane? Where would you go?"

"Somewheres south. Then east. Too many kooks around here."

Banish nodded, pretending to deliberate a moment. "No," he said, shaking his head. "We need you here." He said to one of the agents, "Give him a hundred dollars."

"Whoa, hey," said the man, raising his arms, looking around, stopping things. "The fuck is this?"

"We need an informant inside the WAR camp," Banish said. "You're it."

"Informer?" The man's small eyes flared suddenly. "Hey, man. Hey, hold it right there. Get one thing straight. I ain't no informer."

Banish looked at him, looked around the holding tent. "What do you call this, then?"

"This?" he said. "This is nothing. This is a weirdo and a couple of nut cases. But I ain't no twist, man. I never turned out my friends. Those ATF fucks stood me up under a drug rap and rolled me—OK, fine, so I'm fucked, good. But that's that."

Banish nodded and said again, "One hundred dollars."

"Wait, wait, wait," the man said, swallowing his aggression. "Listen to me. Just listen, OK? You know what they'll do to me, they find out I was in here? They'll slice my fucking tongue out, man."

Banish shook his head. "You know as well as I do you'll walk off this mountain with more respect than ever before. You assaulted an FBI agent. You and your unwitting friend in the other tent will be great heroes once we let you go free."

"Fuck that, man." He was excited again, belligerent. Pleading his case. "They know. Someone's talking and they fucking know. I know they know. So I'm up against it here. I'm fucked everywhere I turn. But I ain't no twist, man. I ain't nobody's whore. You do what you gotta do in life, right? You do what's gotta be done. But I ain't spreading for no one, man."

Banish said again, "One hundred dollars."

The man's face washed white and he almost made it to his feet before the agents shoved him back down in the chair. "Fuck you!"

he screamed, nearly crying. "I ain't nobody's whore, you fucking pansy-ass, nigger-loving, federal fucking faggot!"

Banish stood still and looked closely at the man, watching his dark eyes stare out from inside his face, his thin chest huffing great breaths. Banish looked at the agent behind him.

"Seventy-five dollars," he said.

"Oh, man," the informant whined, deflating. "Fuck you, man!"

Banish said, "Fifty."

"Fucking wait," said the man, hands thrust out now, eyes closed. "Wait. Wait a fucking minute here, all right?" He opened his eyes again, looked around. "The fuck happened here, man? What the fuck is going on? ATF said you'd set me up good, like they did before."

"What was that?"

"Three hundred bucks."

"No," Banish said. "What did you give them?"

"Ables, man," he said, still bitter and unsure, but now fishing around for more money. "They were looking for somebody else they could roll. You know, roll me, roll him, moving higher up."

"But Ables wouldn't buckle."

"And look what it got him. I told you, man, they got me like a motherfucker—"

"Why Ables?"

"How would I know? Somebody who was outside, but inside. They had a hard-on for him, I guess."

"What do you mean?"

"They were pissed at him. They wanted him—I don't know. I said I could get to his truck and they gave me a gun to plant."

Banish was silent a moment. "A Beretta submachine gun."

The man nodded. "And they said it would be my last job. That was two fucking jobs ago, including this bullshit one right here. So they got me by the balls, all right? So I'm in it up to my eyes, all right? So fuck you, assholes! I ain't your fucking whore, man!"

Banish spoke after a moment. "No," he said, nodding slowly. "You're ATF's whore." He looked to the agent. "Give him one hundred dollars, grill the other one for an hour, then let them both go."

Banish waited for more abuse. The informant expelled an empty breath of protest, then looked off to the side. His face showed hard-bitten dismay, lips moving in near silence as he swore bitterly to himself. Then he crossed his marked arms on the table. He lay his head down on top.

Banish wondered then why he had allowed it to get so ugly. He looked once more at the man with his head down on the table, then turned and went out past Perkins into the cool daylight of the clearing.

Office

When he entered his office, Coyle was standing behind his desk looking through some papers. She sensed someone entering and stepped back too sharply, then saw that it was Banish. Her face went from shock to embarrassment to guilt.

"What are you doing?" Banish said, advancing.

She gestured at the desk. "It was open," she said. Then, reining in her nerve, she offered confusion as an excuse for her interest. "A poem," she said.

It ripped through him. He had left his notebook open on top of his desk.

"Not a poem," he said, taking a step forward. "An exercise. Focuses the mind."

He heard himself being defensive, and felt her respond. " 'The Hornet's Nest,' " she said. "It's about this, isn't it?" Then within the framework of her short-cut hair, her face—worn dry from days of mountain living—relaxed its fatigue for a fleeting blush of discovery. "The words," she said, "the images—"

Banish stood fast. "You came in here for something?"

She sputtered. "Seattle special detail releases. And small equipment consignments."

"Did you find them?"

There were two sheets of paper in her hand. She looked up and examined Banish's face from across the room, then her eyes fell. She started the long walk out of his office. She went past him without looking up and exited through the canvas flap.

Sheriff Blood almost walked into her, entering with a stack of newspapers under his arm. He tipped his hat to her back as she left. Banish crossed to his desk before Blood could and closed the notebook and went about straightening up some other items. He had hoped to avoid Blood that day. He did not want to be made to discuss the previous night.

Blood set the papers down on the desk. "You saw the briefing?" he said. Banish gave a half nod. "It's getting pretty unfriendly down there."

Banish said, "I would prefer specifics."

"Well, you killed a twelve-year-old girl over nothing. That's what they're saying. You, meaning everybody up here. You killed her to get back at Ables, and now you're going to pick off his family one by one until you get to him. Or until the protesters can get to you."

Banish expected as much. "Just talk?"

Blood shrugged. He was back on his heels. "Two calls I got on my car radio this morning," he said. "The proprietor of Huddleston Sporting Goods called to let me know by manner of curiosity that he had sold out, within one hour of opening this morning, of batteries, flashlights, camping and hunting equipment, and other such supplies. All gone."

"Sold them to Truth members," Banish said.

Blood's eyebrows arched. "And some locals too. He'll sell to anybody who's buying, of course, that's his business. But he thought enough about it to let me know. Then after that I get a call from the bank manager over at the Huddleston Dime. Two men went in there first thing this morning and put in a change order for fifteen thousand dollars' worth of pennies and nickels."

"Two men?"

"Two bald men," said Blood. "They left cash for it. More than that, though, he said people were lining up at his tellers, regular residents, pulling out all their money. Even cashing in IRAs and taking twenty percent penalties. They want it now and they want it in cash."

Banish looked at him. "Meaning?"

"I was hoping you'd know. What comes to my mind is survivalist activity—we've seen some of that around here before. Comes in waves. End of world type thing. But why the urgency, I can't say. Could be some people took the death of the girl as a sort of sign."

"But the protesters below," Banish said. "They're stable."

"Stable because they're still unorganized, each with their particular gripes and views. But if that mob ever pulled itself together," Blood said, shaking his head, "those folks could just about overrun this place. And if it comes to that, I'd say the tree cover is in their favor. Don't you want to push them back any farther?"

"Too far along for that. It would only raise more suspicion. We can control them where they are."

"Can't control everything," Blood said, picking up a thin, brightly colored, half-sized newspaper off the top of the stack on the desk. "Even these tabloids have taken it up. 'Mystery Mountaineer Foils FBI Arrest Plot,'" he read. "They've taken to calling him 'Grizzly Ables.' Here, there's even a UFO angle."

Banish busied himself.

"I don't know," Blood continued, opening to a page. "Folks around here tend to take these things pretty seriously. If it's printed in a newspaper, then they accept it as the truth. You do wonder where these reporters get their sources, though." He started to read some of it. "'On the other side of the confrontation tearing this family apart, observers are now questioning why federal officials have put responsibility for the standoff—now estimated to be one of the largest nondisaster relief law enforcement undertakings ever witnessed on American soil—in the hands of a mysterious federal agent with a record of criminal violence himself.' "

Banish stopped and stiffened. His chest went cold. His eyes fell and came to stare at a fixed point of nothingness as Blood continued. " 'Veteran FBI agent John T. Banish was fined $1200 in February 1991 for being drunk and disorderly aboard a Washington, D.C.–to–New York flight on Thanksgiving Day, 1990. Through a plea bargaining agreement, more serious charges of assault and making terroristic threats were dropped. "He went berserk," reported an unidentified steward who was on that flight. "He hit me and gave me a black eye when I refused to serve him more alcohol. He was very drunk, waving his badge around."

" 'Banish was also the agent in charge of the World Financial Center hostage-taking in which three people died.

" 'New York District Court records show dual restraining orders filed against Banish in December 1990 by his wife and daughter, who have renewed those orders every ninety days since then and remain estranged from him to this day. "He's sick," said a person close to the family. "John is very dangerous." ' "

Blood stopped reading. He closed the paper.

Banish remained still. Regret tugged at the muscles of his face and he straightened as much as he could and slipped one stiff hand inside his pants pocket.

"Very well," he said.

Blood set the tabloid down. This was his payback for the previous night, to watch Banish slowly twist.

It was as though Banish had heard his own obituary read to him. He saw that this was how he was to be remembered. This was the sum total of his life. Flames of regret burned in his gut, but not new flames. They were a raging, ceaseless thing that even the satisfying of his immense thirst never did quite douse.

"Very well," he said again.

Blood said, "Something happened to you in the woods last night."

Banish nodded. "Fine," he said.

He was certain that there would be no discourse. There was nothing in that for him. Talking was his profession and he knew better than anyone else its limitations. It could take you only so far, and Banish had been there, and he had come back, and here he was now.

He looked at the floor. "We will begin to allow relatives and friends up one at a time to record messages to the family," he said. "Those urging surrender and peaceful resolution will be broadcast to the cabin. Those which do not, won't. There will be no conversations."

He found his chair and managed to sit at his desk. He pretended to go about his work. Blood said, "Fair enough"—to no acknowledgment from Banish, not even an answering glance upward. Then he turned and left without having to be asked.

Alone, Banish allowed himself to stare off again at a fixed point somewhere beyond his consciousness. The telephone was right there on his desk next to him. He recalled the few times during the past two years, the low times, when he had dialed the number in Cincinnati just to hear a familiar female voice say, "Hello." The last time, following a prolonged silence on both their ends, Molly had said fearfully, "John?" and then hung up. He could see her in a long nightshirt, standing back from the telephone in a darkened kitchen, looking at it, wondering if it would ring again. Short, layered hair, lighter than it used to be, as in the hundreds of different photographs he had commissioned. Her left hand near her mouth. Her mother's garnet the only ring she still wore.

He felt for the thick band on his finger. He pictured Nicole in a white wedding dress and veil. But he could not see her smiling. Despite all the photographs, his only daughter's face was suddenly unclear to him. He could not conjure her up. As hard as he tried, he could not get his image of her to lift its lace-covered arms and raise that veil.

Staging Area

Fagin turned away from the Salvation Army truck, hot tray of food in hand. He was one of the last to be served that evening. A bonfire crackled strong in the cleared area before the trailers and most of the marshals and agents were eating their slop there. At a single picnic table separate from the rest he saw a man eating alone. Fagin went there.

He set his tray down without Banish so much as looking up. On the tray was a piece of thick-crust bread covered with chipped beef in a thin, lumpy brown sauce, a serving spoon's worth of beans still settling into its rounded section, a separate cup of sulfurlike bouillon, and a small square of cornbread.

Fagin said, "Shit on a shingle. Jesus H. Christ."

Banish sat up a fraction then, no longer able to ignore him. He was bent over his plate, eating efficiently like a kid in his last days of BT, as a light wave of laughter went up from the direction of the blaze.

"Didn't think you'd OK a bonfire," Fagin said with his mouth full, gesturing with his fork.

Banish swallowed, still watching his food. "No reason not to," he said. "Good for morale. After six days, fatigue becomes a factor."

"Yeah," said Fagin. "Six fucking days. That World Financial Center thing, how long was that?"

"That was an overnight," Banish said.

An agent came up then with papers for Banish, who looked them over and initialed each page. He returned to his plate and started in on the beans.

Fagin said, "So, you married?"

Banish stopped chewing. He stared at the table. "You don't read the papers?" he said.

Fagin gave a small grin of concession. He cut into his food. "Separated or divorced?"

"Waiting for annulment."

"A Catholic." Fagin nodded. He had guessed that, long ago. "Funny because you don't seem to me like the marrying type. And also funny because, I guess you could say, now my own marriage is hanging by a fucking thread."

"Maybe it's your language," Banish said.

"No," Fagin said, "that's the part of me she likes."

Fagin let a smile surface, and then even Banish broke down and bared some teeth. Fagin shook his head amusedly, then looked at his food again and soured on it once and for all, dropping his fork and knife onto the tin plate and pushing the thing away except for the cornbread. Fucking disgusting.

"We met at a Dodgers game," he said. "She was working in their front office there, still does." He looked up at the top of the mountain, orange with the last of the dusk. "In fact, tonight's our seventh anniversary. Yeah." He nodded. "I'm thinking about spending it up in a tree. Sitting up in the branches pointing a sniper rifle at some fucking guy I don't even know, holed up in a dink-water shack on top of a fucking mountain in the middle of nowhere fucking Montana."

He was shaking his head slowly in disgust, wiping an already clean hand on the front of his uniform shirt. He wanted to spit, but could not from the table. It was his upbringing. "Now she wants a divorce," he said. "She's younger than me, couple of years. She's white. It catches me a lot of shit. But who knows, you know? I'm not around much. You know how it is, the job. Maybe she's fucking a ballplayer." He looked down then, thinking he had gone too far. He didn't want to look weak. "Maybe," he said matter-of-factly. He was concentrating on one finger of his right hand, his trigger finger,

dry and pinkish on the underside, rubbing as though to get something off it. "I'm gonna need an outside line later on."

Banish was looking across at him. "OK," he said.

Fagin nodded, looking back up, then skyward again. "What's
with these fucking stars?" he said, meaning to change the subject.
"Jesus. It's like Vegas."

Banish nodded. "You get used to it."

The bonfire snapped loudly and they both turned their attention
toward it. The blaze had lost some of its strength, blowing more
white smoke than before. Fagin's men were obviously lingering at
that point, done with their meals and just shooting the shit, hanging
around the bonfire to kill time and delay the inevitable return to
duty. Fagin let them. This brief fire was their whole Saturday night
and he wanted his men to have it.

He saw then the rookie cop crossing in front of the bonfire and
heading toward the mess trucks, alone. He noticed that Banish saw
the cop too, then turned right back around to the table. He seemed
angry, maybe with a bit of surprise. Then it seemed as though he was
reconsidering it or thinking of something else. Gradually he came to
look heavy-eyed, staring down at the table. He might even have
looked sorry. It was a strange look for Banish.

"That rookie cop," Fagin said with a jab of his chin. "What's his
name?"

Banish was looking at his plate. "I think, Kearney," he said.

Fagin nodded. "There's a story there. The short version is: A
couple of my men were making noise over dinner last night about
you Fibbies, and also a little about how you yourself were handling
things here. Just talk, right?" Fagin leaned forward, pointing toward
the fire and grinning wide. "Kearney here was the only one who
stood up for you. With all the GS grades on this fucking mountain,
the only one willing to take on the entire nail-chewing, bad-ass U.S.
Marshals Service SOG was him. A traffic cop from North Bumfuck.
I don't know—tough, or just shit out of brains? What do you
think?"

Banish gave no response. He was staring at the square of corn-bread left on his plate. He seemed to have been saving it, but now he looked as though he didn't want it at all.

Fagin was about to ask him for it when another agent came rushing up to Banish's side. Coyle, her name was, the librarian from the command tent.

"Sir," she said, talking fast. "Agent Banish. We received a trans-mission signal from the mountaintop and a voice on the CB. I think it's Ables, sir. He says he wants to talk to you."

Command Tent

Banish entered, Coyle in front of him, Fagin behind. Perkins was there already with the other command tent agents, including a few technicians, standing around the CB radio at the switchboard desk. "Hook up the recorder," Banish instructed one of them; to another, "Get this all down." The technician went to work on the CB wiring, the agent grabbing a pad and pen. Banish looked over at Perkins and said, "We're sure it's him?" and Perkins was about to answer in the affirmative when a hiss of static came on over the CB, then the voice.

"Watson. I know you're out there."

It was breathy and not too heavily accented, slight, not deep. Banish licked his dried lips, watching the agents hurrying around the CB. It was a broadcast channel and therefore unsecured. The entire county could be listening in, but too much time had passed and Banish needed to talk to Ables now. He realized he would be play-ing to two audiences.

It was respectfully quiet in the tent. He set himself mentally as he watched the technician work. He reviewed some must-ask questions and fleshed out a rough preliminary strategy. Ables was catching him off-guard but not unprepared. The technician switched on the recorder and the tape reels began to turn. He backed out of the way and Banish sat down and picked up the handset, thumbing down the trigger.

"This is Special Agent Watson," he said. "Mr. Ables?"

The voice came back. "Watson."

"Mr. Ables. Is everyone all right in there? I want you to know first of all that your family's safety is our primary concern."

No response. Nothing over the CB but the hitch of dead air.

"What happened with Mr. Mellis?" Banish asked.

"Don't worry. He made it back safe and sound. We're all here together."

Brick wall. Banish bore down.

"Mr. Ables, listen. I was not injured, and neither was the county sheriff with me. Now I want to work with you to end this thing as soon as possible, before someone on either side gets overanxious and there's a loss of life."

Ables said, "There already was."

Banish said, "We're still not entirely clear on what happened to the marshal." It was thought displacement—Banish feeling Ables out. An isolated suspect could often be made to believe what he wanted to believe through simple suggestion, even when the truth facing him was certain and contradictory.

Ables said, "I'm talking about my Judith."

Banish looked up. He saw the tape reels slowly turning, then glanced beside him and found Fagin. Fagin said simply, "Fuck."

Banish returned to the CB, pressing the thumb switch down. "That is exactly what I'm trying to avoid more of, Mr. Ables. I was actually, however, referring to future charges possibly being brought against you."

Ables's flat voice rose for the first time. "I couldn't get a fair trial in these Jew courts."

"Mr. Ables, I have no bearing or opinion on your current case. I am here simply to expedite your safe delivery over to the proper authorities."

"What's that?" Ables said, as though he hadn't heard correctly.

"You out there are the authorities. You're the FBI. You've got orders to shoot and kill me. It's all one big cartel of freedom oppression come over from the East. You people are the murderers here."

"Mr. Ables, let me say that we regret, deeply, the initial altercation and subsequent misfortune that has befallen you and your family—"

"I don't want your words, Watson. You listen to me now, phone cop. Don't you talk about my daughter."

"Mr. Ables—"

"Shut up. Don't you talk to me about Judith, Watson. Just shut up out there and listen. Here is why I am talking to you at all. You stinking sons of bitches lie. You talk and you double-talk, and all of it lies. You think I'd listen to you now? I got a radio up here. I know what they're calling me on it. They're calling me a child molester. All up and down the dial. I keep hearing it over and over and over."

Banish shut his eyes again. He could feel Perkins standing behind him, but it was not worth the effort to turn around.

Ables kept going. "You dirty sons of bitches. This is how you want me to go out. You're clearing the way for the kill. You, the child murderers, calling *me* sick—"

"Mr. Ables," Banish said, "the FBI has no belief, knowledge, or reason to suspect you of any criminal or immoral activity whatsoever involving your family."

"I have a radio," Ables said.

"Mr. Ables—you have to understand the situation down here. I am but one man. When you don't talk to me, the other personnel here have a job to do, to try and induce you into giving up your family and coming out, and I have no influence over their actions."

"Then put on someone who does. Put on the son of a bitch who called me a child molester."

"No, Mr. Ables—your talking to me now gives me some leeway. If we can make progress together working things out through a dialogue, you and I, then this whole thing can proceed a lot more smoothly and safely. Which is why I am encouraged that you finally contacted me. Why haven't you taken the telephone inside, Mr. Ables?" Banish was trying to regain control over the conversation.

Ables said, "If I step one foot out of this house, you will blow me away. You proved that."

"Mr. Ables—if you give me your word that they will not be harmed, I can dispatch men immediately to deliver that telephone right up to your front porch—"

"I give you nothing, Watson, and anyone steps on my porch, it's the last step they take. I've done too much talking already. I know why you want me on that phone. So no one else can hear. That's shady right there, and you want my trust."

Banish held his mouth with a full hand, slowing down the conversation, picking his shots. The mistakes of New York City weighed heavily on his mind. "I do want your trust, Mr. Ables. And I'd like the chance to prove that to you. Is there anything I can get for you now, anything you need? You must be very low on food and water in there. I'm thinking especially of the infant—clean diapers, baby food?"

"You'd drug the food and poison the water. And nothing you won't give me without a trade. I know what's going on. I am through talking now. All I want from you is for everyone to just go away and leave me and my family alone."

"Mr. Ables, we can't leave."

"Well then, neither can I."

There was a sharp click and then the hiss of dead air. Banish weighed briefly the prospect of trying to get Ables back on the line, then dismissed it and set down the handset.

"He's canny," he said, sitting back, nodding. "He's been waiting for this for a long time."

Fagin said, "He's fucking pissed is what he is."

"He's grandstanding. He knows he has an audience out there and he wants his side told. That's good. That's very good. Twice he said he was talking too much, then kept right on going. And hear him refer to a trial? He doesn't want to die up there." Banish gestured at the CB with confidence. "That's no death wish. He's think-ing about the future."

"But no deadlines," Fagin said. "No demands. Nothing to nego-tiate."

"He was feeling us out. Trying to get a better look at things down here."

Banish stood, recharged. He saw Perkins standing behind every-one in that disappearing way he had. "Stupid," Banish said. "But it got him to talk. He needs more convincing. I want to step up Tacti-cal. More noise, a tighter net. Roving searchlights. Helicopters buzz-ing the cabin every five minutes." He turned to Coyle. "Put some-one on this CB full-time and keep that channel clear. Anything else comes through, I am to be called immediately."

He glanced about the tent. This was progress, solid progress, the preliminary pawn-takes-pawn, slow-dance maneuvering finally pay-ing off. Banish paced. He told himself to be patient. There would be no sleep for him again that night, too many things to think about, to review, to prepare. Too many loose ends to consider. He had to get out of these tents. He needed to get out into the open air and settle his head.

He caught Fagin as he was leaving. "Send someone over to suit me up," he said. "I'm going to sit out a watch tonight."

Paradise Point

Banish crouched on his knees in a gully thirty-five yards below the cabin. The stadium lights were all off now, a single searchlight trawling the patchwork of pitted scrap wood in the distance, illumi-nating in roving circular sections the lopsided cabin that was the focus of all their attention. The refuse of their few days there—the bullet casings, half-devoured dog carcasses, tree limbs, the phone—littered the thinning, sloping land in between.

He turned and sat against the dirt wall with his back to the cabin. His radio and a 7mm Remington rifle were on the ground by his side. There had been no cure for the problem of the decomposing dogs—what the coyotes had not already torn off and taken away— only a treatment, and Banish decided he needed more of it. He brought out the small glass jar of Vicks VapoRub and smeared himself a generous gel mustache over the greasepaint camouflaging his face.

He was positioned behind and to the left of the loudspeaker. The pleading voices he heard seemed to come from ghosts deep within the trees.

Margie. It's mother. Your father's here with me, we're both praying for you. Margie—enough is enough. Glenn, you too. Just come down now. There's no point to this anymore. We've got four beautiful grandchildren, including little Amos we've never even seen. There's nowhere you can all go, and now your father and me can't imagine what you're up there waiting for. The babies' lives are in your hands. Just come to your senses, all of you. For their sakes. You need to keep them safe now. Then we can make funeral arrangements for Judith.

Silence then. Banish heard a helicopter approaching over the trees.

Marjorie. It's your father. Come home.

The Huey roared low, ripping apart the thin air overhead and rumbling the ground. Dead leaves fluttered and fell in dozens and the treetops wagged in its wake.

Kearney appeared standing at the top of the opposite side of the gully. His face was obscured by greasepaint and he wore a borrowed, loose-fitting camouflage jumpsuit, vest, cap. Banish looked up at him from where he was seated. Kearney said "You wanted to see me?" with affected toughness, but it was plain to Banish that Kearney was more than a little nervous.

Banish told him, "You'd better come down from there."

Kearney looked up to the cabin and saw that he was well within the line of fire. He dropped down into the gully, and after a moment of standing there, squatted down and sat back against the dirt wall opposite Banish. From there he looked around. His lips came out a bit and his brow furrowed.

"Dead dogs," Banish said, tossing him the Vicks. Kearney looked at the small jar with suspicion. He unscrewed the cap and sniffed, the folds in his brow evening out. "Under your nose," Banish said. Kearney pulled off a glove and began to apply it. Banish said, "How long have you been married?"

Kearney's eyes shot to the gold band on his bare finger but he managed to check his overall response.

"Almost a year now," he admitted.

"No kids?"

Kearney shook his head. "One on the way."

"You hid that ring when I had you in formation."

"Yes, sir."

Banish nodded. "Maybe you see why I did that now. This is no place for a man with a wife and children."

"Yes, sir."

"But you wanted to be a part of things," Banish said. "Nothing would have kept you away."

"I guess that's so, sir."

Banish looked at him, nodding. "Why do you think I selected you? Out of all those others."

Kearney said, "I don't know, sir."

"Do you think it was anything more than an efficient way of paring down the number of men?"

Kearney looked at him a while. "I guess I don't really know, sir."

Banish slipped deeper into thought. Another disembodied voice in the woods pled with the cabin. Banish looked up and down the darkened gully. "This is where the dead marshal was posted before he was shot."

Kearney regarded the gully solemnly and set down the jar of Vicks, his white eyes showing respect.

Banish set himself as comfortably as he could against the hard dirt wall. "There's an old FBI tradition," he said, "on a surveillance, of telling stories. When I first came up, it was Hoover stories. Everybody had one. J. Edgar Hoover was an idiosyncratic man, he never married, and his assistant, a nonagent named Clyde Tolson—well, they were pretty tight. So there was talk. The kind of stories you could only tell to a fellow agent, because if you talked to anybody on the outside, next week your name could wind up on a list in somebody's drawer."

Banish folded his arms across his vest. "I was the most successful hostage negotiator of my time. I held the position of Chief Hostage Negotiator for the New York City FBI Field Office from 1979 to 1990. In those eleven and a half years I never once lost a hostage, never once failed to effect a resolution. How? Negotiation. Deception. Intimidation. Things I am not now very proud of. My most effective tactic, the one in certain circles I'm probably best known for, was to bring to the scene the wife, mother, child, whatever— some close relative of the hostage-taker—get some personal information from them, and then go to the phone and make veiled indications to the suspect about what might happen to his family if he didn't give himself up. 'Whatever it takes' was my motto. He takes a hostage, you take a hostage. By any means necessary.

"I was a hotshot and I got results, and that was all anybody cared about. Nobody questioned it, least of all me. Nothing else mattered so long as the job got done. And I was a pretty good drinker those days. Never on the job, always after. Interesting thing about a hostage situation: you can never walk away cold. There's a downtime afterward when you have to get together with the other men involved and toss back a few, to relieve that tension, that adrenaline, whatever it is, to flush it out of your system for good. Primitive therapy, but absolutely necessary, because there is no one else you can share it with except those who went through it with you. Not your wife. Not your kids, your clergyman. And that was when I really held court. Those were exciting times—heady—and I guess I came to live for them, situation after situation, triumph after triumph. Like a drug, over and over. I was at the top of my game then. In other words, I was pretty well primed for a long fall." He nodded, surprising even himself with his candor. It relaxed him to tell it. Didn't it all seem so clear to him now. "Ever heard of the World Trade Center?" he said.

Kearney nodded. "Seen pictures. Where that bomb went off in New York City."

"This was almost three years before that. A huge place it is, with two zip codes of its own, millions of people passing through it every week. A large complex of buildings and tunnels and walkways. This was at the World Financial Center, which is part of the complex but separate from the twin towers. Tuesday night late in June. Raining hard, I remember, because this was lower Manhattan down near the Hudson, and Vesey Street was flooded and shiny black when we pulled up outside.

"A Cuban national had taken his wife and daughter and thirty-seven other people hostage on the Fixed Income Trading Floor of one of the largest brokerage firms in New York, seven stories up. We were called in as feds because it was thought initially to be some sort of Free Cuba ploy or other act of terrorism. Turned out later it was just the messy end of a simple domestic dispute. He was a maintenance worker in the building, a heavyset guy who had been beating his Cuban-born wife for more than a year and had started in recently on their twelve-year-old daughter. For this, and various other reasons, the wife had become very unhappy with her life in America and decided to steal the child away from him and move back in with her mother's family in Cuba. But for some reason, she decided to go to his work to tell him of her intention, and brought along the daughter. Two policemen responding to initial reports of a disturbance in the lobby of the World Financial Center were overpowered.

The Cuban took their guns, chemical Mace, and car keys, went out yelling into the street, got the shotgun from the trunk of their cruiser, then retreated back into the building with his wife and daughter up to the seventh floor, where he took over.

"Logistics were a problem from the beginning. The seventh-floor trading area was wide open, an L-shaped football field of rows and rows of desks spaced by white rectangular columns, and two stories high. For security reasons, the elevator did not stop there after six at night, so the only way you could get in was if you had permission—Capital Markets salesmen catching up on work after the markets closed—or were a maintenance man with keys. There was no eighth floor, except for a side flight of stairs leading to a catwalk elevation of desks and offices above the trading area. He had barricaded that entrance and said it was rigged to a bomb. That was nonsense, but forced entry was an operational no-go regardless, as the upper area was visible from almost anywhere on the trading floor below.

"The next lowest floor was the fifth, the Equity Trading Floor, which was also two stories high and therefore prohibitive in terms of gaining access through the ceiling. The floor above Fixed Income Trading, the ninth, the Public Finance Trading Floor, was just one story tall, but too far above the seventh floor to be effective. Even if we broke through the floor itself, Hostage Rescue would have had to rappel unprotected down forty feet of wide-open space.

"The one thing the seventh floor did have was telephones. Hundreds of them, on every desk throughout the trading area. We established a control base on the fifth floor below and evacuated and sealed off all the floors above the seventh. By this time it was late at night, so the evac went quietly and smoothly. I got him on the phone right away. One ring. He was too distraught for English, so we used an interpreter. I made progress quickly, getting some hostages released in exchange for meals he had requested from a small Cuban restaurant off Fulton Street. We had to locate the proprietor in Bed-ford-Stuyvesant and get him to come in and open up the place in the middle of the night. He said the suspect had eaten lunch there every day for more than two years. The waitresses all knew him by name.

"We negotiated through the night. I said yes to everything he wanted in exchange for more hostages, while at the same time moving Hostage Rescue snipers and assault specialists into position, filling the stairwell with guns and men and working on rewiring the elevators. I talked him down finally to just thirteen hostages, seven male and six female, including his wife and daughter.

"The suspect was clearly unbalanced. One moment he was demanding to talk to his mother in Cuba, and the next, Castro himself. He was unstable. His life had somehow gotten away from him, he felt powerless, and he said many times that he had nothing left to live for. That was my main concern. You have to give a hostage-taker some sense of responsibility, some meaning to his actions. Otherwise, there is nothing stopping him from executing the hostages and you've lost him. I remember I convinced him at one point to put his wife on the phone. I can't recall now what she told the interpreter. But I do remember her crying. I remember her praying."

Banish stopped a moment to collect his thoughts.

"The problem with using a public phone line in a hostage situation is that anybody can call in. This was a major concern, as we had been through recent scenarios where television reporters telephoned hostage-takers for interviews in the heat of a standoff. For that reason alone, I wanted to shut down all the phones on the Fixed Income Trading Floor, save one. This was met with resistance on three fronts. First, the World Financial Center managing group had made numerous legal guarantees to the brokerage firm, among them the provision that WFC could secure their offices and operating space against unlawful intrusion and provide adequate communications service at all hours. New York Telephone had made a similar agreement with the firm, and was having trouble anyway locating a technician who could circumnavigate the complex WFC branch exchange at that late hour. Then representatives for the firm itself arrived on the scene. Lack of telephonic access to the Fixed Income Trading Floor during normal operating hours would be devastating enough, they said, but a Wednesday morning shutdown of the Equity Trading Floor, which we were currently occupying, not only meant the instant loss of millions of dollars in business, but would have serious repercussions on the opening of the New York Stock Exchange and various financial markets around the world.

"So I listened to them. And I held off. I sent someone down to talk to the news media camped out in the lobby below, to play up the risk to the hostages and get them to agree not to attempt to contact the Cuban under threat of arrest. I should have just gone ahead and cut the cords and let everybody fight it out afterward, but I did not. I let it go. The phone lines remained open while our people scrambled to get a court order, and I sat back patiently to wait.

"There was this morning radio personality in New York City. Very popular in that market. About six in the morning he comes on, reads the news off the overnight wire, and gets the bright idea to try and call the Cuban. He gets through and puts the Cuban on the air live. We didn't know it was happening until they were about halfway through. The DJ was asking the Cuban questions and drawing him out about his family and his troubles, and basically trying to talk the man down—but using pop psychology. There is nothing more dangerous than that. The Cuban was getting all wound up again and starting to lose his English, after I had worked all night to stabilize him. Then we started hearing phones going off upstairs. One after another, and by the time I realized what was happening, it was too late. This DJ's listeners had figured out that they too could dial the firm's exchange, plus four random numbers, and have a chance to talk directly to the hostage-taker themselves. I sent men down to the communications center with fire axes but it was too late, there were already a hundred telephones going off all around this guy, and every other caller telling him, *Kill them.*

"Then we start hearing gunshots. The Cuban is losing it, firing wildly, at the floor, up into the air. Then he comes back on our phone. He's screaming about executions. He says he's going to kill all the hostages one by one. My people begin to scramble and I get into the elevator at this point. I do not know why. The negotiator never participates in any arrests, but the situation was starting to slip away from me—*me,* you see—so in the confusion I grabbed a portable phone and went inside the elevator. We were jammed in there— myself, a technician, and six HRT members, all just two floors below him. The elevator had been rewired and was ready to go. I called up to the ninth floor, and our sonar equipment placed him not ten feet away from the elevator doors, some forty feet away from the hostages. More wild shooting then. I didn't have any choice. I pushed the button for the seventh floor. I gave the order to fill the room with gas and sent my men in."

Banish was staring straight ahead. He was watching the elevator door slide open, seeing it all happen again through the smoky plastic shield of a gas mask. The confusion, the yells, the pushed bodies. Gunshots, screams.

He heard the single shot. He saw the prone legs kicking, blood darkening the floor. "The Cuban took his own life. A single round to the temple, just as we broke in."

People in business suits screaming, wailing, lying on the floor. "The firm's employees were traumatized but each of them got out OK."

Banish remembered running up to the side wall of the smoky room. He watched it all happening. He saw them there. "But the wife and daughter—he had stood them up against a wall away from the rest of the hostages, tied with a thin wire cord around each of their necks to keep them still. I had sent the gas in. They both lost consciousness just as we arrived. Their own weight dragged them down."

He saw them sagging forward from the wall by their necks, throats sliced open ear to ear. Dangling hands twitching spasmodically, run red with blood. His own men trying frantically to cut them loose from the wall. Mother and daughter dying right there in front of him.

A dark woman in a sundress with a black eye and bruises on her arms. A twelve-year-old girl.

Roaring thunder approached his consciousness and then a helicopter buzzed over them, its spotlight running past, and Banish saw where he was again, the ground and the gully before him, and for a frozen instant everything glowed white. Then the helicopter passed and the shaken leaves drifted like regrets to the dirt around them. Banish cleared his throat.

"So we went out afterward. It was different, of course, all different. And when it was over I could not go home. I didn't, until three days later. And I did not stop drinking from that day on. Gradually, and then rather spectacularly, I fell apart."

Banish was quiet for a while.

"And the freed hostages. More than half of them quit their jobs within six months. That's standard following a crisis like that; people yanked out of their daily routines, isolated, terrorized. One night can last you a lifetime. But one young woman, the first to leave the firm, refused to cooperate with her appointed psychiatrist. Eventually she disappeared altogether. It's what is known as the Stockholm Syndrome. She came to identify her captor as her savior—rather than the police, with whom she had no contact—because her captor held the power of life and death over her and she had been spared. She got my name somehow and tracked me down at a hospital I was staying at. She had a gun and she tried to kill me. Fair trade, I'd say, except that she bungled the job. But that is what you get for playing with other people's lives."

He looked at Kearney then, across the cold mountain gully surrounded by the pleading woods. Banish said, "Do you understand what I'm trying to say?"

Kearney hesitated, then nodded.

"I am nobody's hero. I don't like some of the things I have to do."

I have too much power, too much responsibility. Too many hands. That's why these protesters—I could have pushed them all the way back to the Pacific if I'd wanted to. But I need them here. They will keep me from doing things I might otherwise do. Whatever their motives for being here, that is what they are: eyes, to watch me. Because I am not to be trusted. Because I am a gambler—that's all I am. And a pretty good one. That's my curse."

Kearney was blinking at him. He started to say something, censored himself, then went ahead and said it anyway. "But it wasn't your fault."

Banish smiled weakly at the sentiment. Familiar words of counsel. They must have tasted warm on the tongue. But hearing them again did have the effect of sobering him.

"We talked to Ables tonight," Banish said. "I'm reassigning you to the command tent, starting oh-eight-hundred hours tomorrow."

Kearney's white eyes cleared then. He nodded. "Yes, sir."

Banish realized he was leaning forward. He sat back against the hard dirt wall again. There was an awkward moment of nodding silence on both sides, then a muffled pop. Banish turned his head to listen, uncertain. When nothing followed immediately, he crouched and turned fully to look up through the trees at the cabin. The searchlight was still. Then a crack out of the night like a cap being fired, and a hiccup burst of light—a shot from somewhere high in the trees above. Banish grabbed for his radio on the ground next to him. "Fagin," he said.

Sniper's Nest

Fagin scanned the compound with his NVD. Like looking into a fucking aquarium. He answered the voice in his ear.

"Wasn't me," he said. "Is that fucking HRT?"

Banish said, "Situation report."

"Warning shot. Something moving out there, don't know what the fuck it is."

Banish's voice came back. "Fagin, warnings only. Everyone else hangs back. I'll get someone on the lights."

Fagin clicked off. It was fucking Hostage Rescue. He slipped his finger back in over the trigger and stayed alert. He could see nothing clearly because of the goddamn spotlight burning into his NVD— there was glare, although the light being still now made things easier. A second light came on low then and swept the woods. The stinging odor of the Vicks put a throb in his head. He heard the whup-whupping of the Huey returning. The whining of Ables's family on the speakers down below. Another cold wind wheezing through the trees. He frowned hard. Happy fucking anniversary.

Something moving again in the greenness. He blinked several times, scoping the area.

A figure outside, an adult, standing just beyond an open door at the right side of the cabin where the land began to drop off. Something in its hands, maybe a gun, but impossible to confirm. Fagin heard the helicopter coming faster, the treetops starting to bend. He cursed the glare of the spotlight. The side door was still wide open. He fired once more, another generous warning, this time low and wide to the figure's right. Whoever it was, Fagin wanted the person back inside pronto.

Banish's voice again in his ear, "Fagin."

The Huey roared and whupped right overhead, cruising in on a low sweep. Fagin saw the figure looking up. He saw it raising the object in its hands as the Huey floated over the trees.

He saw a burst pattern of gunfire from the dark figure.

Fagin said, "What the fuck—"

The helicopter was bailing out. Fagin tapped on his radio. "Fucker's shooting at the Huey."

Banish's voice came back. "Who?"

Fagin dropped two more rounds and watched two patches of green ground jump black near the figure's legs.

The figure ducked and swung around toward Fagin, returning fire. The Huey was gone and Fagin could hear the shots accompanying the fireburst as the figure moved back toward the open door. "Stupid fuck," he said. He took aim and paced the running figure with trailing shots.

Rounds strafed the leaves above Fagin's head. He ducked and reaimed. "Motherfucker," he said, angry, squeezing the trigger, plugging away.

Banish said, "Fagin."

Fagin picked surgically at the ground by the figure's feet, chasing it back to the door. It let go one final volley and then ducked inside. Fagin came up on the last one, depositing a single black chip hole in the glowing green door.

The door was slow to close.

"Fagin."

He pulled the Remington off his cheek and clicked back on. "What the fuck!" he said.

Banish said, "Sit-rep."

Fagin was near breathless with anger, but Banish wanted control on the network, a concise situation report. "Hostile gunfire, unprovoked," Fagin said. "One individual. I moved it back inside and left a round in the fucking door. That's all."

Banish said, "This is for everyone: we're hitting the lights."

Fagin pulled off his NVD and slammed the helmet down against the wood planking of the perch. "Fuck!" he said. He was thinking about how long it had taken that fucking door to close.

When the stadium lights clanked on and bleached the cabin, there was nothing left to see.

Sunday, August 8

Command Tent

Banish entered from the light morning rain and wiped the bottoms of his shoes on two muddied towels set down inside the flap door. Kearney was there already, seated at the switchboard and wearing a telephone receiver headset, manning the outside lines. He did not look up. Banish turned to Coyle, who was ready for him.

"The road should be finished later today," she reported. "Nothing yet on the CB. Do you want to try and raise him?"

"No," Banish said. "We have to get him on that phone."

"Excuse me." It was Kearney's voice. He was swung toward them, the single earphone pulled off his ear. "A woman on the telephone just said, 'Stand by for Alpha Four'?"

Banish looked at him a moment, then told Coyle to order everybody out of the tent.

Coyle made the announcement, moving with the rest of them up and out of their chairs, setting down coffee cups and pencils, leaving work unfinished on desks and filing out past him through the door. Kearney looked around and followed suit without question, removing the headset and leaving it on the console and walking out with the rest.

Banish moved to Coyle's desk. He punched the button on her

telephone and took up the receiver, standing and waiting patiently through the silence. Alpha Four was the transmission code name for the Director of the FBI.

"Jack," the Director said, his rich, senatorial voice coming on the line without a click. "What's the good word?"

"We finally made contact with the individual last night."

"I know," said the Director. "I read the transcript in this morning's *Post*. It's not going very textbook, Jack, is it."

"No, sir," Banish said.

He envisioned the Director nodding on the other end. "A funny world sometimes, Jack. What the general public will latch on to. What the media will pursue. But you know there's great interest in a case when you're at a breakfast meeting and the President asks you how it's going in Montana." A pause then, but not dramatic; the Director was a deliberate man. "I know things are escalating out there, Jack. Administration tells me you're up over a million dollars a day. People are watching this very closely."

Banish said, "Yes, sir."

"I've already had the Governor of Montana on the phone this morning. He's going to declare a state of emergency. He was also ready to call out the National Guard, but I scotched that. I was able to convince him how serious a mistake that would be. Just to give you some idea of what's going on out here, Jack. People are beginning to lose their heads over this. I'd say it's the death of the girl, chiefly."

Banish nodded. "Yes, sir." He saw then what was coming.

"Jack, Sam Raleigh's just gotten off that Port Authority situation in L.A. You may know, he was with the first negotiating team in Waco, the one that had so much success in getting the children out before Tactical took over. I know that he was your number two in New York before SOARs was established, and Carlson says he still speaks very highly of you."

Banish nodded. "Yes, sir."

The Director said, "I have a decision to make here, Jack. I was wondering if you could make it any easier for me."

Four days after his reassignment, here it was finally. The arrow pointing home. A few quiet words to the Director, as smooth as an easy handshake, and he would fade back into the woodwork again, perhaps walk off the mountain that very afternoon, without fear of penalty and without disgrace. The Director was making it very easy for him. He could return to Skull Valley and continue the regimen he had set for himself there, and ride out his last few years to retirement and a full government pension.

But the situation. Recently, and in spite of himself, ever since hearing from Ables the day before, he had been thinking more and more about the children inside the cabin. Not so much as hostages, but as children. Three girls and an infant boy. He wanted them safe. Perhaps more than he should have. He wanted them well. It was a new sensation for him, seeing a hostage as anything other than a marker to be bargained for and won, although it was a common enough affliction and something he had witnessed numerous times before. Like a fever, it would strike even the most disciplined of men in the heat of a negotiation, becoming a hindrance only when manifested in the form of desperate acts committed out of frustration or anger misdirected at fellow agents. Either case warranted immediate dismissal. But other than that, this syndrome, Banish's affliction, now seemed to him entirely reasonable. You don't ask a man to carry around plutonium for a week, then have him hand it off to the next man and walk away and wait for the poison. Banish looked around at the vacated command tent. He felt strongly the drag of the small community he had created there. Its purpose had become his purpose. Leaving was no longer a viable option. He must not merely remain on the mountain; he must succeed.

"Sir," he said, "I don't think I could respect myself if—"

"Jack, I'm behind you. I've always been behind you. I think you know that. But my concerns are necessarily broader. I have faith in your talents, Jack, I do, but this operation has become much too significant for us to risk it being bungled. I need reassurance. Besides, Carlson says that as he understands it, you resisted the assignment from the beginning."

Banish was recalling the day almost three years ago when he was told to walk away from his wife and daughter and never return. This assignment was his second chance at redemption, both personally and professionally, and perhaps his last.

"Sir," Banish said, straightening when there was no one to see him there, "I'd like to stay on."

Staging Area

The rain was falling harder and the wind was picking up, and Fagin stood waiting in it, his plastic poncho blown flat and wrinkled against his broad back. Two of Fagin's men stood under nylon rain jackets near him, while a few yards away six members of the FBI Hostage Rescue Team were huddled together in their traditional black ninja uniforms. Banish was late to the meeting as usual.

Fagin turned. Two of the eight HRT agents stared at him coldly. Fagin shook his head a little but did not expend much effort. Stupid fucking mind games. Junior league interagency sandbox shit.

HRT was the FBI's elite paramilitary force, trained to capture terrorists, hostage-takers, and violent criminals in life-threatening situations. Their team was made up of fifty volunteer agents split into three revolving units, with one unit on alert at all times and available for emergency assignment within a few hours anywhere in the country. They were assault specialists and top-flight snipers whose training regimen included what Fagin referred to as the Bayer drill, the ability to snipe an aspirin tablet at two hundred yards. In terms of prestige, equipment, and their five-million-dollar annual budget, HRT made the U.S. Marshals Special Operations Group look like Double-A ball, and Fagin was man enough to admit this professional envy, but only to himself.

He found resentment a much more pleasurable emotion. HRT agents were largely range-taught, not war-trained like himself. Honing their talents by picking off over-the-counter pain medicine at Quantico's Hogan's Alley test range, a five-acre simulated town of pop-up targets, seemed to Fagin like not much more than a parlor trick. Fagin had seen them misused by their commanders, trotted out before the cameras during high-profile but nonessential situations, and media-hyped to no end. That budget game that Congress played. It made men in the USG sing and dance like women in the USO.

Banish finally showed, head ducked to the rain, shoes sinking into the muddy ground. He eyed the two segregated groups of BOLOs. Fagin made no move to cojoin. He was expecting a nice clean whitewash here.

"Who fired that first shot?" Banish said above the downpour.

One of the HRT agents spoke up, name of Renke. Plump-faced but solidly built, big hands. "We spotted a suspect exiting the side of the residence armed with a rifle of some kind, crouching in a furtive manner."

Banish said, "Adult figure?"

"Affirmative. I had the suspect in my Weaver scope."

Banish stopped him there, turned. "Fagin?"

"I saw someone come out, but couldn't make the object as a weapon until they started firing up at the NG helicopter. I was at six o'clock, head-on. The glare off the searchlight fucked my NVD."

Renke stepped in, saying, "SA Banish, Marshals Service has no command or say-so over HRT."

Banish's response was quick. "That's my determination, SA Renke. As your senior SOARs agent on this mountain, HRT answers to me, answers loud and answers clear. Deputy Fagin has been with this operation from the beginning, and if I so determine in the interests of convenience and/or mere whim that you men are to be placed at his disposal, then so shall it be." Banish got in Renke's face then. "Or do you feel the need to seek a second opinion from Quantico?"

Renke turned his eyes straight ahead. "No, sir."

"Good," said Banish, backing off. "Let me review for you men the rules of engagement on this mountain. Do not fire unless expressly fired upon. And even then: with extreme and diligent caution. Do not get drawn into an exchange. Every man will be held accountable for his actions here. If you had been with us over the past few days, you might have known that just last evening we received our first communication from the suspect. That alone renders your initial warning shot ill-advised at best. There are young children in the residence and they are armed and possibly dangerous, and that is what makes this operation such a challenge. And I know how you men like a challenge. That is all."

The HRT agents looked at each other and went away. Banish was showing some spark here. He came back to Fagin through the rain.

"Listen," Fagin said. "I've been giving it some thought. Last night. That side door didn't close right away."

Banish immediately shook his head. "Don't tell me that," he said. "I don't want to hear that. I just got off the phone with the Director and the subject of a gunfight did not come up."

"Well, I'm telling you. Now you know."

"What are you saying?" Banish said. "You hit somebody?"

"I was taking heat. I popped back high and hit the door once. That's all."

Banish looked away, then looked back. "You mentioned night-vision," he said. "Judith Ables was killed in the initial skirmish. How did they get her body all the way over to the barn without your men seeing anything?"

"We assumed they did it in the hour or so after the cease-fire, before we were moved into position."

"Right." Banish nodded. "But this is their twelve-year-old

daughter. This is a child. They've been living together in that same five-room shack for two years now. You think they could get rid of her corpse in less than an hour?"

Fagin thought about it, shrugged. "What I'm telling you is, we've had that cabin under twenty-four-hour surveillance since the original shootout. There is no way they could have carried a dead body over to that barn without me and my men knowing about it."

Banish nodded again. He was rubbing the burn on his face and looking up at the wet mountain.

Barn

A cloudburst on the way up, and the woods darkened some more and thumped with heavy rain. Marshals Taber and Porter stood posted outside as Fagin and Banish entered the run-down barn shaking off their coats. It still smelled of human death, rain rapping on the collapsing roof, piddling through to the ground. Fagin scanned the barn and moved directly to the far-left corner. Banish remained somewhere behind him, near the center, looking around.

There was a stack of old fruit crates in the corner, the only area of the barn where a section of floor was well concealed. Fagin tugged on the top crate with a gloved hand and met resistance. He checked it and saw that the bottom slat was nailed tightly to the top slat of the crate below, and so on. He bent over and stretched to reach the bottom crate farthest to the rear. It slid out freely without moving the rest. Fagin turned it over. No bottom slats. He examined the dirt there and saw that it was looser and finer than in other places and reached out and brushed the top layer aside, then dug in deeper with his gloves. The soil below was also loose. He stepped in beside the crates and dug some more and hit something hard about ten inches down. His fingers found a latch. He pulled on it and there was a rush of foul air and the entire section of dirt came up and out.

Fagin straightened up pissed off. "Fucking tunnel," he said, too loudly, and Banish came over beside him and Fagin lowered his voice. "Sneaky fuckers," he said.

Banish said angrily, "Jesus Christ."

"Fuckers," Fagin spat. "Motherfuckers. We go in there now with night-vision, take them by surprise—"

"No," Banish said. "Even if it isn't booby-trapped, they'd hear you halfway through and be waiting." He looked around. "Put two men in here, grab whatever crawls out. Why wasn't all this broken down in the first place?"

"My fuck-up," Fagin said. "Overlooked. *Fuck.*"

Banish looked around the barn, nodding. "He's been waiting for this," he said, then stepped away. He had said that a few times before.

Fagin checked the area around the tunnel hole. The opening was two feet square, the tunnel below much larger and the dirt walls brown and dark. He was thinking out loud, only half-talking to Banish. "They pulled the girl through here wrapped up in something else besides those sheets, then cleaned her up and took it back with them." He kicked at the hard ground. "Dirt here's tough. Must be the only tunnel. Took them all of two years just to push this fucking thing through."

He dropped the wood board back down with the chunk of dirt on top and kicked the loose soil over it and slid the crate back into position. Then his voice rose, directed at Banish somewhere behind him. "I'll have my people check the other buildings just in case. Can't run too deep. Fucking tunnel rats," he said, stepping back to shake his head. "Picked that up in Nam, huh? What do you say? Charlie could fucking dig. Honeycombs, they were, like those fucking ant farms you see into—storage rooms, kitchens, sleeping quarters. Had to be deep enough, though. I remember these cowboys in one of the units I was hooked up with, they'd take down a village rough, then pull aside all the remaining locals and bring in heavy equipment. They'd go riding in these big trucks, slow, all around the rice huts. That was how they celebrated. The weight of the trucks would cave in the shallow family tunnels, the local routes. You could hear the trapped VC screaming up through the dirt. Fucking ready-made graves, claustrophobic death traps."

He was shaking his head, remembering the war-whooping farm boys wheeling around in circles. He turned in annoyance when Banish did not respond. Banish was standing across the barn, near where the Ables girl had been found. He was looking down. Fagin moved aside a rusted-out lawnmower and started across to him.

He saw that Banish was holding the corner of a cracked sheet of black tarp in his right hand. The tarp was caked with heavy, dark dirt. A good-sized body lay below.

Fagin stopped behind Banish's shoulder, looking down. "Oh, fuck," he said.

Banish dropped the tarp and walked away. He walked right out of the barn and into the rain.

Fagin picked up the tarp again. Charles Mellis's eyes were still open. His face was drained white and his lips were wrinkled gray and curled back. There was a neat hole in his forehead and a dark spit-spray of dry brown blood on his cheek and much of his beard. Exit wound. Fagin tried to roll Mellis's head over but rigor mortis was setting in. His neck turned as much as a board. Fagin felt the dead arm and found it still soft. He knelt down low and eyed the crusted, bloody pulp behind Mellis's right ear, the burnt red hair and dislodged flap of exploded scalp.

Taber and Porter came in behind him, and Fagin stood. "Stay off the radio," he said. "This one's dead twelve hours. I'll start back down and notify." Then he pointed. "There's a rat hole in back. Keep your eyes on it and stay fucking alert, both of you."

Fagin exited into the blowing rain, the trees bending, his poncho whipping out hard. Banish was standing downhill from the barn.

"Flash burn at close range," Fagin said, coming up behind him. "It wasn't me. Whoever did it was standing right like I am here with you." Fagin fashioned a gun with his fingers and pointed it at the back of Banish's head above his right ear. Banish did not move. "Why would he do his own man?" Fagin said.

Banish said nothing. Fagin went around to see his face. Banish was looking far downland, into the trees.

Bridge

Blood was headed back to his Bronco through the rain when he saw Banish standing up on the mountain road just at the point where it began to curve and climb. Blood watched him a moment—Banish seemed to be watching the clustered umbrellas of the hundreds of protesters beyond the bridge, his face shadowed by the ashen burn—then tucked the papers he was holding into his sheriff's coat and started along the slicked road toward him.

"Just missed the show," Blood said, coming up. "Someone from WAR and some others came to the bridge for you. Wanted to make a citizen's arrest, they announced. Here's the warrant." He pulled out the papers. "I accepted it on your behalf. Not just you, though, it names as well the Director of the FBI, the head of the U.S. Marshals Service, the Bureau of Alcohol, Tobacco, and Firearms, the President of the United States, the Director of the CIA, the Governor of Montana, and, proud to say, yours truly."

Banish looked from the crowd on the other side of the bridge to the typed papers getting wet in Blood's hand.

Blood said, "That's some pretty fast company for me. But it was all just a big show of foolishness for the cameras. The arresting party all shook hands afterward."

Banish was looking straight at him. "Mellis is dead," he said.

Blood's lighthearted mood plummeted. His soul, what he thought of as the character of his person, seemed to vanish suddenly and his throat clucked under a swallow. The rain turned up a notch at that point, lashing him, finding a way through his clothes to his skin, raising gooseflesh. He was holding Banish's gaze because there was nowhere else to look. The rain slapped on his hat and it was all he could hear. It fell between them in lines as they stared. It fell all around. Puffs of their breath swirled. Mellis was dead. Blood didn't need to ask how.

He began to shiver. He experienced a weakening chill. He had tasted Banish's world and now felt sick. For the first time in his forty years, Blood wanted to be somebody somewhere else entirely.

"What do we do about this?" he said.

Banish shook his head. "You don't have to do a thing."

Blood looked away. The sound of the rain smashing his hat and the trees and the road grew louder in his ears, and he grew heavier beneath it. He turned back. "Why did your wife and daughter leave you?" he said.

"What?"

"I need to know what kind of man I am dealing with. I don't know anything about you beyond what I read in the papers. Why did your wife and daughter leave you?"

Banish's eyes became distant, pulling away, as though either making up an answer or trying to fit the unsayable into words.

"They were afraid of me," he said.

Any number of questions might have followed, but Blood found neither the strength nor the inclination. None of them anyway would have been delicate enough to broach that admission without breaking something that was already quite fragile. That was what Blood had tasted here. The sway of absolute power and the havoc it wreaked.

There were shouts now and then from the disorganized civil disturbance thriving beyond the bridge, yells sent up like bright flares. Then all at once the calls came in tandem and in force. Banish turned his attention past Blood, looking out over the vast mob with dark consternation.

"Ables," he said.

Blood turned. The umbrellas were beginning to scatter. A marshal was starting off the gloomy bridge toward them at a brisk jog. Banish said behind Blood, "Have the marshal take a Jeep and pick me up on the way."

He said the last of it as he was sloshing off. Blood put the silly papers back into his coat and met the marshal, related the instructions, then continued on to his original, dry destination, the Bronco. He climbed inside and pulled the door shut on the rain, removing his plastic-covered hat and shaking it out over the passenger floorboard. The rain thumped on the roof and hood. He sat watching the various umbrellas collapsing and figures disappearing into cars, wet parkas and hunting macks and raincoats retreating.

He unzipped his coat and switched on the CB. He worked the squelch. He started up the Bronco for the heat, to keep the car unfogged and warm. Then it hit him again that Mellis was dead.

The realization, the truth of it, came like shivers, in waves. That Blood had helped to kill him. That Mellis had tried to kill Blood. These feds were probably used to killings and death, living with it as they did from time to time. But Blood had never before been a part of anything like that. He had never felt so bad or so stained. He sat there and wondered what would become of him.

This swirl of increasingly troubled thought was broken by the crackling of the car radio. "Watson," it said hissingly. Blood recognized the voice from the mountain woods. That seemed like years and years ago.

Command Tent

Banish sat down at the console and Coyle called for quiet in the tent. Banish reached for the handset and flipped the switch. "This is Special Agent Bob Watson," he said.

"Watson," Ables said. "You son of a bitch."

"Mr. Ables?"

"You bastards shot my wife."

Banish stared at the radio. When he looked up, he found Fagin standing nearby, his stern face mouthing curses. Banish tightened his grip on the handset. "Mr. Ables," he said, "someone stepped outside your house and warning shots were fired. It was never our intention—"

"Your assassins missed their mark."

"How bad is she wounded, Mr. Ables? Can you give me some indication of where she was shot?"

"You sound concerned now, Watson."

Banish licked his lips and took a steadying breath. "Mr. Ables," he said, "why don't you just come out now? We can end this thing right here before anyone else gets hurt. Your wife will receive immediate medical attention."

There was a pause then, brief but unmistakable. "No," Ables said.

Perkins, behind Banish, said "He hesitated" as Banish's left hand darted out to shut him up.

"Mr. Ables, I can have an ambulance at your front door within thirty seconds. We have emergency medical technicians here, and helicopters equipped to airlift your wife to the hospital of your choosing."

"No."

"Then why don't you just release her, Mr. Ables? Let your wife go."

"Release her to the men that want to murder her? The men that slaughtered her daughter? You listen to me, Watson. I want bandages. I'm run out. Gauze and disinfectant and antiseptic and tape. And Percocet, something for the pain. And fresh water. Or do you want more blood on your hands?"

Banish removed his thumb from the handset. Fagin was already moving toward the tent exit. He did not need to be told where to go. The protesters down below were getting this word for word.

Banish resituated himself, fighting for concentration. It was still a negotiation like any other. He asked himself what he wanted most.

"Mr. Ables," he said, "first of all, for your own protection, until and unless you are ready to come out for good, I would advise you and your family not to leave the cabin again under any circumstances. Now, I am most certainly willing to provide your wife with the medical attention she requires, right away."

"No doctors," Ables said. "Just supplies."

"Whatever you want. But it has to be a two-way street. Mr. Ables, I know you know that I cannot simply give you something for nothing."

Another short pause. "Sons of bitches," he said.

"Perhaps through a fair and equitable exchange, Mr. Ables, we can begin on a course of reestablishing trust. Why don't you release one of your daughters?"

"No."

"The youngest, Esther. She can be properly cared for out here. We have a nurse standing by, and food, toys."

"No."

"Your infant son, then. Amos. His grandparents are here."

Ables said, "You will never tear this family apart."

Banish released the handset then, instituting a pause of his own. He waited deliberately. Behind him Perkins swallowed and cleared his throat noisily, small sounds of impatience and doubt. Banish turned the handset on again.

"The telephone, then, Mr. Ables," he said. "I want to privatize our conversations in the interest of public safety. If you can give me your word that you will use it to communicate with me, rather than this broadcast channel—"

"I told you, Watson. No men on my porch."

"Your word, Mr. Ables."

"No men on my porch!"

Banish nodded, satisfied. "Mr. Ables," he said, "I think we can work around that."

No-Man's-Land

Fagin took a Humvee and drove himself right up the side of the mountain. The dirt road was cleared and completed, but blocked near the top by a traffic jam of ambulances and fire equipment, mainly caused by a Bradley fighting vehicle being loaded off a flatbed truck. The one vehicle that Fagin could not ID was a small white unmarked van, open in back, a metal ramp leading down and footprints and other tracks in the wet ground around it.

He parked and stepped out into the mud. The rain had let up after midday, leaving a hanging dampness that brought out the fucking bugs again. Fagin crossed the short distance to the no-man's-land through the thinning tree cover, swatting flies.

No music now, no recorded messages. Just the hushed voices of agents hiding in the trees. He found them spread out along the edge of the no-man's-land, crouching behind tall, folding bulletproof shields set up like bedroom screens people dress behind. Banish was peering over one, looking through the shredded tree cover across thirty short yards to the cabin.

A robot, maybe three feet in height, a six-tractor-wheel base supporting a raised metal spine and a long, jointed mechanical arm, was wandering through the trees toward the phone. A remote console was set on the ground next to Banish, operated by a pale-looking agent with a dark crew cut. A monitor showed the machine's camera-eye view.

"The fuck is this?" Fagin said, though he knew full well. He was a practical man with a natural aversion to technology.

Banish did not answer. He wanted to know what had happened down below.

"We took away some guns and rifles, then stumbled onto something big. A cache of plastic explosives and egg cartons of hand grenades, souvenirs from the jungle."

Banish turned. "Veterans?"

"A counteroffensive. They were planning on taking out our microwave communications equipment. They see another brother being screwed by the government all over again. We were very fucking lucky this time, practically falling over them. Sixteen total arrests. But it raises a major concern."

"Post guards around the generators," Banish said. "If an attack comes, it will come there first."

Fagin nodded. "Already done."

It was too crowded behind the shield, so Fagin stepped out into the open and looked on with arms crossed. Severed tree limbs lay dead on the ground, the woods ripped apart, trunk bark scarred with ivory and greenish-white wood showing through. That had been a serious demonstration of artillery.

The robot had the phone case handle in its claw now and was grinding toward the cabin. Two containers were strapped to its base. "He's getting everything he wanted?" Fagin said.

"Except the painkillers. Could be fatal if administered improperly. He didn't ask for blood or plasma, so maybe it's not too serious."

"Water?"

"It's clean," Banish said.

"You can't mickey him?"

"Unreliable. Could be fatal if taken by a child."

The robot pulled up alongside the slanted front porch, its spine straightening hydraulically, arm extending out. Banish said to the pale agent working the controls, "A little closer."

Fagin watched the robot roll back and forth into position. "Hope he doesn't kidnap your robot too."

Banish said to the pale agent, "Not too close."

Fagin grinned briefly. Bureaucrats with their toys. He went and watched on the black-and-white monitor as the robot dumped its gifts on a stack of logs piled underneath a boarded-up window, then pulled back slowly. They watched and waited, Fagin growing impatient. Banish sent someone off to get his bullhorn. Then the boards moved, swinging open a few inches. A sleeveless male arm appeared. It snatched up the first-aid kit, then the satchel of water, then finally the telephone. Then the boards swung shut again.

The pale agent let out a long, gusty breath. In Fagin's experience, whether on bomb squad or crisis intervention teams, these robot controllers were all a little fucking fruity. Talking to themselves while they worked, calling their machines little names, like Buddy or Hal. Fucking ventriloquists without an act. This one mumbled to himself as he worked the slide gears up and down, easing the robot back to him.

Banish peered over the top of the shield again, probably waiting for something to go wrong. After all their waltzing back and forth, the actual exchange itself had been nothing. Secure communication had finally been established, but at a great goddamn cost.

Fagin stepped away from the screen, watching Buddy the Robot return home through the slaughtered woods. "That fucking telephone better be miked," he said.

Banish waved off a mosquito. "Don't worry."

Sound Truck

Banish pulled the sliding door open. The sound man was at his console, dials and recorders along the van walls all up and running. Banish said, "Anything?"

The sound man flipped a switch and a hollow sound came on over the speakers inside the van. Vague, distant noises, echoes reflected off walls, sounds of people moving around. "Mainly footsteps," he said. "Different sets. Some chatter about bandages. Not clear enough, though. He must have left the phone in front and gone into one of the rooms in the rear, possibly the kitchen."

"We're in," Banish said. It was all that mattered.

"You want me to ring him?"

The phone would ring abruptly twice like a bicycle bell, as opposed to a long ring or beeping noise, as different as possible from the sound any sort of bomb might make. The throw phone was just that, in most situations lobbed in through a door or window, and hostage-takers were notoriously paranoid and hypervigilant.

"No," Banish said, easing himself into the other chair, feeling his exhaustion. "We'll wait, and listen. Let him call us."

Monday, August 9

Sound Truck

Banish was sitting back in the swivel-tilt chair in the quiet low light of the van monitors, tired but not sleeping. He could hear the deep, regular breathing of the sound man, who had put his head down to rest for a moment on the console board more than two hours before. Banish realized he still did not know the man's name. But he let him sleep, and wished he could do the same. Banish sat in the humming darkness with his arms crossed over the borrowed parka he wore, the inside of the van not noticeably cold until just then. The van roof conducted the overnight chill. He was watching his breath mist and dissipate.

He had sat up the entire night. From time to time the noise-activated tape recorder reels clicked on and began their slow revolutions, but nothing audibly significant came out of the cabin: stray noises, rustling around, an occasional distant unintelligible voice. Banish was watching the monitors. Without daylight, the black-and-white images ran hazy, like photographic negatives. Now as day was starting to break, the cabin views, the empty road, the staging area, the bridge, all began filling in clearly, as though being tuned.

"Watson."

The sound man bucked his head and jerked awake, clattering his headphones atop the console. He sat up straight and looked around. "Sorry," he said, reaching for his headset.

Banish shook his head to show him it was all right. He picked up his own headset and put it on, adjusting the cushion comfortably over one ear, the opposing brace above the other. The tape reels had resumed their revolutions.

"Watson."

Patience. Control. He had spent all night waiting for this. Banish cleared his throat and fixed the connected microphone under his chin. He pushed the appropriate button, cutting off the van speakers and patching himself through.

"Mr. Ables," he said. "How is your wife doing?"

Ables's voice sounded strained. "She's all right now."

"We have an ambulance available, and two paramedics, just twenty-five yards away from your cabin door. If you look out your window, you can see them."

"She is all right," Ables said.

"Can you tell me where she was injured?"

"Her arm."

Banish nodded, encouraged. If it was just her arm, then Ables with his military background could treat her for days if necessary. Banish said, "I would ask you to put her on . . ."

"But she lost her voice to cancer," Ables said. "I bet you think you know a lot about us. I bet you got files and witnesses and depositions and everything. You're probably some kind of shrink yourself."

"I am not," Banish said. "Mr. Ables, have you given any more thought to coming out?"

"Never."

"What about your children, Mr. Ables? They are much too young to be going through this. Think of the effect this ordeal must be having on them."

"I warned you, Watson. Don't talk to me about my family. Don't talk like you know me. You want to do my kids some good, you all go away then. Because we can outlast you here. My kids are survivors, that's how they were raised. My kids are tough. Tougher than any man you got hiding behind a tree."

"You may be right about that, Mr. Ables," Banish said. "And believe me, no one is telling you how you should or should not raise your own children. But they are just children, Mr. Ables. Minors, all of them. This is a situation for adults."

"You don't get it, Watson. Do you. My kids *want* to be here. We're a family. There's no place else they'd rather be."

Banish said, "I do understand that, Mr. Ables. I understand how close-knit you and your family are. I'm sure a lot of people envy that closeness. That is what I am talking about. Mr. Ables—you must know that you can never get away from here. You are completely surrounded. This entire mountain is cut off from the rest of the world. We can sit out here and wait for you forever, and you can sit in there and wait for us, but the bottom line is, you are caught. You cannot escape. For all intents and purposes, you are already in police custody. Now, you have been charged with a serious crime. And your wife, by virtue of remaining at your side through all of this, has become an accomplice."

"You're trying to threaten me, Watson."

"No, Mr. Ables." Banish was shaking his head. "I am not. I am being straight with you here. I am giving you as much information as I can so that you are able to make an informed decision. If these men have to go in and extricate you from your home by force, then both you and your wife will be arrested and charges will be brought. If you are subsequently found guilty in a court of law, then your children, as minors, will likely become wards of the social services department of the state."

Ables said, "They would go to their grandparents."

"The grandparents could request a custody hearing," Banish said, nodding. "As could the Newlands or the Mellises. But there will be experts involved, child psychologists. They will likely testify that a lot of damage has been done to the children already, from the

psychological effects of this situation alone. I imagine they will rec-
ommend close treatment."

"Sons of—" Ables swallowed his anger.

"There is of course a chance that one of your in-laws could win
custody, Mr. Ables. But the determination would likely be that the
best way to monitor them would be to keep them away from relatives for the time being."

Ables's voice sputtered. "Sons of bitches," he tripped out.
"That's what this government is. Framing people, busting up families. You'll never arrest me, Watson—"

"If these men are forced to go into your home, Mr. Ables, your
children will likely be taken away from you. I am just making you
aware of this. They will be parceled out to foster homes—most of
which are run by good, family people—and then, depending on the
length of term of your and your wife's sentences, and the outcome of
the grandparents' hearing, the youngest of your children will likely
then be put up for adoption."

Ables let out an angry, choked noise. "So that's it," he said. "The
federal government establishment really got its teeth in now. Get
Ables at any cost. Frame him. Kill his daughter. Shoot his wife.
Smash up his family. But let the niggers and the drug dealers in the
streets run free. Let the faggots bend each other over in alleyways.
You tell me there's no conspiracy, Watson. You tell me that."

"I don't know what you are talking about, Mr. Ables."

"Tell me I haven't been selected for extermination by the execu-
tive council in Washington, D.C. Tell me there is no list with my
name at the top of it." His voice was rising. "Why do they hunt me
now, Watson? Because I speak the truth. Because I know what is the
real situation here."

"I don't know what you are referring to, Mr. Ables," said Banish. "I am merely trying to avail you of the facts—"

"So they're the meat and I am the maggot. Right? That's it right
there. They got me lined up so goddamn good."

A long break then, Banish sitting perfectly still. One virulent

"Goddamn!" shattered the silence, followed by more labored breathing.

"Watson," said Ables.

"Still here," said Banish.

"You tell me this, then," he said. *"Sons of bitches"*—a hissed aside. "You tell me what would happen to my family . . . *if* I surrendered."

Banish looked up from the console. Next to him, the sound man's face broadened into a wide, winning smile.

Command Tent

The meeting took place by the glass-wall diagram inside the command tent around nine in the morning that day, whatever day it was. Brian was working the phone lines as well as doing twenty different other things, menial things, messengering papers around and such, because he was the grunt, no different there than at the police station. But he was paying as much attention to the meeting as he could. The fact that it was being held out in the tent and not inside Agent Banish's office showed that things must have been going pretty well. Brian could feel it also in the rush of the agents, who were attuned to the morale of the place the way fish are to river currents. They carried more of a sureness of voice now, a clearer purpose in their ways, a sharper stride.

He hadn't known what he was getting into. He did as much work as anyone else in the command tent, though on a lower level, and got no more sleep than anyone else did. They were all run ragged and operated at such a high pitch that Brian saw you either joined in right off or got trampled underfoot. Luckily he had landed running. This was the inside lane here. He would go hurrying across the clearing for something or other to do with his new assignment and see someone sitting around near the kitchens or the trailers and wonder how they found the nerve to do that here. Why everyone wasn't moving as fast as he was, spinning, spinning. Brian's main responsibility was the outside phone lines, so he kept trying to find a slow moment to sneak out a call to Leslie, but he couldn't. There were none. It never did stop.

First, Agent Banish played the tape of the negotiations for Marshal Fagin, Agent Perkins, Agent Coyle, the Hostage Rescue agents, and whoever else was there. Brian missed most of it.

"Reiterate the order," Agent Banish said afterward. "The children are to be given wide berth. Do not fire. If any doors open, it may be them coming out. Let whatever's going to happen, happen."

These words seemed to be directed mainly toward the Hostage Rescue agents. Brian had helped coordinate the reassignment of trailer space to accommodate them following their arrival.

"Perkins," Agent Banish said, "form an arrest party and have them ready to take Ables into custody. I'll script a press release saying we have begun negotiations and anticipate a break soon."

Naturally, it was Marshal Fagin—who, the scuttlebutt said, would be eased out of his duties on the mountain now that the Hostage Rescue Team had arrived—who disagreed.

"Bullshit," he said. "He'll never surrender."

Agent Banish looked at Marshal Fagin, the grayed burn darkening half of his face. "I'm going to break him," he said confidently.

Marshal Fagin said, "I know this fuck. He's a scrapper, a backstabbing son of a bitch. Look what he's tried already. He won't go down without a fight. This fucker hates to lose."

From the way Agent Banish was looking at Marshal Fagin and clearly weighing what he had just said, Brian could tell that the watercooler talk around there was just about as accurate as it was back at the station house. Even in Brian's distracted state, it was plain to him that Marshal Fagin would be remaining at the front lines. He was one of the few people Agent Banish seemed to listen to. As opposed to Agent Perkins, who had a knack for discovering the obvious. The command tent agents respected him about as much as they would a substitute teacher.

Agent Banish said, "It doesn't fit his profile—all right. But we've got him. We're three hundred beekeepers in charge of one bee. There is no way he can escape, even if he thinks he can. So let him toss and turn. Let him scheme himself out. I'm inside his house now and inside his head."

Staging Area

Banish was sick of sour coffee, but that morning's supply of fruit juice was already gone. He took the coffee black and turned to find Fagin approaching.

"I'll say this only once," Fagin said, standing close when they were alone. "We know where the phone is. We know when Ables is on the line. I don't give a fuck who gets the call, me or HRT. Head shot through the window. Clean. Bang in behind stun grenades, flash entry. The whole thing, I can give you twenty seconds, in and out."

Banish shook it off. He had already considered similar scenarios. "If you could guarantee me—guarantee—safe harbor for the wife and Mrs. Mellis and the kids, then I might be convinced to roll Ables. But you can't, so I won't. Besides, there's no need now. He will come out. The question is when."

Fagin's steady eyes were brought out by his hard-set, deeply brown face. "Your choice," he said sternly.

Then Fagin got that distant look again, receiving something through his ear wire. His eyes righted themselves and he glanced around, his face showing that the news was nothing important. "Here comes Tonto," he said.

Sheriff Blood was drifting over in his laconic way, not looking at either Banish or Fagin but crossing directly toward them regardless.

"Sort of a happening going on down below," Blood said to Banish when he reached them. "Something I thought I'd make you aware of if you don't already know."

"What?" Banish said.

"Kind of an event in these parts. The state troopers got called away on special detail."

Banish looked at him. "What detail could take precedence over this?"

"Well," Blood said. Banish could see then that the Indian was, strangely, embarrassed. "Over in Little Elk tonight." He nodded then and came right out with it: "There's to be a miracle, they say."

Banish could feel Fagin turning and jumped in ahead of him. "What kind of miracle?" he said.

Blood nodded. "The religious kind."

Fagin said, "Here we go."

Blood said, "Jesus Christ, or Yashua if you prefer, is set to reveal Himself over at a church in Little Elk around midnight tonight. They're expecting upward of twenty thousand. Word gets out on a thing like this, people come in from all parts. The troopers needed to keep the highways moving."

Banish regarded the Indian. "Twenty thousand people," he said.

Blood nodded. "Upward of."

Banish was silent a moment. Fagin studied the both of them. "There's this thing," Fagin said, "on the planet where I'm from, called television. It's what most people do at night. Keeps them pretty fucking quiet, usually."

Banish said to Blood, "You're telling me that all those people down there, the entire protest, has evaporated. Just like that."

"It's down to about thirty." Blood nodded. "Markers, more or less, for the hundreds they represent. Quiet down there now, kind of peaceful."

Fagin looked at both of them. "This is fucking retarded," he said. He strode off.

Blood turned more fully toward Banish then. "How did you know about those unattended deaths?"

Banish looked at him.

"That first day," said Blood. "You figured that most of them were Indians."

Banish watched the sheriff's eyes. "Indians are the only minority up here."

"What does that imply?"

"That you believe the deaths are related."

Blood stood fast, looking at Banish, his eyes brighter. "Four of those six were hit-and-runs," he said.

"Which Police Chief Moody dismisses as drunken Indians. Which is why you called the FBI in here so fast. You think you might need some help."

Banish could see Blood bracing there before him.

"The newspapers are right," Blood said. "You are dangerous."

There was something here. Something in the Indian's face. Banish discovered the cup of coffee in his hand and tossed it into a nearby barrel. "I've got a couple of minutes while I change," he said. "Why don't you give me the particulars."

Blood nodded and walked with him across the clearing.

Trailer

Blood went and stood by the bed. Banish closed the trailer door and moved to his suitcase, set on top of the table. Blood looked across to where the mirror had hung and saw only a rectangle of wall darker than the rest.

Blood had been buying time on the stroll over, secretly having trouble figuring out where to begin. This was important.

"The first two happened before I took office," he began. "A sixty-eight-year-old Indian found on a county road after attending a powwow down in Crater, and then a floater washed up on Shoot River. He was a sixteen-year-old who had been missing for a few months, and was pretty badly decomposed, not much left."

Banish had his back to him, rummaging through clothes. He said, "What's the river like?"

"Wide and rough. Can be treacherous, depending on the season.

Runs right through Huddleston. There have been some drownings in the past."

Banish pulled out a pair of pants with the belt already looped. "Just tell me about the deaths you have the most information on."

"Right," Blood said, nodding. He had to present this clearly. "That'd be the last two. This was after my ears had perked up, and other people's too. They—Indians around here—by then were talking amongst themselves. Speculation about a serial killer of Indians."

"Hogwash," Banish said, pulling out a shirt.

Blood nodded, "That *is* hooey. I told them that's not how a killer like that works, but they're just scared. The second-to-last was a twenty-two-year-old male, last name of Kowes, late-generation Shoshoni. Missing for eight days, found floating in shallow water— also in Shoot River. Last seen at a party down near Huddleston Center. Left there late and was headed home when he snagged a tire on a railroad tie while crossing the tracks out by Potter's potato farm. That amounts to what we know for sure. From there, the official speculation is that, afraid of being caught DWI, he abandoned his car on the edge of the tracks and hiked a mile up to the river. The boy was in good shape, an athlete, and may have thought he could swim the Shoot and walk home from there. It would have amounted to a shortcut."

"Blood-alcohol?"

"Point-one-seven. The boy did have a good shine on."

"But people who knew him say he was too smart to try and swim the river," Banish said, "drunk or not."

Blood nodded. "His parents think he was forced in."

Banish pulled his wallet from his back pocket and tossed it onto the bed, where it flopped open, then stepped into the bathroom, fresh clothes in hand. "I'm listening," he said, turning the corner.

Blood cleared his throat, not used to talking so much at a time. He wanted to be sure to leave nothing out.

"More is known about the last one. A seventeen-year-old male, name of Darkin. Last seen at one of the local hangouts in Huddleston. Called the Bunker, a small cinder-block place set back from the road. Used to have a few swastikas decorating the back of it, been painted over since."

"The bar Ables was pinched at," Banish said from the bathroom. The door was open. "What the hell would an Indian be doing in a place like that?"

Blood looked at the brown leather wallet on the bed. It was worn, its faint gold stitching pulled. He could see, poking out of one of the deeper pockets, the top border of a photograph. Blood took a step closer to the bed, keeping an eye on the door.

"That is unknown," he said. "Maybe to meet some others, there being strength in numbers. Maybe to meet a girl. Anyway, he arrived alone by taxi after midnight, stayed less than an hour. Two men at the door say they saw him leave around one, one-thirty, again alone. It's a farm road there, tarred but unlit, a fairly main drag south of town. A motorist came across the body more than a half mile away from the Bunker. That was some time shortly after two."

Banish's voice said, "What did the doormen look like?"

"Shaved bald, suspenders, black boots."

Banish said, "These are the people who place this Indian's time of departure. These are the last people to see him alive."

"We have no independent corroboration. We're still trying to track down some of the patrons of the bar."

Banish said, "Go ahead."

Blood checked the bathroom door again. "First of all," he said, reaching across the bed for the wallet, "why would this boy want to walk home four miles at that time of night?" Blood slid the photograph most of the way out. "It was the middle of February and twelve degrees. He told the cab driver who dropped him that he would be calling later for a ride home. He never did." Blood lingered a moment on the wallet-sized portrait. It showed a trimmer Banish, his face thinner and ten years younger, wearing a dark suit and wide tie and standing with his hand on a chair where his wife sat, her brown hair long and flat, skirt and stockings conservative—and standing at her shoulder, smiling for all she was worth, their daughter, a dark-haired girl of no more than ten or twelve. "Nine dollars in his back pocket," Blood said, quickly sliding the photograph back inside its pocket and setting the wallet open again on the bed, "more than enough for taxi fare. Coroner filed official cause of death as blunt head trauma of unknown cause, but I asked him to take a closer look at that, it seeming a little too speculative to me, and he came back with a fractured skull and other injuries jibing with hit-and-run."

Banish didn't answer right away and Blood took a step farther back from the bed. "Which side of the road was he found on?"

Blood answered, "Dead center of a two-lane tar road. Spread out in the middle of it."

"Blood-alcohol?"

"Point-one-two-five."

Another pause. "What did the body look like?"

"Brian Kearney was first on the scene that morning. He said that it was his feeling immediately, first thing he thought of, that the death had occurred someplace else. That it looked like a body that had been moved. Now, you know Brian. He's a rookie and his mouth gets out in front of his mind on occasion. So I checked these things for myself." Blood ticked off each point with the fingers of his right hand. "No automobile parts on the road. No skid marks, no glass shards. All the driveways and byroads are dirt around there, and plenty of tracks on either lane, but no dirt crossing the center strip within thirty yards. And then this. When he was found, the boy had two T-shirts on under his jacket, both rolled up from his waist to his armpits, and his back all scraped up. Like he had been dragged there. Some say a car could do it, but his back would have been torn to shreds on that tar. And then the next day, Brian comes over to me on the sly. He tells me that Moody talked him out of it. The T-shirt angle got left off the official report entirely."

Blood heard a faucet running, then turned off. "The first one, Kowes," Banish said. "Missing for eight days. What about his car?"

"Found the next day by the railroad tracks and impounded as an abandoned vehicle."

"Parents weren't notified?"

"It was registered in the boy's name. I took his father down there myself a week after the body washed up and we found it tucked back behind some others in the tow yard. Wallet empty on the floor in front, contents scattered on the front seat, the dash, and both floorboards. Also clothes. Also shopping receipts, also check stubs."

"And the parents insist he was a very neat kid."

Blood nodded, now pacing a bit. "And that right there is evidence lost, because it comes out later there's a young lady who claimed she was with Kowes in the car the night he died. Her story was that the boy thought he was being followed, which was why he got a little lost and anxious driving around and wound up blowing a tire. She said he pulled over and told her to get out of the car and hide—she's not Indian. From where she was, deep back in the potato field, she said she heard some other car door slam, and voices."

Banish nodded. "All right, then."

"Problem is, she's changed her story, significantly enough, more than once. And now she's moved away altogether and I don't have the faintest idea where she is."

"So Moody's office had the car and the missing persons report and never connected them?"

"Exactly. He said they didn't because the body was found in the river, which is county land, my jurisdiction, and the car was found out by the tracks, which is his. But that's damn thin to me," said Blood, feeling the harshness in his own voice. "Damn thin."

Banish came out then, around the corner from the bathroom, his shirt unbuttoned and pants half-open at the waist. Blood saw a raw, silver-dollar-sized scar just below his stomach, a red-pink indentation upon the white of his skin, and smaller flecks of pink around it —then looked up immediately at Banish's face so as not to stare.

Banish tossed his dirty clothes on the bed. "It's not Moody," he said. "I'm sure you already looked for some connection between the victims, other than gender and race, and if there is none, then forget it. It's only a cover-up if somebody profits. This doesn't read like a police conspiracy. More likely, Moody just turns a blind eye, or worse, he doesn't care. A couple of drunken Indians to him. Two drownings and some traffic accidents. That's what others will say too. If it's FBI involvement you want, you'll need more than this. No paint on the hit-and-run?"

"From the car finish?"

Banish tucked in his shirt and fixed his pants. "Impact burns paint onto the skin and clothing."

Blood nodded. "There was none of that. You see?"

"What was Darkin wearing besides two T-shirts?"

"Jeans and a leather jacket."

"That's good. Leather picks up paint better than anything. No paint on that jacket, then you proceed right away with an open homicide investigation. Tie in one more similarly dead Indian and you've got grounds for a civil rights case that bumps it up to federal. And I would also consider contracting an outside coroner, one who isn't so quick with his knife."

He ended nodding, seemingly reviewing his own answer. He picked his wallet up off the bed and slipped it into his back pocket. Then he was still, standing there. Then he shook his head. "How could you let something like that go so far?" he said.

Blood looked at him. "What do you mean?"

"What is the overall Indian population up here?"

Blood thought about it, realized what was being implied. "Maybe two percent," he said. "You saying I'm not doing my job?"

"You had questions," Banish said. "You talked to people, you developed theories. Then you did nothing. Why wait for federal help on this? How can you allow these separatists and neo-Nazis around here at all?"

Blood was hot. "They call it freedom of speech," he said. "Lots of good people up here too."

"Sure," Banish said, "but there's a fine line between good people and look-the-other-way-and-keep-quiet people. Freedom of speech works both ways."

Blood nodded slowly. "So I should just take care of them then. The way you took care of Mellis."

It surprised and ashamed Blood how much venom he had in him, but Banish took it, standing quietly a moment. "I'm saying that working in secret is not doing anyone a damn bit of good. Get out and meet these people head-on. They are flaunting their lawlessness and disrespect in front of you. You've got to confront them, you especially. Otherwise, you're the sheriff of this county and no better than any of the rest. You have to show these people to be ridiculous. Humiliate them. Nothing else works as well."

Blood's face burned. The room seemed to drift a little and he looked around, his mind filling with all the things he could come back with: that he didn't have the public's support, that he was just a one-man office. But hearing it loud in his head like that warmed another blush of shame on his face and he realized his excuses were all just as petty as they sounded. Which was why Banish had called him a politician. Ever since the glory of his election-year upset, for some reason Blood had been tipping his hat at these frays rather than running headfirst into them. Storing his pride rather than displaying it. Blood was embarrassed, but more angry now than blushing. Angry at Moody and anyone else who was taunting him. There were shitbags laughing at him behind his back. He realized that he hadn't come to Banish for aid at all—he had come to be talked out of something, to be told he was wrong when he knew he was right. In certain circles Sheriff Leonard M. Blood was a laughingstock. He had been elected to keep the peace. There were good people out there, not just the trash he mainly dealt with, but good, fair-minded people who had invested their trust in him when they cast a vote for change and peace and order and law.

All this put him in mind of another thing he had so willingly set aside, another thorny suspicion he had been shying away from. He brought out the letter he had been carrying around and handed it over to Banish. He waited until it was unfolded and recognized. "The letter to WAR from Ables," Blood told him. "A man last night claiming to be Ables's lawyer passed copies of this around, stirring up the crowd. Said ATF threatened to bring charges if Ables didn't tattle for them, and said he could prove this in a court of law. You ignored that when I brought it to you before. Can you now?"

Banish looked at the letter. He folded it in half, running his fingers slowly along the crease. "If I told you it didn't matter?" he said.

Blood said, "Can you now?"

Banish held the piece of paper. He didn't say anything.

"What would you do," Blood said, "if this whole mess turned out to be one big damn mistake?"

Banish was quiet for a while and seemingly heavy with thought. Then he folded the letter once again and slipped it into his shirt pocket. He nodded at Blood from where he was standing. "You're a dangerous man yourself," he said.

Dangerously inept, thought Blood. A mat for people to walk over, a statue that sometimes even talked. He had thought previously that strength and silence were enough. Chief Moody practically burgling his office. Cops parking in his space. Deke Belcher throwing up insults at him in his own car. All unanswered by him. The thought of them snickering made Blood furious. Why hadn't he acted? Why did he keep so much in reserve? And what was the cost?

He pictured each of the Indian boys—young, drunk, and terrified—surrounded and set upon by a mob.

Banish moved to the door. "I want you up at the staging area from here on in," he said.

"Why?" Blood said. He was mad and frustrated and trying to hide it.

"We're getting into negotiations with Ables now. You know the character of the people, the way around here. I want you in the mix. You might pick up on something I would otherwise miss."

"And?" Blood said.

Banish seemed to think about that. "There's also a saying," he said. "Keep all dangerous men closest to you."

Blood felt much the same. For now, he was in that numb state that followed a thorough beating, the pain that falls over you heavy and starts to settling deep into your muscles and your soul. He went out behind Banish and set off across the clearing by himself.

Command Tent

[PARASIEGE, p. 66]

SA Banish returned to the command tent and instructed SA Coyle to contact the BATF office in Spokane, Washington, for the purpose of ordering the return of Agents Riga and Crimson for further questioning.

Sound Truck

Banish paced inside the cramped quarters, head bowed to avoid the van ceiling. He kept his hands busy, folding and unfolding them in front of him, wringing them, wiping them on the hips of his pants. Blood stood leaning against a wall in the corner near the closed door. The sound man sat monitoring.

The tape reels clicked and started another revolution. "He's coming," said the sound man, pulling on his headphones and flipping a switch. The sound of footsteps over a wooden floor came on inside the van. The footsteps approached the microphone source and stopped, and there were muffled noises, the sound of a man clearing his throat. Then a click.

"Watson."

His voice filled the van. The sound man adjusted the broadcast volume as Banish climbed into his chair. He used the hand microphone only, leaving Ables's voice on the overhead speaker for Blood to hear.

"Yes, Mr. Ables."

"You have a family, Watson?"

The very first question threw him. It would have been an easy lie, but since Banish's aim here was to sympathize with the suspect and establish a rapport, it seemed to him that the best answer in this particular situation was, in fact, "Yes."

"I want to talk about mine," Ables said. "In case something happens to me."

"What do you mean?"

"That was good," Ables said. "That was convincing."

Banish squinted, looking blankly at the console in front of him. "Mr. Ables, you've lost me here. Are you considering coming out?"

Banish would not say "surrender." He would not say "give up." He had to make it Ables's choice. He waited through a short pause.

"Maybe you don't know, then," Ables said. "I figured you were all in this together, but misinformation is legion. Or maybe you're just not high up enough to know."

"Know what, Mr. Ables?"

"About the plans they have for me. How this is all going to end."

Banish pressed him. "Who, Mr. Ables?"

"That I am going to be assassinated when I step outside my house and murdered in cold blood. I know that."

"That is simply not true, Mr. Ables. No one here will take any hostile action, not unless you were to try something ill-advised again."

Banish waited through another, longer pause.

"My wife," Ables said. "If I did come out. She would go free."

Banish paused, as though carefully considering it. "That is certainly something that could be arranged," he said.

"Not so fast, Watson. Not so simple. I have other responsibilities. I know they want my house. They want me and they want my land. I built this house up with my own hands, me and my wife and daughters. Do you understand that, Watson?"

"I do understand, Mr. Ables."

"You damn well should. And I paid for the land on this mountain and have worked it hard."

"Mr. Ables—we are getting into an area here that I don't have much control over. Legally, you forfeited your residence to the courts when you refused to appear for trial."

"It was refused for me. Another slimy sabotage. That letter reached me two months too late."

Again, Ables was way out ahead of him. "What letter?" Banish said.

"The letter from that courthouse. With the date for my appearance. Delivered by the federal mail, Watson. It's all a game to you people out there, ain't it? You sit and act like you don't know that you're all in on this together. You know that you have set me up and yet you will not admit it to my face. You will double-talk and triple-talk and try to fill my head with doubts."

"Mr. Ables, all I am trying to do here is iron out some agreement between us whereby you can come out in cooperation with the proper authorities before it is too late to do so."

"Who is Banish?" Ables said.

Banish started. His chest went cold. "What?"

"Banish. I hear his name on the radio, more than yours."

Banish said, "There is no Banish on this mountain," and immediately knew that it was a wild mistake.

"On the radio news they said he's in charge."

"He is not here now. Mr. Ables, we were talking about your home."

"I want to talk to this Banish."

"I told you, he is not here."

"Where is he, then? I'm on the phone now. Who the hell's in charge out there?"

"Mr. Ables, I think it would be best if we could work this out between the two of us rather than involving the confusion of a third party."

"He's Tactical, then," Ables said. "You're the mouth, he's the trigger boy. Right? Sitting out there in the trees somewhere right now. Watching for me. He's the one, then. He wants me in his crosshairs. He wants me dead so bad he can taste it."

"Mr. Ables, no one out here, no one, wants you or your family harmed in any way. I am personally assuring you of that. Now, if you will be reasonable, we can continue talking realistically about meeting your immediate needs—"

"Does Banish have a family?"

Banish glanced away. He frowned slightly and looked back. "I wouldn't know," he said.

"You, then. If you knew, Watson, that something was going to happen to you in the very near future, if you knew that, wouldn't you want to arrange things for your family in advance? Isn't that your responsibility? Wouldn't you want them to have their house to live in, a house they helped to build, and be allowed to stay together and not be bothered by any shits from the government once you're good and gone?"

Banish closed his eyes. "Mr. Ables," he said, "that does sound reasonable."

A third pause. Banish waited patiently through it. It went on.

Banish opened his eyes. "Mr. Ables," he said. "Mr. Ables."

There was a click. Banish looked over at the sound man. The sound man shook his head. There were footsteps in the cabin, walking away.

Banish switched off the microphone. He sat there awhile, staring at the controls. His head was swimming. Then he stood. "Fine," he said distractedly, without turning, feeling he had to say something before he left. "I'll be right back," he said.

Office

He paced in his office. The noise in the command tent outside did not intrude upon the swirling inside his head. Each time he passed his desk he looked at the telephone upon it. He was troubled. Fatigue, an unsettled feeling. A sense of moving frantically in slow motion. His face itched now, where the powder blast shadow remained, but rubbing his cheek and jaw with his dry hands only further aggravated it.

He was thinking about Molly and Nicole. He was looking at the telephone each time he passed it and he was entertaining possible approaches. He was casting off scenarios. Just friendly congratulations to start with. He could say that he heard about Nicole's engagement from a friend of a friend. Just calling to wish her the best. That would leave the ball in their court. Nothing would happen very quickly, if at all. A few courteous phone conversations over a matter of months. An engagement gift sent by him. An invitation to the wedding. A dance. An embrace.

He quickly walked away from his desk, chastising himself bitterly. Romantic fantasies. They would never take him back. He remembered enough of it to know that. He shook his head. He had terrorized them. He had made them afraid to live in their own house, to sleep in their own beds. He had inspired fear in them. He had wanted them to fear him, to fear everything, that had been his mania. He had never physically abused them. He was nearly certain of that. It was the living environment he had created after his failure at the World Financial Center, after watching that woman and her daughter die. The guilt he felt, manifested in drunken, raving tirades alternating between open threats and manic bouts of overprotectiveness. He had worked to keep them off-balance. To make them ready for whatever danger might come. To make them see what he had seen and learn from what he had learned so that nothing like that, no death or random act of terror, no pain would ever touch them. Witnessing the end of that family, and bearing responsibility for it, lit off something in him that was impossible to contain. He remembered the last weekend, when he tore up the house: every appliance, fixture, wall hanging, door, room. Nothing was safe and nothing was permanent, he had decreed. That had been demonstrated to him at WFC and he was proving it to them now. He was showing them that anybody and anything—*anything*—could be destroyed.

And he had. And it was. The next day they left him for her mother's and never returned. In the restraining order, Nicole had repeated to a judge the various warnings that her father, in his fits of despair, had issued to her. That she could be strangled in her sleep. That she could become anybody's hostage. That she could be raped and killed. That her mother could be murdered. That people die suddenly and for no reason at all. That life had absolutely no meaning or purpose. That the bad received no punishment, and the good no reward.

The warnings were meant to snap her out of her everyday slumber, to make her vigilant. In reality, they were the ramblings of a diseased drunk, and of course came to be interpreted as threats. He had laid their home to waste. He had defiled something there that was sacred. There was no forgiving that. He did not even ask for forgiveness. For wrecking the house, for months of torment—he could not paper over that. Yet still he wanted them back. He was a changed man. He had served two years of penance in Skull Valley and he was better now—yet it was all still not enough. At the bottom of his heart, he knew that it was simply too late.

He went to his desk and sat, wanting what he could not have. That which was once his to keep safe. He looked again at the telephone. It mocked him. He thought about calling out to the switchboard and having them open up an outside line so that he could further punish himself with pathetic dreams of reconciliation. Then Coyle pushed open the door flap and came inside. She had the itemized expenditures list from the previous day. He had to review it, checking and initialing each individual sum, then sign off on the total day's cost. She stood watching over him as he did.

Sound Truck

The man in the headphones signaled and Banish sat up in the chair facing the panel of controls. Blood stayed where he was, again watching from the corner. It was now suppertime and neither he nor Banish had eaten lunch, but there was an urgency in the van, fully realized whenever Ables's voice came through, that precluded the satisfying of everyday human appetites.

"Watson."

When it came, they went into motion. Small lights came on in the electrical works and tape recorder wheels started to turn. Ables's voice was like a fuse switch thrown on, jerking the van to life. The speakers made it sound as though he were right inside there with them.

Banish worked his microphone. "Right here, Mr. Ables," he said into it. He kept his eyes trained ahead and down as he talked.

Ables said, "Is he there now?"

"Who, Mr. Ables?"

"Banish."

Banish sat up a bit, resettling himself. This sort of talk clearly made him uncomfortable. "No," he said, "he is not."

"Even after I called for him?"

"I explained to you, Mr. Ables, that is not even an issue. I am here for you. It is just you and me talking."

"What did he say about me?"

Banish rubbed his face. "He didn't say anything, Mr. Ables. I have not spoken with him. What do you mean?"

"I want to know how it's going to come."

"Mr. Ables—I am assuring you, unless you want to try something foolish again—"

"What about your family, Watson?"

"We are not talking about my family, Mr. Ables."

"I want to know."

Banish said, "Have you reached any decision regarding your coming out?"

"I can guess," said Ables. "Three boys is what I see. Close in age. Real popular boys, strong boys, all-American all-stars. Real friendly at school with their Jew professors."

Banish said, "Mr. Ables—"

"I see a wife everybody in the neighborhood likes, who fake-kisses on the cheek all her Jewess friends. I see her in a red apron waving from a white picket fence."

Banish said, "Mr. Ables, are you trying to insult me?"

"I didn't think that was an insult, Watson. I used to live in America for a while, don't forget. I saw what was out there in the suburbs. I'm saying that I bet you have the perfect all-American family. That is what I am guessing. You and a wife and three strong blond boys, all driving cars with slanty headlights, working to put money in the bearded man's pocket."

"Mr. Ables, we are so far afield—"

"I think you are hiding something, Watson."

Banish relented a bit. "I have nothing to hide, Mr. Ables."

"You do, Watson. I can tell you do."

Banish stared ahead. After a while, he spoke. "I have no sons, Mr. Ables," he said. "I have one daughter, who is engaged to be married."

"How old, Watson?"

"My daughter is twenty-one."

"Young for marriage nowadays."

"It comes as a relief," Banish said. "She seems to be on the right track now."

Blood's eyebrows were up. He couldn't see the strategy in any of this.

Ables pressed him. "You're saying she had some trouble."

Banish nodded as though recalling it. "As a teenager," he said. "Falling in with the wrong crowd. We had some rough years. She ran away from home when she was fourteen, for one day, and when she was fifteen, for three. Her mother had her hands full, and I was away a lot. I regret not being there."

Blood even considered tapping him on the shoulder. Banish seemed to have lost himself in his candor. Blood saw the sound man turn to look at Banish as well.

Ables's voice said, "All them schools are ghettos now. That's what I got my kids away from."

"Guns and violence," Banish said.

"That's right."

Banish nodded. "Trouble is where you find it, Mr. Ables," he said, the irony of the thing not lost on him. He appeared then to come up for air. "Does that satisfy you now?"

"I am not looking for satisfaction, Watson. You get to go home to your family when you are through. I won't."

"Mr. Ables, I am personally overseeing each and every aspect of your arrest. I am guaranteeing you that there will be no shooting, that you will not be harmed in any way."

Ables said, "I trust you, Watson. I do. Truly. You can't guarantee me nothing. Guarantee me the sun'll come up tomorrow."

"Who do you trust, then, Mr. Ables? I can arrange for eyewitnesses to be there to watch your arrest. Who do you trust?"

Ables, apparently thinking it over, said finally, "No one."

"Your wife's parents," said Banish.

"No."

"Television cameras, then. The media. I can have them film the arrest for your protection. How would you like that?"

"What about my home, Watson?"

Banish was nodding. It looked like progress here. "The only thing I can suggest," he said, "is that you arrange to sign ownership of your property over into your wife's name. That is my best suggestion to you. Possession is nine tenths of the law."

"Whose law, Watson? Your law or mine? Mine says free and innocent men are left alone by their government."

"We are making some progress here, Mr. Ables. Let's stick to resolving the terms of your coming outside—"

"Do you think I'm a bad man, Watson? I want your view on this. You think I'm a guilty man?"

Banish let out a short breath. "Mr. Ables," he said, "I have no opinion on the matter."

"I'm as guilty as you are, Watson. I just tried to live my life alone up here. I minded my own business as other folks mind theirs, and if no one came up here meddling in my life, then I wouldn't have gone and bothered anyone in theirs. But it ain't up to me. You came up here, Watson, and you scratched me, but I don't bleed."

"Mr. Ables—"

"You found that out. I scratch back. If this was a fair fight, I'd win it. You might even know that I would. But nothing is fair, Watson. Resist and they will crush you. Deny them and try to stay with your own and they will rise up and make an example of you. That's what this is right here, Watson. Maybe you can see that now. I am the example."

It was obvious by the clattering noises over the speaker that Ables was done with them again. Banish sat back. The sound man pulled down his headphones, saying, "He's clear."

Banish shut his eyes and was quiet for a moment. "He's stringing this out," he said.

Blood said, "He's enjoying himself."

Banish opened his eyes and sat forward. He spoke generally, reviewing things. "Still fairly coherent," he said. "Wants a personal relationship with the negotiator. That's common. They all want reassurance near the end. So you use that, you figure out what they want to hear in terms of similar problems, you empathize and exploit their weaknesses, show them they are not alone in this, even get them thinking you are on their side if you can." He turned and looked at Blood. "What do you think?"

Blood was going to say that he didn't believe Banish for a second, that it seemed as though he had gone too far and was trying to excuse himself here. "About what?"

"Ables."

Blood nodded at that. "I'd say he's sizing himself up to be a pretty good martyr."

The sound man with the Southern accent contributed to Banish's cause. "I think it's good how you let him flex his ego now and again. I think that works."

Blood said, "You going to ask him about Mellis?"

Banish shook his head lightly. "Not the sort of thing I'd want to introduce into the conversation," he said. "I don't think he will either."

He stood then. His shoulders looked heavy. To the sound man he said, "Call over to the command tent, have them get a printout for me. I want to review the transcripts."

The sound man nodded. "We're silent up top," he reminded him.

Banish stopped. "What do you have?"

"Depends. What are you looking for?"

Banish thought. "Something new. He needs more pushing."

The sound man ticked off his selection. "I've got Tibetan monks chanting, military marching music, a clock ticking, baby rabbits being slaughtered, Andy Williams Christmas carols—"

"The clock," Banish said, starting to leave. "Good and loud."

Command Tent

Fagin was reading the transcript when Banish walked in. He had to catch up on the negotiations on his own because nobody fucking told him anything. He looked up at Banish as he entered. "Do you need a hug?" he said.

Banish took the printed sheets out of his hands. Then he recognized Ables's voice on the CB. Banish turned and walked a few slow steps toward it.

"Bible lessons," chided Fagin.

Coyle told him, "It just started."

Banish looked around. "What part is he reading from?"

He was sure to get a quick answer. Half the FBI agents kept Bibles out on top of their desks. "Psalms," one at the switchboard said. Then Fagin saw that it was Kearney, the local cop who had stood up for Banish.

"A scholar," Fagin said to him, wondering what the hell he was doing at the FBI switchboard.

The young cop said, "Not actually. He said the name himself when he started to read it." Then Kearney looked past Fagin. "Agent Banish?"

Banish raised a hand to hold off Kearney. He was standing there listening to Ables on the CB, or thinking. Either way, he was just standing there.

Fagin said, "Cut him off."

Banish waited some more. "No," he said. "Let him go. If we cut him off mid-verse, people listening down below and elsewhere will assume the worst." He looked over at Coyle. "When he finishes reading, jam him. If he starts to ramble on about anything other than what he's reading, jam him. But shut him down for good when he's through."

"Agent Banish," Kearney said.

Fagin spoke first. He was starving and wanted to get in what he went there for. "I'm going to eat," he said to Banish. "You coming?"

Banish said, "Hold on." He was hassled. Ables on the radio obviously worried him. He looked over at Kearney. "What is it?"

"Call for you, sir."

Banish told him, "Give it to Coyle."

"It's the outside line," Kearney said. "A woman."

Fagin watched Banish's eyes hold on Kearney then. They held there tightly, as though seeing something else altogether.

"My office," Banish told him.

"I'm going to eat," Fagin said, but Banish was already moving toward the back.

Office

Banish went right to the phone. He looked at the blinking light. He wiped his hands on his shirtfront and picked up the receiver.

"Hello," he said.

"John? John Banish?"

"Yes," he said.

"It's Dr. Juliet Reed."

Banish's eyes searched.

"From the Retreat," she said.

Banish turned and sat against his desk. "Dr. Reed," he said. He put his hand to his hot forehead and held it lightly. After a moment he closed his eyes.

"Hello, John. I wasn't sure I would be able to get through."

"Yes."

"How are you getting along?"

Banish opened his eyes. The disappointment drained him. "Fine," he said.

"I read your name in the newspaper. You can imagine my surprise. I contacted some people at the Retreat rather on a whim. They got back to me and gave me this number. They thought it might be a good idea that I call."

"I see," Banish said. Hearing her voice again had triggered within him a subtle ebb of passivity. It was as though the years had not passed and he was still living in that small community of sterilized floors and broken men.

"I am no longer associated with the Retreat," she said. "I have a private practice in Boston now. It is so rare that I come into contact with a former patient. Are you keeping up with the therapy, John?"

"Yes."

"Poetry still?"

"Yes."

"You excelled at that. Have you given any thought to publishing?"

"I'm working on a translation now. Just for myself, to keep my mind focused."

"Translation of what?" she said. "If I may ask."

"A notebook of German poems. Kept by a low-level guard at Buchenwald, recovered after the emancipation. Slipped to me by a friend of a friend from the old OSS."

"Well," she said, as though catching her breath. "That sounds absolutely fascinating. I can't imagine—was he humane at all, or an ogre along with the rest?"

"I guess there's no simple answer for that."

"Fascinating," she said. "How is the case progressing?"

"We are into negotiations now." He spoke optimistically, as a matter of habit. "It should break soon."

"An awful situation. And the dead young girl—tragic. I've been following it in the newspapers here. Remarkable, and terrible."

Banish rubbed his face. "Dr. Reed, I'm sure you can understand, I am pressed for time—"

"Are you strong, John? Do you feel strong?"

Her words cut him. "Strong enough," he said.

"You recovered fully from your wounding?"

He touched his lower torso over the scar, a gesture of remembrance. "It was kind of you to visit me in the hospital," he said. "I do remember that."

"An awful thing. I treated Lucy Ames myself, in another wing of the facility. After you dropped the charges. She grew to be quite strong before her discharge. Quite solid and rational." She paused then, reflective for a moment. "I am not sure why I was so moved to call you, John. What exactly it was that compelled me. Concern, perhaps, although it is not at all professional to take an interest in a former patient. Especially, I suppose, a patient from the Retreat, due to the sensitive nature of that place. But I've always felt your therapy there was unfinished. That we did not have enough time. That has always concerned me."

Banish said, "Dr. Reed, I really do have to go."

"But I can tell by your voice, John, you are strong now. You must be to have been assigned this case. I am so encouraged by your progress. You have overcome more than anyone will ever know, John. It is a triumph, and I do hope you understand that. To have come as far as you have. You have much to be proud of."

She went on saying a few more things like that, then they said their goodbyes and hung up. Banish remained sitting there awhile looking at the phone.

Sound Truck

Perkins was there now too. There were four of them: Perkins, Banish, the sound man, and Blood himself. The inside of the van smelled faintly like their chicken-and-gravy dinner, a picked-at plate of which sat on the control panel near Banish.

It was getting late in the day, and this fact was well known and weighed heavily upon all concerned. Banish was sitting back from the desk panel. He was brooding. "Let me hear it again," he said.

The sound man worked the buttons and the distant, eaves-dropped conversation was replayed once again.

Ables's voice saying, "Esther. Get back here."

A young girl's voice, more distant. "Mommy in back room."

Ables's voice again, sharper, "Becca, get her back here."

Then footsteps and off. Banish sat there thinking.

Blood said, "Which one is Esther again?"

Perkins told him, "The five-year-old."

The sound man was puzzled. "In the back room," he said. "Must be her post."

"Watson."

The voice surprised them, but most of all Perkins, who wasn't used to being jump-started by it. He stepped up behind Banish as though they were about to meet Ables in person. Banish moved forward to his microphone. "Go ahead, Mr. Ables," he said.

Ables said, "One: The house will be put in my wife's name. She will not be arrested, and neither will Shelley or my kids."

Banish sat up straighter. Perkins brought out a small notebook and pen and started scribbling. "That can be arranged," Banish said measuredly. "Go ahead."

"Two: I will walk off my land a free man. I will walk out of my house and down to the bottom of the mountain. TV cameras will be set up to film my arrest."

Banish said, "That is fine, Mr. Ables. The only problem I can foresee is the location—"

"These are demands, Watson," Ables said. "Three: I will not be placed in any handcuffs whatsoever."

Banish sat and listened. It was obviously a snag. Perkins scribbled next to him.

"Four: I will read a speech on television at the time of my arrest. Five: The federal government will publicly admit its conspiracy and guilt in the premeditated murder of Judith Ann Ables."

The pause told them Ables was through. Banish frowned. "No deal," he said into the handset.

Ables said, "I didn't offer you a deal, Watson. These are my demands."

Banish took the list from Perkins and quickly reviewed it. "One," he said. "Any statements you wish to make, political or otherwise, may be released through your lawyer at an appropriate time following your arrest. Two: Arresting you at the bridge could incite a riot and may risk the safety of my men; I won't do that. Three: I am not, nor is anyone here, authorized to speak on behalf of the federal government of the United States of America."

A loud click and clatter as the phone was slammed down on

Ables's end. Quiet for a moment, then "Sons of bitches!" heard, then booted footsteps walking away.

Banish switched off his microphone and turned around in his chair. He looked drawn and tired but, to Blood's surprise, not disappointed. In fact, he looked pleased.

Perkins said, "The Ritual?"

Banish nodded. "He's started to fold."

Blood interrupted. "What is 'The Ritual'?"

Perkins turned toward him like a man finding a dollar bill on the floor. "Surrender Ritual," he said. "The suspect preparing to leave. Emptying his pockets, giving things away. Winding down." He looked quickly at Banish, who was looking at the van floor, and then back again at Blood. "A mixed-up process they go through before giving up."

"Like making out a will before a long trip," Banish said, standing suddenly and moving away. "We've got him."

Tuesday, August 10

Marshals Tent

The principals convened inside the marshals tent for a midmorning strategy meeting over breakfast. Perkins had organized the conference and figured to be instrumental in the postresolution breakdown of the staging area. He was seated, spooning out the loose white of a salted soft-boiled egg, between his ASAC, Hardy, and a tieless representative of the American Red Cross. Also seated there were SAs Banish and Coyle, two HRT agents, Fagin and another deputy marshal, two U.S. Attorneys from Helena with whom Perkins was acquainted, a GS-5 stenographer, and the local sheriff. The mood around the table was one of optimism, of anticipating the end of a tough, drawn-out siege and the satisfaction of a job well done, except of course for Fagin, for whom no form of resolution short of a blitzkrieg would have been entirely satisfactory, and Banish, who appeared distracted. Perkins assumed it was because Ables had been silent overnight.

The surrender protocol was SOP and familiar to all involved. They were assembled to iron out the particulars so that the event would proceed smoothly, and to ensure that the arrest would be performed strictly by the book. All agreed that they had come too far to risk being shot in the foot by a technicality.

Following Ables's arrest, the task of removing him safely off-site fell to HRT. They had already secured the services of a UH-60 Black Hawk military helicopter, to be captained by a member of the 160th Special Operations Aviation Regiment "Night Stalkers" unit, currently en route from its home base at Fort Campbell, Kentucky. Ables would be transferred under HRT guard to the U.S. District Court in Helena and held there pending arraignment.

A special medical helicopter would airlift Mrs. Ables to a hospital in Great Falls, where she would be treated and later interviewed along with Mrs. Mellis. The Ables children would be turned over to their maternal grandparents following a nutritious meal, routine physical and psychological examinations, and subsequent individual questioning. Banish spoke up for the first time at that juncture, reminding everyone once again that their primary concern was the safe rescue of the children.

Alert status would remain in effect until Ables was confirmed airborne. Following that, marshals and agents would move immediately up the mountain to secure the cabin and cordon off the surrounding area. An FBI forensics team would enter and complete a point-by-point situational analysis of the cabin and grounds, including on-site ballistics work and color photography for possible future trial exhibition. Weapons would be itemized and tagged, then removed to an outdoor table for press viewing. Perkins would deliver a brief media statement in front of the cabin detailing the harsh conditions inside, and end with a protocol of the various participating agencies. All inquiries would be referred to the Department of Justice.

Fagin, sitting next to the younger marshal taking notes, objected then. "We need a contingency plan," he said. "We need a net in case things go sour up there."

Perkins said, "Our current blanket operation is more than sufficient. We have total containment."

"If the exchange goes bad," Fagin argued, "there's gonna be beaucoup confusion, and Ables could provoke events beyond our control. What do you think he's doing up there now? He's been quiet almost twelve hours. You think they're playing cards?"

Perkins said to him across the table, "We own this mountain. The moment he indicates he's coming out, we go to full alert and collapse in on the cabin."

The debate went back and forth a few more times, then passed quietly, with the majority expressing confidence in the present game plan and no objections from Banish, if he was even listening. The only other point to which he spoke during the briefing was in reference to the postresolution deployment of the Marshals Service Special Operations Group for bridge barricade containment. "At no time are any shots to be fired at civilians," he ordered. "Tear gas and baton battery if necessary, but absolutely no shooting. Make it perfectly clear to all personnel."

No one anticipated any problems on that end. The Marshals Service SOG was well versed in riot control and crowd containment.

Perkins then directed the men and Coyle to the prospectus before them, which outlined his schedule for the dismantling of the staging area. He estimated twenty-four hours from the time of Ables's removal until complete federal evacuation, including: transport of all hardware such as vehicles and generators; inventory and removal of reusable materials such as tents and all unused supplies; plans for the kitchens and latrines to be razed for scrap; and transportation of federal personnel to the airport, with special attention to Banish and Perkins himself, who would be flying directly to Washington, D.C., for postsituation summary consults.

The protesters were expected to disperse once Ables was delivered from the cabin. By prior arrangement, the Red Cross would oversee the return of the mountain residents to their homes following the federal evacuation. No recompense was deemed necessary or was being offered to the residents by the federal government regarding either term of displacement or property damages resulting from misadventure, as per the determination of counsel for the Department of Justice.

Toward the end of Perkins's presentation, which he had spent the better part of the night working on, Banish stood and walked out of the tent without explanation. Everyone watched him go. The county sheriff excused himself and followed shortly after.

Office

Banish entered his office fast. He had had enough of this. He was viewing the situation much too desperately. They were his wife and daughter and he was going to call them on the telephone like anyone else. He went around to his desk and sat down and picked up the phone. He pushed a button to call the switchboard for an outside line.

Blood walked in. Banish pulled the phone away from his ear and said "What?" roughly.

Blood came forward to the desk. "The protesters are back," he said.

Banish nodded curtly. "No miracle?"

Blood shook his head. "The problem now is, we seem to have inherited a good number of people from it. I think disappointment may have carried them over here. They're stretched out both ways down the county road now, easily up over a thousand. They want a show, I guess. They want something."

Banish heard a small voice talking at him through the earpiece. Kearney. He hung up the phone impatiently, his foot tapping under the desk.

Blood said, "The hardware store I told you about was broken into last night. Ransacked. Guns, knives, crossbows, over sixty pieces in all. Ammunition cleared out too."

Banish rubbed his face hard. "Suspects?"

"Two words spray-painted over the emptied gun racks: 'Holy War.' "

" 'Holy War,' " Banish said, nodding.

"Then late yesterday there was a full-fledged run on the Huddleston Dime bank. They had to lock the front door. Near riot."

"Christ," Banish said.

"It's gone past any reasoning now. People are even talking about raids and invasions. Some, anyway—I'm sure others just see all this hysteria and want to make sure their money's safe."

Banish said, "All we have to do is hold them down below."

"It's exploding," Blood said. "I understand it's a race war now too, though I'm not quite sure how. They've taken Glenn Ables and they've fashioned him into a kind of hinge upon which all their beliefs turn. They're preparing for a revolution."

"That's fine." Banish nodded, wanting to push on.

"One more thing," said Blood. He brought out the local paper and started to open it, then slipped it back under his arm and simply told Banish instead. "Today's paper," he said. "They got ahold of a courthouse copy of the letter mailed to Ables. He was right about that court date. It was a clerk's mistake. The wrong date was on it."

Banish looked at him a moment then. "You think he's innocent?" he said sharply, suddenly trying to contain himself. "After all this. An illegal arms dealer. An explosives trafficker with white hate organizations. A racist. A murderer of federal agents, a shooter of police officers."

Blood shook his head. "I think he's guilty," he said. "Of a lot of things. Just maybe not this."

Banish brought his hand up near his head and squeezed a quivering fist. "Christ!" he said. He wanted to stand. "We should all just walk away, then."

"I didn't say that."

"Then why do you come to me with this? Now you're a crusader all of a sudden?"

Blood nodded. "That I am."

"For the guilty?"

"For what's right. For what's lawful. I believe we talked about this yesterday. You pretty well took me out to the woodshed, matter of fact."

Banish nodded and said, "Fine. Just fine. And you might as well bring a hat to a man with no head. Because I have no choice in the matter now. I was put on this mountain to do a job. And I will do it, I will accomplish what I came here to achieve, goddammit—and then they can all fight it out in court. I do not care. If it all comes to nothing—then fine. Let me read about it in the papers."

Blood nodded. "All right," he said.

"What word do you want me to use?" Banish continued. " 'Misguided'? 'Unfortunate'? 'It's a damn unfortunate situation'? There. Now everybody's even. Everybody's got a raw deal, you, me, Ables —everybody. All right? That what you wanted to hear from me?"

"I understand the situation."

"I cannot care. That is not my job here."

Blood was nodding. "I am with you," he said.

Banish saw that he was protesting too much. He curtailed it with a grand shrug of his arms and hands, and Blood nodded again. "Fine, then," Banish said. Blood nodded and went out.

Banish sat still a moment, collecting himself. "Christ!" he said. He picked up the phone and got Kearney back. "Get me an outside line," he said.

"Yes, sir."

A dial tone came on immediately. Banish knew the long-distance number by heart. He dialed carefully. The connection went through and he switched ears, regripping the receiver. He rubbed his itchy face. He waited through six long, empty rings until it was evident that there would be no answer. Then Coyle came in through the door flap. "Ables is on," she said.

Sound Truck

"Watson." The voice sounded tired and strange.

Banish said, "Mr. Ables."

"I don't like that tank out there."

Banish glanced at Fagin standing next to him. The tank was there mainly for intimidation. Fagin showed him a shrug.

"The tank," Banish said into the handset.

"It's too close. I know what that thing could do to my house if I leave."

"I'll have it moved back."

Ables was speaking more deliberately now. "I haven't slept much since this started," he said.

"You didn't sleep overnight?"

"I stayed up with my children. We prayed together. For a sign."

Banish flashed on the sound man's report of having monitored one or more of the girls crying sometime before dawn.

Ables said, "My children don't want me to go outside. They'd rather have that tank bomb us all into oblivion than see me go."

"I'm having the tank moved back, Mr. Ables."

"I will only be arrested by a white man."

Banish nodded. "All right," he said. He could not appear too eager.

"The house will be put in my wife's name. She and Shelley and my children will not be arrested. Cameras will be there when I come out. They will have lights on so I can see them. I will not be handcuffed on my property, and I will be allowed to salute my supporters."

The subtle sounds of disapproval from the men crowded behind him reflected the disappointment and exhaustion Banish felt himself.

"Mr. Ables," he said, "that is unacceptable."

Silence for a while, then Ables's voice again over the speakers. "Watson," was all he said. He sounded tired and dispirited.

Banish said, "You heard on your radio that people were keeping a vigil down at the foot of the mountain. First of all, those numbers have been exaggerated by the press. Secondly, it's been nine days now and there are simply very few people left." In a hostage negotiation, lying was known as *disinformation.* "Still, I cannot allow you to do anything that might bring about a civilian uprising."

Ables said, "I know there are people down there, Watson. I know it. Good people, loyal people. Christian people. You will lie to me when it serves your purpose. They are down there waiting and they expect something of me."

Banish came back quickly. "What do you want from me, Mr. Ables? Would you rather I agree to everything you say, that there are hundreds of people down there, that you can salute them and wave to them and give speeches and do whatever you want when you come down—and then double-cross you once we have you in custody? I am bargaining with you in good faith here. As unreasonable as things might seem to you right now, I am bending over backward for you."

It was a measured risk. Ables was silent for a long while.

"Mr. Ables," Banish said.

He looked to the sound man, who reassured him that Ables was still on the line.

"Mr. Ables," Banish said.

"My children hate you, Watson."

Banish went cold. "Mr. Ables," he said.

"They will spit on your grave."

"Mr. Ables."

"No salute, then—but *no handcuffs either.*"

Banish looked over at Fagin. Fagin showed him a light shrug. Banish turned back to the microphone and made his decision, then waited, then waited some more.

"All right, Mr. Ables," he said. "I accept your terms. Do we have an agreement?"

"I am still a man here, you bloodsuckers. A free man, an innocent man."

"Mr. Ables, do we have an agreement?"

"Bastards," he said. "Cowards."

"Mr. Ables—"

"Do you believe in Yahweh, Mr. Watson?"

Banish, suddenly alarmed, reasserted himself. "Mr. Ables, I have accepted your terms and will honor them. Do we have an agreement?"

"You could take my life." Ables's voice was lower now. "You bloodsucking heathens—you could take my land and trample vilely upon it. But you will never take my faith."

Banish straightened in his chair.

"Mr. Ables, we have an agreement. Will you come down now?" Banish hung on that, waiting a long time for an answer. "Will you come down now, Mr. Ables?"

Ables said, "I believe Yahweh has a plan for all of us."

Then the thin click of the connection being broken. Banish said after him, "Mr. Ables—Mr. Ables—"

Fagin said, "Fuck."

Banish tried again, becoming more anxious. "Mr. Ables—"

"What?" Blood said behind him. "Crazy talk?"

Perkins said, "Worse than that. The thing about the Surrender Ritual is—"

Banish switched off the handset and sat back fast. "It is identical to the Suicide Ritual," he said. He turned to the sound man. "Ring him. Get him back on the line."

"Screw it," said Fagin. "I say fuck him. Let him twist."

Banish turned. A sense of alarm was overwhelming him. "We need him alive."

"Easy for you to say," Fagin said. "I'm a black man."

"He could turn right around and do the entire family."

The sound man said beside him, "Not answering . . ."

"Sweet," Fagin said, nodding, "real fucking sweet. Now all we have to do is worry about trying to save the life of the fucker we were sent here to kill."

Banish stood then. "I wasn't sent here to kill anybody."

"Jesus Christ." Perkins was standing behind everyone, seemingly in a daze. "We can't turn this guy into a martyr. If we give them a grassy knoll here—Jesus Christ—"

"Agent Banish?" Banish swung around at the sound of his name. Kearney was standing outside the open door of the van. "The ATF agents are here."

Banish was reeling. He avoided all faces, trying to rein in his desperation.

"Get HRT up to the cabin on standby," he directed. "And keep trying that phone."

Office

Banish in. Riga and Crimson seated, waiting.

"Why did you sting Ables?" Banish said, dispensing with formalities. No time for that now.

"What's the idea," Riga said, "pulling us off a job to come back here? You have the file."

"Forget the file." Banish was in front of them now. "Why Ables?" he said. "With all of the active WAR members inside the camp, why Ables?"

Riga said, "What do you mean?"

"You had a CI deep inside the WAR camp and you put him on a religious gun nut with delusions of grandeur, a non-Aryan racist malcontent living on top of a mountain miles away."

"What does that mean?" Riga said. "What do you care?"

"Why did you get him on only one submachine gun and no explosives?"

"We told you why."

"Why weren't there any eyewitnesses to your meet with Ables?"

Riga opened his mouth to answer, then reconsidered. Crimson was sitting next to him watching Banish silently.

Banish said, "Why wasn't either one of you wired?"

Neither agent said anything.

"Why wasn't any money recovered from Ables after he sold you the Beretta? What prompted you to take him down without any backup?"

Nothing.

"How much prior contact did you have with Ables?"

Riga glanced over at Crimson.

Banish said louder, "Did you ever visit him at his cabin?"

Nothing.

"Did you ever threaten him with arrest if he did not cooperate?"

Nothing. They sat there.

Banish had worked himself up into a fury. "Why don't you goddamn answer me?" he said.

The agents looked at each other. Riga sat slowly back in his chair, stern and narrow-eyed, while Crimson stayed where he was, his polite facial expression now betraying hints of concern. This was not at all how the game was played.

"You're not asking the right questions," Crimson said.

Command Tent

Agent Banish came back into the tent immediately after the ATF agents were asked to leave. He came up and used Brian's telephone and dialed a number. Brian could hear the phone ringing without answer through the earpiece. Agent Banish waited fretfully. He rubbed the burned side of his face. When he hung up, Brian noticed him whispering to himself. Then he wrote down the phone number, area code included, and turned Brian around in his chair and showed it to him. "Forget what you are doing right now," Agent Banish instructed. "I am reassigning you. Dial this telephone number and keep trying it until you get through. When you do get an answer, come and find me immediately. This is the home number of my wife and daughter in Cincinnati, Ohio, and it is imperative that I speak with them. Do you understand?"

"Yes," Brian said.

"That is your sole responsibility from here on in. Clear?"

"Yes, sir," Brian said, nodding.

Agent Banish went out then. Brian didn't question it. He didn't even tell Agent Coyle. He just started dialing.

Sound Truck

Fagin paced past Banish's chair. Banish was sitting there with his head in his hands. The Indian sheriff was standing off to the side with his arms loosely crossed, leaning back against the wall.

This deathwatch was driving Fagin crazy. "What time is it now?" he said.

Perkins said behind him, "Four."

Fagin said, "Motherfucker."

"Watson."

Banish was quick to react, switching on the mike. "Mr. Ables, are you coming down now?"

"I'm tired, Watson," Ables said. He sounded weak. "I never been this tired."

"Why don't you come out, then. Come down and face your legal problems, Mr. Ables. Then you and your family can put this all behind you and get on with your lives."

"Watson," Ables said. He sighed then, or stifled a chuckle. "You have a forked tongue, Watson. I am charged with the murder of a federal official. I wouldn't ever live to see the outside of one of your federal prisons."

Even the sheriff stood off the back wall then. There couldn't be any bigger flashing red light than that. Banish was sputtering. "Mr. Ables—I know it looks bleak in there—but out here there are no foregone conclusions. I guarantee that you will receive a fair trial—"

"In a federal court of law. The government establishment is looking forward to that. A legalized lynching. Or will your men save the taxpayers' money, Watson?"

"Mr. Ables, listen to me." Banish was leaning into the microphone. "You do not sound well."

"Thorny-tongued . . . bastard," Ables said. He was in-and-out like that, talking tired, taking deep breaths. "Who will you surrender to, Watson? Who will execute your sentence?"

"Mr. Ables," Banish said. "Mr. Ables. Will you come down now?" He said it again, harder. "Will you come down?"

They waited, but that was it. Ables hung up and went away and Banish sat back in his chair. Fagin stepped up to him then, knowing what needed to be done. "He's getting desperate," Fagin told him. "We should go in there right now."

"No," Banish said without turning. He told the sound man, "Try and get him back."

Fagin said, "Listen to me. He's going fucking loopy up there, and growing more dangerous every second. We're not so refreshed ourselves, but we've got speed, surprise, superior tactics—"

Banish turned on him then. "The kids, goddammit," he said, getting to his feet. "What the hell do you think this"—he waved awkwardly—"this whole goddamn thing is all about? What do you think we came here for in the first place? We're here to save lives, for Christ's sake. Not take them. The kids, Fagin."

Fagin looked up at the ceiling and nodded. He knew full well what the hell their job there was. What he was doing now was cutting down the odds.

The Indian sheriff spoke up behind him. "What if he's baiting us?" he said. "What if he's playing possum? We're out here doing a number on him, how do we know he's not in there doing the same on us?"

Banish shook his head at it all. "We wait," he said. "Wait. Wait. Wait."

He also seemed to be convincing himself. This was crunch time and it was all they could do to keep from climbing the walls. Banish went off and moved toward the other side of the crowded van, bumping elbows with Perkins and pulling back in anger.

There was a crackling in Fagin's ear. He put his finger to the wire, then tapped on his radio. "He'll be right there," he said.

Banish glanced across at him. Fagin grinned wide. "You're gonna love this," he said.

Banish turned and studied the black-and-white monitors. Then he and the sheriff left. The rest of them stood there trying not to look at each other. Fagin smiled and shook his head, pacing slowly back and forth.

Bridge

Blood got out of the government Jeep after Banish, halfway between the bottom of the road and the iron bridge. They faced a sea of protesters jammed in shoulder-to-shoulder, filling out the wide area beyond the bridge and extending out in both directions of the access road as far as the trees allowed Blood to see—all standing quiet and still. No speeches, no milling about. Standing silently in the dimness of the setting sun and watching the mountain, and waiting.

The only figures breaking rank were a dozen or more skinheads squatting shirtless on the jagged rocks to the right of the bridge. Large black swastika tattoos showed on their white skin, as did the yellow laces crisscrossing up their black boots. They were shaving their heads in the muddy creek. They crouched there in defiance, running disposable razors in clean strokes across the tops of their skulls and ladling out water and washing it over their smoothed heads.

A bridge marshal came up and gave his name as Orton. He reported to Banish that there had been a bomb scare earlier and the marshals had gone through and shaken down the crowd, and since then, this.

Banish instructed Orton and the roughly forty other marshals around the bridge to ready their riot equipment. He then reiterated his order that no civilians be fired upon under any circumstances.

Blood sensed heads turning. The gathered faithful were recognizing Banish, and the scandal of their discovery rippled, like a whisper, throughout the vast crowd.

Banish stood facing them. "We won't win here," he said quietly.

Blood turned and looked at him. "What?"

"We won't win here," Banish said, looking out over the mob. "It will not end well."

"What do you mean?"

Banish did not answer. A few voices rose out of the horde then, hecklers, their voices growing louder. Banish listened as they taunted and cursed him. He remained there a while longer, seemingly accepting their vilification. Then he turned and climbed into the Jeep and they headed one last time back up the mountain.

Sound Truck

Banish was floating in the black realm behind his closed eyes. He was waiting. His fevered brain had finally cooled. Peaceful there in the darkness, his eyes relaxed and still, soaked black.

He opened them. He was seated on the step of the side door of the van, head down, forehead held lightly in his hands, shoes planted flat on the weedy ground. He looked up. Kearney was standing in the twilight before him. Banish started to get to his feet.

"No answer," Kearney said quickly, stopping him. "Still no answer. I just wanted to let you know I was still trying. I've been dialing nonstop."

Banish sat back down on the metal step.

Kearney said, "They must be out somewhere."

Banish nodded, tired. Kearney was looking at him.

"I'll be getting right back to it," Kearney said. "I just thought I should reassure you . . ." His words trailed off. "I'll get back," he said.

"I just need to speak to them," said Banish.

Kearney nodded quickly. "I understand that."

"I'm better now," Banish said. "I need to get through to them to tell them that."

Kearney nodded. "I understand families, sir."

They looked at each other, then Kearney's eyes fell to the dirt and he turned to start away.

"I—" Banish said, rather than "Hold on," not imploringly but with the same effect. Kearney stopped and turned uncertainly, then came back a few steps. Banish shook his head. "Listen," he said. "I don't have many friends left. But I still know a few names at the Bureau. Some people there I could call."

Kearney's expression flattened out in gradual realization. His mouth opened and he came closer.

"It might not even help you," Banish said.

"Sir, I—" Kearney looked to the ground with a blinking expression. He shook his head slightly. "Sir—that means the world to me."

Banish shook his head.

Kearney went on haltingly. "When all this happened," he said, "I was excited to be here for it, I was just—just ready. I was ready. I watched you. Throughout this whole thing, whenever I could, sir—Agent Banish. And I feel that I have a sense for it now. For what it is to do what you do here, and to be what you are. And you giving me a chance, in the command tent—" He stopped himself and looked down at Banish. "But when I think of Leslie—Leslie is my wife. And the baby we're having."

Banish saw him with clearer eyes then. He watched the expression on Kearney's face. He realized he was being turned down.

Kearney said, "I see what this job can take out of someone. What this life can do to a man. And I think we've got to get our start together first, Leslie and me. I can't let go of that, sir. I've got to think of her at this point. Which is why I'm thinking maybe I'm not quite cut out for this, at least not right now. I don't really know, I guess."

Banish nodded. Kearney came closer still.

"But sir," he said. Kearney raised his arm and extended his open hand out toward Banish. Banish looked at the palm, creased but unscarred, young, then up at Kearney standing there behind it and the expression on the kid's face. He grasped Kearney's hand and shook it firmly.

"Thank you, sir," Kearney said. "Thank you."

He went off then. Banish did not watch him walk away. Another pair of eyes he had opened and then plucked out. Banish smiled bitterly at the dirt. How many years was he removed from Kearney? Was it thirty? Christ. He wondered what it would take to have it all over again. To have the chance, to not make the mistakes. How many chances do you get, he wondered, beyond the one you're issued? And how many had he already wasted? And exactly how many did he have left?

"Watson."

Banish's heart fell with the breathy voice calling to him from behind. He stood and went back into the van, past Fagin, to his chair.

"Mr. Ables," Banish said. "Are you coming down now?"

"Where do you find God, Watson?"

Banish stopped. "Mr. Ables," he said, "there is no time for that now. Are you coming down?"

"Where do you find God, Watson?"

"What?"

"Where you tremble. That is where you find Him, Watson. That is where He finds you. Where your flesh crawls and the hairs on the back of your neck sting. Where you go slack. Where you howl and are struck to your knees."

"Mr. Ables," Banish said, rubbing his face. "Mr. Ables, you do not sound well at all. I am being honest with you here."

"I'll let you in on a little secret, Watson. That bullet that hit my wife through the door. The one your assassins fired. I don't like to give you the satisfaction, but . . . it hit me too."

Urgency surpassed caution in Banish's voice. "Mr. Ables," he said, "you require immediate medical attention. How badly are you wounded?"

"Is Banish there now?"

"No—Mr. Ables—"

"He was the one who set me up, Watson. I know that now. Him and your whole corrupt government machine."

"Mr. Ables—" Banish was desperate. He felt as though he were melting into the chair. "All right," he said finally. "All right, Mr. Ables. Maybe you did get a raw deal here. So maybe you did. You got screwed, all right? We all did. Now come down peacefully and resolve it."

"What did they do with my daughter's corpse?"

Banish was thrown again, scrambling. "She is being turned over to your relatives, Mr. Ables."

"They won't even let me attend the funeral, Watson. Will they. I will miss my own daughter's funeral."

It was there in his voice. Banish could feel the tension in the men moving behind him. He gripped the handset. "Mr. Ables," he said, "I insist that you come down from there immediately."

"I have prayed with my children, Watson. For guidance and forgiveness. But who will hear your confession? You, Watson, who have waged wars of the flesh—"

"Mr. Ables"—Banish was nearly yelling—"will you come down now?"

The sound of Ables's breathing filled the van. Heavy, labored, Banish hanging on every sound.

"Watson."

"Yes, Mr. Ables?"

Ables let out a long, hollow sigh and said, in a voice closer to a gasp than a whisper, "Maybe this tragedy will end in a greater glory."

There was a click. Banish looked at the microphone. People started to scramble behind him in the van. He hit the broadcast switch again, hard. "Ables!" he said. "Mr. Ables!"

Perkins, moving behind him, said, "I better get up there."

Fagin said into his radio, "Go to alert—"

Banish squeezed the handset switch and called after him. "*Ables!*"

"You lost him," Fagin was saying. "We gotta get in there now. We gotta go in."

"No," Banish said. He stood dizzily and turned and put his arms up to stop time and everything else that was clamoring around him. He was trying to think. His head was ringing. He said to all of them running around him, "JUST LET ME THINK—"

Bridge

Marshal Orton stood quietly just before the bridge. From the enormous public gathering on the other side, formerly silent and still, he detected now a buzzing. Glimmers of excitement crackling through the people like electrical charges, growing.

He was not the first to look at the trees. The thick woods riding high on either side. It was nighttime now and he couldn't see well into them. He didn't have to. Movement. Like animals in the trees, where there had been no animals before. The realization of this came gradually. The huge crowd beyond the creek bed, buzzing. Other marshals coming off the bridge now too—standing before and looking deep into the towering woods as though the trees themselves were about to rush out roaring and overtake them. There were people in the trees. It was certain now. They were scurrying and moving up past the marshals.

Orton clicked on his radio. "Deputy Fagin," he said quickly. "Agent Banish—"

There were people running up through the trees.

"Agent Banish—"

Staging Area

Banish leapt out of the sound truck in a swirl. Here was an outlet for his frenzy. He yelled into the Motorola, "I ordered radio silence!"

An explosion from across the staging area knocked him off his feet. He looked up from where he lay on the ground and watched a black-orange cough of flame rise and expand, then puff out like a popped balloon, turning to black smoke. The sound rang in his ears as the ground rumbled beneath him. He registered the general direction of the blast and realized that one or more of the generators had blown.

As he got to his knees, a flaming arrow streaked in a strangely beautiful arc over the staging area. It landed in the ground at the tree line along the low end of the clearing. Banish heard the cracking of low-caliber gunfire to his left and at first thought it was his own men, then he heard the pop-popping of the security lights high above in the trees.

As Banish got to his feet, Fagin came crashing out of the van behind him. He surveyed the clearing and drew his gun, working the radio. "Tactical support, staging area, locked and loaded—"

Banish found his own radio in his hand. He said into it, "Scattering fire only—"

Another flaming arrow streaked out of the woods and whipped gracefully over the staging area, biting into the roof of one of the holding tents. The fire spread quickly.

A strange glow caught Banish's eye. He turned left to follow it and watched in amazement as a red laser dot slid down the black side of the sound truck to its right front tire. A bang then, separate from the other cracking noises, and the big black tire deflated with a whine.

Another explosion across the way. Banish was jerked but not thrown this time, the mountain rumbling beneath him. The staging area was being pounded like a bass drum from all sides. Gunfire took out more overhead lights. Fagin seemed anxious to start shooting.

"No killing!" Banish said, as if he could be heard amid the gunfire. "They want to draw us in!"

Fagin glared at him. A smaller explosion then, and Fagin turned. A second propane tank from the kitchen had gone up.

A brushfire burned across the clearing in the tree line where the first arrow had landed. Banish caught sight of the red beam again, now floating over the right rear tire of the van. The tire broke open and air steamed out and the sound truck sank lopsided, hobbled.

Fagin swore into his radio. Personnel were spilling out of the soft tents and running across the besieged clearing for the shelter of heavier equipment. Banish picked up the laser beam, now slinking down the flattened tire of the van and onto the ground. It was skimming along the dark dirt toward him. It came and skirted the weeds at his feet, crossing his left shoe, then starting up his leg. He did not feel a thing. It traveled along the folds of material at his waist to where his jacket was zipped over his stomach. Banish looked out across the dark clearing and could see the bright source of the beam shining small and steady within the tree cover downland, beyond the spreading brushfire. He looked back down at his midsection as the beam floated up from his stomach. He did not feel a thing. It drifted upward and stopped, vibrating slightly at the center of his chest.

Staging Area

Fagin looked at Banish. Banish was staring down at a red laser dot dead center in his chest. His eyes were vague.

Fagin brought his left arm straight out and grabbed Banish back-handedly, clothes-lining him across the front of his chest and spinning him backward and down to the ground. The intended round cut whispering through the air past them and thumped into a tree trunk some meters behind. Fagin held Banish down with one hand and quickly traced the beam back to its source, raising his gun arm and wasting rounds across the clearing, blasting away at the ground before the guilty tree and the trunk and the low branches above. The laser sight quickly vanished—some Bubba's birthday present getting a dry run.

Fagin pulled at Banish to get up. "The fuck is wrong with you?" he yelled at him over the noise.

Chatter from the front right and wide left, the open clearing a shooting gallery of crossfire. Potshots from fucking everywhere, guns constantly moving. They had decent cover where they were, near the van, with the mountain rising behind them. Fagin would have to hold the place down himself until his troops arrived.

He saw a small flame moving in the trees wide left and the dark figure of a man behind it, crouching by a tree on the edge of the clearing. He was pulling back a flaming arrow. He was raising a curved bow and aiming across the clearing, and Fagin looked past the tents and vehicles to the one Huey remaining there. It had just refueled and was starting up its rotors and making to get off the ground in a hurry. A fat gas pump sat right next to it.

Fagin turned left. He raised and aimed.

Banish said, "Don't shoot him."

Fucking crazy. It was fucking nuts. Fagin pulled off, grimacing, standing there and watching the archer take aim. Banish did the same. The flame-lit fucker in the trees poised his bow.

The arrow was away. Fagin lost it for a moment, behind a tent, then saw it streaking over the staging area, climbing, the orange flame of its head whipping back in a loping up-arc.

Blood stepped out quickly in front of him. He raised his Browning and pulled back on it twice in quick succession, two blasts ripping into the air.

Incredibly, one scored. Part of the pellet shot caught the arrow just as it was beginning its descent, knocking it off its trajectory, and the arrow flailed in the air and fishtailed back behind the Huey, disappearing into the trees.

Fagin turned fast left and blasted the bark off the tree shielding the guerrilla archer, the cowardly fuck, emptying his gun while the figure ducked away wildly and retreated fast into the woods.

Fagin turned and reloaded. Banish stood there, stricken, Blood reloading also. "This is one hopping fucking town!" Fagin said.

Then Jeeps rolled down off the mountain road into the clearing. Fagin's men swept in from the surrounding trees as well, quickly taking back the staging area, guns and rifles forward. "Round 'em up!" Fagin yelled into his radio. "I want every last fucker tracked down and arrested—weapons offenses and assault on federal agents." He looked at Banish then and decided he could afford a little grace. "But no shooting," he added. "Not worth the bullets. Repeat, do not get drawn in."

The cavalry was overrunning the fort. Fagin pulled Banish back with him beside the crippled van, wondering if Banish realized that he had saved his life.

Then the ruckus started on the radio net. Disciplined preliminary reports escalating quickly to shouts and high-pitched yelling overlapping back and forth. Banish could tell that Fagin had something and he pressed him for it, but Fagin wanted all the facts first—

head down, finger pressed hard against his ear. Banish turned on his own radio, but by then it was pure emotion on the line, men overcome with adrenaline, voices over voices over voices.

Fagin looked at Banish and didn't want to be the one to have to tell him. "Shots fired in the cabin," he said.

Banish's face went white. It seemed to collapse. He said, "No," a small word.

Fagin said, "I'm getting up there." He started off at a run past the small fires toward the Huey.

Sound Truck

Banish rushed inside. Only the sound man remained, hands on his headphones, monitoring the chaos.

"Shots fired," he said excitedly. "Movement. Possible escapees."

Banish whirled around to look at the monitors. They were dark. "Flood it!" he said.

The sound man flipped all the switches and the stadium lights came on and brightness blared for an instant into the monitors, like irises opening too widely, then gradually they settled into focus from white-out haziness to abject black-and-white clarity.

Three different angles of the cabin. Black smoke seeping through the cracks of the boarded windows.

Banish stared at it and for a few scrambling moments could not comprehend what he was seeing. He was like a man watching his nightmares broadcast on television. Thick black smoke rolled out of the stone chimney and puffed through small bullet holes in the roof. The cabin was ablaze.

Banish's voice was not his own. "It's going down!" he said, grabbing at the back of the sound man's chair. "It's going down! Go! Go!"

The sound man reached for his handset and stammeringly repeated Banish's commands into it. Banish stood there staring at the unflinching monitors.

Blood said, "I'm going."

Banish stood there frozen. He could not go. The negotiator did not go. The negotiator stayed behind. He stood shaking and watched for the Ables children to come out. It was all falling apart. As hard as he stared at the monitors, no doors or windows opened and the smoke poured out blacker and heavier. Small flames appeared then along the roof.

Banish said "No, no, no" over and over again. He had to stay. He was caught there. He had to remain behind and watch it all slowly burn. Then men came into the black-and-white picture, agents and marshals, guns and rifles drawn as they slowly approached the cabin.

Banish moved. It was a mistake, he knew it was a mistake, but knowing it did not matter. He could not stand there and watch. He could not ignore it and walk away. It was all falling down around him. He grabbed his radio and started after Blood.

Bridge

It happened so fast there was nothing they could do. Giving uniformed men guns and not letting them shoot was worse than giving them no guns at all. After they entered the woods on both sides and stopped the bleeding there, cutting off the last of the trespassing protesters and making a number of arrests, the marshals gathered back out on the road. Orton's head turned with all the rest when the reports started up at the staging area. The enormous crowd rocked with that, making noise. Orton shared their feeling of hearing something, of knowing that there was real trouble close by and not being able to move to it.

So he held fast with his fellow marshals, waiting for reinforcements or some word of explanation or a direct order from above. The crowd saw the black smoke first. Before any of the marshals did, noise spreading through the mob like an avalanche and voices yelling and bodies starting to move. Orton saw their heads upturned and arms outstretched and fingers pointing upward, and then he turned and looked himself and saw the heavy stream of black smoke rising off the mountaintop, lit brightly from below. It looked like a bonfire up there. He heard a voice cry "They're burning Glenn out!" and that was all it took.

The mob turned. They pushed onto the bridge before Orton knew what was happening, the yellow police ribbons snapping across their chests as they surged ahead. Orton and a number of other marshals rushed onto the bridge and took up positions, setting themselves against the vast crowd. They issued verbal warnings and drew and pointed their guns and the people up front held back a moment, but then a blind surge from behind propelled them all forward and the iron bridge was pummeled under the fury of advancing feet. Orton did not fire his weapon. They were quickly upon him, five or six pairs of hands, and he was upended over the side railing, tumbling downward. Falling. He landed smack on his front side, winded, lying facedown in the cold mud. Hundreds of pairs of boots stamped past him on either side, racing across the dribbling creek now, the bridge too narrow to hold them all, running, jumping, charging, bodies scrambling past him in a mad rush. Orton did not fire his weapon. It was still in his hand but he did not fire it. If they gave him a commendation for not firing his weapon, he would hand it right back to them or mail it to Agent Banish.

All he had for a target was their backs. He got his radio working and yelled into it, watching the rear of the mob running up the beginning of the incline of the mountain road. Media trucks pulled rumbling over the bridge above him, following. It was a free-for-all, pure bedlam. Orton's stunned and excited voice joined the shouting match in his ear and the marshals getting to their feet around him.

Whatever he was yelling, he yelled it again and again. He was hoping they could head them off at the staging area.

Cabin

They had to abandon the Jeep halfway up the road. They jumped out and ran the rest of the way, up past all the service vehicles and the Jeeps and ambulances jammed together. Blood could see the black smoke up ahead spilling into the sky and glowing strangely.

They came at the spotlit, flaming cabin from the left, crossing the great divide of shredded trees that had once been the no-man's-land, now everyman's land, firemen, agents, marshals—just chaos. Men running this way and that, holding guns, axes. The wind carrying the stench of smoke and rotting dogs. Blood had to slow down, his leg wound starting to bite again. From where he was he could see the darkly lit rear of the cabin: smaller sheds standing in light tree cover, boulders half-buried in the earth, trash and scrap boards and weedy ground leading out to the cliffs. Blood looked for bodies fleeing but saw nothing he could be certain of. The flames gave everything the illusion of shifty movement.

The front of the cabin was already burned out. The porch had broken full off its frame and slumped forward like an early casualty, charred and dead. Flames darted fast along the roof, fueling the rising stream of black smoke and producing a hollow sucking noise like whipping gusts of wind.

Men in fire suits stood in front. They were entering the cabin in teams of two, charging through ragged pennants of flame as the previous team exited with suits blackened, stumbling out and pulling off their helmets and face masks and seizing mouthfuls of air. Fire trucks were pulled up, hoses partially unrolled but lying flaccid on the ground. The water truck was unable to get through. A spotlight grazed the area and a helicopter ran overhead, grabbing the pluming smoke in its rotors and twisting it and throwing it higher.

Banish stood before the engulfed cabin as though it were his own mortgaged house. His burnt face was flushed with the reflection of the red-orange flames as they surged, his expression and the underpinnings of his face faltering along with the foundation of the dying wood cabin.

Perkins came quickly across to them. His hands were dark with ash and his sandy hair was tossed. He came over from the right side of the cabin in a high state of anxiety.

"There's a body in the rear of the cabin," he said all at once. "Badly burned. Gross head trauma, gun in hand." He gathered his breath, looking pained. "They think it's Ables," he said.

Banish's head pitched a bit and his eyes went tight and sharp. There was a long moment when it seemed as though he were examining the air before his face for something vital. Then he choked on a swallow, or maybe just the smoke. Blood looked down and away.

Beyond the weight of his disappointment, Blood found himself even more worried about Banish. He looked up again and saw Banish still searching, body bent slightly forward. "The children," he said, short of breath. It was issued to Perkins like a final appeal, the answer to which would either loose the steel blade hanging over his neck or pardon him.

"Nothing yet," Perkins told him. He looked to his left, Blood and Banish's right. "Mrs. Ables got out OK, though."

Blood looked. She was away from the side of the cabin near a pair of paramedics, doubled up, coughing. Her arm was in a scarf sling and her clothes were sooty and darkened and some of her hair was burnt.

"She's refusing treatment," Perkins said. "We're trying to get her into the medical helicopter now."

Seeing her alive seemed to lift Banish. He turned back. "Sew up the mountain tight," he said quickly. "Get some order here and forget about the fire. Let it burn to the ground. Just find those kids—"

He looked around in desperation, specifically to the left side of the cabin. He started off after them himself.

Command Tent

Brian Kearney stayed at his post long after everyone else was gone. First the explosions and the gunfire, ripping holes in the canvas and dropping everyone to the floor. Then the generators blowing up outside. Then immediately after that the gunshots up at the cabin and all the shouting over the radio. He was still at the switchboard now solely because he had not been relieved. Even Agent Coyle had left for the mountaintop after the staging-area shooting ended and the cabin fire had been reported. Brian was still in his chair at the outside switchboard line, punching in the numbers again, hearing the long-distance connection, the first, slow ring, then waiting through five more before starting all over again.

There was a great noise gathering outside, which he figured must have been the agents returning to the staging area. They sounded triumphant. Brian's mood lifted and he fought the impulse to run out there and look. It was more relief on his part than anything—sweet relief. But he stayed dialing, and got halfway through the numbers again before realizing that there was no sound coming out through the earpiece now. He clicked the plunger down once, then a number of times. The receiver did nothing in his hands. The phone was dead.

He got up. The noise outside the tent was tremendous now, but first he went around picking up different phones in the tent. All dead. The lines had gone down.

Brian went to the door flap and stepped outside to look, and it was incredible what he saw. Not a celebration. A revolution. The mob of protesters charging through the staging area, hundreds of them, a thousand, up from the mouth of the road and across the clearing like a civilian army. They were out of control. Brian saw people he knew, neighbors of his, racing for the road, yelling and pushing on each other, fists in the air, legs working frantically. He saw a few agents attempt to get in and stop the crowd but it was useless. Like rocks in the river. The dam had already been broken. Then trucks appeared behind the mob, TV trucks, like pistons driving the marauders into the clearing and across to storm up the road. It was a swarm. A whole mass of frenzied people moving as one. As the trucks rolled past the tents and onto the new road, Brian lit out fast from where he was, running after them. It was already a full-blown riot. He feared a massacre.

Barn

Watching the crate slide back in the dark corner, and hearing the commotion going on up at the cabin and in his ear, Taber needed all his patience to remain quietly where he was. The dirt top came up and off and smoke puffed out of the tunnel hole as a woman came out coughing violently, recognizable as Michelle Mellis. She had a gun in her right hand.

Before she could step forward, Taber said authoritatively from behind the old sit-down lawnmower, "Hold it."

Porter, at the barn entrance, echoed him. "U.S. Marshals Service."

Mrs. Mellis's shirt and sweatpants were streaked with dirt. Smoke drifted up around her. She stopped where she was but did not immediately lower the gun.

"Your choice," said Taber.

Another moment of weighing her options. "Damn," she said then, tersely, hacking dryly into a dirty fist and tossing the gun aside.

"Hands above your head," Porter commanded.

Taber stood and advanced with his gun aimed, moving in behind her with handcuffs. "Who killed your husband, Mrs. Mellis?" he said.

Mrs. Mellis stifled her coughing. She looked away from Taber as the bracelets clicked around her wrists. "I want a lawyer," she said.

Shed

A crash behind Banish as part of the roof collapsed and sparks shot out into the open land behind the burning cabin. There were flashlight beams in the trees. Marshals or agents moving along the outlying grounds. Banish quickly scanned the area. He was in the zone directly behind the cabin, beyond what the spotters in the no-man's-land could see.

There were three small shacks and the outhouse between the cabin and the cliffs. The nearest was a skeletal frame of rafters and beams, only half-constructed. He went to the one in the middle ground, made of waferboard and flathead nails, with a box window facing the cabin and a four-foot latch-handle door on the right side. The door was closed.

Banish went to it. He stood and listened over his own harsh breathing for movement inside, then lightly tugged up on the door latch. It lifted and the door fell open a few inches. No noise. He pushed it open wider and stepped inside.

There was sudden, jerking movement from within and he stopped fast. Orange flame light slanted in through the box window. He saw one young Ables girl, then another, seated side by side on the floor, in the shadows between the wooden end-legs of a broad workbench and the far-left wall. The older one, Ruth, was sitting with her arms hugged around her knees, frightened, staring up at him. The five-year-old, Esther, had one arm tangled up inside her sister's. Her other arm hugged what appeared to be a Bible. Esther began immediately to cry. Both skinny girls wore T-shirts and soiled skirts and sandals. Both wore leather holsters. Small-caliber guns hung in each.

Banish was so gratified to see them alive that at first he could think of nothing to say. He took another slow step inside and then showed them, without being too obvious, his empty hands. He saw that Ruth noticed.

"Hello," Banish said.

Esther turned away, burying her face in Ruth's arm. Ruth looked at him with wary eyes, then turned her head back toward the window. Flickering orange played over her dirty face. The cabin outside was now completely engulfed. They had huddled in the small toolshed to watch the blaze.

"Hello," Banish said again. "Are you girls all right?"

Ruth turned and looked at him. Neither girl spoke.

"Where are your sister and brother?"

Again they said nothing. Ruth's nine-year-old face was dark-eyed and tight with suspicion.

Banish entered more fully. He did so slowly and without looking at their holsters, removing his own jacket for further reassurance. Ruth saw that he was unarmed. A helicopter buzzed overhead and for a moment the dark shed glowed under the searchlight.

"No one is going to hurt you," Banish said. Esther's face was hidden. Both girls appeared particularly fragile, like rag dolls tossed into an attic corner. "Are you hungry?" he said. "We have food for you. Whatever you like."

Ruth turned to look at the blaze again.

"What happened?" Banish said.

Ruth answered him then, blankly, bravely, staring at the fire. "Daddy lit a fire and told us to get out and run," she said.

Banish nodded. "He was worried about you."

Esther was peeking out at him now, sniffling, urchin-eyed. Banish took another small step forward into the center of the shed.

"I have a daughter," he said. "She looked just like you two when she was your age. Same dark hair, big eyes."

Ruth said, "You tried to take our daddy away."

"No," Banish told her. "We just wanted to keep you safe. Your grandparents asked us to come up here and get you."

Footsteps rushing outside. HRT. Banish stepped back to the door as agents in black ninja gear ran up. He showed them a harsh face and an open, insistent hand, then turned back slowly to the girls. They were still sitting there on the floor, captivated by the blaze. Their guns remained holstered.

"We're here to rescue you," Banish said, coming back toward them. "To bring you to your mother. She's safe too. She's waiting for you out in front. Do you want me to take you there?"

Esther said, sniffling, "Mommy in back room."

Banish stared at her until his eyes glistened. His eyes glowed. He moved close to them then, almost blinded. "Come on," he said quietly, arms out. "Come on."

Esther stood first, reluctantly, not letting go of her sister or her Bible. Then Ruth. Ruth's head was turned, still watching the flames through the window, as Banish knelt on one knee before them. "You'll be all right now," he said, unbuckling Ruth's holster belt, then Esther's.

Ruth's upturned, vacant face glowed like brass. "Mommy," she said.

When they were both disarmed, Banish waved the HRT agents in behind him. He stood and handed the first one the holster belts, then grabbed the man's sidearm from him and went racing out of the shed.

Cabin

Banish came around the front of the cabin with the gun up and aimed. The medical helicopter had landed in the foreground, rotors whining, waiting to take off again. Two EMTs led Mrs. Ables toward it. She was walking on her own, between them, wearing a loose sweater, a loose gray skirt, and a long, singed dark-haired wig. Banish came up behind them and stopped ten yards away. They were too close to the helicopter for him to risk waiting any longer.

"Mrs. Ables!" he yelled.

She stopped dead. The EMTs on either side of her stopped as well and turned back and looked at him strangely.

"Mrs. Ables!" Banish yelled again.

He was aware of Perkins and the other agents around him turning and watching in confusion as he stood there aiming the gun. The helicopter beckoned. The EMTs were looking at her now. She was not moving. Banish called her one last time, yelling, dizzied.

"Mrs. Ables!"

She threw a fist suddenly and then an elbow with the same, good arm, and both EMTs collapsed to the ground. She turned fast, holding a gun. It was Ables himself. The wig hung ragged and low on his head and his face was darkened with soot, which obscured his identity. The clothes were shapeless on his small frame and soiled with ash, his left arm bent in its sling.

The surrounding agents all dropped and drew. The EMTs realized what was happening and scurried away.

Ables was staring at him darkly from behind the .45. "Watson," he said. "You son of a bitch."

Banish brought out his ID, ten yards away. "Banish," he told him. "FBI. You're under arrest."

Ables's face shook a moment, staring, then regained its outlaw composure. "Son of a bitch," he said. His eyes glanced left and right. "Move and I'll kill him!" he warned, then looked back to Banish. "I'm getting on that copter."

Banish just shook his head.

He saw Fagin moving in front of the helicopter to his right. Fagin knocked on its bubble windshield and gave the pilot a quick thumbs-up sign and the pilot needed no more than that. He throttled up quickly and took the bird into the air.

The rotor wash whipped at Ables as the helicopter turned above, then dipped sharply down behind the tree cover and disappeared. Everything was quiet then except for the fire. Ables looked around desperately. More marshals and agents emerged from the woods and behind the cabin. Each had a gun or rifle out and was aiming at him. Ables saw them all and raised his arm a bit, reasserting himself, leveling the gun at Banish as though to shoot.

"You murdered my wife and my daughter," he said loudly.

"You shot at policemen," Banish said. "You killed a United States Marshal."

"I was framed."

"You wanted this," Banish said, shaking his head. They were standing there pointing guns at each other. "This is what you wanted."

Beyond Ables, the earth was rumbling, shouts and trampling footsteps approaching fast. Banish first saw the tops of heads, then bodies filling in around the vehicles, advancing upon the scene. The protesters had somehow broken free. They had rushed all the way up the new road and hundreds were now charging onto the mountaintop. If they overran the cabin, they would easily obscure Ables. Some of the nearby agents stepped back, greatly outnumbered, guns aimed. There was going to be shooting. Ables's face showed that he knew exactly what was going on behind him and he grinned cockily. This was his dream fulfilled.

A body moved at the top of the road facing the stampeding crowd. It was Blood. He stopped in front of them and fired a single shotgun blast into the air, then recocked the weapon and aimed it at the mob, halting them all. The lead protesters stopped fast, others piling up quickly behind. "Not one more foot," Blood announced. They stood there breathing heavily, pressing against one another, stunned, looking at the local sheriff standing up to them and beyond him to all the armed agents and Banish, and the figure standing there in the skirt and wig.

Ables realized what had happened behind him and his confidence failed. "Back off, all of you!" he shouted to the agents. "I'll kill the FBI man!"

Not one man moved.

"Get back!" he shouted. "I'll do it!"

No one retreated. Barely any motion from any of the men. Only Fagin moved. He started over toward Ables, in plain view from the right. His gun was up and aimed and obvious.

Ables saw him coming peripherally, and surely saw his black skin. "I'll kill him!" Ables shouted, eyes on Banish. "I ain't afraid to die!"

Fagin kept coming. Ables's eyes darted from Fagin to Banish and quickly back and forth again. But Fagin just kept coming. Ables's gun hand shook. His eyes twisted around and saw Fagin's gun nearing his head. "I ain't afraid to die!" he said.

Fagin stopped next to him, arm outstretched, his gun muzzle not six inches away from Ables's left ear. "Here's your big chance, then," he said.

Ables's face was a wide-open display of desperation. His eyebrows ran high as though trying to pull his head back from the muzzle. The .45 shook in his hand but stayed up.

Banish lowered his gun and tucked it loosely into his belt, then started forward.

Ables's head turned just a little. His face could not comprehend what was happening as Banish approached him unarmed. The .45 remained high.

"After all your talk," Banish said to him, halfway there.

Ables's face clouded over in anger. "Son of a bitch," he said, reasserting the .45.

Banish came closer until he was standing right in front of Ables, the muzzle of the .45 leveled flush at his heart. He watched Ables's face under the dark wig, shaded with ash, small and weak-featured, and popping, and seething, and pathetic. He saw the flames reflected in his small black eyes. He saw the man standing there behind the gun. Behind all the rhetoric and the hatred, a small, pitiful man. In over his head and too blind to see it until just that moment. All the trouble he had caused, and all it had cost him.

Banish reached out and pushed Ables's .45 away and stepped up to him. Ables was breathing fast. He was staring at Banish. Banish felt nothing for him. All the time and money spent, the man-hours, the equipment. Everything Banish and his men had gone through to arrive at this triumphant moment of surrender, to deliver this man from his home. "This is all it comes to," Banish said. Fagin came around Ables and relieved him of the .45, ripping off his sling and pulling both his arms behind him. Ables grunted in pain. He twisted his head around to see the black-skinned man taking him into custody.

Banish turned Ables around to face the mob. He saw Deke Belcher pushing his way to the front of the crowd there. He saw Kearney standing next to Blood.

Banish pulled off Ables's wig and tossed it to the ground. He could feel the spirit of the mob, palpably, its cresting triumph dying suddenly there in front of him like a ghost slipping free of a corpse. Here was their savior before them, revealed. Here was their tarnished soul.

Sheriff Blood turned back from the stilled crowd. They were mere bystanders now, as though snapped out of a trance and happening upon this strange scene. Blood came up in front of Ables and took a piece of paper out of his coat pocket. He pressed it to Ables's thin chest.

"Served," Blood said. "Notice of eviction."

Fagin had handcuffs out and was snapping them tight around Ables's wrists. "You have the right to remain silent," he began loudly, adding under his breath, "*you fuck.*"

Banish stepped forward then. He felt a sad sense of piety looking out over the mob. There was no glory here. He eyed the thick stream of bodies stretching down the freshly cut road. "Go on home," he told them. "Get out of here, all of you. It's over."

A lilting silence. Failure brought to the mob a small, ringing moment of true peace. Then the people in front started, reacting suddenly, buzzing again and looking to their left, Banish's right. He turned. A figure was emerging from the woods. It was Rebecca, the fourteen-year-old daughter. She held the infant Amos in one arm, a .38 in the other. Marshals and agents were backing cautiously out of the way. She saw her father standing there in a skirt and handcuffs and was moving toward him, aiming mainly at Banish.

Banish held his open hands out toward her. "No," he said. He said it simply, extending his arms, trying to stop her with sheer will. "No," he said. "Don't do this."

The marshals were all backing off, giving her a wide berth as she walked with the baby and the gun from the trees in toward the burning cabin. The girl was crying. Tears rolled in two clean streaks down her face. She wore a plain, frayed cotton dress and sandals with broken straps.

"Let him go," she said.

Banish moved between her and her father. His arms were out. "Don't do this to me," he said.

"Becca—" said Ables behind him, followed by a grunting noise, Fagin shutting him up.

Tears rolled liberally down the girl's face. "Let my daddy go!" she screamed, the gun shaking.

She stopped a few yards in front of Banish. The baby was waking in her other arm. Marshals moved in slowly around her.

"No, no, no," said Banish. His arms were out and he was simultaneously holding off the marshals and pleading with the girl. "No," he said, trying to stop time, trying to hold everything.

The marshals slowed, remaining close. Banish slipped his gun out of his belt and tossed it away. He started forward toward her. He was shaking his head. If he could not talk her down, he would jump her himself. She was aiming fully at him now.

"Give me the gun," he said. He reached one open hand out to her. "Give me the gun. It's all over."

She shook her head wildly. "You let him go!"

Banish moved again closer. His hands were out in front of him. He was pleading. "I don't want you to get hurt," he said.

"Don't touch me."

"Give me the gun." He was walking forward, close to her. He was shaking his head sadly. "It's all over now," he said. "It's over. It's over."

The corners of her eyes crinkled, then fresh tears squeezed out. One lip came up to comfort the other. The siege had taken its toll. He saw now that she was looking at her father standing there in custody. She was fighting reason. She shuddered twice, two small, silent sobs. A revolution going on within her. The baby boy, Amos, held in a sitting position, looked blankly at Banish.

"It's over now," Banish said. He was getting through to her. Her lower lip quivered as her face crumbled inward. The baby and the gun both heavy. She was fighting hard to hold her composure. He was convincing her. She was only fourteen years old.

Banish shook his head again, nearly crying himself. He was reaching out to her plaintively. "Don't do this to me," he said.

She was lowering the gun. She was putting the gun down. Her shoulders were shaking and the tears were washing her face, and the gun was going down. Two marshals, one on either side of her, started forward. Banish let them. He dared not move. The gun was pointed at about his knees now. He made ready to step forward and take it away from her.

The girl looked once more at her father. Her quivering shoulders stopped then and held still, as though in one final swallow of compliance. But the gun had stopped too. Stopped at about Banish's feet, and now she was staring hard at her father. Only Banish was close enough to see the burning in her eyes, her face changing before him, the burning overcoming all else. It was fierce in her eyes, the flames, reflected from the cabin and not reflected, and Banish saw in a moment of flaring intuition that she was not looking at her father at all now, she was looking at the man standing behind her father, the man who was holding her father in handcuffs, and seeing the black color of that man's skin. He saw it happening as it was just about to happen, a moment of pure vision, and as he rushed at her all at once, propelling himself forward, her gun came back up and she got one shot past him before he threw himself upon her and the infant boy and went crashing down on top of them hard to the ground.

Cabin

It all happened at once. Blood saw the girl's arm stop going down, and then that look she got on her face, like wind blowing sand off a sundial, and Banish leaping forward and the gun going up and her firing off one shot and Fagin pitching back behind Ables, hit, his head snapping back, blown off his feet by a shot to the chest and his body dropping fast and the gun kicking back in her small white hand and the nonlook on her face—it was pure instinct—and the marshals' rifles beside her coming up in their hands, and Banish leaping in the air with his arms out and landing on the girl and the boy, tackling them, smothering them underneath him and falling to the ground, the marshals' guns kicking back and puffing smoke, all happening at once, Banish coming down hard on top of the girl with the baby and the gun and Ables falling forward from the act of Fagin being blown back off his feet and settling still on the ground.

Cabin

He saw the night sky. He struggled up dizzily to sit. Screaming fucking pain in his chest. Fagin said viciously, "Jesus fucking *Christ!*" and looked down and saw the hole in his jacket and ripped it open and saw the fabric torn apart. He saw the shotglass punch mark in his Kevlar vest. Christ, it hurt. Right in the fucking sternum.

He looked up fast, the pain shooting to his waist and neck. Did they get the gun? And why wasn't anybody fucking helping him?

He got to his knees, then his feet. Christ, it fucking hurt. Ables was lying on his stomach near him, hands cuffed behind, unable to move. Fagin stumbled forward, standing on his own. He had to. Everyone else was away from him. He looked over and saw that Banish had taken down the girl himself. He was body-blanketing her and the infant, holding them still on the ground, and the gun was lying clear. The marshals and agents were all moving in around them. Blood reached Banish first and touched his shoulder. Fagin saw then for the first time the two holes in Banish's back. He saw the blood soaking like red ink into Banish's white shirt. Blood rolled him off the children, who were hysterical. Banish's half-burnt face was fixed. His eyes searched the night sky, mouth mumbling.

Cabin

Blood was the first to reach him. Banish wasn't moving. Blood called his name and touched his shoulder, the girl and the baby boy screaming beneath him. Then he saw the holes in Banish's back. Two distinct holes filling up red. Blood grasped Banish's shoulder and rolled him off them and stood back fast. Banish was staring up. His blue eyes were glazed, blinking for comprehension. His face seemed lazy, half-ashen, lips opening and closing without sense. Hands grabbing lightly at the ground. Blood took a full, terrified step backward, then rushed forward and down. The blood was pooling on the dry earth beneath Banish's back, spreading. His head lolled to one side. He was looking at the children. Blood reached for Banish's head and turned it so that he was looking up at him. Blood could say nothing. He tried. Then Banish's weak neck failed again and his head dropped the other way and blood spilled like red syrup out of his mouth. Blood righted him, holding his head with both hands now. Banish was mumbling, incomprehensibly at first. Then, wheezing:

"Call my wife." Blood could hear Fagin saying behind him, *"Somebody get a fucking EMT!"* and sensed the people suddenly rushing around him, the weight of their collective realization. The girl and boy being pulled away, screaming. Banish was looking up past Blood. "I'm sorry," he said. "I'm sorry." He was apologizing over and over again. Blood was yelling down at him, something, holding his head up, watching the red life spill from his mouth.

Cabin

They rolled him over and he was looking up at the last of the shooting flames and the black tower of smoke running up into the night sky. A buzzing helicopter slowly crossed his view. Banish's eyes fell left and he saw Rebecca and he saw Amos and his blood was on their dirty clothes but the gun was knocked away and they were crying and they were both fine. They were fine.

They moved his head again and he asked for his wife. He asked that Molly and Nicole be brought to him immediately. If he spoke at all, that was what he said. He was trying to speak. He was just a head now, nothing in his arms or legs or in his chest except the heaviness, not really tingling but absent now and gone.

He saw Blood over him. The Indian's hat was off and his long black hair was out and hanging and he was wild-eyed, yelling. He told Blood to get his wife and daughter and hurry. He needed to tell them. It was never too late. That was what the songs always said. It was never too late. He saw Fagin now, alive. Others looking over him with paralyzed expressions. Kearney, his face wide. Coyle in tears. Perkins. The smoke funneling up beyond them.

He saw the smoke and the fire and the helicopters and the branches and the night. He heard the buzzing now, full in his head. The buzzing. He was getting through to Molly. "I'm sorry," he said. He said it again and again. "I'm sorry," he said. Everything relaxing in him now. "So sorry," he said. The smoke and the fire and the night. "Forgive me," he said. Everything he had ever done to any-body he had ever hurt.

Blood yelling at him now. Fagin motioning. EMTs working over him, shaking him. Shining lights, talking in his face.

Some things you cannot negotiate. Some things are fixed and cannot be bargained with or for. Banish relaxed completely and let his eyes unfocus, softly, like ribbon raveling off a spool.

Butte, Montana

[PARASIEGE, p. 83]

SA Banish expired at 22:47 hrs. (Mountain Time) on 10 August 1993. His body was loaded into a service truck and transported off Paradise Ridge and flown to FBI headquar-ters in Washington, D.C., for postmortem examination. An intermediate crime scene was declared and the area cordoned off and all weapons surrendered for inspection. Members of the press were briefly detained, camera film and videotape recordings confiscated as evidence.

The subsequent official ruling of SA Banish's demise as death by misadventure was appropriate and the dismissal of all charges against the two deputy marshals justified. No one law enforcement individual or group of individuals could be said to have been at fault or performing outside their duties in the wake of the attempted murder of Deputy Marshal Fagin by Rebecca Ables.

As to the subject of this report, Special Agent John Ban-ish:

As directed telephonically by Assistant Director Richardsen, GID, on 4 August 1993, I insinuated myself as close as possible to SA Banish during the PARASIEGE op-eration in Montana and monitored his daily activities, reporting nightly to AD Richardsen's office and recording notes and observations variously reflected herein. In summary, I find that I cannot accurately estimate the quality or state of SA Banish's mental health and disposition, or whatever limitations it may or may not have imposed upon his reasoning faculties as they impacted his decision-making ability over the course of the siege. I can, however, offer my impressions of SA Banish's job performance as compared to those activities generally understood to befit a federal agent.

SA Banish's methods were unorthodox. SA Banish's actions were suspect and often baffling, and his motivation for these actions secretive and at times wholly unknown to anyone but himself. SA Banish was inconsistent in following both basic negotiator as well as Bureau SOP, and on at least two occasions detailed herein blatantly disregarded or, at best, casually ignored direct Bureau orders. The joint forces' confidence in SA Banish varied widely throughout the siege, but overall would be rated at a level lower than the minimum standard any effective case agent would be expected to garner. SA Banish's interpersonal skills were naught and his personality—that is, his presence, characterized by the caliber of his leadership—was, at best, remote.

Having said this, I find however that I cannot myself join the recent chorus condemning SA Banish's performance at Paradise Ridge. Despite his numerous shortcomings, I found SA Banish to be entirely focused on the case assigned to him and at all times fully and wholeheartedly dedicated to the successful resolution of operation PARASIEGE. I must also contradict SAC Perkins's and others' accounting of SA Banish's professional demeanor, in as plain language as I am capable: at no time in my numerous daily exchanges with SA Banish did I suspect, sense, or otherwise detect any evidence whatsoever of alcohol use. Unsubstantiated allegations as to SA Banish's deportment can only serve to cloud this already difficult and complicated after-action examination. SA Banish was dispatched to Paradise Ridge under unusual circumstances with the directive to end the delicate, highly public siege situation ongoing therein and deliver the suspect individual while preventing any further harm to the hostage family. Setting aside for a moment the question of the death of Marjorie Ables, with which this internal investigation is primarily concerned, and the death of Judith Ables, which occurred before SA Banish's arrival, SA Banish resolved PARASIEGE successfully and at extraordinary personal cost. SA Banish delivered all four of the Ables children into safety, including single-handedly saving the lives of the oldest and the youngest at the expense of his own. In this light, I find the recent backlash and revision of SA Banish's reputation by SAC Perkins and others not only misguided but, frankly, most unfortunate.

I would like to request a personal interview, sir, in support of this report.

SA Mary Grace Coyle
26 October 1993
Butte, Montana
[signature, initialed]
[Stamped "TELETYPE" and "CONFIDENTIAL"]
1—Mr. Richardsen
1—Mr. Carlson
1—Mr. Frankson
1—Mr. Lewis
1—Mr. Patrick

[Printed on the bottom of the page:]
These comments are neither the recommendation nor the conclusion of the FBI. This report is not to be distributed outside this agency.

About the Author

Chuck Hogan lives in Boston, Massachusetts, with his wife, Charlotte. He is twenty-seven years old. *The Standoff* is his first novel.